NO JUSTICE

by Chris Raymondo

Sunstar
PUBLISHING LTD.

No Justice
by Chris Raymondo
© United States Copyright, 1996
Sunstar Publishing, Ltd.
116 North Court Street
Fairfield, Iowa 52556

Computer Graphics Layout: David Carrier
No Justice Symbol, Illustration: William Lancaster
Editing and Text Design: Elizabeth Pasco

Library of Congress Catalog Card Number: 96-069531
ISBN: 1-887472-14-2

Readers interested in obtaining further information on the subject
matter of this book are invited to correspond with
The Secretary, Sunstar Publishing, Ltd.
116 North Court Street, Fairfield, Iowa 52556
More Sunstar Books at: http://www.newagepage.com

*Complacent apathy
is the substance of
destroyed nations.*

• Enrique Deleon •

Acknowledgements

Mom, I love you. You too Dad. Absolutely the best parents the universe could create. Thank you. Thank you. Thank you.

My lawyer too, Robert Levitt of Denver, Colorado. Nowhere does a finer friend nor better attorney exist. You are a shining light of integrity in a profession aptly recognized for its dark corners.

Also I'd like to thank everybody I've ever met. You had something to do with this. Muchas Gracias.

PART I
THE SET-UP

Believe anything is possible,
and anything you believe
will be possible.

• Enrique Deleon •

Chapter One

Taylor Nicodemo Tarrington awoke from a dream-filled sleep at 4 a.m. The cellular phone next to his bed was ringing. He picked it up.

A familiar voice said, "Nicky, your dad's in the twist again. Our friends over there… say, no more. I did what I could, but you better get your feet into it before they put him to bed." It was Tony Mo, crime boss for the Catalano Mafia family, calling from New York.

Tarrington leaned his head back and scratched his neck. The highest echelon of the Sicilian Mafia was about to kill his father. He said, "Did you tell them that would be a terrible mistake?"

"Nicky, you know I told them just to fix it and leave it alone. But your old man took down the Italian government this time. And our friends are taking a lot of heat." Tony cleared his throat. "And you know how hot that gets 'em."

"Where is he?" Tarrington asked.

"Rome… downtown in the jail."

"Who's mad?"

"The Old Man himself."

Tarrington cringed. "Lay some asphalt Tony, and I'll follow up… in what?…an hour?"

"Nicky, I already built you a freeway and your own personal exit. Call the Old Man now."

"God bless, Tone."

Tony said, "God don't got nothin' to do with it," and hung up.

Tony was right. This was all about money.

Tarrington pushed the button to disconnect and the cellular started ringing in his hand.

A woman's voice inquired, "Taylor Nicodemo Tarrington?"

"Perhaps," Tarrington answered, puzzled that she would know his real name.

"International toll from Rome, Italy. Person-to-person collect from a Mr...."

"Wellington James Tarrington," Tarrington finished for her. "Yes, ma'am. I'll take the call."

His father came on the line, "Hello, son."

Tarrington said, "Don't tell me... You're at the circus in India where a gang of disgruntled elephants stage a protest over blackmarket ivory. As the crowd goes wild you are trampled by the throng. You fly directly to Rome for a mud pack, eucalyptus steam and some deep tissue massage. Now the Swedish girl has your leg in a hammerlock and you can't get to your calling card... so, it's collect for a bit of Dad-and-lad bonding."

Welly said, "I like the hammerlock part. Reminds me of the good ole days."

Tarrington smiled, "Pops, the good ole days were officially over the moment they shot Kennedy."

"I thought that was when Clinton didn't inhale," responded Welly.

"Nope. That was the beginning of the End."

"And here I thought that was the season M*A*S*H got cancelled."

Tarrington said, "Read the newspapers, Dad. You're way behind."

Welly chuckled, "What was I thinking?" Then changed his tone and said, "No, son... actually... I was being fitted at Brioni when..."

"When the cops rushed the place and arrested you," Tarrington finished. "Now, how'd I know that?"

"The Psychic Hot Line?" Welly asked.

Tarrington smiled. He sighed. Then he asked his father... "Why?"

"So you heard already, huh?"

"Your profession is hazardous to your health... and *my* wallet... Let me make some calls and I'll get there. Until then, watch who you sit by at dinner. How's Mom?"

"Your mother said she was gonna take a hit out on me."

"She's gonna have to stand in line, Pops. I love you. Sit tight. And I mean *tight*."

Welly laughed, "I always like your prison humor, son. Good show."

Tarrington hung up. He could feel the gentle rocking motion of his yacht beneath him. Breathe in—breathe out, he was thinking. Okay, so his father was in jail. Again. This made number seven in the last five years. When would the old man learn?

Tarrington worked the phone. The Mexican end didn't know yet, and probably never would. But the Family in Sicily was none too pleased. Their stern request was the hint.

Which is why he had to call Tony Mo in New York again—a diplomatic gesture—before he scheduled a flight to Italy.

Next he engaged the morning ritual: shower, shave and straight to his car. He'd buy some clothes on the way to the airport.

———⟶◆⟵———

Tarrington's grandfather, Italian nobleman, Nicodemo Riva, met him in Rome. A lean body shrunk over time, Riva was stooped now like an ancient gardener. He still had a full head though—thick black hair speckled with grey. And positioned to either side of his rocky sloped Tuscan beak, were dark-ringed chestnut brown eyes glimmering with the lusty intensity of a man sixty years his junior. Even sun-scarred and bent with age, he commanded a magisterial presence... one which stiffened with pride as his grandson cleared customs, heading towards him, now.

Tarrington had inherited the Riva hair; his version flowing like a black wave past his shoulders. The quick brown eyes too. But not the nose. The union between Contessa Arianna Riva and Wellington James Tarrington had graciously left Taylor with his father's fine patrician model. And now with the jaw line, permanent tan, and good muscles, Tarrington was the stylish namesake of English-Italian seduction.

Dressed like a page from *GQ*—Gianni Versace, Cole Haan, Vuarnet—Tarrington was camouflaged in his trade garb, but you couldn't call him a label man.

An enthralled gaggle of uniformed Catholic School girls gawked at him as he worked his way through the crowd.

Noticing this, he kissed the tips of his fingers and met their eyes. "Chill a' Cella!" He told them, blowing a kiss their way. It bought him a flutter of embarrassed laughter. None of them actually knowing what the hell he was talking about.

"Happy Birthday, Nicky." The elder Riva was dressed like a peasant. He positioned his walking stick and grey-stubbled cheek for the traditional greeting.

"Yeah,... that too." Tarrington said, and embracing the old man, kissed both cheeks, one after the other. He stepped back and gave his grandfather a quick up and down. "You're looking like a trip to Monte Carlo, *Nunu...*"

Riva grunted. "Why's the bastard gotta do this?" He pivoted on the ivory handpiece of his stick and started through the effusive homecomings of excitable Italians, dodging them as they clutched and cried and kissed in the exit path.

Tarrington adjusted his pace, raised his voice, "You coulda shot him. You didn't have to let him run off with Momma." They doddered together.

Riva colored from the neck up, like a wine glass being slopped full of Chianti. He screamed in his native tongue. "The son-of-a-bitch took me for everything I had!"

Several people stopped to listen, necks craned to eavesdrop.

Calmed a bit, Riva continued, "I let your mother go 'cause I thought it was the only way I coulda got my money back." He dropped his head grumbling, "Stupid son-of-a-..." then raised it with his eyes full of pride, telling Tarrington, "I got you though Nicky. God bless, I got you."

Tarrington said, "You tender-hearted old fart you."

Thirty-one years before, playing the smooth-talking, upper-crust English bloke that he no doubt was, Wellington James Tarrington had bilked the elder Riva out of millions on an ersatz land deal. Some fraudulent deeds putting Nicodemo's credibility on the coals. He'd lost the Riva boat building business that still bore his name. And to top it all off, during the process of the con, the scoundrel Wellington had impregnated Nicodemo's sixteen-year-old daughter, Contessa Arianna. The result: the consensual elopement of the con man and the Contessa: the perpetual festering of her father, the literal death of her mother (the heartbreak of social scorn); and the birth of Tarrington himself.

Two years later the money was gone, and Contessa Arianna was back. No husband Wellington, just baby Taylor in her arms.

And eighteen years after, that baby named Taylor Tarrington had found it in himself to restore the Riva Family Crest, its attendant fortune, and more. Like his mother, there was that inherent shame of father Welly's waywardness. So Tarrington had worked his way from Italy to America's west coast, and while there, on Mexico's Baja, fate's undertow had dragged a rich man's daughter out to sea. Long-haired, pot smoking surf fanatic, Taylor Nicodemo Tarrington had been poised upon destiny's surfboard and the one to ultimately save her life. The reward for which he was still collecting.

"Sometimes I wish I wasn't a Catholic..." Riva was saying, as he stopped to pat Tarrington's cheek. "Silly Pollock and all his delusions."

"Give the old guy a break, *Nunu*. Maybe his miter's too tight, huh? Ya ever think of that? Where's Momma?"

"She's in the car." Riva paused a moment, "What the hell's a miter? Some kind of gilded jockstrap, huh?"

"It's that phallus he wears on his head."

Riva mumbled, "Phallus... *humpf.* I'll show him a phallus...."

At twenty-two, Contessa Arianna Riva's extraordinary beauty had landed her one leading role in Italian cinema. As well as the money she'd made, subsidizing Tarrington's semi-fatherless upbringing, she'd also earned a modicum of notoriety. A celebrated status her embarrassment of husband Welly's criminal bent had possessed her not to capitalize on. She'd been hiding from Welly's infamous reputation most of her adult life.

Outside, Rome was Mediterranean muggy. Clear sky, and a slight breeze coming north from Sicily. Perfect weather for linen, thought Tarrington, fingering his lapel delicately. Then he moved to help his grandfather down the steps.

"Leave me alone." Riva grumbled. "I got up 'em, didn't I?"

"So jump!" said Tarrington.

"Don't tell me what to do!" Riva swung the cane in a wide arc, barely missing Tarrington's head.

Tarrington ducked and grinned.

Now three years shy of fifty, Contessa Arianna Riva was still a heart-stopping beauty. Spotting her son, she raised herself regally from the limo, then immediately contradicted this haughtiness by dashing towards him with tears in her eyes. "Taylor, Happy Birthday, my son!" They hugged, kissed.

Tarrington always felt like a gigolo around his mother. The way people looked at them. She was a knockout.

"His name's Nicodemo." Riva told her.

"His first name's Taylor." Arianna replied.

"Quit, you two." Tarrington interjected.

"You didn't pack?" asked his mother.

"I can buy a toothbrush anywhere, Ma."

"Such a handsome boy," she teased. "You gotta wife yet? I'm waiting for some grandchildren."

"I'm taking applications."

"A girlfriend, then?"

"You and Sofia Loren still fighting?" Tarrington inquired.

"Listen ta you!" she laughed, climbing into the limo.

The driver fishtailed them into the Italian Grand-Prix that doubled as everyday traffic.

Riva arranged his walking stick on the seat beside him.

Tarrington said, "So what's Dad's done this time, Ma?"

"He embezzled around three million Swiss francs from the Italian National Democratic Liberation Party posing as the campaign manager."

Tarrington rolled his eyes, "The trust fund pays him two thousand a day to entertain himself."

"I know, I know!" Exasperated, his mother stabbed the air before her with the back of her hand. "But you know what he says!"

<hr />

"It's not the money…" A dapper Wellington James Tarrington told his son as they left the courthouse, "It's the game."

"You gotta stop, Pops. You're a sixty-year-old kid. Screw the game. You've been pinched seven times in the last five years. They got computers now. Interpol's all over you. Anymore and they might start lookin' into me, or the Riva Trust."

"Old man Nicodemo's got his family crest to cover the money. Nobody knows I lifted it off him before you were born."

"Dad, whaddaya been smoking? Things like that can be traced. Hell, my grandmother died from it. People, those old rich broads, remember? They talk. And what about me? You want your only son taking your heat? In America you don't get no bail. And in my business you don't get no fair trial either. Now retire, goddamit. I can't tap the Boys for no more favors. They're gettin' sick of you down in Sicily. You hear me? If it wasn't for me you'd be dead by now. Hell, one more time with this shit, they'll probably whack us both." Tarrington purposely slowed the pace, looked at his father. Holding him there at bay before they got to the limo. Rome's traffic was a roar of honking horns and rich Italian expletives.

Wellington admired his son's fashion sense, "I always told you: People won't listen to your bullshit unless they love your clothes. I'm glad to see you paid attention."

Tarrington sighed, straightened the fold of his father's silk pocket square. "Dad, did you just hear my bullshit? I got two thousand dollars worth of linen and leather here. You hear me, or what?"

Welly could see he'd pushed it far enough. "No more fake counter checks in Marbella?"

"None." Tarrington nodded.

"No more cubic zirconias in Antwerp?"

"Absolutely not."

"No credit card receipts in Paris?"

"No."

"Not even the cardboard suitcase trick at Cannes…? To stay in practice?"

"Pops, my friend in Sicily will send somebody up here to stick that cardboard suitcase up your ass. Trash the whole idea. Now do I have your word? I'm trying like hell to divest myself of the underworld and you got me callin' in markers every six months with these outdated con games of yours. Just stop. Don't give me that look, either. I can't keep fixin' your bad breaks. Get over it. Go to Lisbon and have a tan. Have an affair. Hell, have an affair with Mom. She loves you, Dad. I love you. The whole world loves you... well, maybe not *Nunu*. But hell. Would you just hold the con and relax?"

Speaking Italian, Wellington stated theatrically: "You have my word, son. May my vermicelli be overcooked the rest of my days should I break it." He could've said it in twelve other languages, emphasized with a wide range of dialect, but he chose a Caltanissetta Sicilian dialect to show his son he knew what was coming next.

"That's right, Pops. Now how much of the money you got left?"

"The Democratically liberated money?"

"What else?"

"It's all been converted to Krugs."

"You know I gotta take it to them."

"To those fucking wops?!?"

"Watch the mouth, Pops. Wops everywhere." Tarrington waving his hand slowly back and forth. "I'm a wop, remember?"

"Your mother was a beauty..." Wellington said wistfully.

"Where's the gold, Dad?"

Wellington kicked his well-shod foot, scuffed the fresh leather sole of his alligator Mauri. "C'mon, son. If it's my last job, what the hell? Explain it to them."

"Dad, we stalled the payoff for DeBeers themselves when you pulled the Belgium score off. But you know these guys down south don't play. Whaddaya tryin' to do here, huh?"

"All right. All right. It's on the Island."

Wellington meant Sardinia.

"It's buried right behind that old peasant's pepper patch." He motioned towards the darkened glass of the limousine, indicating Nicodemo with his gesture and the wince.

"That's your father-in-law, Dad. He's put up with thirty years of your crap. You should be polishing the handpiece of his cane for Christ's sake."

"Yeah, yeah. Tell all those bent noses thanks for me while you're down in Sicily tomorrow…handing over my last heist."

"No thank you, Pops. Thanks for seeing this thing right. Now take Mom to Lisbon. Stay in my villa."

Wellington smoothed back a wisp of brownish-blonde hair, let his lady-killer blue eyes sparkle in the Roman daylight. He patted his son's shoulder, "Happy Birthday, kid. I got ya a suitcase fulla gold coins this year."

Tarrington sighed, "You got me nervous diarrhea is what you got me."

Chapter Two

Purposely laid over in Manhattan, Tarrington changed clothes. A thing with him. The first act was to strap the three-day-old Vuarnet wristwatch to a recalcitrant bag lady's arm. After this little slight of hand, he replaced the Armani he'd flown in with a Romeo Gigli ensemble. Now he was bare chested beneath a dark orange vest with an orange and green striped silk bow tie fastened to an uncollared neck. Covering this with a saffron-yellow, three-button linen jacket and matching cuffed trousers. The Armani stayed behind in the Fifth Avenue dressing booth.

He walked two shops away and deserted a pair of Lorenzo Banfi lace-ups for Reebok Amazone sandals. The full-length mirror made him smile. He could issue a fashion statement the way Welly once issued a ream of bad checks; with perfect flare and relative ease.

A peculiar extravagance for Tarrington. He never wore the same outfit twice. High line retail clerks in his size loved him for this. It also allowed him to travel remarkably light; a checkbook and credit cards.

Feeling pretty good about his father's retrogression from the confidence rackets, Tarrington found the right store and purchased *the* power watch. A quarter-million-dollar IWC Le' Grand Complication. Timepieces were an option. He probably wouldn't give this one away.

Properly attired, he called on his opposite number in the mob. The Mafia boss who represented the Caltanissetta-based Catalano crime family's American interests: Marcantonio Morelli.

Tarrington drank Strego with "Tony Mo" and thanked him

sincerely for his coordinating efforts with Sicily. For arranging the payoff that created a wave of amnesia in Italy's higher courts where Wellington's criminal charges were once a priority. They'd simply vanished. Again.

A favor Tarrington had no doubt been tagged to repay. Somehow. Some day. That quietly wrung leverage common to Machiavellian mob games.

After cocktails, Tarrington cabbed from Tony Mo's Park Avenue high-rise to catch the first flight west out of La Guardia. California was calling.

———⟶●⟵———

Since Tarrington was in the heroin business whether he liked it or not, he'd opted for an alias to separate his identities. Because he believed the best lies contained a carefully measured amount of twisted truth, he felt it prudent to keep his working moniker familiar. So he'd reversed his first and second birth names and developed an extensive "legend" for an entity named Nicolas Taylor. Common enough. Easy to remember. Pretty hard to screw up.

Save for a handful of internationally connected mobsters and a cherished few Mexicans, nobody in the business actually knew Nicolas Taylor was really Taylor Nicodemo Tarrington, descendant of Italian nobility and English con-artistry.

One of the privileged few, Tony Mo in New York, simply referred to Tarrington as Nick the Trick. To keep it simple and to keep a smile going on the running nuance.

Waiting for Tarrington at L.A.X. was a local lawyer converted ten years earlier and slowly groomed to be the heroin operation's maintenance man. James Trowbridge managed the readily collapsible "fronts," where various sports cars were packed with product, and he saw that these vehicles were driven to appropriate mob pick-up points.

Tarrington himself, had not seen a kilo of heroin since his twenty-second birthday. Lately, he hardly ever saw the money that was machine-counted or categorized and weighed then air freighted to Mexico. James Trowbridge was not one of the privileged few to know the real Tarrington, but he was damned efficient. He earned a hundred thousand a month for his sweat.

Sitting in a banana-yellow Ferrari Mondial Cabriolet, James was double parked in the taxi lane. The top was down.

Tarrington strolled up and tossed a *Yachting* magazine into the back. He grinned at Trowbridge.

"Well, if it isn't Mr. Nick. And home so soon."

Tarrington leaned both palms on the passenger door, said, "Top of the day Sir James. And tell me, my good man, before I get in this car, is there anything in the trunk I don't want to be associated with?"

Trowbridge had acne, a ring of flab suspended over his belt, a terrible haircut, and no taste in clothes. He was chewing gum and drinking a Dr. Pepper. He said, "Just the body, Nick."

"No golf clubs?" Tarrington asked suspiciously.

James popped his Juicy Fruit. "Female, Caucasian, 21, 107 lbs., hard eyes, starting to stink a bit. That's it. I promise."

"A blonde?"

James nodded, "Brunette, you're safe."

Tarrington climbed in. There was a fresh six-pack of Coors on the floorboard. He opened one and took a long drink.

L.A.'s night was clouded with the spilled emissions of an infinite number of carbon belching tail pipes. Remarkably though, Taylor saw Venus glimmering where the pollution had temporarily receded. Riding with the top down made his hair dirty. It whipped about his shoulders like advertisement streamers.

"Nice night," he said, and burped.

James said, "It was a good air day."

"I'm hungry." Tarrington proclaimed.

James squealed into the first Burger King and backed around the drive-thru so Tarrington could order from his side.

The usual. Two double bacon cheeseburgers, light on onions, extra lettuce, tomatoes, cheese and bacon, no mayo. "And put plenty of catsup and mustard packets in the bag." Tarrington reminded the girl at the counter.

He wolfed down the first and was doctoring the second in his lap; making sure to rip off just a corner of the mustard pack so the stuff laid down in perfect little squiggles.

James said, "All your money and live on Sushi and Cheeseburgers? You're too old for that Generation X shit. You're a slob. No, not a slob. You're a pig..."

"Bacon cheeseburgers," Tarrington corrected, talking with his mouth full.

"No, wait a minute." James paused, "You dress like a faggot, much too nice. You can't be a slob, or a pig... or can you? What we need here is a definitive reference....."

Tarrington waggled his finger signaling a respite while he chewed. As he swallowed he adjusted the rearview mirror so James could see himself. "That's a slob," he said, "That's a pig. Take it from there."

James smiled and tossed the empty Dr. Pepper can over the trunk onto Santa Monica Boulevard. From under his seat he produced a hand towel to wipe the mirror where Tarrington had touched it.

"You mean...?"

"That's right," James held up his gloved hands. "It's a company car."

Tarrington used the towel to catch up with all the places he'd touched.

"How was the trip?" James asked.

Tarrington said, "No first-class seats to L.A. I felt like a masochist in coach."

James said, "Buy a jet."

"Too high-profile. I'm not a lawyer."

"A bummer trip, then?"

"Definitely not the rave scene," Tarrington said. "Next time I'll check my legs with the baggage guy."

"I see." James pointed, "Drink?"

"Two… actually."

———⟨⟩———

They pulled into a popular night spot and stopped at the front door, parked in the fire lane. There was a long line snaking from the entrance. Tarrington stepped out of the car. James was coming around the front. They headed straight for the bouncers.

"Hey buddy! You can't park there!" Somebody waiting in line had missed their big shot at junior high crossing guard and was still in denial.

James turned his gaze in the general direction the comment came from and yelled back, "Fuck you, I'm rich!"

He and Tarrington advanced to the head of the line and breezed right in. James had to drop a fifty though. He had bad clothes.

When they found a table by the bar, Tarrington wished he'd brought along his *Yachting* magazine. The band hadn't started up, but the piped in music thumped above normal conversation levels. Might as well read. The drink was a tradition between James and him. He stood, yelled over the roar, "Order me a B&B, chilled, straight up."

"Fine, where you going?"

"Get my magazine."

Trowbridge handed him the keys. "Put the top up before somebody shits in it."

When Tarrington was outside, about to open the driver's door, two very attractive young ladies pulled next to him in a Porsche 911 with the targa panel removed.

"Nice ride," the passenger said. She was model-thin, sucked cheeks over high bones, a lot of brunette hair teased with too much styling gel. She wore only a black bra and skin-tight jeans with black pumps. She was obviously doing some serious cocaine. Her eyes were swimming the breaststroke.

"You been cooking?" Tarrington asked her.

She pursed her lips sensually and blew him a kiss.

He motioned to her face, "There's flour all over your nose," and brushed at his own showing her.

She stepped from the Porsche, left the door hanging open, and bellied up to Tarrington. Pressed him against the Ferrari. Ran her fingers through his hair.

"You're prettier than your car," she said.

"Turtlewax," he clarified.

She grabbed a handful of hair and pulled his face to hers. Her breath smelt of rum and tiny beads of sweat clamored at her browline. She stuck her tongue so far down his throat he gagged twice.

The driver of the Porsche, a redhead with jeans and a clingy tie-dye shirt, was smoking a menthol and holding a bottle of Michelob between her legs, wedged towards her crotch. She revved the turbo and yelled over a Zepplin II CD. "Take him to a Motel 6. For Christ's sake, Becky, let him breathe!"

Becky broke it off and said, "Does it taste like flour?"

Tarrington smacked his lips, "I don't know. Feels like a trip to the dentist office, now."

She pinned him to the Ferrari, found him through the thin linen trousers and began to rub and stroke vigorously.

This elicited a couple catcalls from the line of customers. Poised for entertainment as they were.

She said, "You're hung."

He said, "You're toxic."

She said, "I wanna suck you."

He said, "I'm afraid I wouldn't feel it after the first minute or so…"

She smiled and told him, "You're probably right."

Then she sprayed his face with a tiny atomizer full of chloroform. "Nighty, night," she sing-songed.

He fell asleep.

Looked like a CIA job, but it wasn't.

Chapter Three

The man who could make it all happen, who'd played an integral part in the restoration of the Riva family fortune, whose daughter Tarrington had plucked from a frothing oceanic death that fateful day off Cabo San Lucas, turned out to be the Mexican "Malcolm Forbes" of white heroin and green marijuana. It was this benefactor, Carlos Deleon, who'd offered a three-carat emerald ring the day Tarrington surfaced with his near-dead eight-year-old daughter, Sylvia.

Tarrington had laid her on the deck of the sport fisher and performed mouth to mouth. Took her from blue, to sputtering, to smiling, to tears of joy in a small matter of very long moments. But because an inert sense of "the game" (a phrase the gallivant Welly had always used in reference to the long con) had been genetically and psycho-socially implanted in Taylor from day one, he'd declined that emerald ring. The nineteen-year-old Tarrington said, "no thank you" to this reward for selfless bravery and dove off the boat. Leaving in his wake, a pointedly provocative lead for the well-heeled Mexican, Carlos Deleon, to follow.

A trail that led to the Huntington Beach flop house Taylor shared with three other surfers and an assortment of hot-and-cold running beach bunnies. Sure enough, the ethereal Deleon, more prominently known in DEA planning sessions, CIA boardrooms, and the International Drug Cartel clique as the mythical "Lion," had made a rare appearance on Tarrington's doorstep. Invited him to Mexico. All inclusive. "Bring the surfboard if you want, I own half of Acapulco." Reward or not, payoffs constituted a bribe in the Lion's ledger. So what Carlos Deleon wanted to find out was: Who is such a man that can refuse my bribe?

Growing up, on and off with Welly, Tarrington had taken a very astute interest in the machinations of his father's mind. As proof, he'd tamed the Lion Deleon as if the man were a mere house cat. It would've done Welly proud had the young Tarrington ever admitted to the feat. But Tarrington soon learned that Deleon was far from domesticated. Whether it was the fierce Riva loyalty, or Carlos' subtle manipulations, what began as a curious conquest developed into a dangerous career. Carlos knew talent when he saw it.

After two years of indoctrination, Taylor Nicodemo Tarrington was ensconced at the top of the drug trade. His salary: One million a month. His responsibility: A little shuttle diplomacy between the Italian Mafia and Carlos' kingdom, some absentia commodity management, and most importantly… collect the money. No big deal. Tarrington's ingrained life experience provided him the wherewithal of a man thrice his age.

At twenty-four he'd accomplished just what he'd set out to do in America and that was to win back the Riva family fortune one way or another, and to vindicate his father's waywardness.

At twenty-six Tarrington had acquired and/or enjoyed every possible creature comfort civilization could provide within the realm of his personal tastes.

Now at thirty-one, he'd spent the last five years lobbying Carlos to authorize an early retirement plan. It wasn't working out. Taylor had proven himself far too valuable to be let go.

The way Tarrington had it figured there were three distinct retirement options.

Retirement by death.

Federal prison retirement.

Retirement by death.

The latter invoked should he try to sneak off and hide somewhere. Call it a gambler's retirement. The Lion's paw had a world reach.

Unfortunately none of these plans held any promise where Taylor Tarrington was concerned. Though he still plotted... for fate's hand could always intervene....

———⟫●⟪———

The two-bedroom townhouse was clean. It was a safe house. It should be. There were no clothes in the closets. Its owner didn't live like that. There was, however, some chattel of the trade: a money counting machine, a Hobart digital pan scale, beer and cold pizza in the fridge. And furniture: a dinette, a sumptuous pit group, beveled glass coffee and end tables, an extensive Harmon/Kardon entertainment group that included a large-screen Mitsubishi TV, a queen-size conventional bedroom suite in one room, and a king-size waterbed with matching nightstands in the larger bedroom.

It was on this waterbed that Tarrington awoke, fully clothed in the saffron-yellow linen suit with, strangely enough, the *Yachting* magazine clutched in his sweating fist. He still had the Reebok Amazone sandals on. He didn't feel very well. He wobbled to the bathroom and puked. This didn't do much good.

He opened a cold can of Coors. The first sip hissed down his gullet. He finished it, burped, opened another. Two sips later, he puked again.

In the bathroom mirror he examined his countenance. Semisplotchy. He flicked off the light, flicked it back on. Checked. The pupils dilated awkwardly. He felt punchy. Some kind of drug hangover. He cleared his throat and spit. It looked like cotton rust sitting there in the dry sink.

He rinsed the sink, splashed his face, smacked his lips. His tongue looked strange. Like a bad patch of highway. Tasted like it too.

He gargled with Scope and inventoried the apartment. Gone was his answering machine, but the tape had been left behind. The VCR, the Hobart scale, the stereo's smaller components (speakers remained), and several expensive neoclassical knickknacks were gone as well. The closets, couch cushions, pantry, freezer, medicine chest, drawers, and attic cubbyhole had all been rifled.

Seeing this Tarrington climbed atop a dining room chair and looked into the barely functional attic. They'd found the money. Somewhere around three hundred grand!

They'd neglected a Motorola Mobile briefcase phone that utilized military satellites and was supposedly immune to monitoring. They'd left his quarter-million-dollar IWC Le'Grand Complication wristwatch too. They were smart girls. Worked professionally. Didn't fool with the watch because it was seriously high-profile. Registration numbers assigned to its owner. They were obviously cultured enough to recognize this, because the IWC certainly didn't look like a quarter-million-dollar timepiece, it only cost that much. Even if their coke dealer hocked it later there could ultimately be untidy ramifications. What forethought. They left the mobile satellite phone for nearly the same reasons. All the gadgets and dials and meters on the Motorola were like neon lights flashing, Get Busted, Get Busted, Get Busted.

Tarrington checked the garage. No Ferrari. Then he went to the landing for his paper. It was 10 a.m. Should be there by now.

The lawn maintenance crew was mowing the grass. Tarrington sneezed in the sunlight. He waved to Mrs. Hibblemeyer, the spinster across the way. She was out fondling her rose bushes. She waved back. Neither the Porsche nor the Ferrari was out front. But the *L.A. Times* was. He retrieved it and went back inside. When he saw the label, saw the name Nicolas Taylor, he remembered his wallet.

It was there. In his back pocket where he kept it. Right next to the checkbook. No checks were missing. The Nick Taylor California driver's license, an AMEX Platinum, Gold Mastercard, Diner's Club, Visa, and four gas cards in the same name were all there. His Amoco card was gone. The Neiman Marcus card too.

The girls knew what they wanted. They wanted merchandise easily converted to cash with no red tape. They wanted gas. They wanted new outfits. They probably had a connection somewhere with a "chop shop" to dump the Ferrari. They wanted cocaine. Maybe the Porsche had been hot as well.

They'd certainly scored in the attic. Three hundred grand left over from a money counting/weighing session. Money that didn't make last month's move south. Which is what the apartment was for: storage, packing—staging prior to shipment. It was primarily used so people like James Trowbridge and the ever-drunk Al Sharpe would know how to touch base with the phantom Nick Taylor. Tarrington religiously pursued a low profile, yet it didn't seem like such a big deal to sit around and count out a half-dozen suitcases full of cash now and again. He did this so Trowbridge wouldn't feel like he was doing all the work. Though Tarrington knew the real work was in the arena of Mexican-Italian-American relations, and that was where he shined. But why rub it in?

He still didn't feel good. Where the pit-group arrangement had freed up floor space there was a combination chin-up/dip bar. He stripped down to his sulka boxer shorts and buckled on the gravity boots. Fifty inverted sit-ups, twenty-five pull ups, and fifty dips later he'd worked up a nice sweat and the drugged fuzziness seemed to have worn off a bit. So he did it again, reversing the handhold on the chin-ups this time. Then he took a shower.

Naked, he padded through the apartment. Stopped before the fridge, he tried a slice of cold pizza, expecting maybe a revolution from his stomach. Nothing though. Good.   He finished the slice. Pepperoni. He could use a good bacon cheeseburger about now. James ate pepperoni. One of the reasons the man's face looked like a moon shot.

Opening another Coors, Tarrington noticed the Nicolas Taylor passport he usually traveled with laying under the coffee table. He smiled, held the beer aloft, and toasted the girls. "You were even polite about it." He drank, then collapsed in the pit group, locating the remote. Warm up the big screen. Find CNN. Open the newspaper. Business as usual.

Tarrington was a news hound. Tarrington was open minded. Tarrington was a realist.

He knew everything the paper printed and the network news reported was designed to bleed the public's attention from the real news. The news the media masters didn't want publicized.

He knew if you carefully considered what they weren't saying, you could figure out what it was they were covering for. Just squint your brain and read between the lines. The truth was there. It was relative to the lie. You just had to divine it.

He knew, for instance, that when the White House pushed for a national health care plan, it was a tricky way to socialize everybody and get them carrying a microchipped I.D. card. Easier to monitor the masses. A cognizant national data bank. It all spelled control.

He knew that when the congress passed laws to eliminate citizen held handguns and semi-automatic assault rifles, it was not to protect them but to emasculate them. If you disarm people they can't fight back when they realize they've been screwed, bamboozled, brain-washed. If they ever did, of course.

He knew the government had big plans. He knew eventually he'd have to find a nice island somewhere because it was gonna get dicey. Civil rights were on the way out. World Order was in.

True, utopian order wasn't such a bad concept, a little outdated perhaps. Kinda silly when you considered that people were inherently different. Change was the only constant. You couldn't control anybody but yourself. So why try? Yet government tackled these precepts whenever it got the momentum going. Such was history. Greed kindles the desire for power. Power burns with the need for control. Oppression manifests the fires of revolution. But a world revolution was bound to turn into a big mess. It was already. And all these thoughts of Tarrington's were producing some big plans. But right now CNN was putting some kind of large dent in his future.

Pictures of the girls that had mugged him were there on the screen. The yellow Ferrari they'd confiscated for their efforts was in the center of the screen, wrapped around an oak tree like a big piece of flypaper. All this surrounded by official-looking vehicles with flashing lights on top. The announcer's shrill voice:

"...this morning in Santa Monica, California, Camille Abernathy, daughter of Republican Senator Randolf Abernathy, was killed in a one-car accident. The driver, Becky Forrester, is currently at Memorial Medical and listed as comatose and in critical condition. Three hundred twenty-five thousand in cash was found inside the car's trunk and thirty kilos of high-grade heroin was discovered in specially designed fender wells and door panels. Senator Abernathy has denied any involvement with the drugs or money and has called for a full Senate investigation. Relatives of Becky Forrester are asked to notify local FBI authorities as all area federal agencies are working in concert to locate the car's owner.... In Bangladesh today..."

Tarrington muted the set, called Trowbridge. Took about nine rings to get him out of bed.

"Huh? What? It's not even noon yet. Who is this?"

Tarrington said, "I thought you said there was nothing in the trunk."

James recognized the voice. "Was it good? You left me there for it."

"It wasn't what you think. Turn on your TV set. I'll call you back. Battle stations."

Tarrington hung up the phone. His mind was in fifth gear. Redlined. Yet he appeared very calm. He went to the waterbed and peeled back the mattress.

There were four stacks of bills. Twenty-five hundred a wrap. Ten thousand in all. Why he'd put it there two weeks ago he didn't know. But he knew now.

He smiled.

Intervention.

Chapter Four

To be safe, to eliminate the chance of a cab being traced back to the townhouse, Tarrington walked to a Seven-Eleven three blocks away. It was hot. Traffic smelled like kerosene. His mouth tasted of ammonia. He had the mobile motorola briefcase phone swinging, the money counter and the *Yachting* magazine in a hefty bag as if they were dirty laundry. The money counter because it was incriminating, the magazine because he was going to read the damn thing if it killed him. Soon as he could. At present, he was fully into crisis management mode.

Inside the convenience store, he bought two cold cans of Coors, a pen, a small spiral note pad, and a roll of quarters. Outside on the pay phone he dealt with the unpleasantries by priority. He called Trowbridge. The beer was chilling his hand. Cold and wet. His tongue still tasted like Draino though.

James answered, "Jesus Christ, Nick. I'm sorry."

"You told me nothing was in the car."

"Nothing in the trunk.... be specific."

"You're on double-secret probation."

"So what else is new?" James lamented with sarcastic flare. Then he asked, "What do we do?"

Tarrington said, "I need a big storage room twenty-by-thirty. Give me an address, the combo, the gate code."

"An empty one?"

"No, James. One with a view, and a bed. I'm taking a date there tonight."

"Maybe you should try bowling. Stag. Something. These wild dates aren't panning out lately…"

Tarrington yawned loudly, cleared his throat.

James said, "Okay, alright," and gave him an address in Yorba Linda, the combination to the lock, and the current entry code for the facility.

Tarrington wrote it all down in his notebook and said, "Stay by the phone," then hung up.

He hated it when people tore pages from the yellow part. He had to go to the white pages for the number of Allied Van Lines. He picked the one in Westwood.

"Allied."

"Who's the dispatcher?" Tarrington asked.

"I am, why?"

"And you're?"

"Walter Bramhouser. Who's this?"

Tarrington wrote the name down and said, "Customer. How much to move a two-bedroom apartment from Hollywood to Yorba Linda? Not much furniture, hardly any small stuff. No clothes."

Bramhouser said, "Fifteen hundred."

Tarrington told him, "There's nine thousand in it for you if you can do it within the hour."

"Thank you for moving with Allied," Bramhouser said automatically.

Tarrington gave him the addresses. "The money is wrapped up in a newspaper. It's the only thing in the freezer."

"Cash?" Bramhouser seemed amazed.

"Cold. That's legal, right?"

"I'll accompany the men myself." Bramhouser assured his newest customer. "We left ten minutes ago."

"You're a credit to your profession, Walt."

Tarrington wrote: Allied Van Lines, Westwood, 555-7934, next to Walter Bramhouser in his spiral note pad. He guzzled some beer, located a cleaning service in the phone book, called them.

Happy Home Cleaning said they would literally wipe down every square inch of the place for three hundred fifty. Tarrington made arrangements for a Western Union money transfer and got a guarantee they'd begin as soon as the movers finished. He promised them seven hundred. They loved him for it. He wrote it all down.

Next he thumbed to the "Ts" in the white pages, found the name Taylor, Nicolas. An Anaheim address. He removed the latest electric and telephone bills from his wallet. "Nick," he said, "This is your lucky day." He dialed.

A woman answered, "Pacific Gas and Electric. This is Mary, may I help you?"

Tarrington first determined how much surplus money he had in his electric bill account for 8913 Norma Place in Hollywood. About three thousand in credit. He hated having to keep up with the bills so he paid ahead. He had Mary transfer the surplus to his other residence, the one at 1740 Florence in Anaheim. He told Mary that he was the same Nick Taylor at both places; that he was going to reside solely at the Anaheim residence now. He thank her. She reciprocated. Never mind that the Nick Taylor of Anaheim needed his electricity turned back on. Mary thought it was nice the company was getting paid and didn't question the move.

Tarrington did the same thing with the telephone company. He kept extra monies in a credit account there too. Nick Taylor of Anaheim would possibly not pay a phone or electric bill for the next two years. Tarrington making the right move. Random charity.

Final execution, he called a taxi. While waiting, he sipped the second Coors. Sweating like the can, catching a buzz. Still with the chemical hangover though, making him smell the taste in his mouth. Beer wasn't washing it.

After a stop at Western Union, the taxi dropped him at L.A.X. where he lingered before the terminal as the cab drove away. Then to the short term lot where he kept an Audi Quattro. There he switched identities. From Nick Taylor to Taylor Tarrington and vice versa. The Audi belonged to Tarrington. There were things to do.

A 747 thundered overhead as he opened the trunk and retrieved a beige lambskin briefcase. He threw the money counter into the trunk and the briefcase into the passenger seat next to him. First he put Beethoven's *Hammerklavier Sonata* in the CD, dialed a low volume, then he cracked the Motorola mobile phone, plugged the auxiliary in the cigarette lighter, and activated the field strength meter. No electronic surveillance on, in, or around the Audi. Green Light. The immediate vicinity was sterile. He programmed a frequency, clicked on the signal scrambler. Now the line was clean.

Flipping through the *Yachting* magazine, he found a number. It took a few calls but he eventually chartered a 160-foot megayacht out of Cannes for forty-two thousand a week, put the first week on his Master Card. He made verbal arrangements for a bank-to-bank wire to cover the rest of the vacation. He sent the yacht to Sardinia. Then he called his father.

"Whadaya want?" Old man Riva said in Italian.

Tarrington switched to his native language, "Put your son-in-law on."

Riva switched to English, "How ya doin', Nicky?"

"Fine, *Nunu*. You ready for a vacation?"

"Hell no!"

"Take my advice, you're ready."

"What's wrong? I can tell it from your voice."

"Just start packing and put my father on."

"Kiss my ass." Riva hissed. The phone hit the table with a bang.

When Welly got on the line the first thing he said was, "D-Day?"

This was a confidence game term for when the con was over, for when the shit hit the fan, the signification of an impending vanishing act.

"Yeah," Taylor said, "It's not upside down yet, but it looks pretty sideways. I got a boat coming. Should be moored off your beach about two tomorrow morning. It'll be the one with the swimming pool on top. Head for the Canary Islands." Then he emphasized, "I'll handle the finances, understand?" He would make it untraceable, the trip.

Welly understood, he was to take the family and disappear. He said, "A clean break?"

"Just like you stepped out for dinner." said Tarrington, then he asked, "How's Ma doin'?"

"She's happier. Is it the wops?"

"It's nobody right now. But it could be everybody by tomorrow. So pack a bag until you can shop."

"How'd you get a boat this time a night?" It was around 9 p.m. in the Mediterranean.

"Whose son am I?" asked Tarrington.

Welly liked this. He chuckled. "I love ya, kid. Thanks again. Don't worry about a thing. This kinda shit is right in my back yard."

Tarrington understood this all too well, he said, "Don't get any funny ideas, Pop. And tell Mom I love her." He hung up.

Now that he was halfway covered, and the family was five hours from safety, it was time to work on the problem. He started the car. Damage assessment and control was next. Leaving the short term lot, he dialed the number for one perpetually pickled Mr. Al Sharpe.

Al Sharpe. A man whose mouth ran like a river.

Chapter Five

Al Sharpe was a drunk. He'd been one ever since Tarrington knew him. Al Sharpe was Tarrington's unofficial liaison for the mob. Al Sharpe was supposed to advise Tarrington of any policy developments within American Mafia interests. Al Sharpe and Tony Mo had been "made" in the same ceremony thirty years before. Even though Tarrington always dealt directly with Tony Mo on any discrepancy, change of plan, or tactical decision. It was an unspoken agreement between the two of them that Tarrington would look after Al, take care of him. For Tony.

Al was an embarrassment. Al had been given the plum spot because he and Tony had been juvenile delinquents, back in the old days.

Tarrington understood this.

Tony Mo understood this.

Al Sharpe did not understand this.

Al thought he was important.

After Tarrington lunched at the Sushi bar he patronized exclusively, he did a little shopping.

A surprise for Al.

Leaving the flower shop, he set the bouquet on the passenger side floorboard of the Audi. He unplugged the Motorola Satellite phone, placed it behind him on the seat. He'd been burning a secure line for an hour. Talking to Mexico, to Carlos. And talking to Carlos' son Enrique, who'd called Tarrington from his private Gulfstream jet. Enrique was on his way. All kinds of things were going down. Carlos wanted to see Tarrington. Wouldn't tell him what for. Said it was important. They were to meet at a forty-acre ranch south of Las Cruces, New Mexico. Carlos was coming stateside. Very rare. Enrique would be in L.A. to collect Tarrington soon. Tarrington didn't know what to do. For now though, he had direction.

He retrieved his beige lambskin attaché case from the back and laid it gently on the passenger seat. Careful not to scar the delicate lamb leather. He dialed the three-digit combination and opened the case. It was loaded with a vast array of electronic gadgetry; several plantable bugs, all shapes and sizes for a plethora of applications. A miniature camera inside a cigarette lighter, a tape recorder disguised as a cigarette pack, a handheld field-strength meter to sweep for bugs, some multigauged wire, clips, circuits, diodes, chips, and a micro tool kit to make it all easier. This was also where he kept his Tarrington passport and wallet complete with license, credit cards, and a checkbook. Where he switched it out with the Nick Taylor stuff. There was fifty thousand in cash too.

He swept all this towards the hinge and reset the combination, then pushed on the inside bottom of the case. It was a spring catch that floated open. Underneath, fitted snugly in a foam cutout, was a Berretta 92F with two-speed-loader clips full of Black Talon ammunition and a silencer.

Tarrington removed the gun, loaded it, screwed on the silencer. Then he closed the case and started the car.

Pulling into the front lot of the L'Hermitage, he parked well out of the way. He took the masking tape he'd purchased earlier on his shopping spree, tore off eight strips a foot long and stuck them to the steering wheel. He unbuttoned the linen jacket and taped the gun to his stomach. Had the barrel pointing towards his left shoulder. Letting the yellow T-shirt he bought for the occasion fall over the entire rig.

He adjusted his funny round sunglasses just perfectly on his nose and picked up the bouquet with his left hand.

On the way to Al's front door, he wore a smile like he was about to pop the big question. Or something like that.

The L'Hermitage was a world-class, top-flight resort destination. Its property, buildings, linen, booze, ashtrays, and bathrobes all together carried an estimated net worth two notches higher than the upscale. Situated on the grounds were a couple dozen private bungalows. Tarrington didn't know how many. He tried to stay away from Al. Al kept a permanent residence at the L'Hermitage.

Tarrington strolled calmly along the well-manicured pathways, thinking about the years with Al. Through Tony Mo, he'd been introduced to Al early on. Even back then Taylor had figured Al a screaming liability. Nonetheless it had been Al who showed Tarrington the network: Carmine in Vegas, "Fat Frank" in Chicago, Louie the Leech in Florida.

Tarrington ticked off the reasons he had to show Al instant spirituality. Lately Al had been on a binge nine out of every six days. Which was two more than normal. Time and booze had marinated the man's mind. Today Al was mad out of his head, talking about a hit on Tarrington. Actually saying this on the phone while he was speaking with Tarrington. Al's judgement had flown south for the summer. His laxity on the phone had been the deciding factor. Adios Al.

Tarrington knocked on the door. It was a quarter after two. Al Sharpe would be half in the bag by now. He was a real asshole. Especially when he could focus his eyes.

The peephole darkened, then the door flew open and Al held out his arms to give Tarrington a big hug.

Tarrington's eyes got real wide. He looked down and said, "Watch the flowers, Al."

"Yeah, yeah, real nice, Nicky."

Tarrington hunched past Al, checking the premises all the while. "I gotta put them in some water, buddy," he said walking around the bungalow. Looking for a vase. Into the bathroom, the kitchenette, the bedroom, all over. No vase.

Al Sharpe closed the front door, swaying east and west in the entry foyer. Took a couple quick nips off the scotch bottle. He watched Tarrington march back and forth with the bouquet at his chest. Finally he smacked the bottle down on the entry table, wondering why Tarrington was going back into the bedroom. Then he heard it: "Hey Al. Come'ere for a minute, tell me if this…"

Al sauntered towards the summons.

Tarrington was secreted in a blind corner. When Al entered, he waited a moment for the big man to line up exactly with the lighted rectangle of the bathroom doorway.

"Hey Al!"

Beautiful.

Tarrington put a nice round hole, a size seven ring finger type hole, dead center amidst the network of broken capillaries in Al Sharpe's broad forehead. Everything behind that bright red road map exploded like a Roman candle and decorated the back wall of the bathroom. Al's astonished expression stayed with him as he teetered on the big heels of his boa boots.

Tarrington lunged the six feet that separated them and planted a Reebok Amazone sandal squarely in Al's barrel chest.

It deflated with a ragged gasp and Al flew across the bathroom threshold like an epileptic eagle through a roadside billboard.

Tarrington couldn't resist. He looked in on Al. There was a positively one-of-a-kind expression cemented to the big guy's sponge-like face. Tarrington leaned over and prodded Al's cheeks. Felt like sponges too. Now Al smelled like an *empty* bottle of scotch.

Tarrington said, "You look uptight, Al. Relax."

Chapter Six

Returning from Rodeo Drive, with a short stopover at the Ramada Inn for a quick shower before he dressed, Tarrington was ten miles from the marina. Along with his brand new Mafia regulation haircut, he wore a white collared powder blue Burberry shirt and a white silk Countess Mara tie with a dark navy pinstriped V2 Versace suit. On his feet, a pair of white woven leather loafers by Georgio Brutini. He'd never seen a pair of white Brutini's before, so he'd bought them. He actually had a pang about throwing them away tomorrow. He looked just like the kind of guy who'd shoot a high ranking member of the Mafia without prior clearance.

He dialed Tony in New York.

A gruff voice said, "Yo."

"Tell Tony the Trick's callin'."

"Right away, Nicky."

A moment later, the sober monotone of Marcantonio Morelli came on the line. He said, "It sounds like a busy day out there."

Tarrington said, "Mondays are always hectic. Al fell off the wagon today. Knocked him right out."

"Oh yeah?" Tony Mo didn't seem too surprised. "When you think he'll wake up?"

Tarrington said, "No tellin', you know how he likes his naps."

"Ahh, let him go. He needs the rest. At least he sleeps with his mouth closed."

"Feeling pretty sentimental today, huh Tone?"

"The cannolies was stale this morning. I had to switch bakeries."

"Life is full of inconsistencies."

"I just hope my pasta ain't overcooked tonight. It would really turn into a bad day."

"You gotta watch it, Tony. As soon as it sticks to the wall."

"How 'bout you? You eatin' tonight, Nick?"

"As far as I know. If I don't call tomorrow you'll know I got food poisoning."

"Is there anybody I should talk to?" asked Tony.

"You're talking to him now," Tarrington clarified, "don't sweat it. I'll call."

"Try not to put me on hold."

"That's the whole idea."

"Keep your eyes open, Trick. We're all pullin' for ya."

"Enjoy your dinner, Tony. Stand over the pot if ya have to." Tarrington hung up, turned off the Beethoven and pulled into Marina Del Ray.

⸺⊶⊷⸺

Of the docking ganglia that spiderwebbed across the bay, Tarrington's boat, a custom 85-foot Tempest Sport Yacht, was docked at the outside end of a large T-shaped formation stretching well into the water.

Tarrington's little ship, the Pro Bum, occupied the left end of the T and sat transom to transom with a 135-foot Perini Navi ocean crossing sloop, dubbed aptly, the World Affair. This specially made sailing vessel was owned by a Frenchman named Geech LeCroix. Geech had circumnavigated the globe several times. He was revered as a seaman, world renowned for his sailing acumen, had skippered in the America's Cup, won the Whitbread Challenge, and was sometimes featured in yachting and sailing magazines. He was also rumored to be not just rich, but outrageously loaded. His father, long deceased, had

44

passed on a shipyard that had built battleships, destroyers, and various other military monster boats for America and Great Britain during wartime. But most recently, this yard was building ocean liners and mega-luxury yachts for private money.

As the story went, it was on Geech's third circumnavigation that he discovered his daughter. She was seven years old at the time, stranded with nothing but her smile as company. All alone on an out island that was part of the Tuamotou Archipelago of French Polynesia.

Geech and his crew had hung around for weeks and cared for her, yet nobody showed up to claim the child. So Geech adopted the little charmer. She'd stolen every heart on board.

Later, investigation proved her to be the legitimate heiress to a Polynesian crown. She was bona fide royalty, the lone survivor of a bloody tribal feud, left in the care of the nature spirits by her fleeing parents.

Geech had provided her with the best. And she'd grown up to fulfill every vision of what an island princess should be: long willowy legs, perfect breasts suspended tersely over a taut belly. Dusky skin like the shadows of a sunset. Raven black hair worn shoulder length and iron straight, framing almond eyes the color of emeralds. All set in the face of an Egyptian goddess.

Monique.

Three months after Tarrington had first taken delivery of the Pro Bum and rented that slip, Geech and Monique showed up. He never thought twice about their arrival. In fact, he'd gone out of his way to get to know them. He and Monique had been an item for sixteen months now. Self-described as unmarriable, Tarrington had once admitted to Carlos' son, Enrique, that in the race to a joint bank account, Monique was the only contender.

Tarrington parked next to Enrique's Jaguar limousine. He wasn't sure what the hell was going on with the Mexican end of the business, but he knew they'd at least let him explain before they fed him to the pigs. So he marched right past the ship store and headed for the end of the T with all the familiar sights, smells, and sounds of home.

Brine, the screech of seagulls, the water rot of things nautical; and clanging in the sea breeze, that trolley bell suspended from the pilot house of old man Morrison's Grand Banks trawler. Wet hemp was stinking up the walk, but as Tarrington neared the end, the smell of Geech's cherry tainted tobacco hit his nostrils. He could see Geech's bushy-eyebrowed, grey-maned head poking from the aft deck of the World Affair. Geech sipping a brandy-spiked cup of coffee and huffing on the rhino hornpipe. Letting the sun further blemish the skin on his body that the wind and sea had tortured for years.

Tarrington covered the distance, said, "What's up, Geech?"

A pair of delicate gold bifocals balanced on the end of his weather-worn nose. A report of some kind in his lap. He looked up and said, "How 'bout that junkie senator's kid?"

Tarrington nodded, "I saw the news. Crazy world, huh?"

Geech stroked his bushy mustache and told Tarrington, "That asshole Abernathy'll have a helluva time juggling that one up on the hill." Geech gave him that old salt, Herman Melville look.

Tarrington smiled, "I can hardly wait to see the press release," but his eyes spoke of an entirely different curiosity.

Geech saw this, pointed his pipe and said, "She's in your boat with your buddy and his new girlfriend."

"Girlfriend?"

"That's what I said."

"You try that cognac I sent over?" Tarrington asked.

Geech picked up his coffee mug and waved it at Tarrington. "You've got damned good taste, Mr. Tarrington."

Inside the Pro Bum's salon, Carlos' son Enrique sat watching the news. He was slight of build. About 160 pounds. Shorter than Tarrington by a head, with dark features that were distinctively Mexican. But handsome, even with the Mayan beaked nose of his Chiapian ancestors. Today he was dressed in beach thongs with a bright orange tank top hanging over a pair of flower print surfer shorts. A Haliburton Zero briefcase was handcuffed to his wrist. Monique had wondered out loud one day if he were a spy.

Where Tarrington ran a significant portion of just one facet of the retail end, Enrique oversaw the entire Deleon drug concern and was chiefly responsible for laundering the global consortium's wholesaling profits. He'd attended the finest schools money could invade, graduated with a doctorate in International Finance. He owned three banks; Geneva, Hong Kong, and Acapulco. He rigorously exercised his memory and could recall verbatim, pages upon pages of facts, figures, or references of any kind. He detested narcotics, yet his one major goal in life was to see marijuana legalized. Because it was harmless, he would tell you. Because it was beneficial and he had print-out after print-out of reputable scientific verification... all suppressed by the government, and he could prove it. It was entirely feasible he would legalize pot single-handedly should nobody offer to help. Not surprisingly, he had a seething hatred toward all power-aligned bureaucracy. He believed in true communism. He liked the idea of World Order, but had confided to Tarrington the only way it would ever work was if they were to line up everybody on the planet with a net worth over a hundred thousand and shoot them should they fail to disperse their wealth evenly before a predestined date. Himself included. Let the money be used to help the world's populace, not hinder it, as was the current de rigeur. Enrique Deleon was a genius. He was smoking a joint.

"Hit?" he offered Tarrington.

"Makes my nose bleed."

"Stuff wouldn't hurt a fly."

"Maybe not, but it would certainly engender a lackadaisical attitude about eating shit."

"It's all about perspective."

"I don't have an argument."

"Of course not. There isn't one." Enrique inhaled and admired the joint as he blew a stream towards Tarrington, telling him, "It's all political bullshit."

"Give me the goddamned joint, Kiki."

Tarrington took a hit.

Enrique said, "It's Alaskan Thunderfuck."

Tarrington exhaled, "Now why'd you go and do that. I had plans for tomorrow."

"That's what you think."

Tarrington glanced across the salon at an elegant woman snuggled into an armchair. She had her legs tucked under her, sitting as if in deep meditation. He asked Enrique, "You give her some of that?"

At that moment, Monique entered the galley wearing a white two-piece thong bikini. She carried a tray with three mint juleps and a can of Coors. As she stopped in front of Tarrington she practically moaned, "Oh baby, you cut off all your hair."

Tarrington took the can of beer, said, "Growing it was so much fun, I thought I'd do it again."

"You're such a smartass," she told him and served the juleps.

Enrique pointed the joint, indicating the sleek woman perched in the armchair. She was wearing a skin-tight black spandex jumper and silver tipped five-inch black stiletto heels. The jumper told Tarrington she could probably run a hundred yard dash in ten seconds flat. The stilettos told him she may just kick your ass if you beat her.

Enrique said, "Meet your new assistant."

She looked like the kind of woman you'd see in an Austin Martin ad. Or maybe nude, walking her pet leopard down the beach. She lacked only fangs to be a vampress. Her black lipstick a dramatic contradiction to the refined angles of her ivory skin. She wore her dark hair in a stylishly long crewcut. She appeared about six feet tall, and was undeniably sexy in a space station, outer-planetary sort of way. It was a distinct possibility she was a bitch.

Tarrington wondered if she had a sense of humor.

"My what?" he asked.

She rose, offered her hand, "I'm Torren." Her voice was smokier than a Fourth of July barbecue.

Monique looked exasperated. Constipated was more like it. Oh boy, thought Tarrington. "Very nice to meet you, Torren," he shook her hand.

She had a grip like a diamond vice. Her nails were short, black, and nicely manicured. Tarrington winced in exaggerated pain.

Torren smiled. She had good teeth. She was actually quite beautiful.

He asked Monique, "You okay?"

She replied, "Most of the time, why?"

The air crackled with maligned voltage.

"Just curious," Tarrington told her, then whispered to Torren, "Let go."

Torren sat down.

"Come'ere Moni," Tarrington took her by the hand and led her to the forward stateroom. Once there he swept her gracefully into his arms and laid her gently on the big master bed. Carefully he untied her swim top and trailed a line of kisses about her neck and shoulders.

She purred beneath the scrutiny of his lips.

"Look," he whispered to her, "I didn't ask for an assistant. I have no idea what Kiki is up to."

Monique had a look in her eyes, "Torren." She stated with a slight huff. "I'll bet she has sex with animals."

"She's certainly dressed for it," said Tarrington as he stroked the inside of Monique's downy forearms, shucked his shoes and slid onto the bed beside her.

She helped him off with his jacket. He loosened his tie, removed it, and his shirt. She shimmied out of her bathing suit bottoms. He did the same to his trousers.

She said, "Bark like a dog for me."

He whinnied like a horse instead.

———

When they'd finished, he no longer had that ammonia taste in his mouth. He asked her, "How do you feel now?"

She kissed him, "You're so gallant."

"It's only business."

"I know, but I forget 'cause I love you."

"Stop that," he scolded her playfully. "You know how that love word wreaks havoc on my narrow male perception. I'm macho, remember?"

She smiled, "How could I forget?" and stepped into her bathing suit bottoms.

Then he said, "I love you, too."

Monique never asked what he did for a living. She just enjoyed the three or four days a week they managed together.

He would never discuss his true vocation with her anyway, and appreciated her lack of curiosity. He figured she probably had a general suspicion it wasn't entirely legal, but was happy not to explain. They had a great relationship. He was rich. She was an extraordinary beauty with a high 140 IQ besides. Who cared where he got his money. Besides, she'd always been spoiled by her father's extravagant attentions. And Geech was loaded. So being wealthy was normal for her.

If it be known, she loved Tarrington for his body and his wit. She asked, "How long will you be gone?"

"I don't know. I have no idea what this Torren broad's assisting me with."

"Call if it looks bleak."

"Phone sex?" he inquired.

She smiled.

He kissed her on the forehead, told her, "Remember to feed my guinea pig," and left.

Chapter Seven

They rode in the soundproof passenger compartment of Enrique's Jaguar limousine, heading for the airport to board the custom Gulfstream jet. Both part of Enrique's mobile command.

Torren sat with her back to the driver, next to the TV and VCR console, with Tarrington opposite and Enrique on the bench seat beside him. She said, "Did you do her?"

Tarrington replied, "How'd you know I did nails?" He looked askance at Enrique.

Torren said, "You dress like a gangster."

Tarrington told her, "My mother was a tailor for the Mob."

Torren said, "I think we're going to get along just fine."

He said, "Only if you let me win arm wrestling."

Enrique interjected, "I'm glad to see you two hitting it off," then asked Tarrington, "So what's the report?"

Tarrington said, "You saw the news. A senator's daughter is dead. It's like double-helix gnarly dude, two twenty in the shade, et cetera and so on. I've evacuated properly. There's a couple loose ends though."

"Like?" Enrique encouraged.

"Like an Amoco card and a Neiman Marcus card and a girl in a coma and how easy it will be to find the Ferrari's owner."

"I've pulled the plug on the plates," Enrique explained, "In twenty years a Senate sub-committee couldn't iron out the corporate wrinkles in that paper trail. And if they ever do, it'll be the last of the dead ends."

"So what's she do?" Tarrington indicated Torren as if she weren't really there.

Torren spoke for herself, "I kill people, I fly planes, and whatever else the job requires." Kind of leaving it in the air. Being seductive about it.

Tarrington asked, "Is there anything you don't do?"

"Windows."

He wrote: Becky Forrester, Memorial Medical, Los Angeles, Intensive Care, in his spiral note pad, tore out the page and handed it to her. "Make it an irreversible coma. Do you need money to rent a nurse's uniform."

"Negative," she replied.

Tarrington handed her a second page from the note pad. "Get this furniture to another location with no traceable records of the move."

Enrique said, "Is that one of our warehouses?"

"No, one of James'."

"You don't trust anybody, do you Taylor?" Enrique asked.

"I trust Triple A, they've never let me down. Unfortunately, they don't move furniture. And it's Allied Van Lines I'm not jumping in bed with. James is probably safe. I saw a condom in his wallet once."

Enrique asked, "So what about the credit cards?"

"Good question, the girls lifted them. It's a long story."

Torren said, "One you'll tell me some day?"

"Only if you tell me your squat routine."

Enrique said, "Do you like the name Nicolas Taylor?"

"It was fine until this morning."

"Well… here." Enrique went through an exact process and deactivated some booby traps on the Haliburton Zero handcuffed to his wrist. Then he popped it open and handed Tarrington a manila envelope with brand new credit cards and a fresh checkbook. "You're still

Nick Taylor, I changed the birthdate and the social security number though. And you have a Texas address now. Your old social security number has been shut down. But as usual, there's no ceiling on any of the new cards and you pay all the bills. However, I did put three million in the checking account. Consider it bonus."

"For losing thirty kilos?"

"No, you paid for that. I bled it off your trust. So you're actually even with the bonus, well… three twenty-five down with the cash they found in the Ferrari. The car's on the house by the way. We'll call it a business loss and write it off somehow."

Tarrington's salary was automatically credited to his securities trust, but not before it was slipped through a few discretionary accounts. The interest from this trust compounded quarterly, then was wire transferred through a maze of off-shore entities. Mostly financial crevices in and around Enrique's banking charters in Geneva, Hong Kong, and Acapulco, with some friendly charters in Montserrat, New York, and Liechtenstein thrown in for good measure. These monies accumulated in still other off-shore accounts and were ultimately wired into checking and credit accounts in Tarrington's alias and in Tarrington's real name. Enrique had set up the system years ago.

Tarrington said, "Well, losing three hundred thousand is better than three mil. So what about when the Feds figure these other two cards? I didn't always use the drive-thru at the bank, ya know?"

"Ya got a haircut, we'll see. Pluck your eyebrows. Wear colored contacts. Grow a mustache. A fake scar. Makeup. A gold-capped tooth. Try jeans…"

Tarrington's face wrinkled up as if in pain.

"Okay, no jeans. Hell, I don't know. Keep your funny round sunglasses on your nose and let's see what develops."

"I could break it for you," Torren told Tarrington.

"Break what?"

"Your nose," she said.

"That would be natural. Good thinking."

"It would change the color of your eyes, too."

"Nice touch," he said, and smiled as if very happy about this. "So charming."

"It's all in my resume."

"At ease," he ordered her, and turned back to Enrique, "What about a driver's license?" Tarrington was leafing through the identification packet. "A passport?"

"That's what I'm saying. Decide on your new image and we'll shore all that up tomorrow."

"You're such a good little mastermind, Kiki. What's with your father at the Las Cruces ranch?"

"We're gonna hide you out in the middle of a major marijuana operation. It's really good timing on your part, actually. James can run the heroin for now. You've cultivated him well. Torren knows all about the pot."

"How long with the pot thing?" Tarrington asked.

"Until I find a replacement, you're the boss."

"What happened to the old guy?"

"Got hit by a garbage truck."

"Pretty creative, Kiki."

"Not my idea. I think it was the CIA."

"The CIA's trying to steal the patents on this pot machine?" Tarrington showed obvious concern.

"That's why you have Torren. She seduces, tortures, kills, whoever gives you the willies. Simple."

"The CIA?" Tarrington said again, "Why ain't I comin' down both legs?"

"Have you talked to a sex therapist?" Torren asked, "It could be a physical thing too, ya know."

Tarrington kissed her hand.

Enrique said, "My father will explain. It's very important. You've been marked for this for two weeks now so don't think that Senator's daughter had much to do with it. Smile. There's perks. I'm giving you a brand new Gulfstream jet to use. I'm doubling your salary. You have a very capable assistant at your service."

Tarrington said, "Throw in a dental plan and you've got a deal."

"Okay, but there's a deductible."

"For root canals?"

"It's not much."

"I'll take the job."

"Hey," Enrique's tone signaled his sincere appreciation. "Whatever you did to convince that girl she could climb a tree in that Ferrari, thanks. I've been trying to get my father out of the heroin trade for years. It's a nasty business, as you yourself have frequently expressed to me. This might be the ticket."

Knowing Enrique, Tarrington figured that could be the reasoning behind the three million dollar bonus, or not charging him for the lost kilos. Either way you looked at it. Nevertheless, Tarrington could smell his retirement, it seemed so close at hand. He smiled, told Enrique, "The fact that you doubled my salary scares me. But why the jet, Kiki?"

"You're gonna need speed."

Tarrington reached into the mini-refrigerator and handed everyone a cold beer. He popped the top on his and held it aloft, signaling an impending toast.

"Never buy the cashmere at Macey's." He said and drank.

Torren just smiled.

Chapter Eight

In keeping with his wave of motivational awards, Enrique had purchased and registered a new Audi Quattro to the Texas based Nicolas Taylor and had it sitting in the short term lot of the El Paso International Airport when they arrived. More stuff. The whole deal starting to worry Tarrington.

For now, the second helper assigned to Tarrington, pilot Nando, would have first shot sitting behind the wheel of the Audi. That is, after he finished his immediate duties. Flying.

They were airborne in a Cessna Caravan. Nando regularly glancing back to smile at his new boss, Nicolas Taylor, who was balanced next to Enrique on a jump seat in the cargo hold.

Enrique had changed clothes during the flight from L.A. and was now wearing a ZZ Top concert T-shirt, jeans, and tennis shoes. The briefcase still handcuffed to his wrist.

They were on a heading for the Las Cruces ranch. A short hop over the Organ Mountains. Not a cloud in the desert sky, the sun shining in their eyes.

Tarrington caught Nando smiling at him again and vowed to have a word with the man. The drone of the Lycoming single prop and the roar of air sucking past the open bay door made conversation difficult, yet Tarrington yelled, "Why must I die over and over again?"

Enrique yelled back a Syrus Maxim, "Practice is the best of all instructors!"

Tarrington frowned, mumbled something to himself, removed

his double-breasted suit jacket and jumped out of the plane with no further questions. The jacket flapped violently in his fist.

The ranch was actually south of Las Cruces, New Mexico, near El Paso and the Mexican border. It was nestled in the lush Rio Grande River valley with fifteen of its forty acres bordering the river.

The main structure was molded from sand colored adobe with bright red Spanish tiles on a pitched roof line. From the air, it looked half pueblo, half Disney World.

The large kidney-shaped pool was bearing up fast on Tarrington as he fell. He pulled the rip cord, felt his stomach go for that crucial moment when you didn't know if the chute was going to save you, or not.

The Air Force designed BP-15 backpack parachute was originally intended for spies because the parcel was so compact it could be worn undetected beneath a suit jacket. Enrique liked the concept so much, he'd purchased twelve dozen and took the course. Now he was qualified to fold and pack them himself. He once said it was a fine hobby for a man who was as busy as himself because he could circumvent crowded airports whenever the need arose.

Tarrington was not so enthusiastic about sharing in such a hobby. Extreme skiing, minus the chute, was where he drew the line. However, protocol had its sacrifices. He used the steering cords and guided himself to a graceful landing just over the pool, popping the release at the last possible moment to settle the square chute nicely in the water behind him. He then unlatched the harness and took the Versace suit jacket from his clenched teeth. Spittle on the collar. He shook his head in mock disgust. Then shook the jacket as well. Enrique landed nearby and went in the house without a word.

With an aloof dignity, Tarrington put on the coat, straightened the Countess Mara silk tie, smoothed the silk pants and casually walked to a large table at the crux of the rear courtyard.

A uniformed servant, tray in hand, was rushing to meet him.

In stride, Tarrington took the glistening can of Coors from the tray and opened it. His mouth was so dry he could've hung wallpaper with the paste from his tongue.

At the courtyard table he halted, took a long pull from the can, and said, "Chuckie, How's tricks?"

Carlos was even shorter than his son, Enrique, and sported fur on every available skin surface of his body, except for the top of his shiny sun-browned head. He reclined shirtless with his hands folded restfully on his belly, hiding beneath a curly shock of his large blackish beard. Wearing only frayed corduroy cut-offs and old brown leather sandals, one of which was propped against the table's edge. His unlikely grey eyes sparkled mischievously from either side of his hawkish nose when he chuckled and asked, "Treeks?"

"What's going on?" Tarrington restated.

"Ahh," Carlos pushed away from the table, cocked his chair back on two legs. His free leg swung from the chair's edge. "Nada, my son. Jest beesness. How is deese problema por deese muy importante chickeeta who es muerto?"

"I did what I could. We're still cleaning up the mess."

"Es mala?"

"Naw, it shouldn't get any worse. I'm here ain't I?"

Carlos smiled. Thirty-two perfect caps reflected the sun. "Es bueno, you are de sleek one, my son."

"That's a rumor, Chuck, and I'd appreciate it if you'd not repeat it."

Carlos laughed heartily, let the chair legs slam to the patio, then busied himself topping two shot glasses from a dusty bottle of murky yellow liquid.

"Nooooo," thought Tarrington. It was the expected selfless surrender to tradition he suffered every time he visited the old man. "You gonna make me drink that skunk piss again?" he asked Carlos.

"Si," Carlos told him, and with a smile, handed over one of the shot glasses.

It was homemade mescal. Rot gut Tequila. One of Carlos' hobbies. Tarrington was getting hobbied out this trip.

"Salud," Carlos raised his glass.

Tarrington drank it. A gag reflex zippered through his frame to ground out at his feet. His left eye watered a tad.

"Es good, theese batch, no?"

"No," answered Tarrington, "Es pooh pooh."

Carlos got a real kick out of this. He chuckled till his nose ran. Finally, he said, "Come, Raul es here. I have a new friend for you to meet."

While Tarrington was somewhat of an Executive Vice-President in charge of Continental marketing and Distribution in the Deleon hierarchy, Raul was Chairman of the Board. Raul ran all drug gathering, packing, storing, shipping operations south of the border. He also coordinated trans-Pacific heroin consignments with a man named Khun Sa. Khun Sa controlled the majority of all poppy cultivation and white heroin processing in the far eastern region of Burma, Thailand, and Laos, known as the Golden Triangle.

Raul had his finger directly on the pulse of all Mexico's drug activity and could stop this thunderous heartbeat just as easily as he could speed it up or slow it down. He was soft spoken, fit, well preserved for a man in his early sixties. A product of an austere lifestyle. He had that formidable grimness of a leading man: a movie star's profile, tall, elegant in mannerism.

When Carlos and Tarrington entered the rich masculine confines of the sitting room, Raul and Enrique were there. Standing next to them was a man who was unmistakably a general in the Mexican Army. Raul's hand was affectionately clasped to the man's showy epaulets. Turning towards Tarrington with a smile, Raul said warmly, "Nicolas Taylor," signifying that Tarrington's true identity would not be revealed to the man in the impeccably pressed uniform. Raul, of course, knew the entire story.

"I'd like you to meet my very good friend, General Montoya," Raul introduced Tarrington.

General Montoya was well past seventy, brown as maple syrup, wrinkled, weathered, and ugly as a mud fence. He was bent like a well-forged scimitar, yet his coal-colored eyes shone as polished jade and told Tarrington he was sharp as one too.

Despite the spinal curvature, he carried himself and his medaled uniform with a regal pride. His manner was effusive and gregarious, and when he smiled his teeth were as perfect and fake as Carlos'. The expression was infectious. The General offered his hand.

Tarrington found himself grinning broadly as he pressed the flesh. "Very nice to meet you, General."

"Señor Taylor," the General's voice carried well. He effected an expansiveness when he spoke. "It is very nice finally to have met you, my friend."

Like Raul, the General enunciated clearly and spoke English well. Tarrington said, "I didn't know you'd been waiting, or I would've shown a lot sooner."

The General liked this and proved himself by clapping Tarrington vigorously on the back. The old man's strength betrayed his appearance.

Tarrington made a slight correction, turned his shoulder towards the General's affection. He wanted to tell the little guy to relax, but the present pecking order would not permit it. He commented on the rows of decorative medals displayed on the General's uniform.

"Looks like you've championed the Mexican people's cause more than once, General."

General Montoya puffed his chest proudly, and said, "Very good of you to notice, Señor Taylor." He fingered an impressive looking bejeweled ribbon. "For instance," he said, "I received this for moving more than a hundred tons of marijuana in a month!" The General's voice was a boomer. He broke into a jolly self-effacing laugh. Enrique even joined in.

Carlos said, "Mi amigo, Montoya es clown, no?"

"Si," Tarrington responded.

Carlos continued, "for theese reason you will work well together." The furry guy was feeling pretty playful. The General had that effect on everyone around him. Carlos, however, brought the meeting to order in the next breath.

There were five strategically positioned overstuffed brown leather club chairs and everyone found theirs. A huge cypress-stump coffee table separated the players. Drinks were served and the meeting began.

The contextual gist was simple. Raul needlessly explained that he was responsible for the General receiving the marijuana at a well-guarded Juarez warehouse just across the El Paso portion of the Rio Grande. He then turned the floor over to the General.

Armed with an aromatic fat green cigar, the General told Tarrington that he owned and operated most of the Mexican immigration officialdom, a fair slice of local American Border Patrol, a cadre from the El Paso County Sheriff's office, three FBI and two local DEA agents.

He confided that at the Juarez warehouse, fuel tankers with sectioned-off filler hatches were packed with marijuana and driven over the river, unloaded in various stateside holding facilities, some of which Tarrington would administer in his new capacity, and then the process was repeated by stateside crews to trans-ship the product north, east, and west. Using specially designed cars the same was done with Columbian cocaine and Carlos' heroin. Business was good, the General related. He was at Tarrington's service, he said with sincerity noted by all. He handed over a card with two numbers: home and work. And this had him snickering a bit. After shaking hands all around, he said good-bye twice, and finally left. Raul ushered him out.

Enrique and Carlos and Tarrington remained, sitting quietly while a servant brought more drinks and then another followed with dinner. Carlos and Enrique had thick cuts of filet mignon, baked potatoes with sour cream, chives, creamy butter, fresh steamed asparagus under hollandaise and Louis the XIV cognac with Macanudo cigars to compliment raspberry mousse.

Tarrington, naturally, had a serious medium-rare bacon double cheeseburger with extra extras and his choice of three different hot mustards. He tried all of them, drank beer with the meal, and accepted graciously a snifter of Louis the XIV afterward. He passed on the cigar and nibbled at the mousse. He was thinking about the bonus, the jet, the car, the doubled salary, the pilot Nando, and the very capable and obviously very dangerous Torren.

When Enrique and Carlos finally pushed their desserts away, Tarrington said, "All right, what's the real deal?"

Enrique was solemn.

Carlos nodded, a vacant expression looking at the burning ember of his cigar.

Enrique produced a cassette tape, put it in the same telephone answering machine that'd made it originally, then proffered an explanation:

"Your predecessor, Taylor… the man who once ran the stateside pot operation… who was recently killed by the garbage truck… did not know the location of this ranch but he knew the number to this phone. I gave him the number to call in case of emergency. He did not know my father, even though the phone here is usually forwarded to Chiapas where my father stays. This way he could find Raul or myself at any time. The message you're about to hear was left three hours before his death. He called from Jacksonville, Florida."

"Does this guy have a name?"

"Guido, they called him Guido."

"Quaint."

Enrique played the tape. The call was obviously made from a crowded bar. Loud music, drunken laughter, the roar of partygoers and clinking of glassware could be heard in the background. Guido's voice was clear and determined, edged with a little bravado. He said, "They're all over me. It's getting pretty hairy. They pulled me in this morning. They wanna flip the whole system and control the market. They want me to help. I told them "Fuck you in your neck," so be careful. Here comes one now, I gotta go…"

Carlos was close to despondent, he said, "He was a good man, like you, Taylor."

"Who exactly are they?" Tarrington asked.

"Well," Enrique began, "I've eliminated the Mafia, the Jamaican posse, the militias, the Aryan brotherhood, the South American cartels, the Knights of Columbus, masons, Rainbow Coalition, the feminist movement, gay bashers, New Agers, and any possibility of this being some kind of frat house hazing-week prank. So that really only leaves us with the Feds, the secret government, the CIA, the fifth estate, however you wanna phrase it." Enrique held his palms up, shoulders shrugged, "Looks like a Langley thing."

Now Tarrington understood all too well the purpose behind his big promotion. It was going to be his job to square off with the Agency, or at least figure out how.

In his mind he heaved a great sigh. It seemed he'd been poised to get out of the drug business ever since he'd gotten in it. Not that he didn't enjoy the danger, the adrenaline rush, the money, and all the nifty little ego perks being a VIP in some of the big syndicate circles, but now he was all too aware of the federal government's ultimate involvement in the racket.

He knew that every kilo of heroin he inadvertently saw to its final destination was just one more vote up on Capital Hill. One more vote for the World Management Team to propagate their semi-fabricated statistical carnage and pass yet another civil freedom sucking law. One more vote to allow them to further assume their mantle as nosy, over-bearing, control-obsessed nitwits drunk with their own power.

He'd thoroughly examined it from the "heroin and cocaine addiction kills" point of view, but as an enlightened thinker, he'd witnessed the evidence countless times that people would pursue whatever they could in their all consuming search for mental, emotional, and wallet expanding experiences.

And it was this very fact that the governments abroad were cognizant of, wielding the exact same knowledge, they fed it purposely, and turned out a full scale machine that maximized their advantage both coming and going.

It was this very fact that had driven Tarrington to the point of indecision time and time again.

He knew that every kilo passing through the turnstile of his personal assembly line was just another brick in the prison wall the Feds were secretly building around the entire planet.

He knew that if he were to stop… only another would pick up the line he'd left dangling. And this other would most probably work for the government itself.

He also knew that if he quit without Carlos' blessing, he might as well tie a noose with the loose end of that line and slip it around his neck.

It was as if his personal integrity and self-preservation were dressed out for battle and lingering malevolently on either side of the valley of his soul.

And now Carlos had him pitted against the very faction of the shadow government that supervised the entirety of his dilemma.

But for some reason this provided an eerie solace for Tarrington. Perhaps it was the precise opportunity he'd been seeking to drive his self-preservation from its hillock and lead his personal integrity into the battlement.

"What a screaming idiot you are," Tarrington thought to himself as he gave both Carlos and Enrique the grim macho look and asked them:

"Okay, so where can I rent a nice fitting Superman costume?"

Chapter Nine

In his usual room at the ranch, Tarrington lounged in his underwear and watched the eleven o'clock news. He was not pleased to see Happy Home Cleaning service and his freshly evacuated townhouse given a forty-second spot. Not on a local news station. Which meant he was national now.

Leaving the townhouse, three employees of Happy Home were apprehended by the Los Angeles police force SWAT team. One employee, a voluptuous Ms. Narissa Nunez, was taken into custody immediately. Apparently, she had landed a vicious slap to the face of one of the three cops conducting her "pat" search. As a result, she was brutally clubbed and subsequently charged with assault on a police officer. The camera failed to catch the part where the cops "patted" the wrong place.

With the LAPD none too mentally balanced, the townhouse was entered and found "completely cleaned out," said the announcer. Dusted for prints and "nothing usable turned up."

Tarrington greatly appreciated this and thanked higher intelligence for the propitious timing of it all. The two credit cards had been found and traced rather quickly, but not quickly enough.

Unfortunately, Happy Home Cleaning was not so happy anymore. They'd been named a principal accomplice in the flight of "International Heroin Kingpin, Nicolas Taylor." Its bank account frozen, business closed down, employees interrogated. Narissa Nunez herself was being held without bail. Further arrests were pending. It sent Tarrington directly to the wet bar for a cold one. He detected the pungent odor of a nervous sweat breaking out under his arms.

It was not a good development. Of course, being the target of an international manhunt never was.

To relieve some tension, he strapped on the gravity boots and swung onto the combination chin-up/dip bar he kept at the Las Cruces ranch. He had one set up like it at Carlos' place in Chiapas, Mexico too. Wherever he might be staying on business.

After fifty inverted sit-ups, fifty dips, and seventeen and a half pull-ups, someone knocked on the door. Tarrington yelled, "It's open," and continued. Slowly. Working on a set of twenty-five.

Torren was barefoot, but still dressed in her black spandex jumper. She and Nando had just returned from the El Paso airport driving the Audi. She'd stayed behind in LA to take care of things for Tarrington. The first thing she said looking as him was, "Your abs are exquisite."

He said, "I'm bulimic. Puking is really good for them." Then he reversed his handhold and started on the last set of twenty-five with his back to her now.

He did the pull-ups in a concentrated fashion; very slowly going up, holding the body with the chest at bar level, then very slowly going down. He asked her at the top of number five, "How'd it go?"

Her voice was soft and detached, coming from the bed, "Your Becky Forester girl died of complications. There will be no investigation of wrongdoing."

At the top of six, he said, "Please elaborate. It's my policy that everybody in the company feel comfortable talking to the boss. Go ahead, let it all hang out."

"Let me put it this way," her words measured, "I know more about natural poisons than most of your molecular biologists these days. My mother was a Green Witch."

Tarrington said, "So what's that make you?"

"A bad bitch."

"And the furniture?" He lowered himself from number eight, inhaling in proportion to his descent. "You pulled it out of the storage room…?"

"It's done. I've a new address for you."

It was nearly a minute before he said, "No evidence of the move? No way to figure it?"

Her eyes were an icy blue. Had he been facing her, they would have chilled him. She asked him, "What did you tell me in the limo?" not betraying her offense at his imprudent questioning of her professionalism. "There's no need to ask me whether or not I can follow simple directions."

Not that he could detect it aurally, but he did feel the skin behind his ears prickle. So he didn't pursue it. Three full repetitions later he changed the subject.

"Drink?"

"Jack Daniels and Tabasco," she answered.

He smiled to himself. "Why don't you make it? I'd hate to risk a sports injury." He lowered his body. Number twelve. From the corner of his eye, he saw her behind the bar. Sure enough, she poured about a tablespoon of Tabasco over a three jigger shot of Jack Black.

He finished the set, dropped off the bar, and because the bathroom doorway was directly before him, proceeded to the shower. Saying over his shoulder, "Give me a minute or so."

Torren didn't say a word.

<hr />

When he emerged from the bathroom fifteen minutes later, the lights were dimmed and a lone candle burned on the night stand.

Torren was sprawled provocatively on the bed with the sheet and spread pulled back to reveal a long vertical slice of her nude body.

Without hesitation, Tarrington cinched the towel tighter about his waist and strolled casually to the wet bar, removing a bottle of '81 Lafite Rothschild's Blanc de Blanc from the refrigerator. He scooped two champagne glasses from the overhead rack and moved to the bed. Once there he carefully peeled the bottle's cork, opened it and poured the shimmering liquid into the two glasses, serving Torren first.

He raised his in toast. The glasses clinked together lightly in the candlelight.

"To seducing the boss," he said.

She drank, but not without smiling first.

He refilled. Another toast.

"The softest overcomes the hardest as the wise yield to the ever changing currents of power." He hoisted his glass and drained it.

She said, "So, you're coming to bed?"

Delicately, he lifted the bedspread and sheet and covered her bare breast. "Bend like a reed in the wind," he told her.

She uncovered herself, exposing the very same breast, and said, "Fine, I'm bending."

He covered her back up, stood, adjusted his bath towel and said to her, "Never rush the inevitable."

"Where are you going?" she said.

At the door he replied, "I'm leaving before my reed won't bend."

The door closed behind him with a soft clunk.

Chapter Ten

Upon waking in the spare bedroom, Tarrington went to his own room to find it empty. He dressed in the nylon shorts, tennis socks, and Nike Cross Trainers that Nando had shopped for on his first trip from the airport. Before dawn he was jumping rope. Twenty minutes later he ran around the property a few times, then detoured to the Jiffy Mart several hundred yards down the road. There he bought a cold beer, a *GQ*, an *Esquire*, and jogged back to the ranch with a long pause to admire the sunrise and sip his beer.

Tarrington was far from being an electronics expert, but he'd tinkered enough to understand certain functions. Once showered, he had the contents of his lambskin attaché spread out on the dining room table. Next to the table was a foot locker he had brought from the hold of the Pro Bum. It was full of more gadgetry. Now Tarrington had his hands laced with various colored wires. Preparations.

When Carlos shuffled in at eight o'clock, Tarrington bugged his cereal bowl and played back the snap, crackle, pop real loud while the fuzzy fellow was drinking his coffee.

Carlos almost spit up on himself, this was such a surprise. He told Tarrington he had *mala cabeza* (bad brains), and took his coffee to another room in the big house.

Inside his heart though, Carlos was hopeful and happy. His surrogate son would surely figure out the problems assaulting the Deleon empire and fix them straight-away. He'd been praying unceasingly for this to his patron Saint Contraband.

Tarrington assembled a portion of this master surveillance center in the Audi's trunk, running a few extra wires up front, hooking a couple of mikes under the dash. At nine o'clock he called on Torren in her bungalow off the pool deck.

She answered the door nude, had a sheen of sweat covering her sleek body. "Come in," she said and went straight back to her business.

She was kicking a hard rubber baseball suspended from the ceiling by a thick piece of elastic. This target hovered about six feet off the floor. First she'd use the instep, then her heel, then the outside edge of her foot. Front kicks, side kicks, reverse roundhouses, spinning back kicks, and a couple you didn't see at the theater. The ball was zinging frantically from one end of the room to the other, stretching the elastic to its breaking point, it seemed, almost every time. Yet none of the furniture was disturbed. She had a great aim.

Tarrington found a chair and watched her intently for fifteen minutes. Her graceful execution of the kicks and attendant movements were astounding. Tarrington was reminded of the ballet, or perhaps a Degas painting.

When she finished, Tarrington produced a half-dozen pages torn from the *GQ* and *Esquire* magazines, and handed her the stack. Paper-clipped to the top was a page from his spiral note pad. On it, his neck, sleeve, chest, waist, inseam, and shoe size. He gave her the keys to the Audi, pointed out some Donna Karan, Gucci, and a Krizia outfit he liked, told her to use her best judgment on the shoes, and to go ahead and pick up something for herself. He gave her his gold Mastercard.

There was a peculiar tension floating about. "Perhaps she's a little miffed about last night," Tarrington was thinking.

She patted her face with a clean towel, looked at him and then at the magazine pictures she'd set on the table.

"You're an imperious bastard as well," she said.

"Bingo," he thought, and said to her, "We're getting along just fine, wouldn't you say?"

Tarrington went to his room and turned on CNN. He cracked the mobile Motorola and went through the motions: sensor wand, clean frequency, scrambler, and called James.

James had a Motorola too. Same with Al. Enrique had given Tarrington three of them some years back and told him they were "safe" phones. Enrique had actually purchased them from Torren, who had stolen twenty from a high security compound at the Ft. Bliss Military Reservation in El Paso. After only two dates, she'd totally wrecked a young man's mind and he'd let her visit him at his post. He'd actually helped her load them into the windowless van she had brought for the job. That had been three years ago.

Enrique had hired Torren through some contacts in the European Sector of the Deleon empire. On two separate occasions Torren's name had come up where a professional killer was concerned. Both persons recommending her were lifelong confidants of Enrique. Nonetheless, he'd checked her out all the way back to the fifth grade and hadn't found anything he didn't like. She'd won his trust even more so since then. He'd paid her five thousand apiece for those mobile Motorolas.

James answered his on the second ring.

"Up early," Tarrington said.

"Yeah, things to do. You see the news?"

"Try 327.7." Tarrington hung up and dialed in frequency 327.7, cleared it, waited three minutes, and called James back.

Now they had a secure line.

"About the cleaning service?" Tarrington asked.

"Yeah, that and they found Al dead in his bathroom. And that girl who just couldn't distinguish a right turn from an oak tree, Becky Forrester? Well, she's dead too. And your furniture is no longer at my

Yorba Linda storage room. Jesus Christ, Nick, you were pretty active yesterday."

"Scrubbing bubbles, James. Just cleaning up the mess."

"Well Al's an industrial-strength mess now. The FBI looked into his fancy Motorola briefcase phone and linked it to a lot stolen from some Army base in Texas. You realize this is the end of our sterile safe phones?"

"Why's that?"

"The Feds are working with the military to scramble us at the satellite source. I'm surprised we're having this conversation as it is."

"Whoops," said Tarrington.

"Hell," James told him matter of factly, "I'd have been in a hurry to get out of Al's place too. So ya forgot about the phone? So what? You're on double-secret probation. Report directly to me."

Tarrington smiled, "So we're both fuck ups. It must be the weather, huh?"

"Shit happens," James commented. "And it happens to be raining shit. Worst storm I've seen in years."

"Anything else?"

"Not really. They're saying Al was a mob hit from the heroin in the Ferrari. Pretty quick thinking, huh? When in doubt, blame the mob." James paused, "Hey, aren't you watchin' the news?"

"Cable's hard to get here," Tarrington replied. "The greater Rio de Janeiro Cable Company's on strike again. Damn unions."

"But the weather's better, right?"

"It's snowing, yeah."

James said, "I believe I'll keep my head down and my eyes open."

"Good plan. Tony wants no delays, though."

"I figured that," James said, "I shuffled the cars, put all my drivers on a plane for the Costa Del Sol. I'll be doing all the deliveries myself until this thing blows over."

"Nice work," Tarrington congratulated him, "consider your salary doubled."

"That's sweet of you honey. But when will we dance again?"

"I'll meet you in Stockholm. I'll be the one with the Groucho glasses and the broken Nobel Prize hidden under my jacket. How's next week sound?"

"Let me check my calendar…"

"Let's see how it unfolds." Tarrington told him, "We're gonna have to go back to the old system. Figure out some good pay phones. Pull out the February codes."

"What a drag, huh?"

"Nothing safe lasts forever."

"Tell the girl from Ipanema to be sure and use her sun block, " James added.

Tarrington said, "It's winter down here, she must be in Europe with your drivers. All I can see is fat chicks for miles."

"I'll tell them to keep a look out. We'll have her on the first flight back."

Tarrington said, "I'm on my way to the sky lounge."

"Have a nice day, Bob," James told him.

Tarrington hung up, took the mobile Motorola briefcase phone outside and smashed it with an old shovel. About two thousand tiny shards of wire, computer chips and plastic. Then he used the same shovel to dig a hole and bury the remains. "Rest in pieces," he told it.

Back in the bedroom, CNN confirmed everything James had said and more. The more was the heat. More heat. It was getting hot, hot, hot. Becky Forrester's father turned out to be Pierce Winthrop Forrester III, major stockholder of major blue chip companies, major anti-drug crusader, major contributor to too many political campaigns. This manifested immediately as a major pain in Tarrington's backside. And simply because he happened to stop at a particular bar to have that drink with James… where two coke-starved party girls on a head hunt happened to drive by… all for the want of an after-burger cognac.

To keep his mind off the old crap, he thought about the new crap. On a table in the corner of his room was the receiver station for the master surveillance center he'd set up in the trunk of the Audi. The unit he had rigged up for the El Paso play. He dialed the frequency of the two microphones he'd secreted in the dash of the Audi.

Torren was listening to county 'n western. She was singing along to Reba. Sounded just like her. Quite a voice actually.

Now Tarrington was really perplexed. God forbid should Torren return from the shopping trip and hand him a pair of cowboy boots, a plaid shirt with breast pockets and pearl inlaid buttons, and jeans…

Jeans.

Yikes.

He shuddered at the thought, talking to himself, "and you think you got problems now, Mr. T."

Chapter Eleven

On the Chesapeake all was not well. Five miles south of Annapolis, in the library of an elegant waterfront home, three men sat before a videotaped CNN broadcast.

With the huge handcarved mahogany table, the high backed leather executive chairs, and the musty odor of aged binding glue, it could have been the conference room of an old English Hunt Club.

But it was a CIA venture.

One man was so black he seemed purple. He had biceps like cannon balls and legs so thick from weightlifting, his pants were specially tailored. All this wedged tight in his chair. Looking pretty ambivalent about the videotape he was being forced to view for the fifth time. His attention turned instead to a brace of orioles that had abandoned the sharp-leafed sycamore by the boat dock and were relocating their nest to the sill of the bulletproof Plexiglas picture window. He couldn't hear them, but it looked like they were raising some kind of holy hell. Mellonhall, trained CIA killer, simply loved birds, but was careful not to let his over-reactive boss see him daydreaming. He hid the evidence of this behind one of his monster biceps.

The man occupying the head of the table, normally the svelte, impeccably dressed ivy leaguer, had allowed his blue blood to run red. The pressure was on. His tie was askew. A veritable mess by his standards.

He was Robert Preston. And the videotape was telling him he was in danger of failing. The CIA's Domestic Operations Group needed the account. He couldn't fail, simple as that. The establishment would never accept a loser.

Preston was head of the Creative Financing Division, a relative department within the Domestic Operations Group or DOG.

DOG was the section of the CIA the National Security Council's NSC-10/1 and NSC-10/2 conditional memos had helped pave the way to operate in-country, utilizing extra-legal procedures in the name of national security. DOG was, like the National Security Agency (NSA), the premier super-secret intelligence group, by executive order, exempt from all laws that didn't name them in the text as being subject to that law. In other words, DOG operatives could undertake any endeavor; drug dealing, money laundering, bank robbing, terrorism, the issuance of destabilizing propaganda, etc. and not have to worry about the judicial systems' policing of such behavior. DOG operatives were literally above the law unless the law singled them out specifically. And where did that happen? Nowhere. It was their job to operate extra-legally. And operate they did.

DOG was a major player involved in the nurturing in of the New World Order. A concept that would take one of its biggest steps forward when all the pieces were in place to initiate a Martial Law Rule within the United States. It was DOG's primary responsibility to put these pieces in place. Just in case. Cornering the illegal drug markets, then using the proceeds to finance other black operations such as instigating social terror via the direct provocation of violent crime, and then dispersing the propaganda, was Domestic Operation's forte. Frighten the public into accepting an existence governed by Martial Law Rule. These scenarios were a predominate condition of the Domestic Operations Group's unofficial charter.

Robert Preston, as DOG's chief bagman, was an extremely important figure in this particular version of the New Age hierarchy. He was charged with the successful completion of ten identical operations involving the world's ten largest drug cartels.

Distribution networks untainted by CIA influence. Underworld organizations still clinging to their sovereignty. Divide and conquer was the premise behind Preston's duty. It was the premise behind his government's duty.

If Preston did his job correctly, the ushering in of a New World currency would be made easier, and even more beneficial to the ruling elite. As if they weren't raking in enough already.

Preston had business on the brain and high blood pressure thumping in his temples. One-tenth of the operation he was in charge of had just taken a major blow. Its second in weeks.

He fidgeted, but soothed himself by raking his perfectly trimmed thumbnail over the bottom corner of Albert Pike's *Morals & Dogma*. His bible… the book he'd spent the morning reading, waiting for the other two men to arrive.

The third man in the room was sprawled like a teenager before the television. But this man was far from teenaged. Judging from the condition of his hide he could've had grandchildren who were teenagers. His face was rumpled and ocean worn, weather-beaten from countless voyages over the world's waters. He had long wiry salt-'n-pepper eyebrows that matched a swoopy mustache and wavy grey hair. A contrast to the dark scaly hide of his face. He looked twenty years past his sixty and snored softly. His head lulled to one side, rested on the cushioned leather chair back.

The gangly Frenchman was, like Mellonhall, uninterested in the video, even though it was the first run through for him. He'd arrived late, per usual. A busy man with boatbuilding and arms shipments and all the crap going down in Jacksonville, Florida after his number-one agent had run over a non-cooperative with a big blue garbage truck. He wasn't happy flying to Annapolis every time the tautly strung Preston scheduled an emergency meeting. So he caught a couple winks, doing something constructive. Sleep when you can.

Preston pointed the remote control. The videotape froze. The sound muted. Nothing but a picture of a Motorola briefcase phone. He pretended not to notice his French counterpart snoozing beside him. Angry or not, he had to respect the man. The old sailor was the exception, accorded a top position in the Domestic Operations Group to assist in the campaign. He was the chief representative from Europe, a bona fide Bilderberger. Preston spoke softly, "Mellonhall..."

"Yes, Preston," Mellonhall's head snapped to attention. "My man..." So taken with the orioles he'd been startled.

"You said you called the Pentagon?" Preston was on the verge of a nervous tick.

"Yes, Preston," Mellonhall said through a sigh. He acted stoically indifferent, but was ready to reach out and squeeze the boss' head like a bad tomato.

"Well I think we ought to call them back. That idea about jamming the frequency has to keep. God damn Feds, can't they call somebody before they get to spouting off. We've lost the Motorola's surveillance benefit. I'm going to have to accept it."

Mellonhall bore down on the sheen of Preston's jelled hair, saw a trickle of VO5 slide down the ribs in the man's ever-pinched forehead. "You sure, now?" he asked.

"Oh shit, Clarence. I'm not..." Preston's thumbnail increased its tempo on the pages of Pike's masterpiece. His other hand rustled the Frenchman. Delicately.

"Geech... I've a question for you. Sorry to disturb you .. got a question old salt... but I've..."

Geech's wind rutted eyelids raised slowly, the pointy ends of his bushy brows laboring along with them. "Yes, Robert," he murmured, "we jam the frequency..."

"You really think so...?" asked Preston.

"Mella?" Geech looked at Mellonhall. "We got him boxed in, right? We don't need that briefcase tap anymore, right?"

Mellonhall told him, "Right as white, homeboy."

Geech turned to Preston. "Our man Tarrington is far from stupid, on this we all agree. I know first hand. But like Mella says, we got him all boxed in. So let's see how it develops. If I know Tarrington, he's seen the news and the Motorola is already in the trash."

Preston said, "What if he refuses? When we confront him? Like the last guy?"

Geech smiled at Preston as if the man were a child. Told him, "Tarrington is nothing like the last guy. Don't lose any more sleep over this, Bob. When it comes time to choose sides, he'll make the proper decision. We should've run that Guido dickhead over years ago."

Preston seemed appeased with this summation. He said, "Is that mess in Jacksonville cleaned up?"

"Collins made it go away," Geech informed him, "All the right people have received all the right phone calls."

Collins was a life long company man, assigned to Geech for the duration. A good man as far as Geech was concerned, he'd shown no real animosity that some wealthy industrialist with virtually no direct field experience had been placed over him. In fact, he'd given his all to show Geech the ropes, and had taken a bit of instruction here and there himself. Geech had been moving in intelligence circles for forty years. He'd picked up a few pointers along the way.

"Collins is a good man," Preston seemed to be talking to himself.

Geech swung his arm up and consulted the Rolex Submariner, signifying his impatience with the proceedings.

Preston took this hint, said, "Well, I'm cutting it close. There's a group meeting with the DDI and God himself in forty-five minutes. Who knows what traffic will hold. Thank you both for showing on such short notice. It was nice to touch base if nothing else. And please, forgive me for my constant attentions. My ass, though, is literally on the line here."

Geech and Mellonhall nodded in unison.

Preston exited the library, the door making a noise much like the lid of a grand piano being slammed as he left.

"He sure be gettin' worked up over a little spy shit, now don' he?"

"I wish you'd talk right Mella. The government sends you to some of the best language schools in the world and you talk like some ghetto nigger."

"The company found my black ass in the ghetto, knockin' off old farts like you for my lunch money. And all that schoolin' didn't teach me a thing about proper diction in my native language," he said, stressing native with a grin, "All that fancy school I can talk Russian now. You wanna talk Russian, I talk right?" Mellonhall stood. He towered over Geech, glowering.

"Mella, you're gonna have to work on that mean look, doesn't do much for me."

The big man's thick lips pulled back into a wide smile. "One a these days, whiteboy .. I'm gonna sink yo ship." He patted Geech affectionately on the shoulder. "For now though, I'm outta here.." He sucked down his bourbon, threw the cut class tumbler across the room into the trash. "I've gotta be at dinner in El Paso."

"You shoulda stuck with basketball, Mella."

"Tell all yo wrinkled-up friends at the yacht club the big nigger says hi."

Mellonhall walked out the door chuckling to himself.

Geech had a cup of iced coffee before he locked up, spiking it from his personal flask. Some of the brandy Tarrington had given him.

—————⊰◦⊱—————

Leaving a trio of arcing water spouts, he powered away in the triple engined Cigarette boat he'd arrived in. Heading north towards the yacht club, Geech thought about the operation, about Tarrington.

Geech liked Taylor Tarrington. Couldn't find a damn thing wrong with the man. He was a man of honor. A discreet man. An intelligent man who thought things out in advance. A perfect man for the job, the CIA's plans, and perfect for Geech's long term agenda. Perfect for his foster daughter, Monique.

And the last thing Geech wanted was for Monique's heart to be broken. He thought Tarrington would make a fine son-in-law.

Chapter Twelve

"Whadaya mean you got me jeans?"

Taunting, Torren smiled like she'd really gone and done something right. "And raw silk," she explained, "It's very Hollywood."

"Hollywood?" Tarrington was incredulous. "You see me running around with a porta-fax, male secretary and a vial of tar?" He held up the grey Guess jeans, turning them this way and that. Had a squeamish look on his face.

"These guys you're meeting for dinner live in jeans. Go ahead and fit in."

"What?" He looked askance at her, saying suspiciously, "You see my tattoo?" Squinting with the forehead lowered.

"Tattoo?"

He had her. "Yeah, right here." He peeled down his jogging shorts, showed her his upper flank.

She bent down for a closer look, checking the left cheek where the tip of his finger rested.

"Tattoo...?" She was saying.

"Yeah. It's small. Look closely. Conformist, it says."

She stood straight up and told him, "It's really difficult being a bitch around you." She didn't smile. "You know that though, don't you?"

He smiled and didn't say a word.

"So how do you like the jeans?" She asked after a moment.

He went through a very measured routine of lining up the small wicker waste basket by the foot of his bed. With a spritely hop, skip and a jump he kicked it across the room, ran over and pounced on it. Stomping, stomping, and finally crushing it like an old styrofoam cup.

Twisting on the gnarled heap of wicker, he told her, "Just give me a minute or two to work it all out…"

⟶⟫●⟪⟵

After an open viewing for the wastebasket, Tarrington spent most of the afternoon discussing things with Enrique. Getting a few more pieces of the puzzle in order for the El Paso play. Getting ready for the evening's activities. Attacking the problem creatively.

⟶⟫●⟪⟵

Now they were in the Audi, with Torren driving. She had on white spandex for a change. White stilettos too.

Tarrington was reluctantly outfitted in the jeans she'd bought him, with the raw silk blazer hiding the belt loops because she wouldn't permit a belt. He did appreciate the mottled suede jodhpurs. At least they matched the jeans. The argument over the grey suede tie she had failed to purchase had just ended.

"Stop there," he said, pointing up the street toward the parking lot of a strip mall.

"Not if you're buying a tie." She replied.

"Look,… look at the sign out front. The third one from the bottom. Impractical Gifts, it says."

"There's a men's store too in that strip. Fifth sign from the top."

"Impractical Gifts," he reiterated. "They only sell ties that light up and squirt."

"Sorta like what you're doing now…" she told him.

"We're gonna miss it…"

She relinquished and whipped in the lot at the last possible moment.

85

He jumped out, gave her an encouraging look through the window, making it seem like he wouldn't be long.

He purchased a squirt ring. The kind with the little rubber bulb you squeeze when you close your fist and the water shoots out a pin-hole in the ring. Plus a pack of filter cigarettes.

In the car, he rifled through the contents of his briefcase. Eventually a prescription bottle of Chlorohydrate emerged from a leather pocket in the lid.

Starting the car, she asked, "No batteries?"

He ignored this, but grinned as he continued to rummage the briefcase.

"Ah-ha," he said. He'd found it. A UV-100 syringe. He uncapped the needle, and with the Chlorohydrate capsule clasped delicately between his fingers, used the syringe to draw the jelly-like substance from the capsule.

Torren glanced sideways, "What's that?"

"Clear and tasteless," he explained, "Don't go anywhere."

As she watched he disengaged the bulb from the squirt ring, threw the ring part out the sunroof, then half filled the rubber bulb with Chlorohydrate. He syringed another gel cap and topped off the bulb. Next he tore a portion of filter from one the cigarettes he'd bought, twisted it into a point, and wedged it into the nozzle of the bulb. Putting this little sleep walker in the breast pocket of the raw silk blazer, he said, "Let's find a nice record store, now."

When she parked in front of a Hastings Books and Records, he jumped out of the car and ran inside. When he returned a few minutes later, he reached in the passenger door, unlatched the glove box and popped the trunk. He then spent five minutes leaned over the back bumper, tinkering with the main controls of his master surveillance center.

Once again beside Torren, he said, "Now please tell me about these three guys we're meeting for dinner…"

"These three guys," she began, pulling the Audi into traffic, "hold the top management positions under you in Enrique's stateside pot smuggling operation. It was their boss, the guy you replaced, who was ran over by the garbage truck. The one they called Guido. Dead now."

Torren went on to say that Donny and Mike were in charge of all the national logistics; trucks and trains full of pot, making sure it got everywhere it was supposed to go, and on time. They serviced the accounts, collected the money, too. Payouts were done in El Paso.

Donny, she said, was shaped like an upturned pear. A kind of chubby, kind of cute guy. He was more or less the stabilizing factor, where his partner Mike was essentially neurotic and insecure, she related, he simply tried much too hard. But a good looking guy if you could get past that furtive unsettled expression in his eyes.

"And the third guy?" Tarrington inquired.

"Dave," she said, and paused, then said it again. "Dave."

Well, Dave is an enigma of sorts. Stud muffin, but shallow as a teaspoon, and she didn't know exactly what he did in the operation. Before when Guido was alive, he and Dave used to party profession-ally. She emphasized professionally, saying, "Jeeze, did those two party." But since the garbage truck thing though, Dave seemed lonely. No real purpose, she observed. He was making up for it, she explained, by hanging around skating rinks and seducing teenaged girls.

"Dave was… well Dave," Torren said.

Tarrington could tell she might just like the guy. He asked, "What about this Guido?"

Torren smiled. There was a softness to it. She said, "Gweed was your average demented genius type."

"Guido…" Tarrington pondered, "Italian?"

"Like you," she told him with a smile.

The interior of the Bombay Bicycle Club was done in advanced fern bar; backgammon tables, TVs, real-life stuff hanging off the walls and a forty-page, 735-item menu. Typical.

When they got to the table, a small one, Tarrington declined a menu from the underfed blonde hostess. "They look too heavy," he told her. Instead, he slipped her a twenty and asked for a table in a section of the restaurant that was obviously closed until the dinner rush.

She tsk tsk'd him, tapping her tiny sneakered toe with one hand out. Looked at him impatiently.

He put another twenty in the open palm, said, "What's a nice girl like you doing in a place like this?"

She said, "Opening that section. The big table in the corner all right?" She smiled like her bra was too tight, made the twenties disappear somewhere in her Bombay apron, and led them to the potted plant jungle in the corner. "Your waitress will be with you in a moment," The menus sounded like gun shots when they hit the table. She vanished.

Looking after the scrawny blonde, Tarrington got comfortable in his chair, said to Torren, "I'd like to give her a job. Think you could run a security check on her?"

Torren said, "I'm the token bitch. There's no more openings."

"Good thinking," he fingered the white collar on her spandex jumpsuit. "You look very nice tonight, I thought you were cultivating an image with the black stuff."

"I was," she answered. "Now I'm cultivating an image with the white stuff."

Tarrington indicated a wanton looking woman at the bar, openly admiring Torren from her stool. He said, "I think it's working."

Torren checked the woman's passionate disposition and smiled sweetly across the table at Tarrington, "She was probably a virgin once herself. Let her eat her heart out."

"I don't think it's heart she wants to eat."

Torren smiled seductively. "Buy me a drink."

Tarrington signaled the waitress, ordered two beers for himself, a triple shot of Jack Daniels for Torren and told the waitress to bring a bottle of Tabasco.

"Tabasco?"

"Yeah," Tarrington deadpanned.

When the waitress returned he gave her a fifty and explained what he had in mind. Then he handed her a hundred.

"What about the fifty?"

"It's called a pre-performance motivational tip," he said gently, "the hundred's for the tab."

"Oh," she said, and skipped away as if she'd won the lottery.

Torren said, "I thought she was gonna drop to her knees and kiss your hand."

Tarrington quipped, "Don't get your personal feelings mixed up in this." He pointed over her shoulder to a trio of men entering the restaurant. "Is that them?"

"Yes," Torren said as she waved at the men, "that's them."

Two wore facial hair. The third was clean shaven. One with a beard was pure beatnik. Longish, straight dark hair worn unkempt, sort of '70s haircut, a plumpish man with duct tape on his combat boots.

The clean shaven guy's face eclipsed two lightly colored eyes which darted about incessantly. He smiled too hard at the skinny hostess, brown already spreading over his nose. He was wearing jeans and a collared yellow polo shirt.

"Ralph," Tarrington could spot a label at forty yards.

Torren picked it up, " Consider that pony on his shirt a telltale monogram of whom he just might think he is."

"A horse's ass?" Tarrington inquired good naturedly.

The other bearded gent had a head full of lightly-permed shoulder-length dirty blonde hair, a meticulously trimmed mustache to match the chin and cheeks. He wore torn faded Levis, new tennis shoes, a hot pink tank top with an untucked, unbuttoned pinstriped Van Heusen dress shirt over it. There were a pair of 23k gold-trimmed Ray Bans stuck in the perm, resting on his head. He had a cellular phone pressed to his ear. The lithe little hostess practically threw herself at him.

"The guy with the phone?" Tarrington inquired discreetly, "that's Dave?"

"Dave." Torren confirmed.

"Donny's the slob?"

"Correct."

"Mike's the fruitcake."

"With extra walnuts .. no make that peanuts, yes."

"Think that hostess likes Dave?"

"Is that a wet spot forming on her apron front?"

Tarrington told Torren, "Here they come. Be on your best behavior, young lady. Watch for your cues. Remember."

She jutted her chin forward. Cute little Torren.

She said, "Ohh, Daddy."

"Don't let your mother hear you talking like that."

Tarrington stood as they arrived at the table, introduced himself, "Nick Taylor," he said, with his hand out.

Donny shook it, "D. Davis."

Mike said over Donny's shoulder, "Mike Barnes," and waited in line to touch the new boss, glancing nervously at Torren the entire time.

She pretended not to notice as she moved in stealth. Put Donny on one side and Mike on the other and that left only one chair for Dave to sit in. Following her cues.

Tarrington said, "Nick Taylor," again as he and Dave shook.

"Dave."

"Nice to meet you."

"Yeah."

Tarrington let him edge around to the back of the table, then boxed him in, sitting down.

The waitress showed, had a tray of fluted shot glasses. Shooters. B-52s they were called. Kahlua on the bottom, Grand Marnier in the middle, and Bailey's Irish Cream floating delicately on top. She put two in front of each man, skipping Torren, then took the individual drink orders and departed.

"Not imbibing?" Dave asked her.

She tapped the rim of the J.D. and Tabasco, said, "Somebody's got to drive this mess home."

Donny said, "Indeed. Profoundly drunk it is then."

"Biff-de-twos!" Mike said brightly. His eyebrows were like roving caterpillars. He arched them into an introspective pose, swirled one of his shooters at eye level. Some kind of connoisseur. "Full-bodied," he pronounced, putting too much into it.

"Calm down," Donny told him.

"I hate these things," Dave mimicked a whiner.

Tarrington raised one of his, said, "To doing things we don't like." And drank.

Dave didn't.

"What's wrong?" Tarrington inquired of Dave.

Dave eyes went, Me? and he said, "What? Cause I think these things taste like shit?"

"Not at all..." Tarrington replied, "cause they compromise you in the men's room."

Dave smiled and drank, held up the second one, and toasted, "To clever assholes." He stomached the shot by tipping it directly over his mouth, poured it right in. Didn't spill a drop. A professional. No question.

"Good form," Tarrington was thinking, and finished his in unison with Donny and Mike.

The waitress showed up with eight more. Set a draft in front of Donny, a Michelob Light before Mike, a Turkey and Seven with two lime twists for Dave, and another Coors in the can with a freshly chilled mug for Tarrington. She then ringed the table with the third and fourth round of shooters.

The skinny little hostess swooped on Dave from out of nowhere, stretched over the table and inserted a small fold of paper into Dave's breast pocket. Her phone number. She took a moment to swoon. He dismissed her with a haughty flip of his wrist. She scampered away on cloud covered sneakers.

Dave looked the table over. "We gotta serious drunk going?"

"Serious." Tarrington confirmed.

Dave considered this plan, then thumbed through the menu at lightning speed, telling the waitress as he did, "Bring us page three, nine, thirteen and twenty-three."

The waitress was looking at him much like the hostess had just done.

Dave handed her the menu. "Three, nine, thirteen and twenty-three. Some confusion there for you?"

She hesitated only a moment before acknowledgement. Taking one quick glance back at Dave as she walked away.

Tarrington smiled at Dave, thinking, "He's wearing one of those new male pheromone colognes."

Donny toasted away half the next round, saying, "To page three, nine, thirteen and twenty-three. Straight to the neck with 'em." He smiled wistfully at the thought of all that food and guzzled another shooter.

Mike raised part two of the round and said, "To a prosperous future."

Dave said, "Shuddup Mike."

Donny said, "I second."

Mike drank anyway, and didn't seem embarrassed at all.

Tarrington understood the pecking order.

And so it went; six appetizers, five entrees, twelve picked-over desserts, some dozen shooters later, and Tarrington gave Torren her final cue.

Shortly thereafter he squeezed the bulb of Chlorohydrate into Dave's Turkey and Seven.

Chapter Thirteen

Tarrington had summoned a limo for Donny and Mike. And they were no doubt bouncing off the interior of that limo at that very moment. Easy.

Driving Tarrington's Audi, Torren led the limo driver through late night El Paso traffic. Dave, his double dose of Chlorohydrate gestating, snored loudly from the passenger side. Tarrington was in the back, hunched over his open briefcase. He had a pen light clenched in his teeth and the micro tool kit spread out on the seat beside him. Operating on Dave's cellular phone.

Torren practically had to yell over the noise Dave's snoring generated. "What the hell you give him?"

"Chlorohydrate."

"A barbiturate," she stated matter-of-factly.

"You know about your unnatural poisons too."

"Yeah. So how the hell are you doing that?"

"This?" he asked, "This meticulous, exacting, painstaking process, this micro-electro surgery?"

"Yeah. You've been drinking like a drain."

"But I've been puking like a true bulimic? Remember? All kinds of practical applications. I've been drunker off a coupla beers."

She told him, "I thought you were keeping another date in the bathroom."

"I was," he murmured, " with destiny."

"Hmmmm," she went, but Tarrington didn't hear this.

Gagging and sputtering, heaving and sighing, choking and croaking, it was if Dave was about to kick it.

"He sounds Cobainic," Tarrington told her, "Check the food passage."

"Which one?"

"Careful," he admonished, "Ex-Lax doesn't have a thing on Chlorohydrate."

She thought about this, but said, "Where to?"

Tarrington located his wallet, handed her his new Texas driver's license. "Let's try my new place. Kiki should have it ready by now."

She read the address, took a right. From the backseat she heard him say, "Excellent."

She watched from the corner of her eye as he tickled Dave into rolling over. Then he put the cellular in the same back pocket he got it from.

She asked, "Is it fixed now?"

"For a couple days."

Tarrington's new house was a sprawling ranch style conglomeration on El Paso's upper crust west side. Getting back through the trees along the driveway, was a regular journey.

Torren parked in the open garage, asked Taylor, "So what do we do with him," pointing to Dave.

He handed her an unbroken smelling salts. "Wake him up and tell him we're having a party. There should be a pile of cocaine on the dining room table. Being a professional, he should appreciate this. Pop the trunk, would you please." He climbed from the back seat.

With its lights doused, the limousine idled in the driveway. Donny was breathing heavily, trudging towards the front fender. He looked sick. "Pizza," he mumbled on the way.

Mike climbed out with music blaring at his back. He slammed the door on it and stumbled into the night. Spraying a thin sheen of slobber all over the cacti, he screamed at the stars, "JESUS CHRIST AM I FUCKED UP!!!"

The night air was brisk enough to sober. Tarrington was hoping it worked out. "Go inside," he yelled at Mike. "There's hookers and cocaine! Go! Go! Now!"

"Hookers?" Mike fell down twice getting to the front door.

Donny groaned, still mumbling something about pizza, begrudgingly following the path Mike had taken.

Tarrington told the limo driver, "Stick around. Who knows?"

The driver nodded stiffly, looking dour. Jaded from too many drunks like Mike.

Tarrington peeked in on Torren, seeing how she was doing with Dave. He helped by slapping Dave's face as she wedged a smelling salts into his nose.

"Wake up big guy," Tarrington said between slaps, the ammonia of the smelling salt making his own eyes water. "Drink some coffee. Have a beer. Screw a hooker. Snort some coke. It's time to party."

Dave's blue eyes focused. "Coke?" he inquired astutely.

"Try it, you'll like it." Tarrington said, then wrapped Dave's arm over his own shoulders and hoisted him toward the garage access door. Already the music was getting cranked. Over it all, Tarrington heard Mike screaming to the Lord about how intoxicated he was, and some patronizing giggles from the escort service girls Enrique had arranged.

Inside, Donny was spread-eagled on the deep pile shag before the big screen. Two pretty co-eds were pampering him. He's so earthy, the brunette gushed, obviously liking the image the groaning D. Davis projected. The other, not so impressed after unlacing one of his combat boots, said, "He smells pretty earthy you mean."

"Pizza," Donny moaned.

Tarrington caught a yellow blur as Mike chased a squealing redhead down the hall and into a bedroom.

A fourth approached Tarrington. She was wearing a red leather mini skirt, fishnet stockings, a frilly white blouse, and some bright red I'm-extremely-available pumps. The blouse was unbuttoned to her navel and advertising some C-cup cleavage. She was a bleached blonde, looked like a thousand other painted part-time escort service models.

From under Tarrington's arm, Dave came further awake at the sight of her.

She said, "What took you so long?"

Tarrington said, "A hundred fifty an hour, right?"

"Yeah," she replied.

"So what's the big deal?" He said, then asked, "Where's the hawk-nosed Mexican?"

"He left about an hour ago."

"You girls do all the blow?"

"Are you kidding me?" She said derisively, "Who the hell could do all that coke. Dumbo would die. I should've brought a bigger purse."

"Here," Tarrington offered up Dave. She inserted herself under his arm. "Service this guy," he told her.

Dave's nose twitched, "Coke?" he slurred. He was already reaching for his cellular.

Good, Tarrington was thinking.

The platinum blonde walked Dave to the dining room. There was a pile of coke about two feet tall, spilling off the table edges onto the carpet.

Visible white rings were caked around Dave's nostrils when he emerged again. White rings around his pale blue eyes too. Wide open.

His turbo was winding up. "Is the pool heated?" he asked on his way through the house to the back yard.

The blonde had her blouse off already. Her nipples screaming, Cocaine! She chased Dave into the pool

Tarrington went to the fridge, grabbed a cold Coors. After a sip, he toasted the absent Enrique, "Kiki, it's college all over again."

Torren came in from the garage. She was smiling, checking out the big screen, the sumptuous pit group, the color-coded drapery, the glass-topped breakfast nook. Peeking around the corner at the formal living room, she said, "Nice place."

Tarrington said, "If I know Kiki, there's fresh linen on the beds, extra towels, and service for eight in the china cabinet." Then he asked her, "You nosing around in the trunk of the Audi?"

"Nice try," she said, "but I checked out your little monitoring system's mobile command post while I was out shopping today. You like the way I sing?"

"You sing fine."

She said, "You've got this entire house wired up too, don't ya?"

Tarrington said, "Get Donny some pizza," and left through the front door with a fresh beer in his hand.

Chapter Fourteen

After an hour of observation; watching the coke pile slowly disappear, cringing every time Mike screamed, wandering around the grounds; tasting the night air and investigating the perimeter, Tarrington checked the nine cassette tapes in the multi-bank recording station in the trunk of the Audi. Right behind the back seat where the spare tire was supposed to be. The receiver had nine digital readouts keeping time on each tape. One for each bug he had planted. Dave's phone was monitored, six mikes were stashed around the new pad by Enrique. Two frequencies were still to be activated. The whole set-up looked like some college prank time bomb about to blow the Audi into the recent past.

Tarrington noted Dave's readout: eight minutes, thirty-five seconds, the man had been on his cellular phone. How many phone calls would that tally? Tempting as it was, Tarrington put off listening just yet. There were other things to do. Priorities. He opened the lambskin briefcase, found a magnetized homing signal box and an adhesive-applied transmitting mike.

The Executive Protection Corporation of Northern California was the company that supplied Tarrington with all his surveillance gadgets. The spring catalog they had sent to Marina Del Ray, Tarrington's slip, was dog-eared from extensive browsing. Tarrington was on a first-name basis with the company's Vice President and could quote large orders to this man; individual product identification numbers, their prices, verbatim, from memory. And it looked like it was time to do it again, a big purchase. The new mission in El Paso was requiring a lot of ass covering. Plus, Tarrington had a nice twist in mind.

He locked the beige attaché, grabbed his gym bag noticing that Dave was on the cellular again, the digital timer ticking away… and slammed the trunk on this development.

Once inside the limo he pressed the intercom switch and told the driver, "Give me the tour."

"El Paso?" The ceiling speaker asked.

"No just the immediate neighborhood. Take a right leaving the driveway. And by the way, what's your name?"

"Milton," said the driver.

"Well, Milton, I'm looking forward to a nice leisurely, quiet drive."

Milton smiled at the implications of quiet.

Cruising down the driveway, Tarrington changed into his nylon running shorts, tank top, sneakers.

Milton hung the right and Tarrington lowered the privacy panel and knelt on the jump seat so he could look over Milton's shoulder. Sure enough, it was still there. The white 928 Porsche that had followed them from the Bombay Club. Tarrington had seen it in the parking lot, leaving the same time. Had seen it on the Interstate, passing the limo, then hanging back from the Audi. Had seen it at the Seven-Eleven down the street. Now it was parked in the shadows about a mile down the road from his new place.

Tarrington smiled as they drove by. Some big black dude sitting in the front seat. Tarrington moved to the back window to peer out the window. The Porsche didn't move. Perfect.

"Take the first turn after this bend in the road."

"That would be a gated community, sir. We won't get past the guard shack without the proper bumper sticker."

"The next place then."

"Yes, sir."

"Faster."

"Certainly."

When they stopped, Tarrington told the driver, "Meet me back at the place. But take the long route. So you come in the opposite way we left going out."

"Don't worry," Milt told him, "I won't spook our company in the Porsche."

Tarrington sighed.

Milton said, "I've been driving drug dealers, pimps, bank robbers, VIP's, famous people too long not to spot a tail. That Porsche has been following me all night."

Tarrington stepped out saying, "It'll reflect in your tip if you don't run off with this." And he handed the driver his watch. Then he thumped the top of the car, "Mush, Milt."

Jogging, Tarrington had the magnetized homing device in one hand and the adhesive tape peeled off the transmitter mike. Trying not to sweat on the sticky part. He'd run two miles so far. The Porsche was seventy yards away.

Like he was dying, out of breath, cramping, exhausted, past the threshold, Tarrington staggered up behind the Porsche and knocked on the driver's window. He saw the big black dude's eyes go wide and round. Tarrington heaved, wheezed, and bent over.

The first time he bent over he attached the magnetic homing device to the undercarriage of the Porsche. The second time he just kept going; straight to the knees.

"You okay man?" Mellonhall asked him.

"Wha... what's... what's the time?" Tarrington said between gasps.

"It's almost twelve." Mellonhall replied, "You rich white folks can't be doin' all that cocaine and expect it not to hurt ya runnin' around in the middle of the night like this."

"My place is right up the road." Tarrington was holding his heart.

Mellonhall smiled, "Get in, Mr."

Tarrington managed to plant the bug under the passenger seat right before Mellonhall dropped him at the mailbox.

Walking up the driveway, wearing only the nylon shorts now, Tarrington had the tank top wadded in his hand and was sponging the sweat he'd built. He could see the limo, the Audi, and three other cars. Family cars. Mom and Dad's type cars. He took a lap around the house.

Dave was frolicking in the pool with the rail thin hostess from the Bombay Club. He was naked. She was naked. And so were four of her teenaged friends. One of the escort service girls was skinny dipping too. Dave was obviously still stuck in his skating rink adolescent rut. It was as if the escort model were invisible. All his attention and fingers were directed at the girls. Lots of high pitched giggling, and Stop that! and Quit! and giggle, giggle, giggle.

Inside, Mike was screaming something about being a nuclear wart hog, screaming this from behind the master bedroom door. When Tarrington poked his head in Mike was beating his naked chest like Tarzan, bouncing on the mattress in his underwear. The redhead and the once mini-skirted blonde lay naked and apprehensive on the king-size bed below him.

Tarrington closed the door.

Donny and Torren and the brunette that liked those earthy types were still dressed, snuggled into the pit group. There was a high-speed, action-packed car chase on the big screen, but nobody seemed to care.

Smoking a Corona-sized joint and swinging a greasy slice of pizza dangerously before himself, Donny was holding court, holding the brunette in awe, and holding his own with Torren. They were in a cave-deep conversation about the current amalgamation of metaphysical sciences with the physical sciences and about how the alien influence has effected modern technology and about how the government has shrouded all this information from the public.

Tarrington mumbled, "Jesus Christ," and grabbed another beer, sliding on by while Donny talked from behind a cloud of pot smoke.

In the garage Tarrington played back all the tapes. The master bedroom and TV room frequencies were full. Forty-five minutes of Mike screaming and Donny jabbering. Tarrington stopped both after five minutes.

The pile of cocaine in the dining room had logged, on and off, some thirty-three minutes of sniffing and snorting sounds. A few, "Ahhhh's" with emphasis on the nasal.

The bathroom frequency had some farting and some gossip from the girls—twenty-three minutes, seventeen seconds about how cute Donny was, what a basket case Mike was, and how hung Dave was. Torren said, "I'm playing with myself, Tarrington, can you hear me? It's so good."

Now Tarrington rewound the tape of Dave's phone calls, had the headphones plugged in. Cut down on the background noise. It didn't make it any easier to believe, though. Dave was talking to a voice that seemed all too familiar to Tarrington. So he rewound the tape with him and the big black dude in the Porsche.

That one minute, twenty-seven second conversation they'd had on the way to the driveway... And that's where he'd heard that voice before. The last thing the Porsche's bug recorded was, "I'll be damned. White boy went and wired me straight away." Then the noise as Mellonhall destroyed the bug he'd found underneath the passenger seat.

Tarrington knew who he was dealing with on this one. "Huh," he said, and went to the fridge. A naked teenager cut him off on the way.

She was kinda chubby, her make-up running. Chlorine reddened eyes. Goose bumps from the night chill. High on cocaine. Dripping on the floor.

She told Tarrington, "If I told you you had a great body, would you hold it against me?"

He said, "I'm a eunuch. I couldn't even think of it."

She said, "That's all right. I'm Presbyterian. My mother says absolutely no pre-marital sex, but what mother doesn't know won't hurt her... huh?." She batted her eyelashes and tried on a sexy pose, then moved in on him.

He dodged her as if breaking tackles heading towards the goal line. He opened the fridge, got a beer, then turned and told her, "Never on a first date."

She said, "Can I give you my number then?" Will you call me?

"Give it to him," Tarrington motioned to Dave on the pool deck. "He'll pass it on."

This seemed to placate her. She padded barefoot towards the bathroom for a dry towel.

Torren had seen the entire encounter from her spot on the couch. When Tarrington marched over to tell her it was time to go, she interrupted with, "You really love that Monique sexpot back in California, don't you?"

"Moni?" he asked.

"Are there two of them?" she countered.

"I love her, yes," Tarrington smiled, then leaned toward Donny and told him he was coming with them.

Donny indicated the brunette and asked, "What about her?"

"At your own discretion, Mr. Davis."

Donny took the last two slices of pizza instead.

Chapter Fifteen

The Texas Inn was like a giant plastic tarantula poised along Interstate 10, ready to snare tourists.

Tarrington picked it because the jacuzzi was twenty feet from the access road; with the bubbles, jets, and the passing traffic, nobody pointing a parabolic microphone would have a chance.

Once rooms were secured for Torren, Donny and himself, Taylor passed out the keys, saying, "Torren, call Nando at the ranch and get him here driving a windowless van. Tell Enrique first if you have to. And you Donny, figure out what you're gonna wear and meet me in the Jacuzzi in fifteen minutes."

Tarrington edged into the hot water an inch at a time. He was wearing his nylon shorts, had a towel from the motel, a six pack of Coors, and the matrix grid receiver to monitor the homing signal transceiver he'd stuck to the undercarriage of the white Porsche. That's if the black guy hadn't found that too.

The water had to be 105 degrees. Cold from the jog, the strange turn of events, and the night air, Tarrington's skin stung for a while. The reading on the matrix grid blinked, but remained stationary. The Porsche was about a mile away. Or the homing device was in some dumpster a mile away.

Of course, who cared where the Porsche was? Tarrington already knew what it represented. He didn't need anymore evidence to convict Dave.

Donny showed up with moons and stars and lightning bolts on his silk boxer shorts. He slid right into the Jacuzzi as if he'd trained beforehand in a hot shower.

"Beer?" asked Tarrington.

"One of the four major food groups, isn't it?" Donny replied with his hand out, then drank half on the first sip, telling Tarrington, "This thing's parboiling me. I hope you didn't have plans about getting fresh."

"It depends how you act." Tarrington responded, "What I need first is for you to tell me all about the operation."

"Where do I start?"

Tarrington said to him, "I understand nuances, the business in general. Of course. But I'm totally ignorant of what exactly the system is here. Start right after the Mexicans chop the plants down. They're semi-manicured, baled, and sitting in some warehouse down South. But keep it basic. Imagine I'm your brand new pet monkey and you're trying to teach me not to fuck the dog."

Donny smiled, "The gnarled-up little bent-over chubby ugly guy with all the medals on his uniform, who's always smiling and you think he's never gonna shut up once he gets going?"

"That would be General Montoya, yes."

"That's the one," Donny said, "Well, he's responsible for putting it in a warehouse on this side of the river. After that's done, some mysterious Mexican, I've never seen it happen, puts a postcard in my mailbox. Me and Mike keep a place not far from here. One postcard equals thirty-two tons. That's how much we move every ten days. When it's moving." Donny saying this as if he were a little annoyed. "Not a seed shipped since Gweed got trashed. Three weeks now. I got some major pot brokers breathing down my neck…"

Tarrington interrupted him and said, "Should we get something stronger than this," and he held up his beer, "You gonna be okay, Don?"

Donny sighed. "Oh the pain." He moaned theatrically.

"Chronologically, Donny." Tarrington told him.

"Okay, it's easy to stray. I've been suffering from some kind of clinical anxiety lately. There's shit bubbling from several cesspools recently dug in my life. Anyway, me, Mike and like a dozen of the General's best English-speaking workers go to this warehouse and bail all the pot up in these twelve-by-twelve by twenty-four inch ten-pound blocks. Six thousand four hundred of them to be exact. I got around a hundred fifty custom hydraulic pot presses, so the real work is getting the weights right per block. Everybody's got a snow shovel and a digital pan scale and we're dancing back and forth adding a bud to this pile, taking a handful from that pile, and it's a bitch…"

"Basic, Donny," Tarrington interrupted again.

Donny said, "I'll take another beer."

Tarrington passed a can.

"Fuel for thought." Donny toasted, gulped half the can, burped, took a deep breath and began again, "These blocks we vacuum seal in seven mil vinyl and from there we stack them in a special high-impact plastic shell that just fits into a brand new gutted refrigerator. In the plastic shell, we pour a coating of neoprene 571 liquid latex over each layer of blocks, submerge them in the stuff. So the dogs can't smell it no matter what."

"They make rubbers out of latex," Tarrington said, "That's a nice touch."

"Guido's idea, he said we oughta use rubbers for something other than water balloons."

"Good thinking."

"After we've got a load of FWR 400 refrigerators ready, me and Mike dress up like delivery men and truck them across town to the big appliance distributor Guido set up. We got real shipping invoices in triplicate, little name patches on the overalls we're wearin', a company truck, it really looks good. The legitimate aspect of the operation ships the FWR 400s to Dallas by rail and doesn't even know they're in the dope business. They think we're a subcontractor assembling these special refrigerators."

"FWR 400?" Tarrington asked.

"Filled with reefer, 400 pounds. It's our own little private joke."

Tarrington smiled, "Now what happens once the product arrives in Dallas?"

"Crazy Eddie. Big ten-gallon hat, boots, spurs, rides a huge saddled pig down an aisle of fridges and stoves on his TV commercial. Has like seventy-five appliance stores in the chain. Guido and him built it from the ground up smuggling pot. So why not use it to smuggle pot? Eddie's our chief Midwest broker. He manages a Kansas City, Tulsa, St. Louis, Chicago, Indianapolis, and a Little Rock account. He unloads the FWRs and ships by truck. His trucks. What his operation doesn't use gets sent to Jacksonville, Florida. We got an asshole little bastard named Weasel Weinstein there. He's our chief broker for the East coast. He's a major pain in my ass. He's got car lots and jewelry stores. Weinstein Ford, Chevy, Suburu, Oldsmobile, Mitsubishi, Toyota, and Range Rover. The jewelry stores you see in all the malls? He owns the franchise, wholesales all the gold and shit to each location. I gotta put up with him though, he's responsible for making and laundering like two-thirds of my pay check. It's so much easier dealing with Eddie though. Fuckin' Weasy."

"Weasy? His name's actually Weasy?"

"It's a nickname. The Weasel. If the name fits, wear it. That sort of thing."

"Sounds like a great guy."

"He's a real bouquet of roses."

"So what are the numbers. The gross, the net?"

"Me and Mike collect ninety-four million a month. It would be ninety-six, but we pay Eddie two mil to ship to Weasy using his trucks. Plus me and Mike take a half mil a month for ourselves. Everything else goes to the General. I don't know what he does with it. Oh yeah, Dave gets half mil too."

"And everything was running smoothly before this Gweed got whacked?"

"Like K-Y on a waxed floor."

"So what needs to be done to get the machine working again?"

"I gotta go collect like ten mil from Eddie and twenty-two from Weasy. Then we feed the monster."

"When can you do that?"

"I'll leave from this Jacuzzi if you'd like."

"Let's nurse the hangovers, plus I got a few loose ends to tie up myself. We'll begin in a day or so, no problem?"

"I'd kiss you but I haven't brushed my teeth in a while." Donny said with a grin.

"One question, though."

"Yes?"

Tarrington said, "We don't have any seriously large black gentlemen working for us in any capacity, do we?"

"No."

Tarrington looked at the matrix grid sitting beside the jacuzzi on the pool deck. The bleep hadn't moved at all. He said, "Is ten tomorrow morning too early to call your brokers?"

"It's never too early to call my brokers."

Padding across the pool deck, Tarrington said over his shoulder, "Then call them, Mr. Davis."

Donny blew him a kiss.

In his room, Tarrington rummaged around the lambskin briefcase and found General Montoya's card. He called the home number. Even at two in the morning, the old General had a merry disposition.

Tarrington explained the problem, detailed a couple ideas he had about fixing it, and let the General take over, see if he could add anything.

The General mentioned a few possibilities and then after a pause, said, "I believe I have just the answer."

So Tarrington read the address off his new Texas driver's license like the General asked him to do.

"Now you stay clear, Señor Taylor, and leave the rest to Montoya."

Next mission for Tarrington was to just relax for a while and do some thinking, get the head right for the upcoming festivities. He clicked on CNN out of habit. No relaxation. What was he thinking?

Within five minutes, the story aired of how Nicolas Taylor of Anaheim, California, had been arrested in the front yard of his home at 1740 Florence Drive.

Tarrington remembered he'd transferred the surplus from his electric and telephone bill accounts to Nicolas Taylor. An innocent gesture, trying to do the right thing for the hapless, unsuspecting Taylor of Anaheim. He'd done it on Monday in front of the Seven-Eleven. Now it was barely Wednesday. The Feds were working surprisingly fast on this one. It was becoming a media circus. Three rings, all attractions running wide open.

In one ring; a dead senator's daughter.

In the second ring; the hospital death of Becky Forrester, debutante daughter of well-connected, major contributor, Pierce Winthrop Forrester III. That ranting raving anti-drug activist.

And now an innocent man, Nicolas Taylor of Anaheim... about to be crucified in the name of two spoiled brats out to score and Tarrington's great idea about being benevolent.

Tarrington thought about it a long while. Then he got the international operator on the phone, called the charter company he'd used for his family's emergency vacation. After considerable manipulation, waiting, calling back, waiting some more, he got his father on the ship-to-shore.

Welly said, "Can't tell you how much I'm enjoying this son. And to think I didn't even have to pull a job off to get it. Great."

Tarrington said, "You ready to come out of retirement?"

Chapter Sixteen

Donny used the pay phone by the Sambo's restaurant across the street from the Texas Inn. He knew the exact toll to Jacksonville and fed the phone accordingly. It was four in the morning. He absolutely loved waking Weasy up. And with good reason.

When Weasy answered on his end, Donny unleashed a perfect Brooklyn-Miami whine. The quintessential imitation of Weasy Weinstein himself.

"Wake up ya little *shaygetz* bagel burner!"

Weasy recognized the voice right away. Not even his father sounded that Jewish. "Aaaach! Oy-Oy-Oy! You *vontz!* You *zshlub!* Such *chutzpah* from a *schmucko* like you! And the last time we talk you *kvetch* and *kretch* like a real *kronkeh bubba!* So now where's my product already?"

"Hey, do your family a favor with all this shame, and get yourself a circumcision, why don't ya?" Donny tsk tsked him. "You're a *shonda,* I tell ya. A real *shonda!*" He may as well been wearing a *yarmulka* and sidelocks.

"Ai-yi-yi, from a gentile I take this? A *momzer putz* like this? Listen, *schlepo,* enough with the *funpheh,* when already?"

"Christ was a good Jew!" Donny blasted back, "If he were here right now he'd circumcise you with a lightning bolt! Or better yet, a fish! So protect your prick, Mr. *Moishe!*" Donny paused in preparation for the normal diatribe good-bye.

"It's about time, ya *golem!*" Weasy told him.

"Ya Moses lovin' *sctuzem!*" Donny retaliated.

Weasy: *"Schlemiel!"*
Donny: *"Schlemazel!"*
Weasy: *"Gonif!"*
Donny: "Asshole!"
"Oy-veh!" Weasy whined, "Enough already," and hung up.

———>=●<———

In the Weinstein household, Wendy, wife of Weasy, stirred restlessly on her side of the bed and whimpered wantonly. "Everything okay, poopsie?"

"Yeah, yeah, yeah, go to back to sleep why don't ya?"

"Ummmmm," said Wendy, and backed her bare buttocks to his leg.

"Aaaach… such a thing this ass of yours," Weasy lamented. But was drawn from the notion of sex by his strongly ingrained sense of self-preservation.

He slid into his Billy Bunny slippers and went to his office two rooms down the hall. Used the business line to dial his case agent, Hymie Finkleburg.

As much as Weasy loved the extra ten million here, extra ten million there, he had no qualms about shutting down the entire operation and burying Donny and Mike for a mistake he himself had made not two weeks ago saying the wrong things into the wrong body microphone. DEA agent Hymie "The Fink" Finkleburg's mike.

Weasy had been arrested, arraigned, and then released on his own recognizance to work for the Feds. Hymie had been right there to take Weasy to lunch straight from the courthouse.

Now it was time to turn the tables. No way was Weasy Weinstein suffering another night in jail. Who could sleep on those skinny plastic mattresses anyways? *Oy-veh!"*

The phone rang nineteen times before case agent Finkleburg was wrestled from a five-valium narcosis.

"Wha, wha, wha, whosit?"

Weasy said, "Wake up, ya little *shaygetz* bagel burner!"

And so it went. The chain of command... being broken.

PART II
THE FOLLY

Before the wise man
came the idiot,
who taught the wise man.

• Enrique Deleon •

Chapter Seventeen

Dave woke up to the sound of his own teeth chattering. He had willed himself to sleep finally around two a.m. Now his body shivered so profoundly, it made the lounge chair shake and squeak. His blue feet smacking together to keep warm. It was dark outside. He was in the backyard, about two short leaps to the hot tub. Chillin'.

The chaise lounge flipped onto its side as he sprang for the sliding glass doors and warmth. He headed for a hot shower.

Thirty minutes later, thawed out, Dave wrapped a towel around his waist and roamed the house, taking the morning roll. First thing he noticed was two of the girls, the hostess' friends, locked in erotic lesbian embrace on the pit group couch. Dave nodded in disappointment. He'd instructed everyone to cease the coke snorting by three. Watching them pant and moan now, he had to smile, but not for long. Dave knew the backlash from an all nighter. Not good.

He made a mental note to fill them a baggie and call them a cab for Denver soon.

If he'd learned anything as a CIA agent in the last twelve years, it was that young ladies had a way of coming seriously unraveled after too much coke ingestion. He'd seen the evil process played out before his eyes many times. There was no question about it. Having a seriously spun-out coke whore on your hands was like taming crocodiles with a feather duster. He couldn't think of a more dangerous experience.

Yet he left them to their pleasures, and continued checking the bedrooms. Two more in the master, sleeping. Dave smiled. One room empty. Mike and the skinny little hostess in a third. No escort models present. They'd vanished when their ten-hour retainer expired.

Mike, not snorting, but drinking like a dromedary after running the third leg of the Paris-to-Dakar rally, had passed out on top of the bedspread. He was the total antithesis of Dave, and precisely why Dave could barely stand the man.

Mike: the wanna-be stud, flat on his back, a soft snore escaping from a benign smile.

"Simpleton," Dave murmured, and turned his eye to the hostess curled beneath the covers. His entire countenance fell in a relieved, almost reverent sigh. "Quite a young lady, there," Dave was thinking. He'd make her his Bimbo du'jour. He blew her a silent kiss and closed the door.

Rounds made, Dave explained the absence of Tarrington, Donny, and Torren, figuring they'd gone to breakfast or something. No big deal.

He entered the master bedroom and found a spot between two naked girls. He could use a little more sleep. He'd been losing it ever since he'd infiltrated the marijuana operation and discovered cocaine at Guido's hand some four years ago. Everyone had their dues to pay.

Good kids, he thought, feeling a hand creep over his thigh and grab him. Yielding, yet strong. He'd make them all bimbo's du'jour. What the hell.

In the next room, Mike stirred and immediately wormed himself under the comforter to nuzzle the hostess.

She woke up surly. "Would you just quit, Jesus!" She charged from the room, took five steps down the hall, and wedged herself onto the crowded mattress with Dave and her two friends.

Mike remained, nursing his ever-expanding inferiority complex. He was sober now and there was nothing quite as bad as that. His confidence evacuating with the buzz. The ill blessings of his unfortunate birth now officially back to haunt him.

On the couch in the living room, the building murmurs of drug-induced orgasms. Both ladies on the edge. What happened next took them over it.

As they climaxed together, the front door cracked off its hinges and splintered into the far wall of the foyer. The rear sliding glass doors shattered. Six grim looking police officers rushed the place.

Guns drawn, swinging them back and forth, fierce voices yelling, "FREEZE! NOBODY MOVES! POLICE!"

Two from the rear, four straight through the remains of the front door. Fast with practiced precision. A not-so-routine bust. A special job.

The best-time ever duo on the couch went partially uninterrupted. Partially.

One girl at least, shuddering like an old generator, thinking all the shish-boom-bah was part of the experience. Riveted in place on her hands and knees. Her friend, though flat on her back, saw the big black revolver hovering at her nose, and experienced a spontaneous evacuation of her bowels.

The sergeant had seen a lot of strange tableaus in his seventeen years, most unremarkable, but this... this, was a keeper. Definitely one for the boys at the shooting range. He suppressed a sado-masochistic smile and screamed, "HALT! OR I'll SHOOT!"

His partner covered the pile of cocaine on the dining room table. Already breaking out his extra plastic bags.

The four who had blasted through the front entrance finished off the crusade. Down the hall they went, kicking open the bedroom doors.

Mike was apprehended as he clamored in the corner of an empty closet. He'd managed to shake himself into a pair of jeans. Hiding. Busted. The ultimate nightmare. He felt the handcuffs cinch into his wrists... zzzziiiipp. His chin hit his chest.

Dave was a different story. When the noise first sounded, he'd barely flinched. Real cool. Of course, all three of the girls had jolted from the mattress. Dave told them to just relax.

One refused; wailing, tears streaming, standing there with no clothes to wear, nowhere to run. Confused. Another slipped into a state of irretrievable panic; dashing about the room, running in circles, looking for something she would never find—her sanity.

The little hostess watched it all go down, real cool like. Looking up Dave's peach fuzzy chest, she could see her man had the entire situation under control. How though, she did not know. Her fingernails clawed at his arm as the bedroom door exploded.

Dave looked bored.

Three cops galloped in, weapons cocked. The hostess' grip beared down, but she still had that Eastwood look on her face. The screamer was cuffed without ceremony by a stout blonde fellow named Richardson. The panicked young lady stopped running in circles just long enough to land a well-placed snap kick to the groin of the police force's resident karate expert. He crumpled her with a short sharp shot to the neck, then cussed as he jumped around holding his testicles.

Seeing this, Dave said, "Nice ridge hand. Now let this one put some clothes on, she's a good kid." He motioned towards the frozen hostess on the bed beside him, pried himself from her grasp and stood, holding out his bruised arms to receive the cuffs.

The team leader, a Lieutenant with twenty years on the force, had never encountered a "Dave" before. He told the karate expert, "Let her get something on," looked at Dave, "How 'bout you?"

"Nah," Dave shot off, "it's your job."

The Lt. ignored the naked smartass, smiled instead, he told one of his men, "Cuff him."

In the living room, the sergeant worked on his prisoners. First, he shackled the girl stuck in a state of perpetual orgasm while she vocalized a choral arrangement of smiling-eyed vowel sounds. He then threw her incontinent crime partner in the shower and ordered her to clean up. No chivalry there. She would have to ride in his black-n-white.

Everybody was led from the party house in single file. Dave's cool only becoming slightly impaired when he noticed not a platoon of cruisers and armed men, but just three cars. The three cars that the six officers had arrived in. Plus one pickup truck with two shifty looking Mexican Nationals waiting down the driveway. A real bust would've had half the force out, and he would have known beforehand. He craned his neck searching the area for more cops. "Shit," he was thinking, "Those Mexicans are smiling."

Dave, the hostess, then Mike, were shoved into the backseat of the Lieutenant's patrol car.

The sergeant led his two captives to a squad car. He'd given them both a towel.

Richardson, blonde beefcake who'd cuffed the screamer, carried her once-jumpy friend hoisted effortlessly over his shoulder. The screamer had made a remarkable transformation. Now her head was shamefully settled between her shoulders as Richardson guided her towards the car with his free hand. After he'd lowered the groggy one into the rear compartment, safe behind the metal screen, he asked her, "You ever rode in the front seat of a real police car?"

She ground her teeth in frustration but acquiesced with her eyes. She had. She knew the drill. It came with the territory called cute and compromised. The last time, she'd worked it out with a little help from the arresting officer.

Richardson could tell she had so he climbed in the car and unzipped his pants.

She said, "If you were a gentleman you wouldn't make me do this."

He said, "If you were a lady, you wouldn't be talking with your mouth full."

The sun peeked over the eastern horizon, and trails of light crept down the Sacramento Mountains onto the desert floor. The Lieutenant could feel a mild heat through the window as he drove slowly toward the city skyline, morning traffic accumulating with the temperature.

Dave's mind was still with those two Mexican Nationals parked at curb in the pickup truck. He swore he'd seen the Lieutenant give them a nod as they'd driven away.

Mike asked, "So what's gonna happen here?"

No answer.

He continued, "I have the best lawyers money can buy. And I can tell you right now that you won't get away with that bullshit back there. Illegal search and seizure… police brutality…" He lost his listing mechanism and blurted instead, "I'll have your ass! Your job! You haven't even read us our rights! That's a miranda violation! You can't make this stick!" Mike channeling his fear into agitation. He'd never been busted before. The worst of his most loathsome fears coming to pass. Yet the Lieutenant failed to indulge him with a response. "You can't hold me! I'll bond out!" Then Mike's vocal cords cracked and he could only squeak, "Hey, what's gonna happen here?" His voice raised an octave. "Hey, why won't you say something?"

Dave, quiet since realizing things were not at they should be, leaned over and checked Mike's spiral into the depths of cowardice. The man was close to tears.

"Mike… Mike… MIKE!" He got the man's attention, "Mike, you spineless jellyfish! You're starting to worry me. In a minute, this cop will put a dress on you and pimp you out at the policemen's ball."

"My name's Rick…What are you talking about, Joe?" With emphasis on the Joe. Mike flustered as if his life depended on it.

Dave leaned into it said, "Shut up, MIKE!"

"Alright DAVE! There, you wanna play name games, I can play name games." Mike slid effortlessly into a vindictive state.

"Mike, look at you. This young lady here is more composed than you'll ever be." Dave lowered his eyes to meet those of the hostess. He asked, "What's your name anyways?"

She glared at Dave. They'd discussed marriage the previous evening. She pouted and said with some resignation, "Kelly."

"Kelly, you're a hell of a girl. Don't worry about a thing. I'll have us out of this before lunch."

The Lieutenant began to whistle "Camptown Races."

Dave shrugged nonchalantly. He'd never had a serious problem before, and was hard pressed to recognize the one about to rain prohibitionists on his cocktail party.

Kelly gave him the hopeful doe-eyed look. The ordeal was beginning to tear her composure into pieces. Dave saw her uneasiness and did his best, showed her the broad wink. He had it all: the looks, the style, the money, the pink cocaine, everything. Surely he could make good that statement about having them out of trouble by lunch. Kelly smiled, but the moment was fleeting when she cast her eyes upon Dave's incredibly deflated manhood.

He noticed this and quipped, "Cold air."

The Lieutenant slowed the car and pulled off the Interstate. Crossing beneath the overpass, he led the other two squad cars toward the Mexican border.

Mike could not contain himself, fidgeting viciously, he leaned forward and squeaked softly into the Lieutenant's ear. "Excuse me, sir, but this is not the way to the police station." Mike couldn't see a Dunkin' Donuts anywhere. There was no logical explanation for the diversion. "Where are you taking us?" he squeaked politely.

No answer. The Lieutenant was almost through his third rendition of "Surrey with Fringe on Top."

Kelly dropped her chin and began to whimper.

Mike's forehead hit the tops of his knees and he began to wretch.

The Lt. supplied his only comment of the trip, telling Mike, "You puke in my car son, you'll really have a problem on your hands."

Right before the Rio Grande, all three cruisers pulled onto a dirt trail and then into a dilapidated warehouse, parking alongside four late-model sedans. Each sedan manned by a Mexican.

When Mike saw one of the Mexicans pass a satchel to the Lieutenant, everything fell into place.

A calmness came over him. He took a deep breath and chuckled.

Kelly couldn't believe such bravado. Wow, what a man, she was thinking.

Dave sucked air through his teeth, mumbling, "Son of a bitch... mmmmmmm... damn."

Kelly knew it. She took her eyes from the now shriveled Dave to the pillar of confidence that Mike had just become, she buried her head on Mike's shoulder.

Michael Barnes had an instinctive reliance on Mexicans, having worked with and for them for the previous eight years. He didn't know exactly what was going on, but knew whatever it was, it beat hell out of going to jail.

Figuring he had the situation handled, he lowered his cheek to Kelly's dirty blonde locks and began to blubber uncontrollably.

The Lieutenant switched to "Born Free."

And Kelly thought, "Here I am, caught between the incredible shrinking man and a fragmented idiot. And I dropped out of modeling school for this?"

Mike bawled as if he'd misplaced his bottle.

Chapter Eighteen

He'd woken up in the trunk of a car, feeling pretty woozy from the chloroform he'd been forced to deal with. And she'd been there, spooned against him. The two of them bouncing down some pothole littered pavement at sixty-five.

She'd been scared. He'd soothed her, shown her his ascendency, shown her how sublimely his confidence had returned. She'd inched her body around and kissed him, just like that, a reward for his mastery. His new mastery. And she'd kept on kissing him.

When they'd arrived he'd been welcomed by a Mexican general named Montoya as if he were a long lost friend. The general apologized profusely and gave them the tour.

With Kelly in tow, they'd been through every room in the general's ranch. A heart rending story at every stop. The general in full character. Then back to the pool portico... where Mike and Kelly were accorded a private bungalow complete with a uniformed servant to do their bidding.

Now Kelly was lounging naked by the pool. The weather was good in Mexico. She said, "Why don't you come in, the water's nice."

"No thanks, Kel, I've got my refreshment right here," Mike told her and ran his finger along the rim of the margarita glass, making it squeak a bit, then licking off some of the salt..

"Okay," she said, and dove back in with the other naked nymphets. No complaints from anyone. The general had been prescient enough to have a pile of pink cocaine nearby.

The girls were happy. Yet not nearly as happy as Mike. He'd reached a state of profound contentment. He signaled the waiter.

"Yes, sir?" The waiter inquired. "Too much salt on the glass, sir?"

"No, nice and cold, just the way I like 'em. But I'm feeling indecisive. How 'bout an imported beer, not in a green bottle."

"As you wish," The waiter ducked away.

Now Kelly climbed out of the pool, feet slapping on the hot tiles, "Hey, I was thinking… what about my job?"

"You've quit your job," Mike told her, "You've met a very rich man." Mike was experiencing a prime he'd not known existed. "You no longer need to work." He gave her that new smile he'd been experimenting with. The smooth macho look. He'd seen Dave doing it.

This trip to Mexico was doing wonders for his masculinity. He had acquired a completely different outlook on his neurosis. Things were good.

"Ohh, I do love you, baby." Kelly fluttered her eyelashes and gave the new Mike a peck on the cheek.

He knew that. His apparent pre-eminence was like a tool he could use to benefit mankind… or womankind, he was thinking.

Insecurity was a concept in the past. "Ahh, to be young and alive and anal retentive," he thought to himself.

"What about that Dave guy?" Kelly asked, breaking Mike's reverie.

"What about who?" Mike snapped, his ego bubble popping as the contents of his vision dilapidated into nothingness.

"Dave," Kelly said, "What about Dave?"

"Oh… him." Mike paused to consider the fate of David Carmichael, and after a long sigh, said, "I guess Mr. Dave fucked up."

Chapter Nineteen

Tarrington's nine o'clock wake-up call roused him. He parted the blinds, took in some sun. Then he was off to Torren's room in his boxer shorts. She was naked again, doing her Kiai Katas.

He said, "What's that you're doing?"

She said, "I'm breathing. What does it look like?"

"Well it looks like you're hyperventilating on an imaginary horse. Like Lady Godiva at high altitudes."

She smiled and released her stance, said, "What's that you're doing?"

"Staring. What room is Nando in?"

"Two-seventeen."

"Thanks," he said as he left the room. Then he snuck his head back in the doorway and asked "You'll be dressed for lunch?"

She replied, "It depends what I'm eating."

He knocked on Nando's door seconds later. Nando answered immediately.

"Mr. Taylor," he said brightly, "What can I do for you this morning? I've brought the windowless van per your instructions."

"Two things, Nando."

"Yes?"

"First, relax."

Nando tried to slouch.

"Now on the inside." Tarrington explained.

"Done." Nando said snappily

Tarrington squinted at the man, then he handed him a list:

1) three beach towels
2) carton of Marlboro lights
3) hand mirror
4) Velcro neck brace (for whiplash)
5) 50 ft. of extension cord
6) two saw horses
7) propane torch
8) small fire extinguisher
9) 1 pair of hair cutting scissors
10) Norelco portable shaver
11) old fashioned wrought iron birdcage, approximately 24" tall, 30" wide
12) six large white rats
13) a 3/4" sheet of marine grade plywood
14) a handful of 6-penny finishing nails
15) small ball peen hammer
16) battery powered cordless drill with Phillips head screwdriver bit
17) four small brass hinges
18) two speed jigsaw
19) bolt of nylon rope (at least 50 ft.)
20) spool of wax string
21) carpenter's pencil
22) box of Don Limo Peticetro Cigars
23) something from the dentist's office to force one's mouth into an open position

He handed Nando five hundred dollars, said, "Go buy all this stuff. Any questions?"

Nando scanned the list, stopped at number four. He said, "That's one of those things wraps around your neck, keeps it real stiff, like traction."

"Exactly."

Nando nodded, continued down the list, asked, "What if I can't find Peticetros?"

"Try Jamaican Royales, Montecristos, or Hoyo number 5s. Excal-ibers," Tarrington reminded him. "And rapiers if it's Royales. Got it? That's important. Probably more important than the rest of the list."

Nando said, "What about the last one?"

Tarrington said, "Read it a couple times, it'll all come clear. We want those rear molars exposed."

"Like for surgery."

"Nando, I'm putting you in for a bonus."

Chapter Twenty

Dave had accumulated a great many drug-kingpin good-buddy type relationships in the southern Florida nomenclature while posing as something other than a CIA agent. And presently he contemplated dropping some of those names. Maybe that would help. He'd certainly blown it. Though he wasn't sure exactly how.

It'd been back in the Good Ole' Days when the Reagan Administration ran through the streets of America, foraging on the country like a wild band of acid-drunk psychopathic liars. The money flowing like ambrosia from the Greed goblet. With nobody in America caring enough to pay attention to what their government was doing to them in the interim. Most were preoccupied with the prevailing climate of voracious acquisition to stop and research all the Executive Orders being drafted daily in secret. Too busy to grasp the totality of Hot Dog Apple Pie Americana's Constitutional integrity being systematically dismantled.

During this period the CIA's Domestic Operations Group lived out its Golden Years. Major productivity. Field agent David Carmichael in particular. It had been over the course of this era that Dave had made his legend a reality, recruiting several Latin drug lords to help finance the Secret War in Nicaragua. Thus allowing the CIA access to every Central American government in power, because the biggest drug lords in Central America are customarily addressed as "Señor Presidente."

War had always been a concept the CIA promoted. It had been working for years in other regions. Where a myriad of drug-production based cultures had been homegrown by the agency. The covert Political Military Industrial Complex had been thriving on such antics since before Korea. War, drugs, and exploiting the long cultivated American aversion to the evil influence of communism were CIA specialties. Just feed a little propaganda to the public, disperse the promised kickbacks to Congress, and split the tax money handed over to the corrupt regime the Agency created to begin with. CIA Standard Operating Procedure.

And Dave had always been a natural when it came to corruption. He had a knack for picking out the easy ones. The best players. The whores. The true politicians.

The Latin politico drug lords Dave put on the Company payroll were more than pleased to play the game. They collected their end from the CIA's tacit cooperation in delivering their drugs to the United States. The extension of a free ride through U.S. airspace, and in some cases, military assistance at various Air Force and National Guard airstrips around the country. Well-guarded landing plots and plenty of "look-the-other-way" personnel to help unload and further transport tons upon tons of marijuana and cocaine. And dozens of "trade-off" operations like this were still going strong. The Drug War's interdiction methods working smoothly. And Dave had been one of the major grease guns to sustain the process.

Even after the dam broke for him and his cohorts in the Reagan Administration; after the junk bonds were called in; after the eyes of the constituents were partially opened, Dave saw first-hand how easily the entire scandal was patched up with ethereal hogwash. Placation was the name of the game. Or simple misdirection. Whatever worked. And this is what happened when Iran-Contra hit the airwaves. The media masters were put to work and Dave's faith in a corrupt system was put to the test.

He, like all his other co-conspirators in the Nicaraguan caper, emerged unscathed. The few "heroes" who did have to endure some heat were told to just sit tight and wait till the media memory went blank again... and then their appeals would be granted.

The experience showed Dave that the American public was chiefly comprised of nitwits, and that the White House kept those nitwits spinning crazily out of balance with a maelstrom of good ole mumbo jumbo.

Dave saw that; like every other serious government-toppling scandal of recent history, Iran-Contra might play B sides but never long enough for anybody to remember the tune. There were just too many other useless bits of information that had to be conveyed to the American public.

The drugs for money for weapons for war for the hell of it just cause we can do whatever we please scandal blew right over. Dave learned then that the American populous' recall was, collectively, about two weeks long.

The swagger he had demonstrated in Central and South America had escalated Dave to the top of the list for the next major operation. For the CIA would continue to run amok; dashing dreams, distorting reality, dealing dogma and dolling out drugs. All part of the big picture.

As the CIA's chosen contender to head the field aspect of DOG's next biggest civil rights squelcher, Dave was given access to five covert accounts in CIA chartered banks, then sent abroad to make new friends. Carlos and his Asian buddy, heroin lord, General Khun Sa, had been first on the list. Dave approaching them initially through Tarrington's predecessor, who hadn't worked out, so it was on to Plan B: Tarrington himself. And now that'd gone to hell. Who would have thought?

Fifty-one months ago, long before Dave's cover was blown in El Paso, you couldn't have told him he'd be strapped down in some underground meat locker, waiting for the butcher to arrive.

The cell Dave was secured in sat twenty-five feet below ground level and was reached by a secret rotating panel in General Montoya's wine cellar.

It was cold enough to generate a sheen of condensation on the clean tile walls. Dave was inside a thirty-foot square gelid cubicle. The ceiling was flooded with blinding florescent light and hovered imperiously far above him.

The walls and floor were a pristine clean white ceramic. A stainless steel table big enough to strap a large body to was set in the center of the room. It had sturdy metal rings spaced around its perimeter where the restraints would go. There was a stainless steel drain grate beneath it for easy clean up.

It was General Montoya's interrogation chamber.

A stiff-backed stainless steel arm chair had been mounted beside the table, where a crease in the tiles angled toward the drain. There was a hole in the seat. It was in this chair that Dave was tied, still naked from the fake bust.

His ankles and knees were tied to the chair's front legs. His wrists and elbows to the chair's arms. The trunk of his body was wrapped from armpits to navel in one continuous coil of nylon rope. Making it somewhat difficult to breathe. On his shoulders the three beach towels Nando had purchased using Tarrington's list. Balanced on these was more paraphernalia from the excursion; a 36-inch wooden donut-like disc of 3/4 inch marine grade plywood.

Tarrington had used the jigsaw, brass hinges, cordless drill, saw horses, wax string, carpenter's pencil and one 6-penny finishing nail to construct the disc. Dave's head was poked through its center hole, velcroed erect by the whiplash neck brace.

His moustache and beard had been cleanly shaven. Nailed to the wooden collar was an old-fashioned wrought iron birdcage. His mouth was forced wide open with the smooth plastic inserts Nando had gotten from a puzzled orthodontist. The insert was much like an inverted C-clamp mounted to Dave's molars. You could see every filling he'd ever gotten. His tonsils jiggled as he shivered.

He was a naked man tied to a chair with a big black birdcage on his head. And there was nothing he could say about it but "uuuuuh-hhhh."

Dave was thinking how nice it would be to have a cigarette, maybe his Ray Bans to ward off the room's intense brightness, perhaps a hot bath to cure the shakes. How 'bout a couple of muscle relaxers to uncramp the jaw. A masseur?

He wasn't contemplating his freedom. He'd get to that before, during, and after the pending interrogation. Of this he was sure. First, see what he'd gotten himself into.

In answer to his anticipation, the wall before him twisted and Tarrington entered, resplendent in an emerald green surgical smock fastened over a single-breasted Ralph Lauren grey nailhead wool suit, peaked lapels. No tie. Just a grey T-shirt that had "Ask me if I care" across the chest in opaque white lettering.

Tarrington smiled behind his funny round sunglasses as Raul, the general, and Torren stepped in after him.

"Raul Herrera," thought Dave… "Carlos' right hand." He tried to swallow. Raul showing up was a bad sign. The first ill omen of the day was Dave showing up, Dave was thinking.

Everybody but Tarrington carried a box or bag of something. Tarrington held a lit cigar, had a snifter of cognac cupped in his other palm. He smiled at Dave, blew smoke in his vice-open mouth, unlatched the tiny door to the birdcage and set the brandy snifter inside atop the plywood collar.

"Have a drink, Mr. Carmichael." Tarrington said, "Party's in your honor, so you might as well enjoy yourself." He peered in at Dave's exposed molars; clucked his tongue, said, "I'd give ya a cigar, but I'm afraid they don't roll'em that big." Tarrington smiled real crazy, pulled out the Berretta 92F, waved it joyfully before Dave, and then slowly screwed on the silencer. The cigar smoldered in his mouth the entire time.

"I love this gun," he told Dave. "The smell." He removed his cigar and sniffed the barrel.

Dave's eyes got real big.

Behind Tarrington Torren rummaged through the shopping bags, coming up with a welding glove, an ornate butter knife, and a propane torch. She ignited the torch, slipped on the glove, and heated the butter knife to blueness.

The General and Raul spread themselves to either side of the table. Raul wore his usual all-business-deadpan expression. The General smiled amicably, and bent over to dig through the box he had arrived with. Dave could hear the tinkle of glassware, but couldn't see over the rim of the plywood collar. The General came up, still smiling, passed everybody a full snifter of cognac. Then back down for two more cigars, handing one to Torren and lit the other himself.

Torren deep-throated the cigar, then lit it with the white-hot tip of the butter knife she'd been torching. She puffed like a gangster, loud and arrogant.

The General spoke to the ceiling, "Turn on the exhaust fan, Juan. And the tapes… are the microphones working?"

"Si, Generale," replied a leathery voice from the two-way speaker above. The exhaust fan kicked on and cigar smoke swirled upwards.

Tarrington exchanged glances with the General. The General tipped his head forward in a courteous gesture and said, "You may proceed, Señor Taylor."

Tarrington placed the end of the Berretta between Dave's third and fourth finger. The silencer clinking against the two carat diamond pinky ring Dave wore. He motioned for the General to step back, told Dave, "Nice ring," and pulled the trigger.

The ring ricocheted off the tiled walls like a jingle bell in a blender. It landed on the floor about a foot from the pulverized finger.

Dave's eyes assumed the diameter of silver dollars, and he went "Uuuuuuhhhhh!"

Tarrington strolled casually to the ring, bent down and retrieved it, put it in his pocket. He smiled at Dave and tossed his cigar into the pool of congealing blood seeping from the severed finger. It hissed out.

Dave went, "uhhhhh," rather dully.

"Oh yes," said Tarrington, "I see your predicament. There's a considerable amount of blood oozing from a hole in your hand where your finger once was, correct?"

Dave tried to yawn in the velcroed neck brace, staring at Tarrington from behind hooded eyes.

"No need to panic. I've thought of everything, Mr. Carmichael." With this Tarrington laid the gun on the table and leaned into a shopping bag, producing his own welding glove and a portable fire extinguisher. He put the glove on his hand, the extinguisher on the table. Smoothing the front of the smock, he held the gloved hand out, said to Torren, "Hot butter knife."

She carefully slapped the heat warped utensil into Tarrington's gloved palm. "Hot butter knife," she repeated with clinical precision.

"Cauterizing." Tarrington stated and pressed the heated tip of the knife to the hole where Dave's finger once was. The flesh around it immediately caught fire as the wound seared shut with a sizzle.

Tarrington took two steps back, fanning his face, and considered this development.

Dave could smell himself combusting and went, "Uuuhhhh?!?"

Tarrington said seriously, "Nurse?"

"Doctor?"

"That man's hand is aflame."

"Yes, Doctor." Torren agreed.

"You've got the fire extinguisher ready, Nurse?"

"Yes, Doctor."

"Give it a blast then."

"The hand?"

Dave went, "Uhhhhhh! Uhhhhhh! Uhhhhhh!"

"Yes, Nurse," said Tarrington, "The one burning."

"Yes, Doctor." Torren put Dave's hand out, a smug little pout on her lips.

The General burst into a merry fit of laughter.

Raul was still intent on the deeply pained creases of Dave's face, staring at the man as if he were trying to bend it back to normal with his will. He sipped the cognac and sighed.

Dave cycled down, sweat pouring from his head and shoulders and chest. "Uhhhhh….uhhhhh….uhhhhhh," he gasped. The snifter sitting on the plywood before his face clattered he shook so fiercely. Urine ran down the leg of the stainless steel chair and trickled loudly into the drain beneath the table.

Tarrington saw this and sucked air through his teeth in a gesture of consternation. "Nurse," he said, "the patient seems to be dehydrating."

"Yes, Doctor."

"Administer anesthesia," he told her, "He's losing it."

Torren carefully poured from a fifth of Wild Turkey, filling up a spray bottle. She stood about three feet from Dave and angled a stream into his open mouth. He gagged for the most part.

"Hmmmmm," said Tarrington, removing the snifter from the

cage. He leaned over and pulled his funny round sunglasses down his nose, peering through the cage door. "How do you feel in there, Mr. Carmichael? Ready to answer some questions?"

Dave pointedly stopped groaning.

"Uh-oh," sing-songed Tarrington, looking over his shoulder at Torren. "Please bring in the first witness, bailiff."

Torren switched roles and stepped through the twist in the wall and returned dangling a rather large white rat by its tail. The rat squeaked and hissed wildly in reprisal.

"Rats," Tarrington said, nodding at Dave, shrugging his shoulders. "Whadaya gonna do? They'll tell on ya every time. I mean… just who can ya trust now-a-days? It's a crazy business, Mr. Carmichael."

Dave's eyes narrowed. He didn't get it.

A serene smile on the General's face. Stroking the row of medals on his chest. He looked touched.

"Will the first witness please take the stand."

Torren dropped the protesting rat inside the cage, closed the door. Dave's eyes went, "What the…"

Tarrington ignited the torch and barely grazed the rat's tail. The rodent hissed and leapt into Dave's open mouth, started chewing on his tongue.

Dave went, "Uhhhhhh!" so loud the rat leapt back out, hissing at Tarrington now.

Tarrington showed the rat the propane torch and it ran into Dave's unprotected face then bit him on the upper lip.

Dave went, "Aaaarrrrgggghhhh!" and the rat moved on to his earlobe. More urine ran into the drain by the table.

Tarrington picked up the Berretta and obliterated the rat with a 9mm slug. The hair stood on Dave's head. Tarrington said, "I've got five more of these critters, Mr. Carmichael. Did our first witness inspire any testimony?"

Dave couldn't move his head or shoulders or any part of his body except his fingers and toes. He wiggled what ones he had left and seemed to be saying, "You bet your ass," with his eyes.

"Very well," said Tarrington, then asked his first question, "Now who exactly in the federal government do you work for, Mr. Carmichael?"

Dave went, "Uhhh, uhhh, uhhhh."

Tarrington leaned forward, set his funny round sunglasses on the stainless table, smiling in Dave's face. "Okay, three syllables… sounds like uhhhhh." He nodded at Dave, "You're gonna have to do better than that, big guy."

Dave was about to cry.

Tarrington told Torren to take the cage off his head. She motioned for Raul to step aside four paces and then kicked the cage from its 6-penny finishing nail anchoring system. It flew from the plywood collar and crashed in the corner. But not without first opening a nasty gash over Dave's left eye.

"Whoops," Torren said.

"Occupational hazard," Tarrington said, "Right Mr. Carmichael?"

Dave tried to smile.

Tarrington said, "I'm gonna take those plastic braces out of your mouth… you bite my fingers, spit blood on my new suit, or anything of that nature, we start all over with the fingers, *capice?*"

"Uhhhhh."

Tarrington said, "I suppose I'll just have to go on your grunt."

When the braces came out, Tarrington sprayed Wild Turkey on Dave's wounds, gave him a good mouthful, told him to rinse and spit carefully on the plywood. Then he removed the collar.

He lit a Marlboro light and stuck it in Dave's mouth, told him, "Have a smoke. Your favorite. I notice the little things."

Dave smoked and choked and began to spill his guts. He was talking so fast Tarrington had to slap him to slow him down. He aimed the hand mirror Nando had purchased, told Dave, "Look at yourself. Plastic surgery's still an option. Just the facts, man."

Dave told them he was a CIA agent and what the CIA really wanted from Carlos' operation was a full-time business partner. The reason Carlos and the General were so important to the CIA was because they were central figures; Carlos with ties to General Khun Sa, the overlord of the Golden Triangle's heroin production; and General Montoya because he acted as Mexico's chief shipment manager of Columbian cocaine cartels. Dave said the CIA was about to take over all United States drug distribution.

Dave said that because of this the CIA needed a steady producer of drugs. And that they would gladly launder all monies, even after new currency was introduced, because they had the connections to do so. With all kinds of new bills and currency restrictions right around the corner, this was a concept that should be seriously considered.

He also promised the use of the CIA's air force; a half dozen Lockheed MC-130 H Combat Talon II's. A customized version of the C-130, a four-engined turbo prop Air Force cargo ship with day/night infiltration systems. The larger nose radome housing an Emerson electric AN/APQ-170 precision ground mapping/weather/terrain/avoidance radar. The Talons also had short take off and landing capabilities, and automated high-speed, low-level aerial delivery and container release systems. In short, it was a smuggler's dream ship. A twenty-ton payload that could be dropped anywhere under practically any conditions. And to top all this off, Dave would see to it that any Air Force base Carlos needed would be available for safe landing within U.S. borders. No U.S. Customs, no Border Patrol, no cops, no worries, no problems. Nothing but good business.

Plus, (he just wouldn't shut up,) Dave guaranteed the entire cast of any of Carlos' or General Montoya's drug operations immunity from prosecution where CIA interests were concerned. Dave said the CIA had developed such a drug distribution ring that they could handle virtually all of Carlos' business, and the General's too. He even touched on the possibility of the Agency and Carlos' regime co-sponsoring a major automatic weapons assembly plant somewhere in northern Mexico. Dave spoke about a special section within the Domestic Operations Group whose sole responsibility was to foster domestic violence. To make sure underprivileged children had ample access to their favorite TV hero's machine guns. He touched on a martial law scenario coming up in the near future and hinted that it would be wise for Carlos' dynasty to sign on with the secret government while they still had a chance. And he expounded and expounded and expounded.

When it seemed he'd exhausted this well-practiced sales pitch, Tarrington asked, "Anything else? Anything new? Anything juicy? That police-state shit is old news. The agency wanting to deal with us is like so early eighties, dude. It's all you ever hear anymore at the big drug summits. Tell me something I don't know."

Dave had literally divulged everything he'd been given to divulge. He nodded his head, saying, "No, that's all I can offer." Then he asked hopefully, "So, we gotta deal?"

He seemed fairly confident. It was a pretty nice offer.

Tarrington looked at Raul and then at the General, he said, "Hey, sounds like a real bargain, huh?"

The General grinned, "It's what dreams are made of, Señor Taylor."

Raul said, "I'll have to think about it."

About five seconds later Raul picked up Tarrington's pistol, slowly unscrewed the silencer.

The room went quiet.

Dave wore an expectant look.

Raul smirked and very carefully aimed the pistol between Dave's eyes.

Dave's body drew in upon itself as he resigned himself to his death. His eyes seared with a hopeless rage.

Raul pulled back the hammer.

Dave squeezed his eyes shut, his body tensed.

Raul pulled the trigger.

Dave lost control of his bowels.

Raul said, "Go tell your handlers, no deal."

Sweat pouring from his face and neck, Dave had to concentrate to hear Raul. His ears ringing from the blast that Raul had let go next to his head. His body shivered, convulsing with the impact that his life had just been spared.

The General licked his lips, turned his head toward the two-way speaker in the ceiling, said, "Juan, have a car ready to take Mr. Carmichael to Juarez."

Juan's leathery voice floated back down, "Si, Generale."

Tarrington leaned over and whispered in Dave's ear, "If I were you, I'd get to Vegas as soon as possible."

Chapter Twenty-one

With Dave's interrogation concluded, Tarrington dispatched Donny and Mike to head east and collect the thirty-two million. Tarrington and Torren were across the river in El Paso, Tarrington driving them around in the Audi. He stopped at a Burger King for double bacon cheeseburgers—parking so he could eat them in the car. It was almost midnight.

He asked Torren, "So how long was Dave that deep in the operation?" Methodically he dressed his burgers with mustard.

She replied, "Single acts of tyranny may be ascribed to the accidental opinion of the day; but a series of oppressions, begun at a distinguished period, and pursued unalterably through every change of ministers, too plainly proves a deliberate systematic plan of reducing us to slavery."

He said, "What the hell is that supposed to mean? Other than the obvious."

She said, "Think about it. Thomas Jefferson said it eons ago. Since then the Federal Reserve Act effectively relinquished the people's control over availability of currency and credit and handed it to a consortium of bankers. Woodrow Wilson's administration adopted and pushed for the League of Nations, the forerunner to the United Nations. We have Roosevelt's "New Deal" which was no more than part of that plan to reduce us to slavery. We have manufactured World Wars, Vietnam—a war about opium among other unrelated antics, they killed Kennedy because he had his own agenda. Now we have a push to erase the U.S. Constitution and replace it with a treaty called the Genocide Convention which was ratified in 1986, and like it or not, the United States, its citizens, are all legal subjects of the World Court. And not one in a hundred U.S. Citizens in the country is even aware of this. There's also untold famine, poverty, and rampant crime in the streets when it could easily be subverted...."

Tarrington smiled. She was talking his language. But he said, "Some people would call you an alarmist, touting that conspiracy theory like that."

She said, "Those people have been brainwashed by their television sets."

He said, "Bravo. So you're telling me CIA agents like Dave, selling the package he's selling, are inevitable?"

"Correct. It's a sign of the times that the CIA is trying to capture and control all the drug markets and not just most of them. We have a new currency on the way. What better way to crush the existing drug cartels that won't cooperate. And if the CIA can turn the last die-hards with this threat by selling all those extra-legal benefits, well, more power to them as far as they're concerned. The truth of the matter is: First there will be martial law and sometime after that previously illegal drugs will be made legal. It's on the way. The very near future."

"Precisely because," Tarrington interjected, "the government is now working to be in a position to totally control all drug production, distribution, and sales."

Torren said, "Even more than they are already. The idea is to tax the habits they've created. It's a proven fact that drug revenues exceed our gross national product. The country's hooked. The drug war was a real brainstorm for Washington, as well as those individuals that actually pull Washington's strings. The more drugs the better. Government-sponsored criminals fill their pockets, countless front foundations are set up to help wash the financing for the infamous "black" operations. The kind that have total denial written all over them. Plus, the drug problem is given the bellows by a controlled media machine and John Q. Public is more than happy to do whatever he can to help stop the madness that drug-related crime is creating. Not excluding giving up his own constitutional rights to squash the terror in the streets. And the Government created this terror specifically to further their control of the masses."

"Like trying to grab everybody's guns," Tarrington said.

"That and going along with a twenty-year wave of constitutional killing new laws. The entire scenario of our domestic lack of tranquility could easily be turned around, however, the people running this country are propagating it, purposely employing this and many other plans to render the masses weak from poverty and lawlessness in order to one day completely control them. It's the disease of government in general, and of the New World Government in particular."

Tarrington said, "I had no idea you were this adamantly opposed to the current push for a New World Order. Do you realize how much more attractive you are to me now?"

She ignored the second part of this, told him, "If the powers that be weren't murderous, money-hungry, control-obsessed bastards, if they truly were after world peace and harmony, then it would be a great plan. But like Thomas Jefferson said; a series of oppressions, begun at a distinguished period, and pursued unalterably through every change of ministers, too plainly proves a deliberate systematical plan of reducing us to slavery... and our ex-buddy Dave is merely par for the course."

"So what, my illustrious and most beautiful assistant, is your answer to all this?"

Torren said, "Man's got to stand for something, right?"

Tarrington replied, "Not too many of those kind left."

She said, "Regardless. Those that are left, those that have some integrity, some purpose on this planet, will fight. That's my answer. Fight for what's right. Personal freedom."

"Revolution, you're saying."

"Is there another word for it?"

Tarrington broke out in song, "I'm singing in the rain, just singing in the rain…."

———

After Tarrington checked them into a double at the Best Western, Torren gave him the ultimatum. Subtly, by her standards.

First she turned back the bed just so. Then in the bathroom she dialed in the perfect water temperature and started the shower. Finally, standing naked in the bathroom doorway, she caught Tarrington's attention over the news, signaled him to reduce the volume on the TV set and tauntingly beckoned him, curling her forefinger, saying, "It's now or never, big fella."

Tarrington's only concern was the operation. And towards that end there was no sacrifice too great. Given the finality of her manner, he quickly discerned the entire situation.

Without a word, he disrobed and acquiesced. Let her lead him into the shower.

When he'd recovered sufficiently, just prior to dawn, with her snuggled passively against his chest, drooling in her sleep, the first thing he did was turn on the TV. CNN. He couldn't help himself. An innocent man named Nicolas Taylor was being prosecuted in the name of Tarrington's alias. An innocent man now turned into an international heroin kingpin by the machine. Overnight.

The entire deal had been nagging at Tarrington's conscience since he'd first heard about it. He was having a difficult time understanding… no, admitting to himself how easily the Feds had glued the whole indictment to Nick. It was hard to reconcile the ease with which the media and its attendant multitude of "do good" irrationalist supercops could instigate a full scale "witch hunt" on a moment's notice.

It took an hour, a room service breakfast for two, and a freshly opened beer before the story aired. And when it finally did air, it was a Special Live Report direct from the courthouse in Los Angeles.

Tarrington couldn't believe it.

Torren thought it was funny.

Nicolas Taylor of 1740 Florence Drive in Anaheim, the man Tarrington had spontaneously gifted with the surplus proceeds from his phone and electric bill accounts, was a black man. He had a wife and four children. He'd been working the same job for the past eighteen years—a middle manager for one of California's many military hardware development and assembly corporations. It was obvious from the outraged confusion the man exhibited, that he couldn't believe his government was this inept.

What Tarrington couldn't believe were the two key witnesses introduced live at Mr. Taylor's bail denial hearing. One was Mr. Walter Bramhouser, a man Tarrington had hired to move his furniture that fateful day the two girls had stolen his Ferrari.

"Mr. Walter Bramhouser?" the taped-over prosecutor's voice cooed softly, "Currently the dispatcher for Allied Van Lines Westwood California office?"

"Walter, please," Bramhouser responded. "Sir," he added with proper flare.

"Oh boy," Tarrington mumbled.

Torren poked him playfully in the ribs, giggling when the camera panned Ms. Narissa Nunez, a recently jailed employee of Happy Home Cleaning Service—the service Tarrington had hired to clean his apartment immediately after Bramhouser had dispatched a crew to empty it.

Now Narissa Nunez too was an unlikely witness to the newly crowned kingpin's purported flight from justice. And the story got even better.

It was these two people who were being used to identify Mr. Nicolas Taylor for the court. Telling the cameras that this hapless black man from Anaheim was the genuine article. A *bona fide* International Heroin Kingpin.

Bramhouser recounted for the court and camera how the defendant Taylor had phoned him the previous Monday morning and paid him six thousand in cash, for a job only requiring around fifteen hundred. Bramhouser omitted the part where he had pocketed three grand, and continued by pointing out the obvious hurry Mr. Taylor was in to evacuate his apartment. He told the court that he'd found it to be suspicious behavior and that's why he'd come forward to assist the authorities.

Ms. Nunez, in her halting English, explained how she'd been having an affair with Mr. Taylor and this was precisely why he'd used Happy Home to clean up the mess he'd made there "… having filthy dirty sex with deese Americano putas." She elaborated with overdone vehemence.

Nunez was apparently crushed that her beau could be so callous. He deserved everything he had coming, and by the way, she knew nothing of his drug dealing. And that's why she'd cooperated with the police. At least that's what she said.

Nicolas Taylor's bail was denied and he was dragged from the courtroom kicking and screaming, two U.S. marshals on each flailing limb.

"I'm innocent! I'm innocent! I'm innocent!" he wailed on the way out.

The camera panned his emotionally distraught wife of twenty

years sitting beside his two oldest daughters. All of them huddled together, suffering from media mangle.

Interviews with the prosecution revealed that the death penalty would ultimately be sought. Mr. Taylor's actions with Senator Randolf Abernathy's daughter Camellia resulted in her death. The latest federal crime bill said you couldn't even conspire to harm a government employee, or a family member of such an employee, and not be liable where the ultimate penalty was concerned. The prosecutor appeared angry. Perhaps the severe Napoleonic complex he was harboring. He finished up with a snorting exaltation against earth's demon drug dealers.

Tarrington clicked off the TV and sighed.

Torren said, "They're framing the shit out of that poor man."

Tarrington said, "More like crucifying."

"I wonder if he'll rise up on the third day."

He told Torren, "Only if the bullshit they're burying him under floats."

Looking into his eyes, she asked, "What are you thinking?"

He said, "Man's gotta stand for something, right?"

Chapter Twenty-two

Mellonhall had been recruited from the inner city by the CIA. Something about his grade point average in school being perfect. And his record as a one-man crime wave after school hitting the same mark.

He was originally used as an information conduit to and from the welfare initiated desperation of the ghetto. A case study the CIA profited from in their calculated manipulation of the underprivileged. Their creation of the nihilist.

Mellonhall and his people had been a pawn of the government since they first were brought over in chains. It was through some of Mellonhall's work that he advanced his race to victim, and soon to be special weapons. That crafty nihilist.

Mixing cultures was a key to agitating the populous. High profile episodes of violence was the goal. Fostering this dichotomy was a major tool of the establishment in its construction of the police state. There was a New World Order in town. And it was riding a Neo-Victorian social structure.

Mellonhall had always been blind to the overt grand plan and figured he'd been doing the patriotic thing all along. If he were ever to realize how badly he was being used by his government, he would employ all his special training to retaliate.

Unfortunately, Mellonhall would be dead before glimpsing this truth.

Just as Tarrington suspected, Mellonhall had disassembled the homing device Tarrington had fastened to the undercarriage of the

Porsche. He'd left the transmitter in a garbage dumpster. Now he was nervously sitting in his fancy white sports car, parked near Tarrington and Torren's hotel room, putting a couple of the pieces together.

First piece, as much as Dave enjoyed his party, it had never interfered with the operational aspect of his job. The fact that he failed to adhere to the agreed-upon contact schedule meant there was a problem.

Knowing only the aspects of Tarrington that Geech had provided in the personal section of the man's file, plus seeing the way Tarrington had planted the transmitter in the Porsche, he was convinced Dave had been compromised. Which didn't make Clarence Mellonhall very happy.

The fact that he had been been parked at the Best Western most of the night, crammed in the car, only chancing it once to grab a ham and cheese sub, merely escalated his discontent.

He did think it was funny though that Tarrington would have the wherewithal to plant a homing device in the Porsche and not look for one on his own car. Mellonhall had been following the Audi since it first came back across the Mexican border from General Montoya's ranch. For the past nine hours he'd been watching the door Tarrington and Torren had disappeared behind late last night.

Nine hours they had been in that hotel room. And now Mellonhall was sick and tired of waiting. It was time to take an active position in the matter. He climbed out of the car and performed his version of the cold call.

When Tarrington answered the door Mellonhall shoved him backwards and walked in.

Tarrington said, "I didn't order any take out," and set himself into a fighting stance.

Mellonhall waved the empty homing device shell in front of Tarrington, then tossed it aside casually. He said, "Cut the bullshit boy, or I'm gonna take you out. Now we all know the players here. Where's Carmichael?"

Tarrington said, "Oh Dave? He a friend of yours?"

Mellonhall untucked his shirt, stripped it off. His shoulders were so big, it looked like he had a loveseat on his back. He was easily a head taller than Tarrington. He said, "Whiteboy, if he be dead, you be dyin'."

Tarrington said, "Dave joined a traveling bowling team. They've got a ten-game double elimination series in Lubbock, Texas starting tomorrow morning."

"You be a smartass motherfucker," Mellonhall said and moved in swinging.

Tarrington ducked outside, but it didn't matter. Mellonhall was still on the attack. He mauled Tarrington, got him in a bear hug, lifted him by his leg and his neck and heaved him into the big mirror over the dressing area sink counter.

The mirror crashed over Tarrington as he bounced off the counter and rolled onto the floor.

Brushing glass off his back he noticed no bleeding and said to the exasperated Mellonhall, "How 'bout fast pitch softball? I know ole Dave really loved his sports. Beer, hot dogs, skinned knees."

Mellonhall said, "I bet I break your face you keep runnin' that lip," and kicked Tarrington.

Torren was dressed now, had her white spandex bodysuit on with the stiletto heels. She'd been careful to maneuver herself between Mellonhall and the exit during the first round. She yelled at him now, "Hey big boy, ever seen a pair of tits like these?"

When he turned around, she pulled the top of her jumper down to her waist, pushed 'em out there a little.

Mellonhall's jaw dropped.

Torren kicked him right below it, driving the heel of her right shoe at an upward angle through his windpipe, through the aortal artery, and into the brain stem.

He toppled like a tree, backwards into Tarrington's lap.

The shoe was stuck to his neck like a size 7 vampire bat.

Tarrington said, "Now why'd ya go and do that? I had 'em, ya know. I coulda taken him…" Then he grinned at her and said, "Nice shoes."

She said, "They don't call 'em stilettos for nothing."

Tarrington asked her, "What's next?"

She said, "I thought you were the boss."

"I am, but you're displaying such initiative, I thought I'd let you clean up your own mess. I have here in my lap, about two hundred seventy pounds of rapidly decaying flesh."

"Well, for starters, don't remove the shoe. I'm sure the aortal artery has been severed."

Tarrington looked down, "Yeah, he's starting to leak."

Torren said, "Bath tub, quick."

They went about it in short order.

Tarrington was huffing afterwards, "Jesus," he gasped, "Make that three hundred eighty pounds of dead weight." He handed Torren the keys to Mellonhall's Porsche, "Go ransack the car. It's a white 928… probably around here somewhere.

"What am I supposed to find?" she asked.

"Evidence," he said.

Chapter Twenty-three

Three hours east of L.A., Death Valley was fifteen thousand square miles of arid sand, parched plants, malnourished birds, and thirsty reptiles. The Mojave.

A nicely polished maroon Mercedes sedan, heading out from Barstow, cut across the vast expanse of desert. Not too suspiciously fast or slow.

Waves of heat wiggled from the sand and danced with the cactus under a harsh noonday sun. The hood of the car glimmered.

James Trowbridge, Tarrington's west coast operation manager, was driving. He had the air on, the windows down, a smiling face, and a heart filled to its veritable brim with avarice. He was running late by his own schedule, thirty minutes from the Nevada state line. Delivering the heroin. Since dismissing the regular drivers in the wake of the Ferrari incident, he was doing all the tedious stuff himself.

Upon arrival he would park the Mercedes at a strip mall next to the Alladin, right in front of a place called the Little Caesar's Racing-Sports Book. Then he would approach the bank of pay phones outside and jockey for a line out with the bookies. Contact made, he would catch a cab to no casino in particular and do a bit of innocent gambling. Then it was off to the airport to catch the America West shuttle back to L.A. Same as always.

This highly organized, totally foolproof, weekly dope run was about to plummet into a macrocosm of complete disarray.

Having been dispatched by Tarrington to fly east and collect the money, Donny and Mike were now doing just that. Both were more than pleased to be reconnected to the adrenaline rush that doubled as their career of choice.

Upon landing in the Cessna 310 Mike was licensed to fly, they rented a Dodge Caravan and drove south towards the Jacksonville, Florida downtown skyline. A sleeting rain obscured a dismal day.

Mike was driving. "Is the Weasel ready?" he asked.

"Yeah, I called him from Dallas. He said go straight to the safe house off Ft. Caroline." Donny swiveled his chair to display the giant joint he had designs on. "You bring a lighter?"

"Just happen to have one right here," Mike said, reaching into his pocket.

Red-faced, holding his breath, the color crept up Donny's neck. After exactly twenty-seven seconds, the smoke poured from his lungs and curled off the windshield.

With somewhat of a religious reckoning, Donny performed his traditional post-mortem commemoration to his one real hero, the late Bob Marley, saying, "Irie mon, dat be da raggamuffin stash, mon."

A serene smile shone amidst the miasma of Donny's psychedelic experience. Exactly twenty-seven seconds he held it. He'd raised the consciousness level of pot smoking to an art.

"You gonna bogart that thing?"

Donny handed over the Thai stick.

They drove through the sleet, passing that prodigious puffer back and forth as if it were a pipe bomb neither wanted to be associated with for too long.

"Things are good." Donny said to nobody in particular.

Mike turned up the radio.

James drove in silence across the Nevada desert, appreciating the time alone. He checked the dash clock: 12:12. Guiding the German sedan skillfully around a long left, he came into a small valley. At this point his eyes turned into a couple of brown and white targets.

In the valley, he saw a line of cars, some pulled over to the side. James swallowed with much difficulty. The glands just weren't working. Raspy. He looked around the car trying to find something... he didn't know exactly what. He felt the terror in his breath.

After crossing the St. John's River in Jacksonville. Mike turned off Ft. Caroline road and wrestled the rented Dodge Caravan onto a narrow dirt pathway. Here the trees and tangles of overgrowth that bordered the swampy trail slapped against the vehicle. The windshield wipers splashed mud away, then splashed it on. Slipping and sliding. Mike plowed the minivan through the woods to a clearing where a two-bedroom cottage sat nestled below a stand of oaks and maples.

Donny reluctantly snubbed out his Thai weed splif and prepared to load the money. It would be his last toke till the operation was over. Before leaving the cottage, the ashtray would be emptied, the van thoroughly vacuum-cleaned. Time to work.

Once they had broken into the clearing, Donny noticed the Weasel's Lexus parked right in front of the cottage door, "What a douchebag," he grumbled, "Pull right behind it, Mike. Geeze, he knows we gotta load..."

The front door was unlocked. The Weasel, who had been working as the east coast distributor of the Deleon Empire's marijuana, sat in a dusty old Lay-Z-Boy rocker, watching TV. He could smell the rain whoosh in with Donny and Mike, could hear them stomping their mud-caked feet on the foyer rug. "What took you idiots so long?"

"Life," replied Donny.

"I've been waiting three weeks for you guys to come get this money and bring some dope back. Are you gonna make this a habit?" Weasy was doing his very best to incriminate Donny and Mike. It was per his agreement with the Feds. Since he himself had been fooled by the DEA, arrested, then cut loose to help the government round up more of his cohorts, the Weasel was now circumventing trouble the easy way. As a snitch. The conversation between Donny, Mike and himself was being transmitted to three DEA tape machines running smoothly on the top shelf in one of the bedroom closets.

"You know what happened to Guido."

"Guido this!" Weasy complained, showing Donny his middle finger. "Now when do I see more dope? I got a business to run. Guido gets run over by a garbage truck, it's not my problem. It's his. What's next? You guys gonna start recognizing federal holidays?"

Donny very calmly replied, "It's obvious we're back on regular operating status right now or we wouldn't be here." Then he pitched his voice a little higher and said, "So enough with the *funpheh* already."

Weasy rolled his eyes at Donny's Jewish slapstick whine, then turned his wrist to check the antique Brequet watch strapped there. "So what's the holdup?"

"Your car is blocking the entrance," reminded Donny.

"So give me the keys already," Weasy said, "And I'll pull your van up."

With dulled reactions, the sneaky little paranoid-squirrel look on his face, Mike gave a thin grin and fumbled for the keys.

"What the hell's wrong with him?" the Weasel asked.

"He's stoned," Donny declared. "Just cut him some slack, it's Mike we're talking about."

"Yeah," Weasy scoffed. "How could I forget," and he grabbed the keys from Mike's loosely clenched fist and scampered out the front door. Neither Donny nor Mike would ever see him again.

"C'mon Mikey, let's load this cash." And Donny gave Mike a shove to follow him.

They single filed to the larger bedroom where the cash was always kept. Stepping in the room, the ring of DEA agents startled Donny so much that he backed right into Mike.

"What the hell...?" he murmured.

The fact that there was only five cartons of money was the second thing that Donny noticed.

Ten armed men; pistols drawn, flack jackets zipped, all told Donny and Mike in unison, "Don't move."

Frightened from his stupor, Mike turned to run, but was repeatedly clonked about the head and shoulders with the butt of a .44 magnum. He fell to the floor like a heap of dirty laundry.

Very calm. Ramrod straight. Silent. "I'm gonna kill you Weasy, you slimeball, skid pigeon, cum shot, flea bag..." Donny was thinking as he cycled through his arsenal of regret and watched three agents viciously kick Mike to sleep. He stood there as the remaining seven tripped clumsily over each other, spreading themselves around the room, pointing their shaking pistols at him.

"They've been watching too many Miami Vice re-runs," Donny thought, and grinned to spite them.

"Hold it, don't move, stay right where you are," he heard them say.

"Believe me," he thought, "I'm not going anywhere."

Didn't they know that real marijuana men abhorred violence. It just wasn't in the code. And Donny-Do was a prime example.

Two agents grabbed his arms and twisted them to unnatural discomfort. They slapped the cuffs tightly on his wrists. Donny didn't complain. Almost ten years in the business and he'd acted out this part in his mind many times.

An older, coriaceous-faced cop questioned him. A hospital type vodka smell wafted from the man's mouth and found refuge in Donny's nostrils. "What's your name?"

Donny was polite about it. "Fuck you," he said dryly.

The old cop considered this reply for a moment and then gave it another shot. He pointed to Mike as two agents dragged him from the room by the cuffs. He said, "One more time. What's his name?"

"Fuck you," Danny said resolutely and with perfect diction.

The old cop became visibly upset. Just before the steam erupted from the abyss of his hair-lined cherry pastel ears, he spoke, "We've got you red-handed with eleven million in cash. We've got six hours of expert testimony from a key witness, your employee, Mr. Weinstein. Don't you realize, you don't stand a chance in federal court. We'll bait and bullyrag the public sector till they scream for your head. If you go to jail forever, you'll be lucky. Now… are you ready to cooperate?"

"Eleven million," thought Donny. Weasy had skimmed half the pick-up off the top as a nice parting shot. Donny said, "Faaaayyuck Yooouu."

The old cop drew from his well of experience, assimilated a little calm and said, "You can talk to me now… or you can play this game and ruin your chance at a reduced sentence."

They looked at each other for quite some time. "Reduced from forever?" Donny was thinking.

The old cop posed another question, real nice about it.

"Now, who's the new boss? Since the last one's dead now."

Donny checked the faces of each agent. They stared back impassively, yet there was expectation in those faces. The room was silent. Donny creased his forehead, giving them a show, going over his options for the audience. Thinking about it for quite some time. Looking slightly worried as he got into it. Meeting the concentrated gaze of each agent in turn, scanning the periphery. All of their expressions a product of what being above the law bred. Donny had them thinking though… thinking he was going to do what ninety-nine percent of all freshly apprehended criminals did of late.

Cooperate. The American Way. Tell on somebody. Defer your responsibility.

The old cop smiled, he could see it coming. Could see where he was gonna hang that picture of him with the Mayor pinning that commendation on his chest; right above the kid's football trophies in the den. He could see the magazine people making appointments with him, the papers, could see this one going national. This Donny guy cooperating could send him to a desk in Washington. Eleven million dollars in cash was a serious deal.

Donny whispered something.

"What was that?" The old cop asked. He leaned towards Donny. They were face to face now. "What was that?"

Donny had a nice ball of phlegm coddled on his tongue. When the guy was about ten inches from him, he spit this projectile from professional dentistry's private hell, directly into the corner of the old cop's astonished left eye.

"Fuck you!" Donny yelled and began to laugh uncontrollably.

Six agents tackled Donny as their boss stood stricken with stupor. They punched wildly at every exposed part of Donny's body.

Donny found a little air in between blows. "And Fuck You too!" He was cackling like a madman.

The agents worked him over like one.

James had his Mercedes lined up in a slow procession of twelve cars, moving slowly. James was number ten. A sheen of sweat covered his face. The ticker tape of life's highs and lows reeled through his mind. His oft-rehearsed cover story embossed in bold lettering upon that tape.

At the head of the procession, a cadre of California Highway patrolmen, two drug sniffing dogs, and a team of newsmen. Every car leaving or entering the state of California was being routinely checked for drugs. Part of Senator Randolf Abernathy's public appeal in lieu of his daughter's death. Something for the voters. A drug detection gauntlet. He was cracking down on crime. Great sound bites.

On the side of the road, a blue Chevy Scottsdale stepside pickup with New Mexico tags was being dismantled by three State Troopers. The news people filmed the removal of door panels, bucket seats, and the Yamaha Daytona 400 cafe racer that had just been wheeled down a special ramp. The dogs had alerted on something. A bottle of Quervo Gold sat upon the hood of the pick-up. One dog in particular was howling happily. It wasn't tequila he'd found.

The shakedown was a perfunctory action Senator Abernathy was employing to get the media off his back. The plan was to milk it for all it was worth, then disappear back into the recesses of ambiguity. Get back to the job of mishandling tax money.

Thirty minutes elapsed. James felt as if he'd pass out from dehydration. What substance he'd had was leaking on the sheepskin seat cover. He rehearsed the cover story once again.

Then all of a sudden he thought, "To hell with it, who am I kidding? These last few years at a hundred grand a month will have to suffice." He pulled the Mercedes abruptly to the shoulder, stepped out of the car and approached a nearby cop.

The cop saw this and said, "Hey, what are you doing? Get back in your car."

James went right up to him and asked, "Who's running this operation?"

⟶⟩●⟨⟵

Mike floated in and out of delirium. He'd woken up on the way downtown. Nothing was working properly. The eyes wouldn't focus. The arms felt broken. Too much pressure pulling him around by the cuffs. Bad shivers. A bad, bad headache. He was cold. He'd been lying on the concrete floor of the holding pen because it was too difficult trying to climb to the bunk. He felt like a scrambled egg when it was still a little runny. And this time he wasn't on his way, but actually in jail.

This realization sunk into Mike like hot pepper juice. "This is the real thing," he thought. "Uh-oh," he attempted to speak but could only produce a high-pitched warble. Again the vocal cords were responding negatively to the situation. Even worse, his testicles were in his belly. "Hey you!" he squeaked, "Hey you! Hey you over there!"

Two agents were talking by the coffee machine, banging their fists on the table between them, excited about their participation in the big bust, about the commendations they would receive, the media exposure, the possible promotions already in the first stages of development.

One agent motioned for his friend to slow down, to shut up. "The punk's trying to say something." He looked across the break room to the cage Mike was in and barked, "What the fuck do you want, scum?"

Mike gave it a moment. He was dizzy from the attempt. But his thoughts wandered to all that money he had stashed in safety deposit boxes across the country. Then they flopped around like a landed sportfish as he thought about jail, about the retention of his heterosexual values. Still squeaking, he said, "Who's running this operation?"

The agents practically tore the door frame out trying to get to the boss first. Bringing the good news. We got us another cooperator. We got us another one to bleed dry.

Chapter Twenty-four

The Gulfstream Enrique had given to Tarrington was a luxurious affair; burled walnut cabinetry contrasting with powder blue chiffon upholstery. The carpet was cushioned with so much foam under it, Tarrington and Torren were compelled to remove their shoes. Like walking and flying on air, simultaneously.

Tarrington and Torren barefoot in the tail section, elbowed around a circular walnut conference table and sunk into two plush arm chairs. Spread out before them were the contents of Mellonhall's briefcase.

Tarrington said, "What do you make of all this?"

"It looks half-operational, and half-indoctrinational," she answered.

"Like they were running him and brainwashing him at the same time?"

Torren said, "Is there a better way to do it?"

"Look at this," said Tarrington, "This is a brief on that treaty you were talking about, The Genocide Convention. It says right here that treaty law supersedes constitutional law. Quotes Article VI, Section 2 of the constitution as proof. This Genocide Convention is fundamentally the law of the land."

Torren said, "I know all about it. The guy who dreamed it all up was a professor of International Law at Yale. The U.N. refined it and submitted it in Paris in '48. It was adopted unanimously as prevailing U.N. ideology."

Tarrington said, "I sure feel safe knowing the U.N. has power over the Constitution. Whew. What a relief. They did so well keeping that war going on in Bosnia, hell... I guess they deserve it."

Torren, however, was taking it rather seriously. She said, "It took thirty-eight years before Congress finally ratified the Genocide Treaty. Truman, Eisenhower, the Kennedy Administration, Nixon, everybody took a shot selling the country out. But it took..."

Tarrington interrupted, teased her, "But it took ole Ronnie and George to run the final con." He'd picked away some of the documents.

Torren declined comment. She was absorbed by the mass of confiscated paperwork. "Look," she said, "Here's Article III of the Convention, says genocide means any of the following acts committed with intent to destroy, in whole or in part, a national, ethical, or religious group. Sub-clause (b) says, causing serious bodily or mental harm."

"Ahh," Tarrington said, "Humanity's biggest foible... thinking too much. Nothing worse than the hot air of mental harm... except, perhaps, litigating it."

"Yeah, Article III says any of the following acts are punishable under the scope of the Convention; Genocide, conspiracy to commit Genocide, direct and public incitement to commit genocide, attempt to commit genocide, and complicity in Genocide."

Tarrington said, "So you can't do it, think or plan to do it, talk about doing it, attempt to do it, or know about anybody thinking, talking, planning, or attempting to do it, that is, unless you tell on them... or you're guilty too. Looks like they got all the thought crimes covered."

Torren said, "This is crazy."

Tarrington said, "Step one, stop thinking."

"Here we go," she said, picking through Mellonhall's briefcase, "The operational aspect of Shaft's assignment. Prosecution and Imprisonment via Rex 84 Concentration Camp System."

"The martial law stuff," Tarrington observed.

"That's exactly what it is…" She mumbled, reading ahead, "Russia…"

"All over again," he finished, accepting the first page and quoting with interest, "Rex 84 is a Presidential Directive whose primary purpose is to silence and hold prisoner, citizens and groups the government considers dangerous."

Torren said, "In other words, anyone they want."

Tarrington said, "They do it all the time."

"If they don't gas 'em first."

"That's only if they're women and children."

Torren arched an eyebrow and read the document. "Here's Order #11490 authorizing the President or his designee to declare a National Emergency and thereafter a total government take over; rationing, confiscation of public and private property; food, guns, precious metals, business, and homes; reorganize local and state agencies under a single centralized federal bureau. Order #11490 creates ten federal districts, called Newstates. These ten are already used by the Post Office, IRS, Social Security, and keyed banking establishments."

Tarrington said, "Must remember to quit my day job and get that passport."

Torren read, "Rex 84 was created under the guise of a highly classified National Security Decision called Directive 84, thus Rex 84." She handed Tarrington page three, saying, "This directive authorizes the activation of a multitude of huge prison camps, conversion of present prisons to up capacity, and the utilization of abandoned military bases; all at key defense positions nationwide… one of these is a specially designated one million acre restricted area in Alaska to be used for brainwashing during takeover phase. This restricted area in Alaska has been aptly named a mental health complex."

"For all those found guilty of thinking," Tarrington added.

She smiled, said, "This says there are currently three hundred and fifty federal record centers containing computer printouts on civilian/political activities; that there are twenty-five million citizens with files. And that these computers will automatically print twenty-five million arrest warrants the minute Rex 84 is instigated."

Tarrington was thinking out loud, "That's why prisons are such a hot franchise deal now. And why there's a push for a national police force to get this done. You know a national emergency gives the government power to close banks, freeze assets, accounts, kill export capital, call in gold and silver, reissue devalued currency, and control prices and wages."

"Where'd you learn that?" she asked.

"Page three," he pointed.

She calmly removed the sheet from his hand and read aloud, "Executive Order 10995 authorizes takeover of all communication media."

Tarrington said, "That's already in effect."

She let him smile at himself, then read, "Order 10997 authorizes the takeover of all electrical power, petroleum, gas, fuels, and minerals; Order 10998 rations all food resources and farms; Order 10999 takes over transportation, highways and seaports. Order 11000 mobilizes civilian work forces via direct government interdiction; Order 11001 for all health, welfare, and educational functions.; 11002 authorizes a nationwide registration of all persons, microchipped ID's…"

Tarrington added, "The mark of the beast. No man may buy or sell…"

She read, "11003 to takeover airports and aircraft; 11004 to takeover housing and finance authorities… relocate communities… build new housing with confiscated assets…" She stopped and took a breath. "Fuck," she said. "this is nuts… power to relocate, takeover railroads, inland waterways, public storage facilities."

Tarrington began reading from across the table, "And Order 11051 gives the Office of Emergency Planning juice to manage the entire action of…" Here he paused for emphasis, "… those troubled times."

Torren read, "Increased international tension, domestic tension, or economic crises."

Tarrington said, "Sounds like a laxative commercial. Listen to this…" and he read from a random sheet. "Garden plot and Cable Splicer," paused, "…utilizing resources from the U.S. Army's Civil Affairs Group, the Law Enforcement Assistant Force, the National Guard. And the up and coming, National Police Force." He leaned back and sighed, said, "Step two, begin thinking again."

Torren said, "And all you gotta do is watch a little TV, see just how the media masters are preparing the public for these exact scenarios. Funny…" she rifled through five or six of the pages, "I've never seen this Rex 84 stuff before."

Tarrington said, "Well, judging our source, I'd say label it accurate."

"No question." She looked him in the eye. "What are we gonna do?"

He smiled. "We?… Was I that good last night?"

She almost laughed.

He said, "Let's try to stop thinking individually and start thinking simultaneously. I heard that works."

"You're gonna do what?"

There was a wistful bleakness about him. "Move back to Indiana and take that teaching job at Highstreet Elementary, I guess. I mean it's either that or suicide. And what would Momma say if I did myself in?"

She said, "What happened to all that bullshit about a man's gotta stand for something?"

He said, "Hey, call 'em like ya see 'em, right? It was bullshit. You're absolutely correct."

She was trying to figure him out.

Chapter Twenty-five

Nando made a well executed landing at L.A.X. and brought the Gulfstream to a halt at the private section. When Tarrington stepped onto the tarmac, his father, Welly, was there: dressed for success. Had one of his lace-up Santoni's displayed nicely on the bumper of a silver stretch Lincoln.

Tarrington set the lambskin briefcase down and hugged the man, whispering in his ear, "Thanks for coming out of retirement, Pops. I really need ya on this one."

Welly replied softly, "Who you talking to? You know I love to work."

Torren and Nando had emerged from the Gulfstream. Now Torren looked at the two men embracing.

With Tarrington wearing Zileri, a Tino Cosma tie, and lizard Loisis, and Welly standing next to him in a pinstriped Novecento, with those four hundred dollar shoes, well… they only lacked a plucky photographer to make it a fashion shoot.

Tarrington told Torren and Nando, "I'd like you to meet a very good friend, Sir Reggington Colby-Smythe the third. Sir Reggington, this is Torren, my new assistant, and Nando, my pilot."

Welly bowed gracefully, lightly kissing Torren's hand, "To meet one as lovely I knew not the pleasure until this moment."

She fluttered her eyelashes and played along.

Welly then squared off with Nando and shook his hand. "Very nice to meet you. Fine piece of machinery and a fine man to fly it."

Nando replied, "Very nice to meet you."

Tarrington said, "Polly want a cracker."

Nando didn't get it.

Tarrington's eyes met his father's.

Welly said, "I'm at the Hyatt. Suite 1023."

Tarrington looked at Nando. "Your turn."

"The Hyatt, 1023," Nando parroted. "I'll touch base as soon as the plane's ready to fly."

Tarrington gave Nando a wad of bills, said, "Here kid, get something nice for yourself."

Nando said, "Two hours."

Tarrington made a funny noise, shrugged, told Nando, "Don't forget the Eagle snacks."

———⇌>●<⇋———

Once inside the limo Tarrington re-introduced his father. "Torren, this is my father, Wellington James Tarrington." With Nando out of earshot, it was okay to tell the truth. Nando's operational knowledge was accrued on a need-to-know basis only.

"Nice to meet you, Sir Reggie," Torren joshed, and fingered Welly's lapel delicately, looking at Tarrington too. "Like father like son," she said.

"Mom too," said Tarrington, "She's a cross dresser."

Welly smiled. "Please call me Welly."

"So Pops, bring your kit?"

Welly hoisted a large cosmetic case onto his lap, spun the dual combinations and opened its lid. Inside was an assortment of various disguises and identifications.

Welly said, "I've got it all; FBI, DEA, State Department, medical doctor, three different attorneys (criminal, corporate, and civil), heavy equipment operator, ship's captain, building inspector, insurance agent, college professor, private investigator, chauffeur, gemologist, bank president, psychiatrist, philosopher, Burger King employee, skid row bum, a large-breasted blond, a birthday clown, and a Barney costume."

He smiled and asked his son, "What is it you have in mind?"

<hr/>

In Anaheim, on a once quiet residential street, a tan Chrysler sedan strewn with antennae, weaved through a scattered cadre of illegally parked cars.

The cars were all full of television, magazine, and newspaper reporters. All of them camping out, diligently laying for a story, a photo opportunity, or the ultimate—an in-depth interview with the wife of the biggest heroin kingpin in the United States, possibly the world... Mrs. Nicolas Taylor.

But she wasn't talking. She'd had enough. Her life had been reduced to a rambling roller coaster ride of manic depressive sensitivities.

She was now barricaded in with two faithful friends whose jobs were to run errands and screen telephone calls. The four Taylor children had been airlifted to their grandmother's house in South Carolina. Until the travesty subsided. But would it ever? Mrs. Taylor was near her wits end. She looked bad, like a Metamucil hangover and two six-packs of Bud.

The tan Chrysler halted directly in front of 1740 Florence Drive. A slouchy grim-looking fellow sporting a nice Sears & Roebuck ensemble, maroon shoes and a pale green shirt with a plaid tie stepped from the car. He had a thick manila envelope tucked under his arm. At the door, he rang the bell.

Some lady answered and Welly noticed she wasn't black. He said, "My name is Bill Drake." He flashed a badge. "State Department. I need to speak with Delilah Taylor."

The lady's facial tension softened, looking Welly up and down. She smirked. "Alright, step in. Close the door. I don't need those fools charging the place again." She motioned toward the street. "I'll go get her."

Three steps later she turned around, gave Welly a sterner than stern look, "The State Department?"

Welly gave her a sterner than stern nod, "Yes, ma'am."

Mrs. Delilah Taylor came from the back of the house. Rounding the corner, Welly could see she'd been losing sleep regularly. Not even AlkaSeltzer Plus could have helped her.

She mustered a smile and admitted it, "I look like shit."

Welly produced the manila envelope, laid it on the coffee table, placed a letter on top of it. He said, "So what."

She dropped her chin.

He said, "Ever hear of the Fairy Godmother?"

She gave him a weird look, then shook her head, "You ain't no fed, Mister, I can smell from here you brushed your teeth this morning."

Welly said, "We Fairy people are behind you a hundred fifty percent, Mrs. Taylor." He indicated the envelope and the letter, said, "Little present from the gang, read the letter first." He gave her a wink and left, slipped out the door like a cat.

—————⊱◈⊰—————

In the living room of 1740 Florence Drive the telephone rang.

The stern lady answered, "Yeah, we'll accept… How ya doin' Nick? Yeah, we're holdin' on… I'm glad to hear it. Yes, she's in the back… let me get her."

At that moment in the master bedroom, Mrs. Delilah Taylor began to scream. An overjoyed completely excellent wonderful type scream.

Shrilly she professed, "There is a God! He exists! There is a God!"

When her friend ran in, Delilah began to do-si-do with the woman. Dancing.

"Your husband's on the phone."

"He is!"

"Yes."

"Perfect!"

Delilah danced all the way to the living room.

The stern lady took a look around, saw three pages from the letter tossed haphazardly about the room; page one near the nightstand, two on the floor, three in the adjacent bathroom. Then she bent and pulled the flap back on the manila envelope. "My Lord," she intoned.

It was two hundred fifty thousand in cash.

"Jesus Christ," she said.

A religious experience right there at 1740 Florence Drive. The stern lady departed at a brisk pace for the living room. Mrs. Taylor was on the phone…

Nick Taylor: "So what do you hear from my lawyer?"

Delilah Taylor: "Oh nothing dear, he hasn't really been keeping in touch."

Nick: "Damn, I think that man is positively corrupt. Nothing? He hasn't even called or anything?"

Delilah: "No. Nothing dear."

Nick: "What about the private investigator? Has he found anything? Geeze, I need to get out of here." He was starting to whine. "Did you call him, honey?"

Delilah: "Yes I did honey."

Nick: "And what did he say?"

Delilah: "He said you'd probably fry, sweetheart. I'm gonna fly to South Carolina and see your mother, see the children. Good luck baby."

She hung up. Delilah Taylor was now officially oblivious to her innocent husband's plight. She was tired of the United Police States, tired of her long loyalty to husband Nick, tired of their nine to five existence, tired of just about everything. She dialed the phone. There were a million things to do. First was....

Delilah: "Hello, this you Suzy?"

Suzy, who recognized the voice: "What's gotten into you, girl? You sound great. Did Nicky get out of jail?"

Delilah, on top of the world: "No, he's still in. I need a favor, sweetheart. When can you get out of that place?"

Suzy, perplexed: "Soon. Why?"

Delilah: "I need you to bring all the stuff. It's an emergency housecall. Two perms, a cut, three manicures, and three facials. I'll pay double for it."

Suzy: "Don't worry about it, hon. I'll be there in two hours."

Delilah: "Ciao, baby."

Delilah hung up the phone, took a deep breath, and ran her hands through the hair that would soon be fixed.

She asked the stern lady, who was now beginning to smile, lips parted in expectation, "How do we go about getting our passports?"

The stern lady shrugged.

Delilah: "And where can we rent a couple of gigolos?"

The stern lady's composure melted into ecstasy, she pumped her fists in the air and screamed, "Yeessss!"

Chapter Twenty-six

James Trowbridge was now working for the Feds. A rat, snitch, stoolie, confidential informant, however you wanted to say it. He'd turned on Tarrington to save his own skin.

It began the day before at the Nevada state line. Rather than have the dogs discover the heroin, James had propositioned the officer in charge of the highway shake-down. Thereafter he'd been promptly whisked from the Mojave Desert at 160 mph in the back of a California Highway Patrol car, and taken straight to the Federal Building in downtown Los Angeles. There, he conferred with several FBI big wigs. In three hours he'd hammered out a deal. James said he alone knew who the real Nick Taylor was, who the real heroin kingpin was. Said he could produce him.

The surprise had been when James' beeper went off listing the number to a pay phone in Santa Monica. It was Tarrington calling.

That's when James said to the Feds, "See, I told ya so."

The Beverly Center was a large shopping mall, sprawled like a yogic squid in California's commercial wonderland. It was tall enough to accommodate four stories, but only housing two. The architects vying for high ceilings, expansive indoor terraced gardens, big open spaces. James and Tarrington agreed to meet there.

Tarrington figured it was a good spot to discuss the permanent handing over of the heroin operation to James. Tarrington wasn't aware the FBI felt the same way, or he would have rescheduled.

James had convinced the Feds that with enough manpower, there was no way the suspect could escape.

Now Tarrington climbed from the limousine he'd leased for the day. Several people took a second glance, thinking he was a celebrity. Eccentrics with frayed gym shorts, worn t-shirts, and tattered sneakers stepping from limos, were usually subjects of the paparazzi. Everybody wanted to get caught in a star's photo. Famous for a day. Two girls beamed at him. He beamed back. Their beams beamed. He had to be someone.

Los Angeles was clouding. Monique's forecast earlier on the Pro Bum was becoming a reality. Tarrington had just proposed to her. She'd said, "Hell, yes." Now he smiled inside thinking about her; thinking about their impending marriage, the cute little way she ate olives; thinking about the yacht club in La Paz, Mexico... just the two of them parked at the southern tip of the Baja, their new home... it wouldn't be long now. Take that cruise into the sunset with the pretty girl and all the money. He wanted to make it storybook all the way.

Stepping into the Beverly Center, the air conditioning hit him like a bag of crushed ice. The coolness peppered his legs like a dozen depraved squirrels.

The time. 5:37 p.m. The meeting scheduled for six. Tarrington decided a little shopping would further distort his image. He was hiding behind casual clothing. A different modus operandi.

First he stopped at the pizza place in the food court where an old Italian man sold him a large cup of cold draft. Tarrington paid cash from a five thousand dollar roll he was keeping in his jockstrap. He wasn't going to risk a purchase using a credit card.

Walking around, sipping the beer, he spotted a white Adidas track suit, green stripes, it would have to do... so he spent money and put it on. Then caving in to merchandising, he bought a pair of Reebok Pumps. That nifty little basketball in the tongue was just too neat. Why ask why? Just do it.

Now he looked like he belonged in a mall. Right away though he had to loosen the high tops. He took a moment to pump up the little basketball and forgive himself. Then, back to the upper terrace of the food court to meet with James.

James was waiting, just where he said he would. Tarrington was five minutes late. He saw James at the table, caught his eye, and motioned him to the rail. Had his elbows resting on the stainless top, looking down into the lush foliage thirty feet below. There was a multi-level indoor garden growing in all directions. Tarrington could almost reach out and touch a rubber tree.

James was wired for sound. Literally. Had two transmitting mikes strapped and taped on. One beneath the silk tie, right behind the pin, and another tucked under his shirt collar. Stereo. Dressed as he'd never been dressed before. This was a special occasion. His emancipation insurance.

There were fifty-two suits in the mall, all fully aware of James Trowbridge's deceitfulness and loving it. Half the FBI agents in the area had been recruited for the big bust. A spectacle. All of them wound tighter than your average alarm clock, ready to annoy. Six were each equipped with a mini-speaker snugged into an ear, and would be privy to the conversation James and Tarrington were about to have.

Two agents, parked outside the mall in a rolling sound studio, were ready to commit the dialogue to tape.

James lined his elbows up with Tarrington's on the rail. Getting close.

Tarrington said, "As you know, this Nick Taylor thing has clogged the blades of the fan. Just too much shit."

"Good," James was thinking and said, "I know even more about it now. The poor bastard hired a friend of mine to represent him."

"I'm going on vacation." Tarrington said.

"How long?"

"Forever."

"Oh," James said, and stole a quick glance over his shoulder.

Then eye contact with the man he was betraying.

Tarrington paused looking at James and said, "You can count the money all by yourself now. They did teach you to count at Princeton, didn't they?"

"I took two semesters of it. Good marks." James was fidgety. Tension hung in the air like Spanish moss. Tarrington's big cup of beer hung loosely from his fingers, suspended over the fern garden. James' future hung in the balance. He was sure the Feds were taking advantage of the photo opportunity; him and the big boss moments before the bust. FBI agents itching to score what would surely amount to the biggest media sensation since the silicon went bad in a famous actress's breast implants. James could feel the anticipation as if it were a blanket wrapped around him. Wondering how Tarrington couldn't. The body wire he was wearing was quickly becoming obsolete.

James saw them coming as he checked behind again…a dozen heading their way. The bust was on. They'd heard enough. He jerked his head back around. Tarrington was talking: "…later tonight you will meet the pilot who flies the money, and we can deposit last week's proceeds as well. I take it you've put it in a safe place…?"

Now the agent in charge signaled the primary assault team to cease, halt, stop, Stop! Damnit! Some frantic gestures as he pressed the speaker deep into his ear. Trying to get this new pilot information loud and clear.

The advancing row, twelve agents wide, slid to a stop and turned, retreating in haste. Several shoppers noticed this comic routine. A mall show? A dance troupe? A small crowd was gathering. Two agents nervously shooed them away. The bust was beginning to fall apart.

"Yes, I've taken good care of it," James lied, then asked, "What pilot?"

"Name's Hector. We'll all get together later on. I've made sure he's in town for this. Everything's smooth here?"

"No problems at all," James lied again. He had specialized in lying at Princeton Law.

Now the bust was back on: clicking heels, squeaking soles, and stomping boots. And James actually felt guilty for a split second. Even though he'd already done all the justifying a guy could do. Funny how that worked.

From everywhere they converged, yelling, "Halt! You're under arrest! Drop it! On the ground!"

"What's going on?" James pretended to act frantic.

Tarrington slapped him. You could hear it above the excited roar of advancing Feds. "What's going on is that you're a punk, Trowbridge," he said calmly.

Five agents rushed Tarrington, surrounded him, pointing pistols. Just out of reach. "FREEZE FUCK FACE!" You could see the satisfaction in their eyes.

Everybody within a fifty yard radius stopped. Some dropped their packages. Curiosity and fear stabbed at a dreary silence, the only punctuation the footfalls of Feds.

Post stampede, forty-seven agents took positions along the rail across the garden observation opening. Hunched, perched, aimed, and ready. Weapons trained on the suspect's head. It was very quiet. Someone had turned down the Muzak. Just the labored breathing. A baby started to cry. Echoes.

Tarrington glanced behind him, checked the ferns below. A woman's gasp, then whispering to a friend. The baby screaming now.

Nothing else. Tarrington turned to his assailants, smiled, and threw the beer at them.

The five agents took it standing up. Right in the face for two, across the chest for three. Wet shirts, cold cheeks, generally pissed off now.

The largest of the five holstered his weapon and attacked.

Tarrington retaliated by reaching behind, grabbing the rail and kicking the fed as hard as he could. The agent grabbed Tarrington's feet, pushed him backwards over the edge. Holding him there. "What cha gonna do now, huh scum? Can you fly?"

"Good question," Tarrington said. Then slipped from the sneakers and rolled backwards off the rail. His arms flailed. The funny round sunglasses went. He did a perfect back somersault, landed feet first in the soft peat.

Then his glands took over.

Escape.

On the second floor fifty-two cops looked dumfounded at one another, then into the fern garden. Back and forth.

The agent in charge yelled, "What the fuck are you idiots doing? Follow that son-of-a-bitch! Now!" He pointed his pistol in the air and fired. Get them going.

The huge skylight above him spiderwebbed, sagged from its moors, then crumbled into a thousand tiny shards of razor sharp glass. Falling into the crowd.

Three dozen people clawed at their faces and arms. Screaming pandemonium ensued. Sixteen wounded. Two dead. Total damage: four hundred thousand, not including lawsuits.

"GODDAMNIT!" he thundered, waving the smoking pistol at four of his men. "FOLLOW HIM!"

They quickly leaped over the rail, falling... One hit a cement partition and broke both his legs. He commenced to howl.

Above him, a mad rush for the elevators, escalators, and fire stairs. Several people were trampled in the frenzied fed attack. Two more dead, six wounded. A wave of human freight. Forty-eight agents running full out to capture Tarrington.

James was safe. He'd taken refuge disguised as a mannequin in a store front display. He was wearing a nice floral print summer dress. In losing his nerve, he'd acquired a fine sense of style.

One of the agents who had jumped down into the fern garden happened to be the FBI's reigning champ at the shooting range. He screamed at Tarrington, "HALT! OR I'LL SHOOT!"

The crowd of people Tarrington had been running through now parted like the Red Sea, forming a gauntlet of quivering flesh to either side of the mallway.

"I SAID HALT!"

Tarrington wasn't listening. He was looking for a break in the wall of people, thinking, "... no cop would shoot an innocent bystander."

Dan Winter was a bouncer at a posh Los Angeles nightclub. "And a damn good one," he would tell you whether you wanted to hear it or not. When he saw Tarrington running from what appeared to be the police, he decided any day was a good day to be the hero. Thinking about that foxy anchor chick on Channel Four's Action News, Dan knew this was his big break.

Now the cop on the terrace steeled himself, aiming the gun, one knee dug into the soft peat, the other on the hard concrete partition. He had the bead sitting right between the suspect's shoulder blades. The shot was a seventy-five yarder and steadily increasing. No Problem. Last Chance. Final warning. "STOP! OR I'LL SHOOT!"

Tarrington was about to make his move into the crowd, looking for a weak link in the human chain when he heard the woman scream at him.

"Watch out!" She yelled.

The huge body builder, Dan Winter, was ten feet in front of him, looking like a Sumo wrestler in a Levi's ad.

Right then the marksman's gun exploded, ringing like a bad ear down the mallway.

Tarrington stretched out and dove. Hitting the tile on his stomach and sliding right between big Dan's legs.

Dan had been ready. Then the scream, the man in the track suit falling forward, the crack of the bullet and the burning sensation in the center of his chest.

The .44 caliber hollow point had passed right over Tarrington as he slipped along the tile floor, and torn through Dan Winter's sternum, lifting his body from the floor. And Dan went sailing backwards.

"OOOOOOOOOffff!" said Tarrington, as Dan's dead hulk hit him square in the back, punching the air from his lungs.

People standing on the sidelines were appalled; gasps of horror, most covered with a spray of Dan's blood.

As Tarrington and the dead body slid to a stop, a plan came to mind. Crisp. As if he'd been thinking about it all day. He rolled the corpse away from him and peered down the mallway. A wave of federal agents were charging at him like a panzer division on nitro. He unzipped the sweat jacket's front pocket, pulled out the thick wad of bills, fanned them carefully for the crowd to see, and then tossed them elegantly in the air.

The once apprehensive crowd immediately lost all conception of fear and jammed the mallway in a frenzied free for all, grabbing every bill they could. Thoroughly blocking the fed's line of attack.

Tarrington stood up, casually brushed the dust off his jacket, and trotted towards a recently abandoned woman's boutique. Passing through he was forced to stop in mid-stride.

"Hmmmmmm," said he, rubbing his chin introspectively as he circled a display. It was Nicole Miller's latest release.

It would look great on Monique.

Tarrington looted the deserted shop. Parting the rack, he found the perfect size five. Then out the back door to hail a cab.

It was a bright day, he reached for the funny round sunglasses and found them missing. The limo was two hundred yards away at the front entrance.

Tarrington saluted and looked around.

That's when Torren drove up in a rented Oldsmobile and said, "Going my way, big boy?"

He climbed in and draped the stolen dress across the back seat, saying, "Let's try a bar first. I seemed to have lost my beer."

Torren said, "And your shoes too? You sure you need another drink?"

Chapter Twenty-seven

Geech drove a confiscated Seville, burgundy on burgundy. It was still raining in Jacksonville. One of the wipers screeched on the window. Geech used his Motorola briefcase phone.

A woman answered, "Yes?"

Geech said, "This is day code, Twister, word is Seven."

She said, "The amount sir?"

"The transaction totaled two dollars even."

At this juncture Geech was patched through to a different operator. A man's voice, "Your phrase sir?"

Geech said, "Pandora was a bimbo."

Six rings later Robert Preston picked up, saying, "Hello Geech."

"Hello, Bob."

"The general consensus here is that Mellonhall has been blown."

"No contact, eh?"

"He's missed all his nominal relays. And the NSA desk tells me the heat sensor on his implant chip is reading below ninety." Preston cleared his throat.

Geech said, "Well, Bob, he's either dead or trapped in an ice chest somewhere. So what's Tarrington's condition? Where's Carmichael?"

"Word is Tarrington just slipped through the FBI knot... with no positive identification, so the scapegoat theory still holds. As far as Agent Carmichael goes, he was delivered to the El Paso station chief last night, in a somewhat tattered condition. Apparently Tarrington made him too, and succeeded in coercing a confession." Preston's voice was close to quivering. "Geech, what the hell are we going to do? Your man Tarrington's a loose cannon. He's destroying my operation."

Geech paused a good ten seconds before he answered. "Bob... we're just going to deal with it. I told you from the onset Tarrington was no dummy. What did you expect? Until he's completely debriefed I can't see him acting any other way. But consider his natural instinct for self-preservation. When he gets our ultimatum, what do you think he'll do?"

Now Preston paused a moment. Then a reassured tone to his voice, he said, "You're making a good point." He shuffled some paperwork and changed the topic, "So what's the situation there with the DEA?"

Geech answered, "Michael Barnes has been dispatched to reel Tarrington east. It looks like the gauntlet is closing. We'll have our additional leverage soon... that is, if Mr. Tarrington doesn't dodge this too."

Preston asked, "Do we bring him in without the leverage?"

Geech replied, "Let's hope we don't have to use the leverage to begin with. Though it appears we might just need it."

Preston didn't like the sound of this.

Geech asked, "How's the frame-up coming?"

"The L.A. operation? Scapegoat?" Preston's voice had pepped up considerably.

"Yeah."

Preston said, "Well, that black guy Taylor is fucked. Domestic Violence Section says before the trial begins the entire country will know he's innocent. Media Desk is coordinating right now to portray the man as a fine upstanding citizen... family orientated, excellent father..."

Geech interrupted, "He was that already."

"Precisely. We're just making sure everybody knows it. That way when he's handed the death penalty and they fry him, the entire black community should hit the ceiling. We're hoping this does more damage than the Rodney King scenario. We're expecting a National Emergency Status on this one. DVS is counting on it. It sure was nice of Tarrington to hand us this one so perfect like it is. If anything else, the man's a natural."

"Yeah," Geech responded, "I'm just not sure if he realizes it yet."

Chapter Twenty-eight

When Torren and Tarrington arrived at Marina Del Ray, Enrique was already there, inside the Pro Bum watching TV. Monique was below decks, preparing for the long anticipated honeymoon cruise.

Tarrington's marriage proposal four hours earlier was a development her foster father, Geech, was not yet aware of.

Enrique pointed to the TV screen as Tarrington entered through the sliding glass door of the aft deck. "Funny, that fellow looks a lot like you. Same track suit even."

It was an emergency broadcast. Someone in the stereo shop had filmed half of Tarrington's getaway with a mini-cam. The part where the marksman shot the wanna-be hero, Dan Winter. Nice angle on Tarrington sliding between his legs. Now an all-points bulletin was being issued to capture the culprit who had tossed the bills then escaped through a lady's boutique. The police composite, for some reason, didn't look like Tarrington at all. Strange.

To add to this, not one word was mentioned about Tarrington being the actual heroin kingpin, Nicolas Taylor. That information was being adamantly suppressed by higher FBI authorities on orders from their superiors at Langley. Instead, Tarrington was being identified as a long sought suspect in a large drug conspiracy case.

Tarrington watched the news clip, whispered to Enrique, "Where's Moni? Has she seen this?"

Monique appeared at that moment coming from below deck. She handed Tarrington a beer, said, "Don't worry. I'm not calling off the wedding just because you're an internationally hunted criminal.

Besides, it seems to me the authorities have a scapegoat anyways. That poor black man, Nicolas Taylor. So they aren't looking for you as hard as it seems. I know."

Tarrington grinned and told Enrique, "Did I tell you she was smart, or what?"

Monique kissed Tarrington on his nose. "I figured you out months ago, baby."

"My business, you mean?"

"That too."

Torren came in through the sliding glass doors, said, "I've got the ship's store working on all those supplies for the cruise."

"Confer with Moni," Tarrington told her, "She's much more experienced when it comes to the voyage. I'm sure I've missed something."

He asked Enrique, "What are you doing here? I thought you were in Paris?"

"That's this weekend. Tonight is a big benefit dinner the Anti-Defamation League is sponsoring. Grand a plate. The topic is the legalization of marijuana. Can't miss this one."

"The ADL? I don't get it."

"Who does anymore?" Enrique stretched down the couch and pulled a box from beneath the end table, careful of the Haliburton Zero handcuffed to his other wrist. Inside the box was a gross of soft covered booklets. "Take one. It's Jack Herer's *The Emperor Wears No Clothes*. The bible for marijuana freedom fighters everywhere. The total exposé on how the government made pot illegal for all the wrong reasons." He handed the book to Tarrington, "I'm gonna pass 'em out tonight and talk about hypocrisy."

Tarrington looked at it, waved it up and down and tossed it on the couch beside Enrique, "As soon as I get this boat to Mexico. First thing I'll do is read that... for you, honey."

Enrique raised his eyebrows, "And what about other things?"

"Other things?" Tarrington inquired, glancing at Monique.

She grabbed Torren by the arm and led her to the galley, "C'mon honey, this sounds like man talk."

Torren smiled, telling Monique, "I love that bikini on you. Tell me where to buy one just like it," as they disappeared toward the forward hull.

When they were out of site, Enrique whispered, "El Paso."

Tarrington said, "Donny and Mike should be there with the money late tonight or early tomorrow. I'm headed that way."

"So you're letting Moni take this thing to Mexico alone?"

"Why not? She drives the damn thing better than me. Plus I'm sending Torren with her for company. The Bum cruises at thirty knots, I should have Torren back by Saturday. Besides, somebody's got to keep Willie distracted while the ship is being manned… or womaned, shall I say. Ever since the mutiny he's been real uptight about long passages."

"Ahh yes," said Enrique sardonically, "Where is the highly esteemed Captain Bligh anyways? Haven't seen him today."

"Who knows," Tarrington said, then whistled, and called out, "Yo! Sea Pig! Where ya hidin' Billy boy?"

From the corner of the dining room came the squeaking warble of a large guinea pig lost in the throes of owner worship. Making a run for Tarrington, it disappeared for a moment then poked its head from between Enrique's box of books and the leg of the couch.

Tarrington smiled warmly, bent down, "C'mere Billy! Come to Poppa!"

Oinking in delight, the pig waddled over, stretching his little pig neck skyward as he ran small circles around Tarrington's ankles.

Tarrington picked him up and stroked the long mohawkish

thatch of mottled red and black and beige hair on Captain Bligh's head. The rodent chortled in bliss.

Tarrington said, "You're about ready for a nice catholic she pig, aren't cha Bill?"

Chapter Twenty-nine

Welly drove into Tarrington's old neighborhood and parked across the street from the erstwhile townhouse of one heroin kingpin, Nicolas Taylor. It was stilled barricaded off with yellow crime-scene tape.

He grabbed his briefcase, adjusted his bifocals, and approached the doorstep of Tarrington's old neighbor, Mrs. Emily Hibblemeyer. The nice lady across the street who was always pruning her rose bushes as Tarrington retrieved his morning paper.

Welly knocked on her door. When she answered, he handed her a card that said he was Miles Steinberg of the criminal law firm of Steinberg, Fleecem, and Howe.

She didn't seem too impressed.

Then he told her how beautiful her rose bushes were and she invited him inside, gave him a cup of coffee, and asked him how she could assist him?

He made a show of slowly opening the alligator attaché, producing with a flourish an affidavit with Tarrington's picture copied onto the top right-hand corner. The affidavit was written as if by Mrs. Hibblemeyer, attesting to the fact that the man who'd once lived across the street from her at 8913 Norma Place was the white man pictured and not a black man named Nicolas Taylor, of 1740 Florence Drive in Anaheim.

Using a variegated stutter, legal doublespeak plea from the patriotic heart of America, Welly had Mrs. Hibblemeyer so confused over the document she fed him chocolate cake to shut him up and signed it in triplicate.

Welly thanked her profusely and left her standing in her own doorway wondering exactly what it was that had just happened to her.

As far as she could tell, she'd just helped out an innocent man in the name of American justice. But she still wasn't sure. She felt positive that a younger Caucasian man was the actual resident of the townhouse across the street. But she'd seen so much hype on TV the last three days she wasn't sure if the black guy had been wearing a wig and white make up all those times she'd seen him picking up his morning paper. After all, her eyes weren't what they used to be. A woman gets old.

Then again, she had been ready to do practically anything to get that stuttering, blubbering Steinberg out of her kitchen. She couldn't believe she'd misjudged his character so. Of course, she'd always thought the heroin dealer across the street was a nice guy too.

"Ahh shit," she grumbled, and clipped a couple roses for the kitchen vase.

Chapter Thirty

Twelve hours after Welly had initiated his part of the Liberate Nicolas Taylor—Free the Innocent plan, Tarrington began his part, skidding the rented Lincoln to a stop at the airport Ramada's front entrance. He slung open the car door and tripped out onto the pavement. There was a six-hundred-dollar anteater overnight bag in his hand. For the authentic touch. Leaving the car running, he smacked into the glass entrance door of the Ramada, fumbled around, and found the handle.

He had a wig on. A good wig. He had a two-thousand-dollar suit on too. A good suit. He had whisky scented breath. And every time he grunted some guttural slur in further testimony to his condition, he was in danger of spontaneous combustion.

He played the desk bell like an old pro. Some twenty-two bars of "She's a Grand Old Flag."

The kid working the desk showed up after three bars and frowned through the remaining nineteen.

When Tarrington finished, the kid asked, "Can I help you, sir?"

Tarrington giggled, then stared aggressively at the kid, "Listen Asshole," he sprayed the desk and the kid in spit, "I want a room! What's taking so long? Where's the goddamn manager?"

Then coming over the desk a bit, blowing the breath all over the kid, he switched demeanor, "They thought they could catch me... Hah! Showed them assholes!" He moaned, then turned it into a whine, and said, "Pleeease can I have a roooom?"

The kid said, "Eighty-nine dollars and some I.D. and I got ya a nice clean bed, Mister." He dangled a key before Tarrington's face.

Tarrington tried to focus his artificially reddened eyes on the swinging key, his head bobbing and weaving like an old boxer. Then, out of nowhere, an unexpected, yet grand gesture. He pulled a wad of cash from his pocket and flipped the kid a hundred.

"Eighty-nine bucks," he scoffed, "I remember when I could get an ounce of shit for fifty down in Rosarita... yeah, those were the good ole days. Shit... Now I'm getting a quarter mil a kilo in New York!" he yelled like a conqueror, "Silly Feds! They'll never catch me!"

Like a whip he grabbed the key from the kid, and skillfully flicked his old Nicolas Taylor California driver's license across the counter. Hitting the astonished kid right in the chest, it fell behind the desk.

Tarrington stumbled out the door saying, "Send it up with room service... I gotta blow chunks... aaahhooaahh," moaning on the way to the car. He bounced off the fender four times getting around to the driver's side. Then he screeched away.

The kid was looking at the license. It said Nicolas Taylor. The address given was 8913 Norma Place. The kid scratched his head. It didn't make any sense. The past three days all he'd heard about was Nicolas Taylor, some black guy from Anaheim. Just last Monday a hot looking Mexican chick working for Happy Home Cleaning got busted scouring this same dude's townhouse.... 8913 Norma Place... the kid was sure of it. He looked at the license again. The picture matched the drunk he'd just given a room. The drunk's dialogue matched a drug dealer's.

The kid scratched his head again. Then he picked up the phone and dialed 911.

A lady answered, "Nature of Emergency?"

The kid said, "Yeah, I think I got something big here."

The lady asked, "Are you giving information in regards to a crime in progress? We only handle emergency distress stuff on this extension."

The kid said, "I'm not sure."

The lady told him, "Please explain then."

Tarrington found his room, turned on the shower, opened the overnight bag and spilled twenty-five thousand in cash all over the bed. He intentionally fingerprinted the entire premises, the TV, tossed the suit jacket, and vanished.

Chapter Thirty-one

Mike, one-half of the Donny & Mike duo who helped manage the Deleon Empire's El Paso marijuana operation, was now working for the Feds. A rat, snitch, stoolie, confidential informant. However you wanted to say it, he too turned on Tarrington to save his own skin.

As Nando pulled Tarrington's Gulfstream jet into Enrique's El Paso hanger, Mike was there supervising the servicing of his Cessna 310. Apparently there was some kind of fuel mixture carburetion problem that nobody could properly diagnose. Mike had made sure of it.

Tarrington invited him into the Gulfstream, asked him, "Where's Donny?"

Mike said, "He's negotiating."

"With who?"

"The Weasel."

"For what?"

"For the money."

"It's ours isn't it?"

"Yes."

"Then why the negotiations?"

"The Weasel's mad that it took three weeks to get the dope moving. Now he's paranoid that it'll happen again and screw up his thing. Says he's not paying till we deliver the next load. Says he'll pay for three loads in advance from now on. But not until we make the first good faith showing and deliver."

"Did you discuss the possibility of delivering a bullet to the back of this little fella's head?"

Mike blanched, "I'm not authorized to convey that type of information."

Tarrington told him, "So fake it…"

"You mean fly back there…"

"Yeah. Go tell the Weasel he acts right or we kill him. Can you remember that?"

"One problem," Mike said, "The ship's down."

"Come again?"

Tarrington leaned forward in his bolster.

"My plane's fucked up," Mike said, "I almost crashed the son-of-a-bitch getting here. Something to do with the fuel mixture killing the engine at high rpm's or something…"

Tarrington sighed.

Mike stopped talking and just squinted at him.

Tarrington said, "On second thought…" and opened the beige attaché to show Mike the Berretta 92F, the extra clips, and the silencer. He said, "Here, when your plane works, take this gun and shoot this Weasy fella in the kneecap. Start the next round of negotiations like that. Also, here's an extra clip. It's full in case you're a lousy shot. And here's a silencer should you be inspired to really make a statement and shoot him in public. How's that?" handing all three to Mike.

"Take this negotiating kit to Jacksonville and bring back the money. We don't have to take this shit from this Weasel asshole. We're the guys with the dope, for Christ's sake." He looked at Mike, noticed the man's lower lip was quivering. He sighed again, depressed the intercom switch, "Nando? This is the boss calling his pilot. Do you copy, Nando?"

Nando's voice came from the two-inch speaker by the switch, "Yes, sir. Loud and clear."

Tarrington said, "Do we have the fuel to fly to Jacksonville, Florida, Nando?"

"In approximately thirty minutes."

"Fine. File a flight plan. Pray for sushi, and perhaps this will turn out a worthwhile endeavor."

Nando snickered.

Tarrington turned to Mike, said, "Happy?"

Mike sang, "More than I can saaaay.... you take my breath ahhwaay, you take…"

"Shut up, Mike."

"Okay."

⟶⇒●⇐⟵

Jacksonville's crying sky had sobered after a two-day bout of rainy depression. A full moon ignited a thousand glimmering specks against the night's inky backdrop. It was muggy… like an Armenian steam bath. Around three in the morning. Not a good time to get busted.

The stage was set: Federal Stranglehold, take two. Tarrington had slipped through the California knot like Houdini with an appointment.

Mike had the rented Dodge Caravan's window open, and was whistling badly, trying to match the elusive unordered movements of Beethoven's B-flat quartet. Tarrington listened, amused. Mike was happier than Tarrington could have known. He was moments away from the 166-foot motor yacht the Feds had promised him, and just figuring his cut of the proceeds after Tarrington's Gulfstream was auctioned off. He was in for twenty-five percent of all confiscations by contract. He was grinning from ear to ear.

Swerving off onto the access road and then into the parking lot of the Holiday Inn, he jumped out, said, "Just a minute boss, and I'll have us a room momentarily."

The idea Mike finally conveyed to Tarrington on the flight was that the Weasel should be brought to the Holiday Inn where Tarrington would be introduced as some lower-on-the-rung kind of tough guy. Then Tarrington would wave the pistol and get Weasy to do the right thing. Shoot him in the kneecap himself.

Of course this was bullshit.

They appeared out of nowhere; from stationary automobiles, from moving Wonder Bread trucks, from panel vans, from shrubbery, from the Starvin' Marvin Food Mart on the corner. Swarming Tarrington and Nando like mosquitoes on a blood clot. No bull horns. No helicopters. No screaming sirens, strobing bubblegum machines. Nothing. They weren't even yelling. Seventy-five DEA agents seemingly fell from the sky, four calmly asked Tarrington to step from the vehicle. No sudden moves please. Your hands sir, keep them up. Thank you. Very professional.

Tarrington relinquished his freedom to the home team; out the door, slamming it closed behind him.

Then the cops peeled the van open like alley cats in a fish market. Nando was hustled from his spot on the floorboards, quietly cuffed, then shoved along behind Tarrington. Both were marched past Mike having an argument with an old raisin faced cop.

The old cop: "You left two of my best agents in Dallas like they were the plague!"

Mike: "I told you in the beginning you would have to trust me. No tails. At least I called, Jesus!"

Tarrington felt his escort tug on the cuffs. No lingering by the boss and the snitch. One of the cuffs zippered onto his wrist, digging in. Pain. The pain of betrayal. He hadn't expected it here. James either, for that matter.

A mild-mannered cop led him, being nice. A blue Caprice sat waiting, both rear doors slung open. A marching line of Feds were strung on either side of the pathway. Moonlit faces, darkened shadows, Tarrington met their eyes one at a time as he walked past. Arrogance, all of them, flushed with the glib acknowledgement of his dilemma. Behind him, Mike's voice trailed off in laughter. A hyena laughing off the day's kill.

A mockingbird perched on the Caprice's open door sill, looked at Tarrington and sang a requiem for justice, flying at the last moment.

The nice cop motioned for Tarrington to get in. All the way over, he told him. The pressure on the manacles ebbed momentarily and he was crowded into the Chevy. The cop rubbed his pointy red nose. "Cold," he explained needlessly.

Tarrington hunched down and slid across the bench seat. Freedom right there. The opposite door was open and unmanned. He slid faster, scooting nervously across the smooth leather seat, mind racing, two more feet, smiling now, head double checking his back. None of the cops seemed to be paying any attention. The trunk of Nando's body neared the other door, filling the space. Tarrington's temples glistened, he dropped a foot onto the pavement, purchase, one last look. Nothing.

He turned, poised to flee.

"Well whada we got here? A coked-up rabbit? Bad luck, scum sucker." An angry young DEA agent stared impassively, his nose practically touching Tarrington's. Like the seventy-five cops to begin with, this one had appeared out of thin air.

Tarrington could smell light beer and Happy Hour broccoli dip on the agent's breath. There were veins bulging on the man's flat forehead. Tousled blonde hair. Pits in his face from too many steroids. Cold green eyes even in the dark.

The car's suspension dampened as Nando slid inside.

Tarrington heard his original escort, the nice cop, addressing the steroid baby, "Leave 'em alone, Druthers. This one's rich enough to ruin you."

"Ah shut up, LaSalle," A beer breeze wafted through the car. "You're such a faggot sometimes."

"Suit yourself," the nice cop retaliated, "this one can kill you..." LaSalle let it hang, smiled at Tarrington and slammed the door on Nando's shoelace.

Druther's whispered in Tarrington's ear, "You feel that pressure on your pooper, punk? That's the federal government bangin' on your backdoor. And we're comin' in whether you like it or not. We're about to dry rod you."

Pouting his lips, sultry for a man, Tarrington told him, "I like it dry, big boy," and blew a kiss to the angry agent named Druthers.

Druthers backed out of the car so fast he hit his head on the door frame. "Ooouch!" Fuming, he banged the door shut. The window cracked. Druthers was vigorously rubbing the sore spot on the back of his head.

Stretching his face, Tarrington showed the man all his teeth, pressed his lips against the glass.

Druthers spit on the window.

"What do we do?" Nando asked.

"Absolutely nothing," Tarrington said.

———❈———

Good Cop—Bad Cop. That's what it was. Druthers was driving; continuous derisive commentary, full of malice, telling the captives how bad it was going to be in prison.

LaSalle was riding shotgun, explaining their rights, about phone calls. He even complimented Tarrington's choice in clothing, knew the designer. "Veri Uomo, I love him. Very nice, Mr. Taylor."

LaSalle had been the one to frisk him. "I can't wear dark colors," he was saying.

But Tarrington wasn't there. His brain ticked off one drastic scenario after another: Did Mike bury Torren as well? If so, things were looking pretty grim. Of course, Kiki could probably come up with the proper personnel to get him out of the mess. But Torren was right there. Who was he kidding? He was toast.

Then thinking about Moni and what would become of the wedding plans. Shit.

He couldn't begin to fathom the damage Mike had inflicted, nor did he want to at that moment. It was enough, he was sure. He shifted forward to ease the pain of the cuffs, tearing into his right wrist. The glow of streetlights passing over the car gave LaSalle's sugary dialogue a strobe-like effect. Still talking.

Druthers plowed through a deep puddle. Sounded like a machine gun on the fender wells. Then LaSalle's voice once again, saying something about helping the Feds, "..you cooperate and there's a chance we let you out tonight, to work for…"

"Stop." Tarrington cut in.

"You were saying something, Mr. Taylor?" LaSalle and Druthers both in the front seat with high expectations. Their faces saying, Victory?

Tarrington said, "You're wasting your time."

"A hard core!" Druthers ripped him. Bad Cop. "We're gonna show you stand up guys a thing or two, you punk piece of shit faggot scumsucking low life dirt bag dog dick licking fuck! Can you feel that big bureaucratic dick sliding up in ya? Huh punk? Does it feel good?"

"I can't feel it," said Tarrington, "It must be yours then, huh? Forget to put the erection cream on it this morning, did ya big guy?"

Druthers smashed his fist against the wire mesh separating the front and back seats. "Fuck you, bitch! I'll break your arms."

"Before or after you take these cuffs off me?"

Druthers failed to respond.

Lasalle straightened himself in the front seat, eyes on the road. His part was over. No rats on board. No more Mr. Nice Guy.

Silence.

Nando said, "Testy fellow."

Tarrington said, "Too much bran cereal, does it every time."

—————⇒●⇐—————

Tarrington couldn't see anything but dirty water splashing in the Caprice's head lamps. He could feel the car sliding along some kind of muddy trail, heading into the woods. Didn't seem like the way to jail. Tarrington figured he was in for some good old fashioned ass kicking. His. Redneck style. Welcome to Jacksonville.

They pulled into a cavernous clearing. A small cottage was set back in the trees, its front visible. Light from a single porch lamp and two double glazed windows. There were five Florida Highway Patrol and seven unmarked DEA vehicles haphazardly arranged in the boggy clearing. Druthers pulled up close to the front door and stopped. An astroturf mat had been laid in the mud. The door opened and LaSalle told Tarrington to come. He walked in the cottage with Nando close behind.

Donny was sitting on the parquet floor, over in the corner. The cuffs were secured in front of him. He was wearing the same jeans, sneakers, and Harvard sweat shirt as the day before. "Mike's a rat," he said.

Tarrington nodded. True.

"And the Weasel lives up to his name." This was a melodious voice, up-beat despite the scene. It came from a stoutly built man set next to Donny on the floor. The man wore a scraggly unkempt beard and mustache which belied his gussied up appearance. (A three-piece Hart, Schaffner & Marx.) He looked financially healthy.

"This is Domino Joe," Donny said. "He's been held incommunicado for the past three weeks.

Tarrington figured right away that Domino Joe was a part of the

Jacksonville cell that had decided not to cooperate when the chips fell down. And he was correct in this assumption.

LaSalle refastened Tarrington's cuffs in the front and Tarrington lowered himself to the floor.

"Nice suit," he told the Domino man.

"The food's terrible here. Hey, where's my fuckin' waiter?" Domino Joe verbally attacked Druthers.

"Shut Up!" Druthers blared.

Domino Joe snickered in delight. Right away Tarrington liked the guy.

Then a rough voice spoke. DEA area chief, Kevin O'Malley. It sounded like he was gargling sand and chocolate ice cream. Tarrington recognized it from the airport. Mike had been arguing with that voice. O'Malley said, "Let 'em talk."

Druthers deferred, yet nobody took advantage. Donny, Nando, Domino Joe, and Tarrington; all sitting on the floor. An hour passed. An hour without words. It could have been a western.

Checking his watch, Tarrington wondered what the hell.

"They're here," An unidentified agent blurted from the window.

"See how she wants to do this, Simmons." An order from old lava larynx.

"Right chief." The agent went out front.

The prisoner's eyes met, all asking the same question.

"She?"

She indeed.

She was an anchorwoman. She brought two grips, two cameramen, three lighting technicians, a crew for sound, stage, relays, and a makeup and wardrobe gal named Marge.

"Okay," she was all Hollywood, "Let's get them together for a look here!" She was running the show, framing each prisoner's face in her hands, giving them the artist's eye. First Donny.

"I'd like to see a wool, no… linen on this one," she pointed to the hapless Donny, "But open in the front so we can see the Harvard."

"Did you go to Harvard, by chance?" she asked D. Davis, as she straightened Tarrington's collar. Donny answered by way of a disbelieving gloat.

The production was… well, a production. "We'll pan out from the cocaine in the bedroom," checking with O'Malley on this one, a quick nod, she went with it.

"Yes, we start on the stash, and keep your fingers out of it, Jerry!" telling this to one of her camera men, the one with the bandana.

Cocaine? Tarrington's face asked Donny?

Donny said, "Yeah, we're coke dealers for this one."

Tarrington understood perfectly. Framed. Like Nicolas Taylor. Yes, it definitely happened here in the land of the free.

She was flitting back and forth, directing the grips and lighting techs, looking over the merchandise she had to market, You're a handsome one, she told Nando, great cheekbones.

"Marge!" Her wardrobe assistant appeared. "Let's put some colors on the Latin one here, the Aztec print! And bring me the gold chains!" She had Simmons and Druthers remove Nando's cuffs, and proceeded to refashion Nando's outfit. Exasperated, he just stood there. She had him in a peach garibaldi open to his belly button, and completely annoyed. Marge strung three heavy ersatz gold medallions around his neck, arranging them just so against his dark skin. "Nice contrast," she told her wardrobe assistant. "Let's put him in some harrachis!" Yes, this sounded like a fine touch. For the Latin Coke Lord effect, she told O'Malley. He merely nodded.

Marge ran to the wardrobe truck, in search of the perfect harrachi.

She yelled to Marge, "And touch up the grey at the temples. More grey! This is a man of substance here!" She gave the orders. Nando was relieved of his shoes.

She smiled at Tarrington. You really know what you're doing when you shop, don't you? And you're going to look great on film. I know your type. Is that an IWC Le'Grand Complication? She said all this and more. Told Druthers and Simmons, "You should pay attention to this." Inferring perhaps, that they should consider expanding their own fashion repertoire beyond the Men's Shop at Sears. Druthers snorted.

"Marge! Trim those beards," she motioned towards Donny and Domino Joe. "Close-cropped on the Harvard, like a record company exec gone bad, and leave the big guy's bushy. He's my lawyer stuck in the counter culture movement. Yes! Yes! Yes! This is good! I can see it now. This is good!" She was having a time with them.

"And put the fake Rolex on the Latino. He needs more gold. Make it the President with the diamond bezel." She stopped to think, but just for a second, she was on a roll.

"… Diamonds!" she yelled. "Marge! The pinky ring! Bring me the pinky ring! YES! Hurry Marge, we needed this in the cutting room yesterday!" We're going to give you a little more yuppie, looking at Donny now. "The round wire frames, Marge. The polos. For our Harvard man!"

Tarrington didn't want to believe it, but why denial? It was all too easy, and besides, what would he accomplish with intelligent debate? This was a government operation. Facts didn't matter.

It was evident; the DEA pumping the bust for all it was worth, wringing every ounce of moral and monetary support from the media, the congress, the public… the game was fixed. Had been for years. Now they played every angle: stereotyping the kingpins, working on the public's already profusely brainwashed misconception of drugs and their actual part in society.

Torren's words rang in Tarrington's memory. He hoped she wasn't on Mike's list. Because her expertise would soon be needed. For there was truth to uncover. Death to be dealt. That much was sure.

Tarrington thinking, Hope?

The planting of the cocaine would add to the arrest seizure printout and this would help the government—the Jacksonville DEA in particular—to continue its War on Drugs… or human rights, however you wanted to look at it. And with a hard and high profile. Planting the coke would boost their power to fight the smaller battles, the ones that filled up the prisons but never seemed to make any difference to actually stop the flow of drugs into and around the country. It was a war for control. Tarrington was seeing it clearly. Better than normal, from the inside looking out now.

So he watched the anchor woman get him a life sentence. Death row? What was next? Hire a lawyer? All he could think about was James Trowbridge, the last lawyer he'd hired. Did it really matter?

She was going to bury him. If she failed, the DEA and its savoir snitch would pick up the slack and finish the job. Tarrington had the televised odyssey of Nicolas Taylor's tumultuous plight to base this on. There was no justice and he knew it. For to see it in person was to truly understand.

Chapter Thirty-two

The trip to court began at 7:30 Thursday morning.

Spaced a half hour apart, surrounded by a heavily armed contingent of hypertensive agents, Donny, Nando, then Domino Joe were taken in separate cars.

Tarrington was last. Druthers was driving. LaSalle next to him. Usually this was a U.S. marshal's job, but the area DEA didn't want to take their hooks out. So the marshals were only helping.

Tarrington felt gloomy; the entire side of his face was still chapped red from where Druthers had belted him. "Good morning punk," the agent had said.

As soon as he got ahold of Torren through the proper channels, arrangements would be made to have the arrogant Druthers slowly beat to death. Simple as that. For now, he would conform to the situation. He squinted, met LaSalle's gaze in the passenger side mirror, then turned away. Resting his head against the window he could feel Florida's morning chill.

Devastated. He'd never thought twice. Mike's story even went with his personality.

There was a procession the likes of an artillery division. And Tarrington was cradled in its middle flank. The procession's point car was a beige Mercury Marquis carrying two U.S. marshals, six fully automatic Mac-10 submachine guns, 2800 rounds of ammo, hand grenades, stun guns and fun guns. Behind them, a sienna-colored Ford LTD with two DEA agents and an identical assortment of weaponry. Everybody armed to the molars, with Tarrington surrounded like a gold filling. A rather self important crew, defenders of the State.

Tarrington's reverie broke as they slowed to a stop.

A flagman and two others in survival orange hard hats could be seen over the roof of the point car. There was a giant caterpillar road grader, two tarnished steam rollers and a dump truck scattered over several hundred yards, but no movement in the interior of this construction site. It was marked by three dozen orange cones strung evenly along the dashed center line of the road. Another flagman stood at the opposite end. No other activity.

Tarrington heard Druthers mumble some derisive comment about not remembering any damn construction site....

The flagman spoke into a walkie talkie and his counterpart down the street waved the traffic on. A big blue garbage truck and two shiny black limousines were the only vehicles permitted to pass.

Tarrington had that something's-not-right vibe. He was looking at the beige Marquis in front when the big blue garbage truck sheared off the Caprice's rear fender and plowed into the LTD behind. The Ford's headlights exploding, grill curling, glass breaking and tires squealing. The garbage truck flattened it.

Then everything moving at once; Druthers yelling, the Caprice quaking, LaSalle with the machine gun. The hardhatted men with theirs...

Then gunfire. It came from everywhere. The flagmen. The men in hard hats. From a man jumping from the garbage truck. LaSalle had his Mac-10 running. Druthers was panicking. The limousines halted in the middle of the road and a team of mercenaries used the vehicles for cover. Just orange hats, four flaming muzzles and a hail of lead.

Molded to the floorboards, Tarrington had seen the glass and blood blast from the beige Marquis in front.

The roar of automatic weapons. Metal twisting as the Ford

behind them was pushed into the ditch and rolled onto its side. The garbage truck grinding. Druthers howling. More gunfire. The LTD blew up.

Tarrington was planted on the transmission hump as the windows of the Caprice imploded. Marty Druther's cranium burst like a highjacked watermelon. Blood and brains sprayed Tarrington in the back seat. The howling ceased. Druthers a memory now few would cherish.

LaSalle's defensive deafened. He emptied a clip in a 180 degree field. Just him against the rest. You could hear him bellowing above the noise.

Lasalle spreading bullets. No damage done. Just sparks. Bullet-proof limos.

Covered in Druthers' blood, LaSalle screamed as his face was torn from its moors, tufts of hair flying.

From his position tight on the drive shaft, Tarrington heard a familiar voice. Heard it cussing the Caprice's key chain. Heard the keys splash, the clunk as the rear door opened. He could hardly believe his eyes.

"Geech!?!" Tarrington said, "I had no idea you were in the prisoner retrieval business. Great show here. Bravo. You hear the one about the two catholic priests and the lesbian dolphin?"

Geech literally dragged him from the backseat, tossed him in the limo with the help of two hardhatted men. He jumped inside and said, "We'll talk later," signaled the driver, "Collins! We're clear."

Collins dunked the accelerator and Tarrington's head was thrown back into the leather seat. The second limo following the first. Two miles later both sailed into a strip mall parking lot, past the Big Lady's Dress Shoppe, past Frangi's Pizza, past the Hallmark Card and Gift Shop, tires spinning and rear ends sliding, heading around back where an open tractor-trailer waited.

The first limo galloped up the loading ramp and disappeared inside the trailer.

Tarrington's ride screeched to a halt. One of the orange hats was there to take over.

Collins, Geech, and Tarrington, free of his restraints, moved quickly to a nearby Jaguar 6. Fueled. Idling. Poised with all the props; rumpled McDonald's wrappers, Pepsi, empty beer cans, ash trays full, mud artfully splattered on a Georgia license plate.

The second limo went up the ramp and two men locked the trailor's doors, ran to the custom sleeper cab. The jaguar and the semi parted in opposite directions. The semi in a roiling cloud of grey black diesel fumes, heading south towards the carnage. The Jag north to Atlanta.

Tarrington's trip to jail, in reverse.

Efficiency and convenience only the CIA could arrange on such short notice, but Tarrington didn't want to admit it. Free and easy wholesale murders were also CIA trademarks. He'd just seen it. His mind reeled, flashing on Monique, the entire set-up. Anger blinded him. Trying to connect the dots scattering like confetti in his mind.

He fought to accept the new information and the truths it contained. The third betrayal in a matter of hours. Too much. Too fast. And too many slick plans in between. But he couldn't escape it. The facts dangled tauntingly, teasing him with their revelations. A string of unanswered, unaskable questions lulled on his tongue. He looked at Geech, Monique's foster father. Monique. The woman he loved. The woman who'd betrayed him to... what? What the hell was going on? The truth hurt. He was a patsy. A government patsy.

And this realization was punctuated with a sharp prick. The point of a needle stabbed his deltoid. A metallic taste filled his mouth. He tried to focus but could not. Geech said something entirely unintelligible and he felt his head being submerged in a hot tub of quaker oats, then his body by degrees as the drug spread. An icy sensation flooded his bowels as his head caught fire. He forced movement to his lips, but failed to express himself.

What he didn't want to admit was all he'd ever been afraid of. A giddy happiness swarmed over him as normalcy was banged out of proportion and his grief whizzed by at the speed of light. He slumped and his chin hit his chest.

"What was he trying to say?" Collins asked from the driver's seat. He'd watched the entire scene unfold in the rearview.

"CIA," Geech told him, "I'd bet on it."

"Boy, won't he be surprised in the end."

"Yeah, but let's keep him ignorant for now."

Collins had always been Geech's agent.

Chapter Thirty-three

Silk sheets. Clean comfortable rose hued silk sheets. He lay spread-eagled. His eyes flickered open momentarily only to close again. A minute passed and he willed the lashes to part. Which they did, but reluctantly, as if thoroughly glazed with prehistoric amoeba spit. Focusing, he could only detect an undulating sea of rosy pastel. The pillow. Then a pale green wave of nausea crashed upon this....

Squeezing the eyelids shut, he did his best to quell the lurch, scare it from his fragile mid-section. Shit. Erratic messages were sent to shaky hands, feet, legs, and arms. He skipped the stomach. Enough of that. The present mission was inventory.

What a headache.

A pleasant smell of fabric softener and the whoosh of some heating or air conditioning vent. It sounded like the flight deck of an aircraft carrier. Far too loud. He pulled the thick foam pillow to his chest and let his face sink in. Take some time to think.

A pulse throbbed at his temple. Torpid thoughts lurched across the landscape of his blotto consciousness. Retracing the events that had landed him on the bed deck: the arrest... the escape... the needle... the CIA. It was chronologically accurate. It was a drag.

After thirty minutes, he rolled onto his back and rose up. His stomach went flopping like a boomerang in a wind tunnel. The rest of him in thirty-foot seas, balanced in the cockpit of Hell's sportfisher. He quelled the gag reflex by curling his toes into the shag carpet. Some kind of drug hangover. His second in days.

Standing was a dizzy kind of thing. He used the furniture to get to the lighted rectangle at the room's edge.

He was in a bedroom. A nice bedroom; dark colonial furniture of polished walnut, carpet like the leaves of a New England October, rich wood paneling tacked to every vertical surface. A five blade ceiling fan at idle. The air was warm and crisp. It made his lips stick together. Finally, reaching the target, the rectangle of light, he smiled. The excursion across the bedroom was not made in vain. He'd been correct about the light. It was a bathroom.

He coaxed his bare feet on the cold tiles. In the mirror a blotchy complexion stared back at him.

"You look like an elbow," he told his reflection, then smelled the bathroom glass and drank from it. Water and more water until he felt equalized. In the shower he did some thinking. Damn good drugs. He burped. When the skin at the tips of his fingers was sufficiently puckered, he stepped out.

One thing was clear; the body may heal, but the heart would never be the same. A goner. Was Monique a plant? A honey trap, like they said in the spy novels. Was his livelihood nothing more than that of a government controlled marionette? He didn't want the answers. He wanted to kill… no… talk to..no… fuck. He didn't know what he wanted to do.

How long had the CIA been hiding right in his ass? First the mobile Motorola, then Dave and now Monique. What was so goddamn important? He relived the details of agent David Carmichael's interrogation. What had the man said? A little Burmese warlord? The opium crop? Control of the Golden Triangle? Well, those reasons didn't make any sense. The British controlled the Golden Triangle, had for a 150 years. And the British controlled the American Political Military Industrial Complex, the intelligence networks, with the Jews controlling the British cash flow so they could have a say in the matter. Anyone who understood, understood that. So what else? A patch of land in Mexico under CIA control? That was something, but the CIA had tremendous influence in Mexico already. For decades now. But they didn't control Carlos' dynasty. And that had made them jealous if nothing else. It had to get in their operational way now and again. But why me? Tarrington asked himself. "How do I fit so snugly in this?"

He was the lackey. The highly paid, well-respected lackey. Carlos was the man. Raul was the man. General Montoya was the man. Shan State potentate, heroin lord Khun Sa was the man. Tarrington though, he was the easy manipulation. Just as Carlos manipulated him, trusted him to do the right thing throughout, the CIA sought him for the same reasons.

He was the respected, irreproachable man of honor the Mexicans deferred to in the states. He was a somebody whether he wanted to admit it or not. The CIA had discovered this and targeted him accordingly. His perfect record afforded him the adeptness to move about them all. He knew everybody and everybody knew him. He'd never done a damn thing wrong to any of them.

He was the thread that wove them all together.

Through him, the CIA could work the whole crew at once. He frowned, telling the mirror. "But of course. But why you, Moni? You cunt. I actually loved you."

"It wasn't Moni. She loves you too, Taylor. Always has," the voice came from around the corner in the bedroom. Unmistakably Geech.

Tarrington raised his voice, mangled his consonants, and gave it a Japaneese twist. "You lie like rug, round eye! Yankee bastard! Rememba Perra Harba!" Then he stepped around the corner and padded barefoot across the carpet.

Next to Geech sat a silver-haired man.

Tarrington felt like punching that man. Geech too. Then he'd have a good cry about Monique. All the crap.

The man was Robert Preston, head of the Domestic Operations Group's Creative Financing Division. The fountain from which all black operation funds were drawn. The old timers called it the get-killed-quick or do-you-need-any-cocaine section.

Geech ignored Tarrington's remarks, said, "This is Robert Preston."

"Ahh… ahnabal Preston." Still Japaneese, Tarrington steepled his hands in prayer before his heart and bowed low. When he straightened himself he told Preston, "Fuck you in you neck."

Then held his arms aloft, and stood there nude. He said, "Do we torture me with or without clothes?" Sounding like himself again.

Preston smiled, "Torture is not in your cards today, Mr. Tarrington."

"Good, I'm ready for a spot of tennis then. Who's up first?" He feigned a nice backhand.

He was ready to have his way or die. He asked, "By the way, how long was I out?"

"Twenty-two hours," Geech said, "We thought we'd lost you. It's Friday."

Tarrington gave them both a long serious look, then said, "Food."

———◦○◦———

The master bedroom Tarrington woke up in, just happened to have a closet full of clothes. All in his size too. What a coincidence. He picked out some preppy stuff to go with his latest mood swing; grey slacks, pink polo, grey suede lace-ups. He was to meet Preston and Geech in the conference room.

The conference room was also the library and it was too bright and vacant when Tarrington found it down the hall. His thoughts gravitated to the funny round sunglasses he'd lost at the mall in L.A.

Outside the window a large lake was jostled by a brisk wind. The sun levitating on the horizon, easing up over a rolling deciduous tree-line—oaks, maples, beech—and a few evergreens. The absence of negotiable landmarks left Tarrington no closer to discerning his locale. The hills across the water could have been anywhere; Russia, Canada, Nicaragua. He wasn't in the desert. "So where the hell are you, Geech?"

"I'm right here."

Tarrington spun around, startled, "Sneaky Yankee Bastarrr!" he screamed viciously. Then checking himself, fell back into the preppie mode.

Preston and Geech were seated at the long hand-carved table. Tarrington assumed a finicky composure, and primly positioned himself at the head of the table, opposite Preston. Fifteen feet of hand-rubbed teak stretched between them. He toyed with the engraving on a leg, tracing the lines of a gargoyle's tusks with his finger. He grinned at the two men.

Geech opened the conversation with some mishmash about operational logistics, getting right down to it. Tarrington immediately cut him off reminding them that food was an imperative and the discussion could not proceed without it. "Either that or you bring me your arm and some salt," were Tarrington's exact words. The drugs he'd been on didn't help matters.

"Breakfast first then," said Preston, nervously

Tarrington finished his meal with a chalice of strawberries and cream. Which is when Preston began his pitch. And a pitch is what it was.

Tarrington wasn't prepared for blatant honesty. If you could call it that. What they needed was to make General Khun Sa in Burma, or Mayanmar… Preston corrected himself, mumbling something about third-world political unrest being a bunch of bullshit… then recovered his speaking voice; a sousaphone stuck in F sharp, and he was off…

"Khun Sa is a key figure in the future, especially with the Hong Kong treaty expired. Our plan is to win the General's favor. Then as the triads realign with the shifting power base, we move in and take the opium business away from the Brits. General Khun Sa is the man who can make this happen for us. And to tell you the truth, Taylor, as our New World Order comes into focus, we're gonna need some real big ears over in that section of the planet." Preston put on his sincere face. "We'd like to get closer to the Chinese, study what we're calling the China Model. Communist China's gross national product is mainly manufactured by prison labor, slave labor. And we're building an empire of prisons here in the United States now. A conclusive study as to how the chinks did it would help. We have long term plans to incarcerate a majority of the population here in the U.S., put them to work in a controlled environment. It's big stuff here, Taylor. Khun Sa is the beginning."

Tarrington said, "But don't you guys have a contract on Khun's head? Like a hundred thousand for his ears, or something like that?"

Preston waved this away, "Yeah, yeah, but we're ready to change that position. We did that when he appealed for a trade agreement and wanted to eradicate the opium crop if the U.S. would only recognize his territory as sovereign. How stupid could he be? The last thing that little yip is gonna get is his own embassy. Destroy the opium crop? Craziness. Anyway, we need to open negotiations again."

Tarrington shrugged, and since Preston seemed in a benevolent way, parlayed with three questions.

Preston answered them all in turn, counting them off with his fingers, "Yes, we'll see to all your identification from here on. The CIA has their own passport printing shop. Yes, we'll make sure all the funny business in Jacksonville and Los Angeles gets taken care of. And number three, No." Preston paused, "No, Taylor. I'm sorry. There's nothing I can do to save this black guy, Nick Taylor. Nothing at all."

Tarrington froze in mid strawberry, "Why not?"

"Because the FBI and the DEA have their claws in him and he is dead meat. They need the victory, they need the coup, they need all the media bullshit, the Nick Taylor Dog and Pony show for mo' betta budget proposals." Preston slipping into his ghetto dialect, smiling at his own joke. He'd failed to explain that the Domestic Violence Section was planning to use the execution of one innocent Nick Taylor to incite a national riot. Nick Taylor could be the precursor of Martial Law Rule. Preston hadn't yet reviewed the report that Tarrington had studied the contents of Mellonhall's briefcase, or he would've touched on the martial law plans.

He noticed Tarrington frowning. "Mr. Tarrington, I understand about the gallantry, but damn it son, you can't just save the entire world…"

"Sounds like an ex-president," thought Tarrington.

"… innocent people get fucked everyday…"

"Sounds like the current president, hell," Tarrington kept thinking.

"…and there's nothing we can do about it, it's just the way things are. Or how they've been made to be. Hell, at least we've still got money… right?"

Definitely a government pitch, Tarrington thought. Rolling his eyes, but making sure the lids were closed as he did, he said, "Alright,

alright. So what you want me to do is sell the entire Khun Sa package to Carlos and get you guys an above-board intro, correct? You're calling off the six-figure contract, let's be buddies. That sort of thing?" He waved the strawberry atop his cocktail fork to make the point.

Preston and Geech looked at the strawberry, then at each other, then at Tarrington, "Yes, that's exactly what we need." Preston told him.

"We must be able to do business with Carlos too." Geech spoke up for the first time since Tarrington shushed him. "We, meaning the CIA, have a large, terribly large share of the retail drug business right now. And it's getting ever larger with every cooperating drug dealer's territory we move in on." Geech paused, "Carlos, I mean your operation, however you'd like to put it, could handle our, that is, the CIA's entire account, no matter how big it gets." Geech sighed. He was a Bilderberger, not some drug dealer. His mission was to usher in the cashless society; to convert the black markets for when drugs were legalized world wide. A major play utilizing the CIA position deep within the drug trade as a starting point. "It certainly would make things a whole helluva lot easier," Geech was saying, "As it stands right now, we're dealing with several sources, most of which are prone to unheeded violence, theft, and much trickery—that coupled with the egos we encounter, delusions of grandeur, seditious assholes, the works, well… getting a responsible flow of drugs into the states is riddled with unnecessary complications right now. We need to proceed with a plan. What we're talking is a two hundred billion dollar yearly gross to begin with, just here in this country. We'll work on expansion later."

Tarrington's eyebrows raised.

Geech noticed, said, "How amenable to logic is Carlos?"

"Numbers, Geech, he's amenable to numbers. Those sound like the kind of numbers he'd be highly amenable to. But there's gonna be a war when the other big guys find out…"

"'No problem,'" said Preston, "You'll have all the United States armed forces at your beck and call. We could've knocked out the cartels years ago, but we were limited in our resources. We had to deal with someone. So in this consolidation plan, we have no qualms about wiping out the entire South and Central American contingents. The ones that aren't on our collective side that is. So don't worry about a war, Tarrington. We've got experts for that type of thing."

It sounded like complete bullshit to Tarrington, so he went with it, taking care of some personal problems. He asked the big question. Seeing how far they would bend.

Preston smiled and handed Geech an envelope. Geech scoffed for a moment, for Preston was actually in his service yet it wasn't supposed to appear that way. But he went along with the surface pecking order and walked the envelope down to Tarrington's end of the table.

Preston spoke, "I figured you'd ask that question sooner or later. My intelligence reports told me this, actually." Preston wore his "I've got your number" face. "Just look inside that envelope and you'll find the locations where the Feds are hiding all the snitches in yours and the other fellow, Nick Taylor's case. My secretary typed them up real neatly for you."

Tarrington smiled, peeked over the edge of the list.

"Yes," Preston told him, "You can kill them all if you'd like, I don't care. Just don't drop my name. Okay?"

"Sounds fair." Tarrington nodded, then asked, "So where the hell are we anyhow?"

Geech said, "You're fifty miles south of Annapolis."

"Thank you."

"Welcome."

"Oh, yeah, one more question…" Preston asked.

"Do you know The Answer?"

"Accept Jesus Christ as your savior and you go directly to heaven, no matter how narrow minded and idiotic you act while on earth, right? The Answer, correct?" Tarrington grinned.

Preston said, "No, this is some fellow in the Midwest. Been stepping on our toes for years."

"The Answer?"

"That's what they call him, or her... nobody seems to know."

"So why ask the question?"

Preston just shrugged, "I though I'd give it a shot." Then he said, "So what do you think?"

"It all sounds fine," Tarrington replied, "But it's gonna take some time to sell Carlos on this. He's the big banana here." Tarrington's plan unfolded as the words came out of his mouth.

"Okay, so how much time?"

"Oh, I don't know. Maybe a couple months. We'll start by doing a few loads together, check out this drug distribution network you've been bragging about. I'll have to meet with my people... which reminds me... some of my people are in jail. What's their fate? Can you fix it?"

"That's gonna be difficult, Tarrington." It was Preston's turn to bullshit. "They're kind of in that same media-budget proposal, drug-war propaganda limbo that Nick Taylor's in. Remember the China Model I was talking about? The government has a thing about that, doesn't like to let you out once they've got you. Federal prison is big business nowadays. The prison industry is booming. What I can do for sure is the same we're doing for friends like Tony Noriega. Free phone calls, male prostitutes, all the dope he can do, better food, that sort of thing. How's that?"

Tarrington's brow folded like a dinner napkin. "Yeah, that sounds nice, Bob. But as far as I know Nando and Donny are straight."

"Yes, Mr. Tarrington, they are. I've read their files. So we go with female prostitutes." Preston smiled big. It was old home week in Annapolis. The CIA Drug-Lord Summit.

"It's a start," began Tarrington, "How long for me?"

"You won't be much of a problem. You're not behind bars, Taylor. You lay low for a while, keep out of trouble. I'll see to it that your mug shots are conveniently removed from the U.S. Marshall's walls and lost in a file cabinet somewhere, swept under the carpet."

"Sure," thought Tarrington, and asked, "And if I don't go with the plan?"

Preston said, "I'll have you crucified like some modern day Christ."

Tarrington scraped the bottom of the silver chalise; one last strawberry, a dollup of cream. He popped it into his mouth, chewed a moment, said, "You won't have to worry about me. This is a perfect opportunity, a second chance. And I'm gonna take it...."

———⟶⦿⟵———

"How do I know you're not lying to me?" Tarrington gazed across the Chesapeake; two skipjacks were on a graceful reach, pruning for marine life. He could hear a chestnut-sided warbler giggling to its mate. The scent of honeysuckle and wild mountain laurel danced past his nostrils as if disco weren't dead.

"What difference does it make?" Geech answered with a question.

They were walking along the bay, behind the spy-house.

Geech's Arronow speedboat challenged its spring lines as the transom bumped a docking fender. They stepped onto the creaky wooden pier and started for the end.

Geech had a point. If Tarrington was going to do the government's bidding, there was no need to worry over small details such as honesty. That was the government way. As far as Monique went, she loved him. Between Geech's words in support and Tarrington's heart, that point had been settled. To a degree. Whether she was an agent or not hung in the balance.

There was one problem for Tarrington though. He had no intentions of doing the government's bidding.

Geech said, "We're going to have to learn to trust each other in a completely different way."

"Yes," Tarrington replied.

PART III

THE FUTILITY OF IT ALL

—➤◆❦—

*When a fighter
has mastered his art,
he ceases to fight.*

• Enrique Deleon •

Chapter Thirty-four

Tarrington flew from Annapolis to New Orleans, then chartered a small twin to take him to Lake Charles, Louisiana. Once there, he cabbed, ducked and dived just to see how many tails he'd picked up since New Orleans. The same guy who followed him from Annapolis was still following him. Guy named Collins. Geech had introduced them, told Tarrington that Collins was his guardian angel.

Tarrington had waved to Collins once outside the terminal in New Orleans, now they were in Lake Charles together. So he ordered Collins a beer at a place called Mr. D's, winking as the waitress set the pitcher down.

Then paying no attention to his CIA chaperone, Tarrington had a heaping tray of the crayfish, a couple of beers, and climbed out the bathroom window in the men's room. Just left Collins there, nursing the beer, the cajun fried shrimp platter and the tab.

Down the street, Tarrington slipped into a phone booth, called General Montoya. Then he hailed a cab, and paid the guy for the rest of the evening.

"Take me to Houston," he told the driver, peeling a couple of hundreds from the four thousand Geech had fronted him in Annapolis.

Houston was a three-hour drive. When the cabbie dropped Tarrington at Houston Hobby Airport, it was almost Saturday morning.

At 12:06 Tarrington caught the Southwest shuttle to El Paso. General Montoya was there dressed in civilian duds, waiting for him at the baggage claim.

Collins was there too; big grin, leaning on the Hertz Rent A Car desk as Tarrington and the General walked by. He waved this time.

Tarrington, in the spirit of the game, flew Collins a well manicured bird.

The General saw the whole thing go down. He raised one of his crooked grey-black eyebrows in speculation, looking at Tarrington sideways.

Tarrington just shrugged and said, "Guy's pretty good."

He explained everything to the General as they drove towards Juarez and the General told him, "They have planted a microchip in the cheeks of your ass, Señor Taylor, while you were drugged… it is a common practice, I know."

Tarrington said, "What do I do?"

The General smiled, "We start with your friend there," and he thumbed over his shoulder at Collins, who followed indiscreetly in a rented blue Pontiac.

Per the General's word, Collins was detained at the border. He would later call Geech from a Mexican jail and be given another assignment. A temporary damage control mission. But relative.

From the General's ranch, Tarrington phoned the Executive Protection Corporation early Saturday morning. Had to get the vice-president of sales, the man he usually dealt with, out of bed. Called the home number.

Tarrington placed a seventy-five thousand dollar order. Micro-miniature closed circuit video cameras. A mobile satellite dish to monitor them through. A special gadget the V.P. recommended to detect any microwave radiations (the type that might be associated with a body implanted chip). Plus, all the necessary gear to completely wire up the address on Tarrington's Texas state license; the party house Enrique had furnished. While talking to the V.P., Tarrington clarified exactly what he wanted done, then he sent the cash with two of the

General's men, told them to meet the Executive Protection crew at the airport. Take 'em to the place, get 'em working.

It was all part of Tarrington's sneaky little plan. The sneaky little plan he was tucking into the big picture.

After lunch, the General loaned Tarrington his old Saberliner 75-A twin turbined business jet. Tarrington flew to La Paz, Mexico to see if Monique and Torren had made the ocean voyage on time. He was getting around.

When Tarrington arrived at the yacht club in La Paz, the Bum was right there in the slip he'd arranged. The harbor master said she'd come in late the previous evening, nearly no fuel at all. Apparently, Monique had made a record passage.

Once he'd traversed the creaky dock and climbed inside the Bum, Tarrington followed the soft moans and crept up on Torren and Monique. They were in the forward stateroom very much entwined together. Tarrington sat quietly and watched them go at each other for a while, then finally he tapped Torren lightly on the shoulder.

Torren raised her glistening face from between Monique's legs and smiled at him. Her usual black lipstick was gone. Tarrington smiled back, and said, "I thought this was *my* honeymoon?"

Monique said from the head of the bed, "Take off your clothes honey, we missed you…"

Tarrington admired their nakedness, loosened his tie. A moment passed and then he said, "If you insist, dear."

⟶⟩●⟨⟵

Much later, Tarrington met Torren on the flybridge deck. She was topless in a black thong. He was attired in his favorite sulka boxers. The sky blue ones.

He sipped a cold Coors and appreciated her state of undress. The warm wind was raising the fine hair follicles of her upper arms into miniscule goose pimples. He reached over and touched her face. She smiled at him, and her eyes crinkled from the sun.

He told her, "It looks like Monique has accepted you as my assistant, or hers... I imagine."

Torren replied, "She's so beautiful. We're lucky people."

Tarrington wondered at the implications of his luck, knowing as he did that Monique's foster father, Geech LeCroix, was a master spy doing a job on him. He gazed over the harbor to a seagull diving for lunch. Not looking at Torren, he said softly, "Yes... we're very lucky."

Then he turned to her and produced the envelope from the map compartment of the upper helm station. Stretching over, he flicked the latch and coaxed it from the space.

It was the envelope Robert Preston had given to Geech who'd walked it down the table in Annapolis. The envelope with the list of names and addresses of all the government witnesses against the innocent black fellow, Nicolas Taylor. The other witnesses too, James Trowbridge, Mike Barnes, Weasy Weinstein.

In the interest of advancing the New World Order, the CIA had been kind enough to have this death list typed up real nice. To show Tarrington what a great bunch of guys he'd just signed on with. A little good faith between conspirators.

Tarrington handed the envelope to Torren, "But the party is now officially, yet temporarily, adjourned. You've got some work to do."

She said, "Bodies?"

He said, "Yes, so put on some panties. We're flying north in a bit."

She was going to say something smart, but decided against this, observing his evident repose.

Instead she said, "What about your honeymoon?"

He replied, "What about it? Give me an hour or so," and he left her there.

Monique was still naked, laying on the tangled sheets of the king-sized berth, the back of her head tilted forward on a pillow. Her hair washed over it like a coal black halo. When Tarrington walked in, she said, "I've got a real good idea. Wanna hear what it is?"

He asked her, "Is there a reason you failed to tell me your step-father was a big wig in the CIA?"

She raised her torso from the bed, leaned back on her palms. Her perfectly browned teacup-sized breasts lifting slightly with every quickened breath. Her mouth was open, the eyes just wide enough to convey surprise.

She said, "Same reason you failed to tell me you're a bigwig in the international crime syndicates."

He said, "Good point."

She said, "Well?"

He'd already shucked his boxers. The reaction he was looking for hadn't come. So he would. What the hell. No way was she gonna make it easy for him. She was way too smart for that.

Chapter Thirty-five

While his son had been getting busted in and out of jail, Wellington James Tarrington had been getting busy with his portion of the con job Tarrington was working.

Welly had acquired affidavits, first from Tarrington's erstwhile neighbor, Mrs. Hibblemeyer, then from the broker who'd originally sold Tarrington the townhouse, and finally from the kid night-clerking at the Ramada. Posing as an FBI agent, Welly had actually procured the tape recording of the 911 call the kid had made. He'd finagled the police report too. Which backed up the kid's signed statement quite nicely.

Welly delivered this and separate pieces of Tarrington's furniture from the vacated townhouse at 8913 Norma Place to the feature editor of the National Enquirer. Tarrington wanted the furniture presented as an extra source of his fingerprints. To drive home the fact that the black guy from Anaheim was not the international heroin kingpin named Nicolas Taylor.

After the National Enquirer heard Welly's side of the story from Welly, posing as a private detective hired by the innocent Nick Taylor, the tabloid sent out its own people to verify and re-interview all the subjects of the investigation.

This blockbusting, case breaking, rumor spawning, speculation forming edition of the Enquirer hit the newsstands and supermarket aisles late Saturday afternoon.

Tarrington's picture, slightly touched up, was on the cover. The headline: The Real Heroin Kingpin Revealed!

Which is why the CIA agent named Collins had been pulled from his personal safeguarding of Taylor Tarrington, and sent to clean up the mess that Welly was making.

⇒⟫◆⟪⇐

Collins didn't look like your average trained killer. He had taken to wearing old jeans, long sleeved western shirts, big belt buckles, and work boots. His hairline was past the deeply receding mark. And with the age etched around his dark circles of eyes, he looked more like your average hard working dad nearing retirement.

He had a kindly compassionate smile and wore this as often as his big turquoise belt buckle. Rather than walking, he hobbled. A bullet he'd taken in the ankle stalking an Arab terrorist one summer in Beirut.

Now two hours after he was bailed out of jail in Juarez by the CIA station chief in El Paso, Collins boarded a F-15 fighter jet at Holloman Air Force Base and was spirited to a private airstrip outside Los Angeles.

He'd been rushed to a Brentwood safe house for the job debriefing. Then all night in a cheap hotel room, a blue foam oxygen mask on his face, boiling tobacco from two cartons of Camel non-filters. Skimming nicotine residue, then prepping it beneath the incandescent bulb of a cheap food dehydrator. The CIA had taught him the most inexpensive ways to kill.

Now Collins hobbled from his bed to the dresser where the hot plate, skillet, and food dehydrator were. He no longer wore the oxygen mask. There was no airborne danger from the purified nicotine as it dried on top of the hand mirrors. He opened the dehydrator and pulled the last two mirrors out.

The nicotine extracted from the boiled tobacco was concentrated and pure. Highly toxic. Reduced to a brownish powder, he scraped it into a petri dish with a razor blade. One mirror per dish.

There were five petri dishes arranged on the dresser. Each with a different dosage of purified nicotine.

Collins opened a ten pack of UV-100 syringes and set five out. Using an eye dropper, he mixed distilled water one drop at a time in the first petri dish until the nicotine was a syrupy brown. Not too thick.

Stirring it with the swizzle stick he'd picked up at the bar down the street, he brought the mixture to the proper consistency and drew the contents of the first petri dish into a syringe. About 40ccs. He held the syringe to the window for the afternoon sun, checked it, shook it, and checked it again. Perfect. Capping the syringe, he wrapped a thin strip of electrical tape around it, and placed it on the bed pillow.

Then he mixed up the four remaining petri dishes of powdered nicotine. Marking each syringe differently, for they were each of different toxin levels.

These four doctored syringes he placed into a little custom wooden box, not much larger than a cigarette case. The box went into his back pocket. The torn up cigarette packs, cellophane, foil, and cardboard from the cartons, he flushed. The skillet, hot plate, hand mirrors, swizzle stick, leftover foam face filters, rinsed petri dishes, food dehydrator, and five unused insulin syringes went into the Walgreen's shopping bag.

Collins looked like your typical working class hero about to embark on your not-so-typical drugstore assassination.

He tossed the Walgreen's bag into a dumpster on his way to meet the first person on his hit list.

Along with the thrown together victim bios to provide some background and the proper toxin levels to be used for each untraceable heart failure, the message relayed from Robert Preston was for Collins to discourage any further tabloid coverage. This was a priority.

Collins' first appointment was with the feature editor of the *National Enquirer*. More cloak and dagger than legitimate business. They were to meet in the darkened corner booth of a dimly lit, run down, gin joint. Once there, Collins would send Preston's message to the tabloid sector.

Collins had called and conveyed to the feature editor that he had a story for him only. An exclusive. And he'd given enough verifiably juicy tidbits to reel the guy in.

The guy was eating it right up. The clandestine meeting in the seedy bar, dark corner, had been the feature editor's idea. Collins didn't understand people sometimes.

"Poor slob," he thought, entering the beer and vomit stained foyer of the bar, fifteen minutes late.

He took a seat on a stool by the TV at the end of the bar.

It was easy to locate the editor from the National Enquirer. The guy had dressed as the lead in some cheesy Victorian murder mystery. Sure it looked like rain, but the London Fog and trilby were a bit much.

"Hope he remembers his lines," Collins was thinking as he spied on the man from his position at the bar. Sipping a shot of sour mash, Collins let the guy stew. Let him wait. Let him fidget. It didn't take long. The eye contact. The funny signals. The forced noncommunication.

Ten minutes passed and Collins knew the photographer the editor had brought along for that Enquirer exclusive secret photo.

Collins approached the photographer, told him, "You wanna see something real strange? Just follow me..." and he gave him the look to go with such a proposition. Gave him a wink too and went straight into the men's room. The shutter bug had to follow.

When the bathroom was clear, Collins smiled at the photographer, looked down at his own turquoise belt buckle, and began to unzip his pants, saying, "I caught this in Korea last winter... can't seem to get rid of it..." He knew the guy would go for it.

Sure enough, the guy's eyes locked on the first button. Collins took the opportunity to ridge hand him behind the left ear. The guy's knees gave like threads breaking. Before he even got close to the ground, Collins had him sitting upright in one of the stinking toilet stalls. There he snapped the guy's neck because he hadn't hit him hard enough. He wasn't gonna wake up screaming now.

Collins wedged the stall door shut and went to meet the editor.

It took about twenty seconds.

After introducing himself, sitting down, and nervously ordering a drink, Collins let his shaking hands drop the piece of paper all his pertinent information was on.

The editor, excited and unaware that his life was just about over, bent from his seat and reached under the table to retrieve it.

Collins spiked him in the neck, emptying the nicotine filled syringe. Then he limped out, dragging the bad ankle along behind.

The guy was pronounced dead on arrival. Cause: heart failure. The kingpin story died with him.

The photographer wasn't discovered for three more days. It took two days after that to make a connection. By then it was too late. Just more fodder for the media to fling.

Chapter Thirty-six

After flying up from La Paz with Torren, Tarrington left her in L.A. with the list and explicit instructions for her part in the master plan.

Then he flew back to La Paz for another day to figure Monique. Yeah, right.

Now Torren was preparing for the her first target. It was 3:33 a.m. It was raining heavily. She sat in a stolen Bronco a hundred yards from James Trowbridge's Malibu beach house. Along with her, the black bag of her trade. The kill kit she called it. Full of its tricks. Throwing stars dipped in curare poison. Specially cased darts with just a hint of potassium cyanide. The custom CO_2 pistol that fired them. Telescopic fighting staffs, folding razor knives, balanced daggers, black mahogany nun-chukas, grappling hooks attached to pre-knotted rope, night vision goggles, etc…. just a few of the items she liked to work with.

Smiling nice, she folded the list Preston's secretary had prepared for Tarrington. The snitch list. Had her work typed out for her. Confirming the address of the second name, she put it back in the glove compartment.

Dressed in a black body overall zipped to her chin, properly covering the sneakers, with the tight hood puckered around her night blackened face, she stepped into the deluge and disappeared. The waterproofed kill kit bouncing at her side as she jogged towards the crashing surf.

Sunday morning.

Tick... tick.

James Trowbridge wrestled with his bed sheets. That sound. Same one. Again. Scared the shit out of him. That noise, every thirty seconds it sounded against the sliding glass doors that led to his beach-front patio. He stared blankly at the green LCD readout from his nightstand, not to check the time, he was well aware of that.

Tick... tick.

... but just looking at the damn thing, mesmerized by the neon, thinking about the rigid time frame some unknown wind god was keeping as it hurled rocks at his sliding glass door. He wanted to ask the U.S. marshals that guarded him to secure the premises one more time, but it was raining and he'd already asked them twice to no avail. Both times the answer had been, "I'm sorry, Mr. Trowbridge, there is nothing outside but the ocean and the sand and the rain... nothing else, that I can see...."

James hated this answer because he knew, deeply rooted in the garden of his guilt, there was somebody out there going to get him. The boogie man assigned especially to James Trowbridge.

Italians were famous for their vengeance. Killing snitches. Tarrington, whom James had always known as Nick Taylor, was definitely Italian. James shook with fear.

Tick... tick.

And that sound shook him more. A metal-against-glass sound. James wanted to blame it on the storm. The U.S. marshals playing cards in his dining room wanted him to blame it on the storm. But there was something unnatural about its persistence. The schedule it was keeping.

The sound expanded James' fear of himself, the fear that he'd promulgated betraying those who'd taken such good care of him. The fear they were now about to take care of him for good. Heckling him as a vagrant after a quarter. There was no cessation from the boomerang of his actions. He'd have to face the facts....

Tick... tick.

... and the sound. He'd have to face that too.

Jumping out of bed, he shrugged into the full length bulletproof coat he'd purchased at the behest of a friend. Twenty-five hundred bucks to make him feel like a fool. But a bulletproof fool, so what's the big deal? He accepted his foolishness. It was better than being in jail. Maybe.

He paced.

Tick... tick.

Damn it! He jumped at the sound, headed for the door, looking behind him, expecting the mob bullet with his name on it. Italian mob, Mexican mob, who cared. Dead was dead. So many people familiar with firearms out to get him.

He wasn't safe anywhere. And the government had only supplied four U.S. marshals as protection. Four. "Who the fuck these people think they are?" James reasoned, "I'm an important witness!"

Tick... tick.

James was in the dining room. "God damn it, something's at my fucking window and it's fucking with me! Check the goddamn grounds again!" Yelling at the marshals, he broke up the card game for the third time.

"Alright, Mr. Trowbridge," one of the four spoke up. "You don't have to get excited now... we'll get right on it. Please, calm down."

"You don't have to talk to me as if I were a child having nightmares! There's something out there and I want to know what!"

"Okay, Mr. Trowbridge, please... relax." Now another marshal was involved and grinning at his pinochle partner, had that what-a-looney-motherfucker, can-you-believe-this-guy? look.

James caught the inflection in the marshal's voice, in the marshal's manner, and in the marshal's smile, but didn't cave into it. This was his life on the line, not theirs.

James Trowbridge thinking, "I'm an important witness. It's the marshal's job to protect important witnesses." He would see to it. Employing the uppercrust tones of his almost forgotten courtroom voice, he told them, "I implore you to indulge me one final time." Sounded convincing.

The marshals obeyed, but only after a tournament scale, double elimination, paper-scissors-rock game. To see who would take the walk. James watched the loser slouch into his rain slicker and felt some satisfaction. Temporarily though. Then he stalked off to his room.

Now the marshal who had scoured the grounds was back inside, banging his feet on the entry rug, to get the wet sand off. He hung the raincoat on a peg and sat down.

"Anything?" his pinochle partner prompted.

"Just a couple ghosts," the marshal replied, smirking hard. This elicited smiles all around the table. "I implored them to indulge me and stop hammering the rat."

This statement brought a grin, a chuckle, and another choking on his beer taking a drink.

"Yeah," one volunteered, "I've seen it happen to all the big rats. It's really tough on some of them." He laughed. The other three laughed. Four compassionate guys.

<hr />

Tick… tick.

James was through. Bounding from the bed, slipping into the kevlar coat, he grabbed the Walther PPK from the night table.

First the lamp, setting it just right… good, now the weapon, shell chambered. Fine. I'm gonna kill me a noise.

James slung the drapes open and stalked onto the redwood deck. Rain beaded on his face and the pounding surf crashed in his ears. Dawn's faint etching fell from space and rested on the warped horizon. James standing at the railing, swinging the pistol like a rehab victim, checking twice. One way, then the other. Malibu Beach at 5:37 a.m. Riding the storm out. All it took was money to live there.

———⟫●⟪———

Torren shifted positions beneath the redwood deck that had taken exactly one hour to dig under with the army shovel. A soupy mixture of sand and soil and rain had been the natural elements she'd become one with during the night; laying low in the mudhole. Now she used these elements to her advantage; dawn's waxing, the reading lamp's glow coming out onto the redwood slats. Sighting her weapon, she gritted her teeth. Damn. The material of the long coat was too thick for the weapon she'd chosen. So she changed tacks and ticked….

She pushed the dagger up between the redwood slats again and tapped on the sliding glass doors…Once.

James wheeled around so fast there was no time for another. She pulled back the dagger's tip, watched James come to the window and bend at the waist, looking curiously at the sliding glass door, trying to figure what had been harassing him.

With the penlight clenched in her teeth, peering up under James' duster, she smiled so broadly she almost swallowed the light. Then much to James' discomfort, she squeezed the trigger.

The ocean concealed the tiny pop of the CO^2 pistol and James grabbed frantically for his testicles, trying to get the buttons on the long coat undone, to get through the zipper, fastened so securely… to finger… to kill the spider… to figure out… to collapse on the porch.

A scrotum shot. Cyanide. "Blue balls indeed," Torren whispered.

She traversed the muddy passage on her belly, made it to the Bronco.

Standing over a hefty garbage bag, she used the truck as cover and stepped out of the ninja suit, dropping the mud-caked clothing inside the plastic sack. Twist the attached tie, throw it in the back. Doing the same with the kill kit. Keep the stolen vehicle clean.

She drove away.

Next victim please!

Chapter Thirty-seven

With the morning sun just over the glistening treetops, Collins pulled the rented Chrysler close to the curb, four townhouses down from Mrs. Hibblemeyer's place. He'd idled through the complex twice before deciding on this particular vantage. The Sunday papers hadn't even hit yet. Collins checked his Seiko, a little after seven, kept his eye on Mrs. Hibblemeyer's front door. Kept his ear out the open driver's window.

About eight, the papers started hitting the porches. Collins opened the wooden box and selected syringe number five. The weakest of the batch. No use overloading the old woman's system and having traces of nicotine poisoning show. Collins was your thinking man's assassin.

When Mrs. Hibblemeyer came out at half past nine to retrieve her paper, Collins just happened to be walking by, just happened to notice her beautiful rose bushes and just happened to say something to this fact.

She blushed, thought he was talking about her. Batting the false eyelashes.

Collins sighed, smiled to himself, and moved in for the kill, telling her, "Your roses are beautiful too, Miss."

She liked the Miss part.

"I'm Abe Isenburg," he offered his hand.

"Emily Hibblemeyer. I haven't seen you around before… Abe." She touched her hair.

"Visiting my daughter, two blocks over. Just out for a morning walk, Emily. Nice quiet neighborhood here." He gave her his endearing fatherly smile, reached out and pulled a stem down to smell a damp rose.

"Especially in the morning…" Mrs. Hibblemeyer said, "but we've had a ruckus here lately…"

Collins' eyes gleamed, "Kathy was telling me about it."

"Kathy?"

"My daughter." Collins winked, looked across the street to Tarrington's vacated townhouse. There was still a piece of yellow crime scene tape on the front door. Collins said, "I thought I'd scoot by and see how the kingpins are living this end of the country."

Mrs. Hibblemeyer said, "He seemed like such a nice man," gazing across the street sighing, "I guess you never can tell nowadays." She gave Collins a lopsided grin. A little flirtatious perhaps. "This end of the country?" she asked.

"Virginia Beach," he told her.

"Virginia Beach!" she was pleasantly surprised. "I was born in Virginia Beach."

Collins used that smile of his. He knew that. Her bio had included birth certificate information from the Social Security Administration.

He said, "Yeah? I was at Norfolk, retired from there. To the beach."

She gushed, "My, my, what a coincidence! My first husband and I met on that base. He's a retired Commander now…"

Collins grinned, "Just an enlisted man myself, dear. Chief Petty Officer, twenty-six years, nine on the Saratoga."

She loved it. "Won't you come in and have a cup of coffee, Abe?"

"Why thank you, Emily."

They talked about the recent and not so recent scandals involving the Navy's newest female recruits.

"It's really a shame, wouldn't you say, Abe?" Mrs. Hibblemeyer balancing her cup primly on its saucer. Being dainty. "All those randy adolescents, Abe, stuck out there in the middle of the ocean, you'd think a young woman would know what she was getting herself into and not be such a prude when it slapped her in the ass." She looked sideways at Collins.

He couldn't believe the direction this termination with extreme prejudice was taking.

She said, "My second husband was an enlisted man, just like you, Abe. More coffee?"

On the way from the percolator she spilled a little. When she bent over to wipe the mess, Collins was afforded a bird's eye view of her ample backside. He poked the syringe through the dress, bloomers, and the girdle, emptied it there.

"Ooops!" she stood straight up, turned on him with a rather mischievous smile. "Oh Abe, you ruddy old salt, you…." Had that seductive leer in her eyes.

Collins was thinking, "Oh, my God."

———>•<———

"Oh my… oh dear… I must of… I don't… I…"
"Shhhhh," he told her.

She was laid out on the couch, had her head in his lap. "I don't feel very well, Abe…" her voice was weak. "I'm sorry, I must of…" she trailed off, eyelids fluttering.

Collins smoothed back her hair. "It's okay, Emily. Just relax. You'll feel better in a while."

Her head swept slowly from side to side. "I just don't know… I…"
"Shhhhh," he scolded her softly.

Ten minutes later he removed her shoes, positioned a pillow under her head, and covered her with the well-worn quilt he found folded at the foot of her bed. Tucked it in real nice and walked out the front door.

Chapter Thirty-eight

Torren raised the Steiner Admiral binoculars and examined the front facing of Walter Bramhouser's apartment building.

She could see the curtains parting again. Bramhouser peeking out for the tenth time in thirty minutes. This had her thinking Bramhouser was doing a lot of coke or something. Blowing the cash he'd received from the Feds for his testimony against an innocent man. Or maybe just an acute case of paranoia? Perhaps both.

One thing was sure, there were no U.S. marshals assigned to protect Walter Bramhouser. No way would they allow that incessant peeking from the windows. Apparently, the government knew the Nick Taylor they'd locked up in Tarrington's place was not a drug dealer at all. Torren figured this was the case. Smiling, she mumbled, "No, Mr. Bramhouser, the government is famous for not keeping their word. You, my nervous friend, have been converted to a statistic now."

Then, as if on cue, the statistic poked his head in the curtain again.

Torren said, "Enough's enough," and started the Pacific Gas & Electric truck she'd temporarily borrowed. Steering slowly through glassy puddles, she navigated the parking lot of Walter Bramhouser's apartment complex. She was wearing a PG & E uniform. The man she'd borrowed the truck from, Murry Simpson was gagged and tied at a nearby Motel Six with the Do Not Disturb sign swinging.

Murry was a little shorter than Torren, so the jumpsuit uniform that zipped up the front, rode up her backside provocatively. She had the legs cuffed to midcalf. Pair of sneakers, no socks. If PG & E had put out a calender, she could have picked her month.

Knocking on Bramhouser's door, she hoped he wasn't gay, or worse yet, too terribly oversexed. She waited, waited, waited. She watched the peephole darken and lighten, darken and lighten.

Finally, she spoke up, "Look buddy, I know you're in there and I really don't care if your tubes blow or not. But if you would, just sign this release so your heirs can't sue PG & E and I'll be on my way." Torren held the clipboard up and poked its page at the peephole, showing off the perfunctory form she'd drawn up at a printing shop not one hour ago.

"Tubes blow?" Bramhouser said from behind the door.

"There's a manufacturer's recall on every florescent light in this apartment complex. And six others. They've been blowing up and the dust in them is highly toxic and can kill you."

"How do I know you're a real PG & E lady?" came the thin reply.

A cheap wooden, almost balsa door, separated them. Torren could've easily pulverized it, but she didn't want to do that. Hers was finesse.

"Look asshole… You don't know if I'm the real PG & E lady and I don't really care to prove it to you. Hell with it." She waved her hand upward, gave Walter a funny look, and put her eye to the peephole, saying, "Who cares if you explode?" Then she left.

Behind her, the deadbolts, door chains, one chair back and chest of drawers were being removed. Torren heard this leaving the corridor.

"Wait! Alright! Alright! Come back…Please!"

She stepped in Walter's apartment and gagged from the pungent odor of cat.

Bramhouser was a cat person and his unadulterated fear of one heroin kingpin's revenge had left him in a serious kitty litter shortage since he was not about to leave the apartment for anything. His girlfriend, who was working at the moment, was the designated shopper/errand runner until the trial was over and Walt was placed in the Witness Protection Program. It was her fault his trio of cats were initiating the place. Walt had put off questioning her about why she kept forgetting to pick it up at the store. He was afraid she'd tell him the truth and call him a ninny. She had her own apartment, of course.

None of it made any sense to Walter Bramhouser, how the government worked, that is. Why wasn't he already in the Protection Program? Why he'd trusted that slick talking FBI agent the day he'd called to pledge his support, he didn't know. For now it was the shaft and the cats for Walter.

Torren's eyes watered. She leaned a half-dozen fluorescent light boxes carefully against the wall inside the front door.

Three scruffy tabbies mewled and coiled and meowed about her ankles. She reached down, petting them, and stroked one into love. Show Walter what a swell girl PG & E had sent. She popped her bubble gum.

Walter jumped straight up into the air. "Ohhhhhh!"

Amused, Torren smiled. "... kay, first thing is I kill the juice," and she walked to the circuit box and knocked all the breakers off, popping the gum again.

"Oooohhhhhh!" Bramhouser went again.

"Open a window in this place, Mister... fthuew!"

"NO. NO WINDOWS!"

And they argued in the dark.

Torren said it chewing, "... kay, things blow up ya know...."

"Alright! Alright! Jesus, you're hard to deal with." Bramhouser flitted about the apartment and opened windows, staying clear though. He opened them from the side.

Torren popped the gum again.

"Hey," Walter getting a grip now, "Would you just stop that?"

Torren smiled, stroked a cat, careful to breath through her mouth. "Thank you," she told him when there was enough daylight to work in.

"Sure, but hurry." Bramhouser said, doing well to avoid any direct sunlight, staying clear of the imaginary cross hairs he knew were out there trained on him. He shook. His eyes bulged. He vanished.

That's when Torren installed the fluorescent tubes she'd doctored. After, she doused the pilot on Walter's gas stove, turned up the gas all the way, and closed all the windows she had just made him open.

"Hey, where the hell you go?" she called out.

Bramhouser appeared from a darkened recess of bedroom doorway. "I really appreciate this, thanks," he conveyed, still jumpy.

Torren grinned, wagged her finger at Walt, "You turn your breaker box back on and check those kitchen lights… I got ya five new ones." She showed Bramhouser the spent tubes in their thin boxes. "You're some kinda lucky fellow, Mister. All the ones I replaced were about to blow, including these. Fortunately, this complex has a maintenance contract to cover this shit. You got some kind of good karma or something, buddy."

Walter concentrating on the good karma remark, hoping that he did have some. Then he went for the circuit breaker box.

Which is when Torren vacated in haste.

With the truck started, engine roaring, she watched Bramhouser make the rounds, lock all the windows, put clothes pins back on the drapes.

Five seconds later, pulling away, the explosion rocked the neighborhood as Walt checked out those brand new kitchen lights. She'd impregnated each fluorescent tube with a little gas. Regular, unleaded, ethanol… it didn't matter. Just syringe in the fuel, shake to evaporate, install, and then boom, boom, on go the lights. Or out, however you wanted to look at it.

The windows of his apartment burst into the street, crinkling and shimmering like snowflakes in the sun. One yowling tabby cat followed, soaring through the air and smacking the side of the PG & E truck with a dull thud. Torren felt it in the steering wheel as she took off.

Fire sprouted from the broken windows of Walter Bramhouser's place, fire from the five sticks of electric napalm.

What she didn't see was Walter clutching at a curtain, tearing it down, falling backwards, igniting it; a caterwauling fireball, rolling about, popping and fizzing, arms flailing, legs kicking, hair, skin, eyes, pants, shirt, furniture, carpet, and cats o' burning.

Just in time for lunch, Torren was thinking.

Chapter Thirty-nine

Collins had two more names on his hit list. Cleaning up after Welly and son. Disinfecting their hasty shot at a pile of unneeded publicity for the innocent Nick Taylor.

Left on the list was the kid at the Ramada Inn working the night desk, and the brokerage salesman who had originally sold Tarrington the townhouse. Their statements to Welly were getting folks at Domestic Violence Section a bit on edge. Citizens implementing their inherent human rights were the bane of Domestic Operations.

The Domestic Violence Section in particular this time. They had a major coup planned around the criminal conviction and subsequent death penalty for the innocent Nicolas Taylor. Since the guy was black and obviously not guilty, and since they were going to make sure everybody knew both facts, quite a bit of social unrest could be fostered. What an opportunity. Collins was there as insurance. People that didn't understand why the country was so messed up, read too many newspapers.

Killing a few patriots in the name of establishment rule was merely a logistical convention. A means to an end.

Collins picked a sandwich shop in the Huntington Beach area to buy the brokerage salesman lunch. A sandwich shop wedged in the middle of a strip mall, with a view of the surf breaking across the street. Collins figured he'd take a nice walk on the beach after. He'd given the salesman some story about being ready to invest in some commercial property. Strip malls, for instance. The location they were meeting for lunch was for sale. The entire mall. Collins had dropped enough hints. The salesman was stoked.

Mario's was a quaint little place. Ten tables and four booths. An old Italian smell. You had to order at the counter and carry your lunch to one of the tables. No wait staff. There was a neon Rolling Rock sign flashing over the chalkboard with the daily special: Mozzarella Meatball Melt, $2.99 with purchase of large drink or bottled beer.

Collins elbowed up to the counter and ordered a Steinlager, told the counter girl he wanted the special, but not until his lunch date showed.

She opened the beer, handed it to Collins. He chose the booth with the best vantage, considering the fact he was about to end a man's life. The man was already five minutes late…

Ms. Narissa Nunez was dressed in her usual attire; four-inch heels, skin tight blue jeans, and a paper thin cotton T-shirt tied halter style at the waist. She liked the way the humidity made her T-shirt cling to her body.

The weather was cool because of an early morning rain. Every time the wind blew her nipples hardened. She liked this too.

She liked the way the high heels flexed her calves, brushing the soft underside of the Victoria's Secret jeans, the way they kept her rear end gyrating every time she took a step.

That afternoon, several onlookers from the Huntington Beach community liked the way Narissa and nature worked together as well. She was as bright as the new sun in the dank aftermath of the storm.

Off on a lark, doing some shopping, spending the ten thousand she'd been paid to sign a statement about some black guy she'd never even seen before. The freedom and privilege of being an American. When she told her story about Nick Taylor to the federal grand jury, there was the promise of more money. What a great country, she was thinking.

She loved the new beachfront condo that story had bought her. The government had provided both: story and condo. She had ditched Happy Home Cleaning service, living beachfront now with no ties and a couple lies to tell.

The government told her not to worry about her family in Mexico, they would take care of their citizenship after the trial of Nicolas Taylor was concluded. The good people at the U.S. Attorney General's office had introduced her to a nice older woman who came by the Huntington Beach condo to help her with her English. She would have to be ready for the trial, the woman would tell her, and encourage her to buy only the best clothes and accessories with the money the government was doling out.

"You've got to look real nice and be real smart and ladylike," the older lady would say, "Only the most beautiful, most glamorous women get to be the girlfriends of international heroin kingpins, remember that."

The woman telling her these things during the English language lessons. Prepping her for the jury as the Pacific washed up in Narissa's new front yard. Narissa loved the ocean and she loved her new life. One man at the U.S. Attorney General's office had told her to imagine she was a famous actress doing a movie about the criminal trial of a ruthless heroin kingpin. Easy.

Those people at the U.S. Attorney General's office were so nice to her. One of the secretary ladies had even asked her to the health spa and then arranged for her membership. Narissa hardly imagined such a good life existed. She had no concept of what she was doing to Nick Taylor. All she knew was that since she'd agreed to say those things to the television people, and to the court, her life had become a dream. The dream she'd always wanted it to be.

Now, after shopping she was to meet the nice secretary lady at the health spa. They were becoming very good friends. Now more than anything, Narissa didn't want to wake up from the dream.

She had it all. Especially the health spa. She liked the way the men there would goggle over her in the brand new red tights the secretary lady said looked ravishing on her. "Ravishing." Narissa repeated this word as she window shopped at the strip mall three blocks from her new condo. Ravishing is what she looked like. The ugly bruises from where the L.A. cop had pistol-whipped her had disappeared just as the assault on a police officer charge had vanished. She was ravishing… and free. She liked that.

Her father had always told her she was very lucky and that she should take advantage of what God had given her. So she flexed the new muscles she was working on at the spa every time a gawking man or woman passed. She liked men. Leering men. Smiling men. She liked women too. A rich man. A rich woman. Either would do. It was as if she'd been an American girl for quite some time. She strutted into her favorite dress shop. The good people at the U.S. Attorney's office had opened a charge account there for her. As she entered the store she heard the familiar voice of the nice lady behind the counter. And Narissa's dream colored.

Torren pulled over and stopped at a meter. She watched Narissa enter Le'Bodice Boutique. She had stalked her from her condo, watching her shop, walk along the boardwalk, flirt with the other pedestrians, and then cause two minor traffic accidents in a row; wet streets and hydroplaning vehicles. She'd seen it all go down. She'd seen her innocent charm. Narissa Nunez was in a fog. But a very attractive fog. In the right light, Torren could do nothing but appreciate this fog.

The brokerage salesman arrived at Mario's restaurant. A definite swish to the man. He wore tight grey slacks, a tighter 21 Club pullover, and good shoes. Wavy brown hair, plucked eyebrows, and a full mustache manicured like his fingers. He had a blue name tag stuck to his breast that said, Clifton Flowers. He spread two cases of demographics on the table after finding and introducing himself to Collins.

Collins said, "Can I get you a coke, a beer, some wine?"

Clifton Flowers answered, "No thank you," and reached into his hand bag producing an Evian bottle and a clean glass. He set both on the table and moved the ashtray. Clifton had power lunch written all over him.

Collins frowned at the water. Water was clear. Liquefied nicotine concentrate was not. He said, "I'm having the special, you hungry?"

Clifton Flowers said, "None for me, thank you. Wheat germ, fresh fruit, and raw veggies. Keep the body pure…"

"Well, Mr. Flowers…"

"Clifton."

"Ah… Clifton, you don't mind if I…?"

"Oh no, not at all." Clifton flapped his hand, "You go right ahead and feed yourself honey. And I'll just go over some of the area's demographics, if you don't mind…"

Collins smiled real fake, thinking, "This is gonna be a long one."

He said, "No Cliffy, I don't mind at all."

"Ummmmm," Clifton liked 'Cliffy'. He smiled encouragingly at Collins.

Collins smiled encouragingly back. There was no end to operational depths he would sink to. "Jesus Christ," he was thinking….

Torren entered Le'Bodice Boutique and began to shop the same racks as Narissa. She gazed longingly more than once at Narissa's fine example of the female form.

After a few exchanged glances—Narissa seemed to appreciate Torren's choice in tight fitting clothing as well—they began to chat.

Soon, Torren was holding the utmost is skimpy pieces to Narissa's shoulders and telling her how sexy she would look in them.

Soon, Narissa was doing the same to Torren.

When Torren began speaking Spanish, and in Narissa's homeland dialect as well, the friendship blossomed.

Within moments Narissa was in the changing booth and beckoning Torren to help her with this thing.

Torren entered the booth and saw Narissa was having a problem getting all the fishnet arranged on a provocative top. Standing there with the top in her hand, nude from the waist up, saying, please help me. So Torren unzipped her jumpsuit to the waist, bared her own breasts and demonstrated to Narissa exactly how the fishnet was worn.

When she saw the way Narissa's eyes traveled the length of her body, zeroing in on her breasts, saw how Narissa's nipples hardened further at this pause, she knew what her next move would be.

She kissed Narissa full on the mouth as she ran her hands along the side of her breasts, plucking a pulse into Narissa's large brown nipples.

Narissa reacted by lowering her jeans and dipping her fingers. No panties.

The temperature in the changing booth was rising…

Collins had listened and waited. Bullshitted and waited. Watched and waited. There was a lovey dovey couple in the next booth. Three surfers at a nearby table. Spiking Cliffy in the neck with a syringe full of nicotine was out of the question.

Collins was thinking he'd have to seduce Cliffy… maybe make a dinner date and bring a silenced pistol for the parking lot afterwards. Then Clifton Flowers said, "Please excuse me for a moment, I must use the bathroom."

When Collins said, "Me too, Cliffy," one of the surfers leaned across his table and smiled at the other two, saying:

"Wooo dudes, looks like a rendezvous," real soft under his breath and the other two chuckled at the insinuation.

Collins heard this as he scooted from the booth, but was playing the sanguine homo role and didn't bother to give them even a dirty look…

Torren left Le'Bodice Boutique, walking quickly to the rented car.

As she passed Mario's she took a quick glance behind her and ran into an older fatherly looking gentleman hastily leaving the sandwich shop.

"Ooopps!"

"Oouch!"

"Oh, sorry Miss, excuse me," Collins told her, "Are you okay?"

Torren rubbed her ear, "No, no, excuse me. I'm a klutz today."

Collins smiled his compassionate smile, "No problem, Miss. You have a nice day, okay?"

"And you too sir."

They parted quickly, leaving the bodies behind.

Chapter Forty

The Executive Protection Crew had worked through Saturday night and into Sunday's brunch installing miniature closed circuit television cameras in the vents of Tarrington's operational party house. They re-wired Tarrington's microphone system too. Even brought along a wave radiation meter to see if Tarrington had been implanted with a microchip. Which he tested clean for. So the apparent omniscience of the agent named Collins—arriving at the El Paso airport before Tarrington, when he was supposed to be following him—was nothing more than the pursuit of a good hunch. That or there were more people watching Tarrington than he thought.

Now Tarrington had the fruits of the Executive Protection's labor sitting in his bedroom at the Las Cruces ranch.

Two large cowhide-covered steamer trunks laid on their backs.

Tarrington opened the trunk positioned near the sliding glass doors. He depressed a switch and the whir of an electric motor sounded. From the depths of the trunk a 42-inch mini-satellite dish ascended, clicking into place at the apex of its arc. Tarrington set another switch, dialed in the locator and sent the dish rotating southward. Next he opened the other trunk to turn on the screens.

There were twelve 9-inch television screens set in the lid of the trunk, with their respective tuning banks recessed into the trunk itself. Each screen corresponded to a miniature camera at the party house and on its grounds.

Screen one was the driveway; two the garage, three the family/TV room; four the kitchen; five and six different angles on the back patio and pool (the cameras hidden in nearby pecan trees); seven the dining room; eight a shot of the hallway; nine and ten for the bathrooms; eleven and twelve for two bedrooms.

Tarrington tuned camera three and captured Enrique eating a combo burrito from Taco Bell, then zoomed in on his Pepsi can, Enrique's lips smacking, the hair in his nose, and when he laid his hand on the armrest, his class ring. Tarrington enlarged the class ring until he could read the inscription. Class of '79, it said.

Then he dialed the phone, watched Enrique pick it up, told him, "This is the best Christmas I've ever had."

Enrique said, "It's June."

Tarrington said, "I'm on the New Guinean Calendar."

"I see." Enrique's head turned towards the door bell.

Tarrington told him, "That's Torren and my father. They just drove up in my Audi."

"I wonder how everything went in L.A." Enrique said, taking the cellular with him as he walked out of screen three, through screen four, a rear shot of him on eight, then disappearing for a moment as he stepped into the foyer.

Tarrington said, "Knowing both of them, I'm sure everything's fine." He could hear Enrique greeting Torren and Welly, "How was the flight?" Tarrington saw all three of them in screen eight, back across four, then sitting down in the family room, screen three. Enrique telling them it was him on the line.

Tarrington said, "Just bullshit for a while, let me save some video, get the sound dialed in, just to make sure I know how. Then I'll drive down."

Enrique said, "Bring my Mercedes."

Tarrington had been laying low in a '69 hippie wagon. Even had a peace sign painted on it. Right next to the flowers. He said, "What? You mean you're tired of driving my VW van?"

Enrique said, "I don't know, maybe it's the funny round sunglasses."

Tarrington told him, "They do make your nose look big?"

Enrique replied, "What can I say? Mom watched a lot of Jimmy Durante movies while she was pregnant with me."

———⋙●⋘———

Scot was 192 pounds of deeply tanned fast-twitch muscles. About six feet tall, constantly clean shaven, hazel eyes glowing with the vibrancy of a macrobiotic diet. His hair, streaked from ocean and sun, he wore long. There was a braid down the middle of his back with three ten-ounce stainless steal beads laced into it. He was dressed like a beach bum.

Enrique introduced Scot to Torren first, then Welly, then Tarrington. They were all sitting in the dining room of the party house. Behind Enrique was an aluminum presentation stand with a large map of Montana balanced on it.

Enrique said, "Scot is the most dangerous man I know," deferring to Torren, "You, of course, being the most dangerous woman."

She seemed happy with this.

Enrique looked at Tarrington, "I think he's perfect for your plan."

Chapter Forty-one

Los Angeles was still cool from the rain. Collins had one more name to cross off his list. He parked the rented car two hotels from the Ramada, snugged on a pair of thin leather gloves, dark shades, and walked the rest of the way. It was 12:43 Monday morning. After listening to the 911 recording the kid had made, Collins called the desk to verify the voice. Sure enough, the kid had been clerking since midnight.

Collins approached the front glass door semi-sideways, saw a bellhop sitting just inside.

"Hmmmm," he thought passing through the doors. He rang the desk bell. The bellhop looking at him funny for a moment because of the dark shades, but eventually blowing it off. This was L.A.

The kid came from the office on the second ring, said, "Welcome to the Ramada Inn, can I get you a room?"

Collins looked around, nobody but the kid and the bell hop. He said, "No, but you can tell her to get her ass out of that office." Looking pretty stern about it, with the hard voice, he pointed behind the kid.

The kid's eyes bunched up, "What?" he turned towards the office, "There's nobody in there."

Collins said, "Good," produced a silenced .380, shot the kid in the forehead, took three long steps to the bellhop and popped him behind the ear with the second slug, then back to the counter which he jumped over.

He cleaned out the cash register to make it look good.

Back at the rented car, Collins was unlocking the door when another nondescript four-door sedan pulled up.

The passenger window hummed down and the driver leaned over, telling Collins, "Get in, Preston wants you in El Paso."

Collins relocked his rental, climbed in the other car, asking the driver, "Anything else?"

As the driver pulled away, he smiled and said, "Yeah... don't kill the messenger."

Chapter Forty-two

The Mooney MSE Scot owned was a low wing that came stock with retractable gear and four seats. Two of those seats he'd removed to make room for greater storage space behind the cockpit. In that compartment he kept a selection of explosives, all kinds of firepower, and a plastic coated copy of the license that said he was allowed to have it all.

Scot was flying to a concealed airstrip high in the mountains of Montana for his particular part of Tarrington's plan. For the job, his regular inventory was augmented with the half-dozen remote-control cameras supplied by Tarrington.

The second-tenor drone of the two-bladed McCauley prop whined in his ears. He'd been flying most of the night at 166 knots, intentionally gauging the airspeed and his holdover stop for fuel—in Billings, with breakfast included—to arrive at the Big Timber strip in the full light of morning.

He was flying low, having just taken off. A copy of the Billings Gazette sat folded on the right-hand seat. He liked to investigate an area as much as possible before killing people there. Call it propriety.

With an average of 5.4 people per square mile in Montana, it was a perfect place to land a CIA cargo ship chock full of dangerous drugs. It pleased Scot so that he whistled.

Beneath him, a meager collection of early morning traffic crawling along Interstate 90; headlamp duos winking in the haze. Dawn was breaking now, nipping at the Mooney's tail at 186,000 miles per second. Scot could see a single patch of cirrus about ten thousand feet, due south of his heading, shimmering there. It was going to be a nice day.

He rolled to starboard and executed a long wide turn, the Yellowstone River sparkled below. Climbing through the turn and then leveling with a slight touch back to port, he aligned the Mooney with the coordinates of the clandestine strip as given by Enrique. He checked the faint green liquid crystal diode display on the Loran and yes, he was right on target. Fifty miles to the strip.

He eased back on the controls and climbed a bit more, passing over the settlement of Melville and then over the sweeping plains of Sweetgrass County. The bluegrass swayed below him, pushed north and south by a crisp Canadian wind, shining with the moisture of morning. Foraging cattle formed dark dots in this grass soup.

Scot could see the isolated range called the Crazy Mountains looming in the distance. A volcanic formation, the Crazy's poked from the flatlands as if a giant shard of black ice had tumbled from the cosmos and driven itself into the earth. He could see Crazy Peak eleven degrees to the north, topped with a snow hat pulled down to its timber line.

Two huge arms of the range seemed to unfold before him, as if beckoning the Mooney to come play in its gloomy purple canyons. Which is exactly what Scot was there to do.

He dipped the starboard wing and checked the arrow straight dirt road he'd monitored running out of Melville. Towards the canyon's left arm it went, twisting up to it, and, after a series of spindly switchbacks, climbing that arm and bending onto the lowest plateau. He followed the thin brown line into the first meadow with his eyes.

The canyon had three levels, like three gargantuan grass-covered steps to the mountain top. Each sided by two sheer walls of jagged rock. Each ending in a wet stone wall of green moss. Box canyons. Trailing down the moss, a rain, snow, and spring-fed stream. Enrique had said it began at the top of the third canyon as a ninety foot water-fall. Extraordinary… beautiful… were the two words he used to describe it.

Back on the stick again and climbing… the Mooney had a 780 foot per minute capability and Scot knew he'd be using every last ounce of the power. The third step of the canyon was to level at nine thousand feet. That's where the strip was located.

"How some crazy man lugged five thousand feet of concrete up that nail biting, ass-grabbing, rim road," Scot was thinking, "I do not know."

Yet anything was possible when working with Enrique Deleon. He pondered this, remembering Enrique's reluctance to divulge the name of the strip keeper, or even a brief description of the man. "You'll know him when you see him," Enrique had said.

Scot flew over the first meadow. A thousand yards wide at its entrance and narrowing back to four hundred. There were cows in the valley, munching peacefully on the buffalo and blue gamma grass, some taking note of the low flying aircraft, placidly, with that partic-ular brand of bovine indifference.

Scot watched them watch him.

They had obviously taken the rim road to get into that first valley. Scot looked down at the rutted passage, dangerously hugging the mountain side, rising steadily toward the first step's apogee. That ass-grabbing rim road could come in handy…

More altitude and he cleared the first step. The terrain on the second step was much the same as the meadow he'd just flown over, but devoid of the grazing cattle. The second grassy step cut deep into the mountain. A vibrant green line wove lazily through its untamed pasture. Flickering in Scot's eyes, portions of an icy mountain stream disappeared above and below the overgrowth. He followed it much the same as he'd followed the rim road over the sweetgrass flats.

The road was important. It was the only ground route in or out of the canyon. The escape route. Scot paid careful attention; he may have to come barreling down that road in something. Running from the Feds he'd pissed off. And piss them off he would.

Who cares if more than one fed dies? Scot asked himself, checking the glossy print of his target, Geech LeCroix. He had it taped to the cockpit coaming, letting its subliminal quality sink in. Scot was to assassinate Geech. A nice long shot with a silenced rifle. But why not just kill them all? The job surely permitted such a grand opportunity. It wasn't every day you had fifty Feds trapped in a box canyon. Scot grinned, but was mindful of the grass wall before him.

Up, up, and over the second step to the third pasture. Much narrower than the other two.

"What the…?" Scot whispered.

Nothing.

Grass, three hundred and fifty feet wide, pressing inward six thousand feet to the waterfall. Rock walls forming a corridor chiseled straight into the mountain. But no airstrip. Unless you wanted to land in the llama dung.

A shaggy horned goat, edged precariously on one wall, looked on curiously as the buzzing Mooney passed it at eye level. It nonchalantly resumed its morning ritual of eating.

Scot pushed his nose against the cockpit coaming and peered down. There was nothing to the left side of the meadow but the brook and the canyon road which was now just a couple of brown lines split by bluegrass. Both ended at a small log cabin set in a stand of aspen and cottonwood. There was also the ninety-foot waterfall Enrique had mentioned. It terminated in a crystal clear pool near the cabin.

"Awesome," Scot mumbled, "But no strip, Kiki. Pretty damn secret."

He tugged back on the stick and catapulted from between the

walls, higher and higher until he was straight up in the air, prop wailing, a controlled stall, then drifting, falling, hard over on the rudder, the port wing tip on an imaginary pivot, dropping back in, diving towards the cabin.

Checking the other side of the meadow, charging the sun, he set his forehead on the cockpit dome and stared down. Passed right over three white-tailed deer, who didn't seem to mind low flying aircraft. They barely noticed him.

"No," Scot was thinking, "Nothing in that meadow but stuffed deer and an abandoned cabin." He did the controlled stall and dropped back in again.

This time a man stepped from the cabin. Red-faced, pot-bellied healthy, blinding white hair sprouting from his head as if it were a fountain, flowing down his chest to become a beard. The man waved his hand, holding up a two-fingered peace sign with the other hand pressed to his cheek as if he were talking on a phone. The guy had a baby blue beach towel cinched around his bulbous belly. That's it.

Scot climbed from the canyon again, and switched on his radio. Channel two, taking the old man's hint. The voice he heard had a south Florida twang and conveyed with force, sounded pretty flabbergasted, "Come in, Damn it!"

"Mooney MSE, flying over your house," Scot answered.

"Yeah, yew! Yew in that God damned single…land that fucker why don't cha? Yew some kind of fuckin' idiot er whut?"

"Where had he heard that voice before?" Scot thought as he keyed the mike, "This is a low-winged retractable, not a tail dragger. I'll bury the prop in the dirt."

"Well I'll be goddamned," The voice said, "Yew silly little sheeit, yew git the fuck outta here. Round in five, gear down. And pay attention to the fuckin' cones!"

Whoever the owner of the strip was, he'd signed off in such a vehement good natured kind of way, Scot's memory was piqued. That drawl… he couldn't place it yet.

He climbed out of the canyon for the third time, took a long circuit around the snow capped peaks, then centered back on his original heading.

The radio crackled to life, "Now listen, Goddamnit, throw her down on the cones, right between the fuckers and yew got five thousand foot of grass harder than yer goddamned head. Now radio silence, yew stupid sheeit!"

Scot lowered the gear, and prepared for final approach. There were two safety cones seemingly set in the grass at the edge of the clearing. He crossed his fingers and planted the main gear right between them. The tires chirped. Pavement. He sighed. Looked just like grass. Paint, no doubt.

He taxied to the end, screaming past the three deer as he did. The six-point buck pausing long enough to take note of the visitor. Domestic deer. Right then Scot connected the voice.

Stopping forty feet from the cabin, he leaned out the mixture and killed the engine. The old man was not an old man at all but around forty or so. The blinding white beard was not blinding white up close. Scot could see how time had altered it; first the black, then fading into brown, or was the brown always there? and then red strands interlacing and then finally the white, silver, and grey…grey? Scot watched as the man approached; eager and with a purpose he came at the Mooney.

Scot reached over and popped the canopy. The roar of the waterfall filled his ears. The cool Montana morning surged in and caressed his skin to attention. Scot examined the cherubic looking man as he approached, now six feet away. He said, "Trammel, I thought you were dead."

The man mumbled something as he plodded the last three steps, moving the big hair in on Scot. "Now I know Kiki didn't tell you my name 'cause he wouldn't tell me yours…" His milky aquamarine eyes widened, "Weelll sheeit son! I'll be damned iffen you ain't growed up to be a big ole motherfucker, now ain't cha? You git the fuck outta this plane and let me whip your ass, boy!"

A small world. The man named Trammel and Scot's father were old buddies. Scot's memory flashed on the many evenings he'd spent deep in the muck and mire of the Everglades National Wildlife preserve, high above the water moccasins and the floating gator eyes, in a made-to-look-dilapidated shack, listening to Trammel and his father trade lies, swilling homebrew and skinning the latest poached alligator.

Trammel was a smuggler. Always had been. And true to form, he'd been running a drug drop distribution point right in the middle of Florida's biggest quicksand pit. When Scot's father worked, moving parachute-dropped bales of pot with a group of five, and a fleet of high powered air boats, getting drunk with Trammel had been the after-work tradition. It had been years ago.

"You old swamp monster, my daddy told me you were dead!" Scot climbed hastily down the wing and dropped both feet on the airstrip, relieved to be working with family on this one.

Enrique's skirting of who-runs-the-strip had been solved. An intentional surprise for both of them.

They hugged, rapping each other on the back. Trammel's hand hit the stainless steel beads laced into Scot's braid.

"Whut the hell, boy? Ya got a damn streak of hippie in ya, just like yer daddy. Goddamn platinum plated puma nuts in yer head, boy."

Trammel stepped back, grinning beneath the fountain of hair. "How's yer daddy?" He looked Scot up and down and gave him no time to answer. "Jesus, boy. I can remember when you were no bigger 'an the head of a katydid's dick!"

Scot smiled, but he had to assuage the curiosity before he fielded any more questions. Stomping on the custom painted concrete strip in his flip flops, he said, "What the hell is this, Tram?"

It was Trammel's turn to smile. He rubbed his round belly and stroked the beard at the same time, pondering. "Well, that there's a long story, but the short of it is I donated fifty thousand in small bills to the Art Department down at the University in Boozeman and the whole damn class came up and painted grass on my meadow. Pretty sneaky, eh boy?"

Scot shook his head, "You wily old coot."

"Watch yer mouth son, forty-nine ain't no coot." Trammel led him off the camouflaged tarmac. "What ya bin doin? Helping Kiki I see." Trammel had forgone the first questions. So much catching up to do. "Me too, and thank God for it…"

"I brought ya some money, Tram, from Kiki." Scot was looking around, took a deep breath. "Gee, this is nice up here."

Trammel's eyes shined. "It's been good to me… but it's time to move on. God damn that Kiki saved my ever lovin' fat ass when he rung the radio last week. I needed a cash infusion like a half-dead camel needs a cold beer." His face grew solemn, "I got the house all packed up," indicating the cabin. His voice had risen and dropped thirty decibels as he'd spoken.

"You leavin?"

"Leaving…? What the fuck, son? Acid dealer took your brains back to San Fran one summer? Man can't very much stick around after the Feds land a load of dope on his property, now can he? Huh, son?" Trammel knew a portion of the plan. Enrique had explained the drawbacks of renting the strip.

"Where you going to?" Scot was persistent, and he knew if he got tied up in any long explanations, Trammel would make fun of his penchant to strew subject around the conversation.

Trammel steadied himself on the front porch, "Hell, I don't rightly know that son. How ever far a case of whiskey and a sack of money will take a man, I s'pose." His eyes narrowed. "I've been broker than Marconi's shortwave and running like a wounded bear since them damn Feds came down on the swamp play. They got me indicted on some crazy shit conspiracy with people I ain't never met, saying things I ain't never said, goin' places I ain't never been. I tell ya son, them thunderdolts got the deck so stacked yew can't even have a decent game a crazy eights no more!"

"Yeah, Dad's on the run too," said Scot.

"Now what'd he go 'n do?"

"He retired. Quit. The indictment is twenty years old. Feds won't recognize the statute of limitations."

"Ya can't win fer loosin', son," added Trammel.

"You're not telling me nothin'." said Scot, "How the hell you end up here? What have you been doin' brother?"

"Now don't start with that surfer shit son. Talk English so's I can talk with ya. Yew still live in that goddamn ocean seven days a week, I see?"

Nobody wanted to answer, just ask.

Scot nodded, "Beach too."

Then Trammel began the tour, showing off his hideaway. He'd built a hydroelectric generator in a cave that rose four levels above ground, running the entire ninety-foot drop behind the waterfall. The cave was reached by jumping into the gelid rock-bottomed pool, and sinking twenty feet. There an opening was cut. That's when Trammel said, "Follow me, son." And stepped off the edge into the icy water. Just like that.

Scot dove after him.

It was a custom cave. Trammel had fortified it with months' worth of munchies, huge stores of kerosene for the space heaters. He even had a TV set wired to a VHF antennae. Feds chasing him or not, he wasn't going to miss his "Leave it to Beaver" re-runs.

Soaking wet and shivering, Scot followed an unaffected Trammel and the tour continued. Back in the water, they exited the cave where there was a hand-dug subterranean garage Trammel had commissioned. Nestled in the stand of trees near the cabin, it housed a 1962 bi-winged crop duster and a '49 Willeys Jeep. Trammel's babies.

Then on to the cabin, which had been completely modernized much as the stilt shack in the Everglades. Your typical five star accommodations in the middle of nowhere.

Scot stood in the living/sleeping/eating room and shook like a wet cat.

Trammel said, "Son .. yer teeth 're chatterin' like a castanet quartet, let me plug in the 'lectric blanket."

With Scot thawing, Trammel hustled back outside, moved the Willeys Jeep and parked Scot's Mooney in the hanger. A tight fit, but he did it.

Together in the cabin, they talked for an hour. Trammel, draft dodger that he was, wanted to know all about the hardware in Scot's airplane.

So Scot explained the line of work he'd taken up since he and Trammel had last seen each other. He explained the huge bolt of detonator cord, the pistols, the laser pointers, the Claymore mines, the flare guns, the stinger missile, the dynamite, the .50 caliber sniper rifle with the 10x Marine Standard scope, the plastique explosives, the knives and daggers and rope and repelling gear and telescope and blasting caps and Trammel eventually had to stop him, saying, "Damn it son, yew still ain't learned to talk straight, now have ya?"

He made Scot go back through it all again, this time explaining why, and about the cameras and the battery packs and the sending units and the job Scot had come to do and he stopped him again, saying, "Now you done growed up to be some kinda dangerous moth-erfucker, now ain't ya, son?"

With Scot warmed and ready, eight hours and twenty-one minutes into the Montana morning, they began to set up the cameras. Setting up the sting.

But the three deer had other plans. Seeing Trammel outside again—it being breakfast time and all—they came up and cold-nosed the chubby meadow tenant, prodded him playfully.

Trammel had a fit, but it hardly deterred the deer.

"You'd think I was god damned Dr. Doolittle… three times a motherfuckin' day they come knockin' around fer food, them and about five dozen other motherfuckers I'm feeding around here. Make ya wonder why I'm so goddamned broke," then he elaborated for Scot's sake, "Yep, them damned shit-eatin' spics up and left me. We had a two-hundred-kilo-a-week thing goin' for the last five years. Coming straight outta Canada like time, going to some cigar chewing motherfuckers from Chicago, used to drive out here in a goddamned limo fer Christ sakes! But it's all over now son… time to go south, boy… time to go south."

Then out of nowhere, he vowed to stick around for the fireworks Scot had planned. Which confused Scot because the man was packed and ready to leave. Who could second guess the true crazies?

"You're family boy," Trammel told him earnestly, "Can't much leave ya here to fend for yourself, now can I? Besides, this is too goddamned good to be true. Hell, I may even ring a coupla buddies, invite 'em up for the party." He paused, "Fifty dead Feds…" looking at Scot with those dancing aquamarine peepers, "Now that's gotta be some kinda record or something, huh son?"

Chapter Forty-three

It was Monday, exactly one week to the hour Tarrington had woken up to find his Ferrari on TV and parked in a tree. With a dead Senator's daughter riding shotgun. It had been downhill ever since.

He dialed the number he'd been given by Preston, recited the series of passwords, and eventually was jawing with the man himself.

"Ah, Mr. Tarrington, good of you to ring. How are things?"

"Fine. Been running a few words by the boss here and I believe we're ready to take that first tentative step."

"Oh good," Preston's voice indicated elation, "What a fantastic way to begin the work week. So what do you have in mind?"

"I'll need to sit down with a crew of yours, work out the logistics for our first joint venture."

Preston said, "A mass suicide? Car bombing? Propaganda drop? Assassination? Please, be specific Tarrington."

"Let's start with a nice non-violent load. Dope stuff."

"Indeed," Preston was cheery. "Geech is at the Embassy Suites Hotel on I-10. He'll have a table for you at noon in the center garden. That good enough for you, Mr. Tarrington?"

"Pretty flashy, Bob," said Tarrington and hung up grinning.

—————

Tarrington met Geech and Collins in the open air garden with the fountain and the gazebo and the ferns and flowers and small trees planted along the cobblestone pathways. Geech and Collins were sitting at a three-legged table by the fountain when he arrived. Nice ambiance, tranquil, with the gurgling water and the piped in elevator muzak floating down. Falling into their ears from the eight stories of balconies squared around the center atrium.

Tarrington sat down. There was a cold can of Coors waiting on him. He took a sip, said, "I hope you haven't vaccinated this beer."

Collins said, "All out of AIDS virus today, sorry. The lab guys are working on a new batch though. Ebola they're calling it. Maybe next week."

Geech said, "I talked to Moni, she says hi."

Tarrington said, "Gee Dad, let's not bring the family into this. If you'd read the file you wrote on me you'll see I've always felt that way."

Geech said, "Hummm, sounds about right. So you're a little edgy today, circumstances and all. I suppose I wrote something applicable in your psyche section."

Tarrington said, "Touché."

Collins smiled, "Thanks for the beer in Lake Charles, by the way."

"You tip the waitress?" Tarrington asked.

"It's the thought that counts" said Collins.

"Well, at least you guys have a sense of humor. That's a plus, eh?"

Geech said, "It's hard to work for the Feds and not have one. Right Collins?"

"Righto chum."

Tarrington asked them, "You guys been drinking?"

"It must be the spicy food this end of the country." Geech replied.

"Or the LSD they're treating the water with," Collins smacked his lips, "It feels pretty clean though."

"Must be some of yours," Taylor told them.

"That portion of MK Ultra has been phased out," Collins

explained, "Now we just cook crack and air drop it into the ghetto with the AK's and extra clips."

"One of our more successful projects," Geech added.

"Jesus Christ," Tarrington said, "We're talking shop."

"Isn't that what businessmen do at lunch?" Geech asked.

"I think I need another beer."

Collins yelled, "Waiter!"

With their drinks freshened, Tarrington said, "You got a crew together? We can start with a load. I got a man preparing one of our strips right now."

Geech said, "We use our strips. They're safer. Plenty of security at an Air Force Base. No local cops nosing around."

Tarrington said, "First-load jitters. We use your men, your plane, our dope, our strip. Simple and fair."

"Sounds reasonable." Geech told him.

Collins said, "He's a very reasonable kinda guy," and smiled at Tarrington, patting him on the shoulder.

"Barrel a monkeys," Tarrington said of himself. "So when can I sit down with your people and hash this out?"

"They're right upstairs," Geech said, "We can go up now and settle."

Tarrington stood up, guzzled his beer and set the empty back on the table, "How 'bout you guys come with me?"

"And ride in that VW bus? That dope wagon?" Collins asked, "Without Ken and Pranksters it just wouldn't be the same. How 'bout we follow you?"

Tarrington said, "Not much for nostalgia, huh? Okay, last one to my place buys the beer." He turned and walked away.

Geech and Collins followed, left the check unpaid. Three cars with drivers and passengers waited outside.

Tarrington saw this and said to Geech, "I thought your men were upstairs?"

Collins answered for him, "It's that all-seeing, all-knowing Big Brother shit, Taylor. It took me a while to get used to it too."

<hr/>

The party house was clean save for a remnant of its very latest party; a marijuana roach the size of a St. Bernard paw, atop the glass table where Enrique had left it.

Once they were inside, Tarrington gave a handheld transmission detector to an agent he'd never seen before, told him, "Sweep this place, I want everybody to feel safe… especially me." He said this with just the right inflection and it made three of Geech's mercenaries chuckle.

The unnamed agent swept the house inside and out and pronounced it clean. Just as Tarrington and Enrique had planned. Now Enrique, sitting in Tarrington's bedroom at the Las Cruces ranch, would activate the miniature satellite dish and closed circuit television cameras.

One o'clock was when this would happen. Tarrington and Enrique had synchronized it. So Tarrington wasted exactly eleven minutes, thirty-seven seconds cooling the three cases of beer he'd bought on the way.

At one o'clock, he said, "Okay, let's get this on the road," and passed out beer, directing everyone into the dining room. "Bring in the bar stools, Collins. Only eight chairs in here!" Tarrington the congenial host.

At the head of the dining room table was an aluminum presentation stand with a large map of Montana. Five Rand McNally foldouts were spread around the table.

The meeting commenced.

Tarrington talked and talked, being explicit about the first operation between the CIA and the People's Resistance Liberation Front, as he was calling his faction in Mexico. He divulged a detailed scheme between the two groups to smuggle marijuana, cocaine, and heroin into the United States. The profit for which would be split and used to fund various projects that the groups were engaged in separately. He recited word for word the long list of options and advantages the agent Dave Carmichael had laid out, prompting help from Geech and his men whenever he needed it. All the advantages that came to those in a drug distribution partnership with the United States government.

Geech, Tarrington, Collins and three CIA pilots hashed out the range and payload capabilities of the MC-130 H Combat Talon II, the air cargo plane Carmichael had offered for the mission right before Raul had scared the shit out of him. It was decided that the Talon could easily carry twenty-one tons loaded and fueled. And it was decided what dope would be carried and to where: Big Timber, Montana.

Tarrington gave them everything but the exact coordinates of the strip, thanked them for the successful rescue mission in Jacksonville; thanked them for not interfering with the unlawful prosecution of one innocent Nick Taylor back in L.A.; thanked them for supporting and working with the People's Resistance Liberation Front... Muchas Gracias!

And all through the intentionally drawn-out planning session, he sent one CIA man after another for beer. Camera angles. At least two per agent. Kitchen, bathroom, dining room. Everybody.

The meeting carried on through the afternoon and finally adjourned around five. Tarrington purposely steered away from the topic of Burma, or Mayanmar, and General Khun Sa, each of the three times Geech raised it. In the end, what Tarrington had was irrevocable proof that the CIA had a major share of the U.S. drug market. What he had was proof that Geech and crew had killed United States drug enforcement agents and U.S. marshals. What he had could be linked to all the sermons Torren had given about the Drug War being a well thought out plan to undermine the U.S. Constitution and induce a Martial Law Rule. The conspiracy she believed stretched from the White House to the United Nations, from secret boardrooms in Europe and even into the Vatican. World Order for all the wrong reasons.

Tarrington had the seeds of proof that could flower into a major upheaval of commonly held beliefs. But could the population be reached? And if so, would they ever listen? Major scandal had a way of having no impact. The media had its way of propelling the truly useless news to the top of the heap and pushing the ugly truth out of the picture completely.

Tarrington wanted to get people thinking, get them moving, before the world powers had everybody's civil rights so jeopardized there was no room to run, to work, to reverse the flow of injustice. He wanted to start a revolution, that's what he wanted, but he knew that could not happen, not with what Torren had said; that the government wanted a revolution so they could instigate martial law, that they had been preparing and fostering a social uprising for just that reason.

But Tarrington wanted one. A mental revolution. People needed to break down the barriers of their belief systems and get motivated to make it a better place, this world. Before it was destroyed, too far gone to fix. There was truth to be had. He wanted people to see what he had seen. He wanted people to realize the United States wasn't any better or different than the third world. Civil rights violations in other countries that were routinely highlighted by the White House controlled press corps and given to America as mind food. Misdirection, it was called.

Tarrington wanted to show people that it did happen here. That it happened more often and to a greater degree than it happened anywhere else in the world. Just more subtly.

Something needed to be done.

And he knew he couldn't do it all.

But the videotape of that afternoon meeting would help. And there was more to his date with destiny. If he could catch the government red-handed, he could really expose them. So he got on with the gig.

Chapter Forty-four

Torren arrived in Jacksonville early Monday evening. Forty-eight hours and so much to do. Before killing Mike Barnes and Weasy Weinstein, she had a lawyer to retain.

Dirk Feldspar, the lawyer Donny hired to represent him in the upcoming federal trial, was the same lawyer Torren would hire at Tarrington's behest. Tarrington had instructed Mr. Feldspar over the phone to draw up four "Cooperation Agreements" with the Government. Now all Dirk had to do was get the right people to sign those contracts, and to sign them at the right time. Wednesday. The same day Scot would be calculating the Montana airstrip assassination. If Dirk could pull it off, he was about to make an exceedingly gross, almost disgusting amount of money for one sales pitch.

The people he needed to sell were the DEA's Southeastern regional chief, Kevin O'Malley; the prosecutor in Donny, Nando, Domino Joe, and Tarrington's case; and any extra D.C. suits pertinent to the ploy that Dirk could manage. There were signature lines for everybody.

Once clear of the trouble, when the papers were signed, Tarrington, Donny, Nando, and Domino Joe would go home—no strings attached.

The trade-off was Tarrington's promise… and the eleven mercenaries who had sprung him from jail. The delivery gift wrapped in a stolen Air Force cargo plane so full of drugs the seams would sag from metal fatigue. Tarrington promised to be a good rat.

This was the last hurrah, a piece de' resistance. When the DEA busted the CIA.

Tarrington's epilogue. Promises, promises.

In theory, a great moment in American Justice.

Torren had an edited version of the party house meeting on videotape. Tarrington had run through and cut all the CIA stuff so the DEA wouldn't know they were busting colleagues. Call it a sales aid for Feldspar. That and a half million in cash.

Which really wasn't bad for a day working the phones, as Dirk had said himself while speaking with Tarrington Sunday.

However, not knowing of the video, Feldspar had relayed his doubt any agreement would be signed before the bust.

Leave that to me, Tarrington had told him. "My representative will be in contact Monday night."

So it was Monday night and Torren dialed Feldspar's number from a pay phone in the Regency Square Mall. Dirk picked up on the first ring.

Torren told him, "The coercion, the ammo you'll need, you can find in a changing booth at the Merry-go-round, Regency Mall, 8 p.m. Be there."

"Is this my Monday night associate?"

Torren said, "Did we hire an idiot?"

"I'll be there."

Forty minutes later, Torren watched Feldspar pick up the video. Then she did a little shopping herself.

———⟫●⟪———

The "Do It Yourself Center" was her first stop. There she purchased fifteen feet of yellow safety rope, a two-hundred yard spool of heavy cloth thread, a one-gallon gas can, a Phillips screwdriver, a box of large Ziploc baggies, a package of variable grade sandpaper, and a section of 3/8 inch PVC pipe which she asked the salesman to cut into two four-inch pieces.

Inside Spencer's Gifts, she picked up a box of pops—gag gifts that resembled small paper tadpoles, the head of each as large as a pencil eraser, the body about an inch long. In the head, a pinch of gun powder, wrapped in thin paper twisted to form the tail. When hurled by their tails and struck against a hard surface, the head exploded on impact. About as loud as a hand clap, some louder. A hundred to a box. Torren had a few surprises in mind.

She went to the poster rack and found a life sized tousled blonde wearing only a white thong bottom and a comely smile, walking away from the camera with her hair piled up in her hands. The famous three-quarter pose.

Moving on, Torren stopped for a second at Wicks-n-Sticks, bought several small candles from a guy named Gene. "Whew," she thought, vacating the store, "Weirdos everywhere."

Leaving the mall, she swerved into a Wal-Mart and finished the preparatory spree. A pack of Bic lighters, two vinyl covered suitcases, four cheap sleeping bags, a tie-your-own fly fishing kit, a twelve-ounce bottle of Charlie perfume, a pair of wire cutters, a small bolt of rigid .10 gauge wire, scissors, box of straight pins, a red magic marker, some sewing needles, a roll of Scotch tape, and a container of unwaxed dental floss.

At a gas station on the way to the beach, she filled up the can she'd bought. Premium unleaded.

Basing her decisions on the preliminary scouting reports of Enrique's associate Scot, she would mix these things together and trick Mike Barnes into killing himself. Scot had been in Jacksonville the previous two days looking over the rats and the cages they were kept in.

Without any investigation on her own part, time constraints were forcing her to trust Scot's professional judgment.

The Sea Turtle Inn sat on the oceanfront, at the end of Atlantic Boulevard. Torren checked in, paid for a week in advance, was told to try the Sunday brunch buffet, and went to her room, loaded suitcases in hand.

Once inside, she opened all the windows to allow a fresh breeze in. Negative ions to provide a headstart on relaxation. Killing required calmness. She laid her suitcases on the bed and went back to the rental car for the sleeping bags.

All of her tools in order, she unpacked. Then to work. First, rearranging the furniture, pushing the chest of drawers against the hall door, upending a small circular table, rolling it away. Now she had a five-by-twelve area with a clean wall.

She taped the life-size poster of the bikini girl there, the bottom of the poster flush with the baseboard, because Mike Barnes was a little taller than the blonde.

She uncapped the red magic marker and drew a two-by-two inch square just behind the blonde's exposed right ear, the mastoid fontanel area. This is the point in a full-grown human skull where the parietal, temporal, and occipital bones meet, sometimes called the asterion. Located right behind either ear, this fontanel, or membrane covering, is a soft spot. The mastoid fontanel is a repository for some of the body's more dangerous bacterial toxins.

Torren, too well versed in the many dialects of death, was going to use Mike Barnes' unclean living against him.

Poster hung, she detoured to fix the wick.

The gas can had two openings. Torren threw away the spout attachment and unlatched the breather cap. She used the .10 gauge wire, bent at just the right angle, curled it into the wide opening and out the breather cap's tiny hole. She skewered the cloth thread with the wire and pulled it into the can, then up through the breather hole. It fit snug in there. Then she unraveled the remaining thread and pushed it into the gas, treating the wick.

Nothing like a creative kill to get her juices flowing.

Next she turned down the bed for a clean white surface. She unwrapped the tie-your-own fly fishing kit and examined her possibilities. Laying out the sewing needles and the straight pins, she frayed the yellow safety rope and nipped a small sample with the scissors. She arranged these bristly pieces on the sheet next to the multicolored fly fishing fuzz, then used the wire cutters to shorten several straight pins and six of the sewing needles. Sixteen millimeters is all she would need.

She used the candle wax for counter weight, the dental floss to tie, and built blow darts. Looking like insects with sharp points where their mouths would be. Three hours of silent concentration produced nine darts. All differently weighted, designed. Each fit perfectly into the 3/8 inch PVC pipe she'd had the salesman cut into four-inch lengths.

She squared off with the poster girl, raised the PVC blowgun to her lips and coughed into her fist.

Twack.

The first dart smacked the pouting blonde in the shoulder area and bounced onto the carpet.

"Sorry honey," she told her target, and tried again. But with a heavier dart.

Twack.

This one stuck. Five inches from the red square she'd drawn behind the poster girl's ear.

"Nice," said Torren.

And so it went, three more hours of casual aiming and forced coughing until her throat hurt.

Practice from as far away as she could get.

Chapter Forty-five

Jacksonville beach was muggy on Wednesday morning. With the sun rising; a smudge of translucent red painted delicately on the ocean's edge, Torren could feel more heat coming on. She jogged, the chilly Atlantic splashing at her bare feet. Chasing the seagulls. The surf banged at her ears.

She'd hung around all day Tuesday researching part of the Weasy Weinstein job, waiting for the lawyer Feldspar to do his. With her now, was a grocery sack full of money. A half million in cash. A rendezvous had been scheduled with Feldspar. Torren had instructed him to be somewhere on the pool deck, beachfront at the Howard Johnson. She'd told him to be wearing beige seersucker and she would find him. He was to leave the signed contracts in a manila envelope on the passenger seat of his BMW. With the aid of Tarrington's video, he was able to have all the cooperation contracts signed.

The Howard Johnson loomed in the distance. She stopped at the Holiday Inn where she used the deck shower, then padded through the lobby to the front parking lot. Holding the grocery sack at her chest, she waited. In a moment, Feldspar would park his BMW forty yards away.

Besides the money, the bag contained a detailed account of the landing strip at Big Timber, Montana. The deal was the Feds got the coordinates after they signed the contracts.

Nevertheless, Tarrington really didn't expect the authorities to release Donny, Nando, and Domino Joe or himself from any legal entanglement until after the Montana bust was completed. And he was right.

The package Feldspar left on the passenger seat of his BMW had an attached note explaining as much. Nobody was free and clear unless the Montana bust was a complete success.

Torren picked up the signed contracts and was back on her job by lunch time, ready to kill the snitch Barnes. She entered the Ponte Vedra Marriott wearing a brunette wig, frumpy dress, converse tennis shoes, and a double stuffed 44-D bra for the full frump touch.

Two of the three rooms Scot had rented directly under Mike Barnes' government subsidized penthouse suite, were connected.

Torren sifted through the hotel keys and opened all three, finding the two adjoined by the door inside. She immediately went to work in the center room, placing a chair beneath the main light fixture and unscrewing the glass shade. Then she opened the two suitcases.

Wrapped in three perfume drenched Sea Turtle Inn towels, was the one gallon gas can with the treated cloth wick inside. Next to the towels, two sleeping bags.

Torren unzipped both, laid them on the bed. The sleeping bags were to fill out the suitcases mainly, extra fuel for the fire too.

With the Phillips screwdriver, she removed the rest of the ceiling fixture, reached into the space between the ceiling and next floor and felt around for the equipment Scot had left there. Just as he'd said, a set of Sony headphones and a transmitter receiver. She activated the transmitter and slipped the headphones on. Loud and clear. She could hear a conversation between two U.S. marshals above her in the penthouse suite. She turned the dial and two more voices were eating lunch. Mike's familiar patter was evident, asking to pass the drawn butter. The other belonged to a young girl. Torren listened, curious who the marshals had set Mike up with. Turned out to be the ex-hostess from the Bombay Bicycle Club, Kelly. Saying some cheesy stuff. "Young love," thought Torren, "burnt to a crisp."

She tuned the dial again and found the channel Scot had set up across town for the Weasel's phone, eavesdropping on another conversation, this between two women. Weasy's wife Wendy talking to a friend, saying how sick she was of anchovy pizza. But that's all the Weasel would eat in times of duress. Some crazy belief about the oil in the anchovies reducing cholesterol and his risk of heart attack, cause he was so freaked out. Needing every advantage he could get. "That Weasy's a real card," the other woman said.

"Nice," Torren murmured, and disconnected the outfit Scot had wired to monitor the rat holes. She bound the outfit up in a bath towel, put it in the suitcase.

Now to help Mike Barnes kill himself.

First she took the suitcase with Scot's electrical bugging devices downstairs, put it in the rental. It would come in handy when it was time to tune the Weasel in again. Right before she tuned him out.

Torren waltzed back through the lobby, a relaxed pace, getting a good take on every possible exit from the penthouse floor. There were two sets of fire stairs, one on each end of the hotel. Both led to the large hallway where the bank of elevators emptied into the lobby. "It's possible," thought Torren, and she stepped out front once again.

Just as Scot reported, the U.S. marshals were parked right there, ready to move the snitch in times of crisis. Like a shopping crisis for instance. Torren had a real crisis for them this time. She was about to snip the stool pigeon's wings.

Back in the center room, directly below the Barnes' luncheon, Torren opened the other suitcase, removed the remaining two sleeping bags and her weapons, the mini blow guns. She stuffed one PVC section with about a dozen Pops. The other with her favorite blow dart. It looked like a big bumblebee. She laid both of them on the dresser.

Next she put towels, wash cloths, sheets, bedspreads, and pillows from all the rooms on the queen-size bed in the center room. Pulling the wick from the gas can, she felt along its surface to see how much gas had been squeezed out. Not soaked, but damp. Just right. Removing almost the entire wick, she walked to the adjoining room, weaving it around the beds, through the bathroom, up along the mirrors on the dresser, along the window seal, below the wooden furniture, along the carpet, criss-crossed over the bare mattresses, then back to the center room for much of the same, ending at the heap of laundry.

Pulling enough wick out to get her to the front door, she poured most of the gas on the bundle of linen, leaving a touch in the can which she shook to create a vapor for better explosiveness. She buried the can at the very bottom of the heap.

The blow guns next, one in each pocket.

Leaving the room, she checked the elevators, made sure nobody was about to pop out of them, stopped to listen at the fire stairwells— no marshals sweeping for bombs—then rushing back, she lit the tiny piece of wick she'd left protruding from under the door.

In the fire stairwell, she leapt down one staircase at a time until she was walking casually through the lobby. She dialed the house phone, "The penthouse suite, 1535 please."

"I'm sorry ma'am, I can't connect you to that phone."

Torren was expecting this. She cupped her hand over the receiver and got real gritty. "Listen bitch, this is United States Marshal Cindy Clements. You don't connect me right now, I'll have you arrested for violating a Title 18, Subsection 1503, Congressional law, that's Obstruction of Justice, you silly cunt. How'd you like to do five years for being a bitch?"

Torren didn't get an answer because the phone in Mike Barnes' penthouse suite was already ringing.

She checked her Timex. Forty-seven seconds.

"Hello?" Mike answered.

Looking at her watch, thinking, any time now. She didn't say a word.

"Hello?" Mike said again.

When she heard the muffled explosion through the receiver, she hissed, "You're a dead rat Mikey boy, like Trowbridge, Bramhouser and Nunez. Deeeeaaaahhhhd."

"Oh my God," was all Mike could add before he dropped the phone.

Torren kept the receiver cradled between her shoulder and ear, plunged her hands in her pockets and waited. All around her, the hotel staff began to panic; reports rolling in, a fire near the top floors.

An alarm went off.

People looking towards the ceiling, back and forth, at each other, wondering what all the noise was about. An assistant manager named Rently tried to direct the lunch crowd away from their tables, tried to direct the people in the lobby out the front door.

Use the fire exits, he was saying. Calm and collected, just like the Marriott Management Training Program had taught him.

"Fire!" someone screamed.

A roaring stampede ensued. Consecutive throngs of people simultaneously spilling from both fire stairwell exits, surging toward Torren. The peaceful Wednesday lunch crowd tossing their shrimp remoulades and hitting it. The beginning of a news day at the Marriott.

Torren faked a conversation on the house phone, yelling to an imaginary boyfriend to get her jewelry and hurry, baby, hurry! Looking desperate, eyes wide, on the verge of tears.

A hotel employee understood and left her there.

Up on her toes, checking the eastern stairwell, then the opposite end of the large hallway, then the bank of elevators before her. Droves of panicked people were streaming past in time-elapsed waves.

Then a closely packed unit of blue and brown and grey suits emerged from the east fire stairwell and began moving down the hall toward her. Torren saw the cute little ex-hostess, Kelly, child-bride of Barnes, following this roaming suit. Mike Barnes tucked securely in its watch pocket.

Heading directly for her now. She grinned and tightened her hands around the miniature blow guns in each frumpy front pocket.

Marshals shuffled by, shoving people forcefully aside.

"MOVE!" one yelled, adding to the confusion.

A clear spot. Torren raised her left fist, coughed. Some dozen Pops sailed across the lobby, smacked into the front desk, and exploded on impact with a chorus of loud claps.

The marshal unit fell into a unified full combat roll. Several on the floor now, crouched with weapons drawn, screaming for everybody to hit the deck, damn it!

This startled many of the already nervous hotel guests and the previously confused screams turned into curdling wallops of death and destruction.

Torren smiled because Mike Barnes was standing completely alone after the protection collection of suits had abandoned him. And he was screaming the loudest. All by himself. Just standing there. Screaming....

Torren raised her right hand and coughed.

The bumblebee dart rocketed the ten feet separating her and the snitch Barnes. Struck him an inch below the hairline, right behind the ear. The mastoid fontanel. A perfectly executed shot.

Mike freaked because he was allergic to bee stings, swung his hand around in a wide arc and smashed the thing against the back of his neck.

"Oooouch!"

The very tip of the 16mm needle punctured his mastoid fontanel. Slowly, his body's poisons seeped through the tiny opening. Slowly, the fontanel membrane at the asterion of Mike's skull was inundated with deadly bacteria. Deadly because it was spreading across the grey fields of his very exposed, very vulnerable brain like a heathen gang of stew-eating banditos.

Torren saw the bumblebee dart flip off Mike's hand and fly into the crowd. She followed it with her eyes.

Having realized that there was no threat to the government witness they were charged with protecting, the marshals jumped to their feet and led Barnes out among the over-reactive masses, throwing him into a bulletproof vehicle.

Torren picked up the dart and was carried out with the crowd.

Mike slipped into an irreversible coma as the marshals drove him away in the armor-plated four-door sedan.

He would die later at St. Jude's Memorial Hospital.

Last on Torren's list: the world's only pizza-eating Weasel.

Chapter Forty-six

3:45 p.m. Thursday. Montana.

The cave behind the waterfall was warm. Trammel's kerosene space heaters kept it that way. Yet at the same time the ancient waterfall had chilled the rock around it, so alternating cool/warm sensations could be felt. The walls damp, sometimes dripping, sometimes dry.

Leaning on the inner wall of the first ledge, Scot squinted through a two-inch fissure in the rock and checked the meadow. It was crowded out there. Pressing his face against the heater dried rock, his tunnel vision increased to a band twenty-feet wide. He could see portions of the fed convoy that had been rolling up the rim road and into the meadow all day. There were, at last count, twenty-seven pickup trucks with two Feds per truck.

The cabin, after Trammel stripped it clean, had been leveled by seven strategically placed plastique charges. Nobody would ever imagine it was once a luxurious mountain retreat. And thus, nobody would contemplate the existence of a generator.

They'd labored hard the previous two days, installing the remote-control cameras and the Claymore mines in the faces of the rocky cliffs that walled the meadow to the north and south. In anticipation of Scot's tidy amalgamation of murder.

The set-up consisted of two Claymore mines mounted in opposite rock walls of the box canyon. Each fifteen feet from ground level, hidden behind a thin shield of innocent-looking brush and aimed slightly downward to create a large field of crossfire. Between the two

Claymores, 1400—5mm steel pellets would rain a lethal hail onto the CIA's plane as the DEA was unloading it.

Trammel had flown into town to purchase ten gallons of white and red latex paint while Scot blasted cubby holes in the cliffs. Upon Trammel's return, the paint was mixed and diluted with spring water. Trammel crop dusted the camouflaged strip, turned it into a five-thousand-foot pink stripe. Then he employed a pole roller to paint a giant red cross where the Claymores would converge.

Using the scrambled signal Dirk Feldspar's cooperation agreements had indicated, the DEA would guide the CIA cargo ship in and have it stop right on that red cross. Scot would then see that fourteen hundred steel beads mulched the entire production.

To activate the Claymores in stealth, Scot would utilize a modern aspect of his training; a laser, a silicon photodiode laser detector, and two eight-thousand-foot sections of detonator cord.

The det cord was wired into each Claymore and then hidden along its respective rock facing, running to the very beginning of the strip where each met at the photodetector's circuit box.

The photodetector was buried under an innocuous pile of sod with just a cardboard light discriminator poking out, lined up perfectly with a crack in the cave on the fifth ledge.

At this level, Scot had a Tasco 30X telescope mounted on a tripod with a helium neon laser pointer. Eight AA batteries would get the det cord smoking, powering the laser beam through the crack to be corralled into the light discriminator at the photodetector's receiving point, thus concluding the circuit. Whereupon the det cord would burn at 22,000 feet per second—a whispering blue-grey fume of smoke zipping towards the Claymores.

At which point, Scot's mission to kill one fed, Geech, would be expanded to include them all.

It was a beautiful thing, he'd told Trammel. Rarely was he

accorded a job where he had so much opportunity and such anonymity combined.

Now they waited, settled in for the duration. Both airplanes were tied down at the Billings Airport. The Jeep had been driven away courtesy of two of Trammel's good buddies in the area.

When the time was right, Scot would climb the crude wooden ladders Trammel had rigged to connect the vertical levels of the cave, and flick the switch that would send the laser beam across the meadow—circuit complete; det cord ignited; Claymores blasting; Feds dying. Silence. 1-2-3.

Then they would hide in the cave until it was all over. Body bags, news crews, surveillance planes, television stations, the works. They were prepared to stay three years if need be. Trammel had that many supplies stockpiled.

Scot could hear the "Leave It To Beaver" jingle playing on Trammel's television one level above him. Oddly enough, the roar of the waterfall was no more than a barely audible shhhhh within the cave.

He discontinued the meadow surveillance. It was time to relax with the mind absorption box, lounging on the pile of goose down sleeping bags Trammel had designated the TV ledge.

The meadow mass murder. And all of it on videotape.

Chapter Forty-seven

It was an old Eskimo trick. Used to kill polar bears.

The hunters in the tribe would marinate fish bone slivers in vinegar base, make them soft, roll them into balls and hide them in a chunk of seal meat. This tampered seal meat was then slung to the polar bear from as great a distance as possible. The bear always took the bait. Meat was meat. The Eskimos would build a fire and wait.

Sometimes it took an afternoon, sometimes a day or so, depending on how much food was already in the bear's stomach. Eventually its stomach acid would react to the bone splinters, causing them to straighten into nail-like spikes. Whereupon the two-ton king of the ice flotilla would slowly die, indiscriminately pawing at its underside, wailing great lamented cries along the tundra as its intestinal tract was torn to shreds. The Eskimos would grill fish, sculpt ice, play gin rummy, rub noses, whatever it was they did to pass the time, and when the bear died they were right on it. Cruel, but effective. It also kept the pelts in good condition, and beat hell out of chasing a polar bear around with spears, or vice versa.

Torren liked the method for those hard to reach people. She'd take a job in their favorite restaurant as a waitress if need be. Killing demanded extraordinary patience sometimes. She always kept a vial of fish bone slivers marinating in her kill kit. Just in case.

Now she squinted behind the tinted glass of the stolen Mercedes, focused on the pizza parlor's storefront window. There was a stack of pizzas accumulating on the counter.

She started the Mercedes and tore the coat hanger antennae from the dash, throwing Scot's monitoring gear setup into the back seat. She'd listened in on the call from Weasy as he ordered pizza for himself and the cadre of marshals assigned to protect him.

Torren would've killed him on Wednesday and been done with it, but the Weasel had been nursing his ulcer and wasn't ordering out.

The pizza delivery driver looked about twenty-three or so; light brown hair pulled back in a pony tail, with a chipper bounce to his walk. He carried the seven pies to a Chevy Suburban. "Nice," thought Torren, as she watched the driver carefully place the pizzas on the front seat.

She followed the truck from the parking lot, turning south with it onto University Boulevard, towards Argyle Forrest, the country-club community Weasy Weinstein called home.

At the fourth stop light, Torren ran right up the rear end of the Suburban, smashed her headlights and folded the Mercedes hood into a motorcycle ramp. Angry motorists honked and swerved.

There was no evident damage to the Suburban. "Just plain wonderful," thought Torren.

She'd chosen pink. Looking at the young man's eyes as he came around the back of his truck, she could see it would be a winner. She climbed from the Mercedes and let the frazzled female side of her take over.

The sandy haired delivery driver was not in any mood for some freaked-out broad. This much was apparent the way his face went sour as soon as she started on him.

She was babbling, very close to tears. What was she going to do? It wasn't her car! It belonged to Freddie! He was gonna kill her! Darn! Darn! Darn! Darn! She jumped up and down, stomping her heels on the pavement, then burst into tears.

The pizza delivery guy calmed her. First he pulled the Suburban over, then her Mercedes, and handed her his insurance papers. Which made her cry louder because she'd left her purse at the hotel.

He offered to drive her there.

She looked at him through tear stained eyes and said, "Thank you so very much."

⟶➤◄⟵

The Weasel's Tudor mansion was resplendent with several towering oaks thoughtfully spaced along an ample stretch of curved driveway.

Torren was wearing the pizza delivery man's baseball cap. The Suburban idled on the street, magnetic pizza logo sign displayed on top.

She squared off with a set of double entry doors, rang the bell. The pizzas stacked on her hand were warm through the padded red delivery bags.

She had a surprise for Weasy's house guests this evening. A surprise for the Weasel as well. Terminal indigestion.

A U.S. marshal answered, scowling, "What took you so long?" He examined her pink outfit with an evident macho fascination, took a second glance at the Suburban. "Hey, where's Chuck? That's his Chevy." He pointed towards the street and grunted, belched.

"Chuck's sick, asked me to take his shift. Even loaned me his ride. He's so sweet." She smiled demurely.

The marshal held up his hand like he was a directing traffic, signaling Torren to stop.. "Okay, okay, thanks." His hand rotated downward and slid under the stack of pizzas.

Torren was taken aback, dramatic, "The bags belong to the… I couldn't…"!

The marshal interrupted her, "Yeah, yeah, I know, I know. Give me the pizzas. I'll bring the bags back. God damn Chuck didn't tell you that?"

"Oh." Torren gave him the wide eyes.

The marshal grimaced in disgust and snatched the pizzas. He

stalked back into the house. The door slamming shut as if propelled by an unseen force.

Torren smiled. The peephole darkened once before the bags were brought back out.

"Here," the marshal threw the bags at her, didn't seem to care that five of the seven landed on the porch. "Your money's in one of them, I don't know which."

Torren picked them up in perfect subservient fashion, saying "Try the anchovies, they're new. Imported from Italy."

"Oh yeah?" The marshal's eyebrow arched in the middle.

Torren smiled at the thought of all those little fish bone slivers snuggled up inside the anchovies. Then she said, "Yeah."

Chapter Forty-eight

The FBI, DEA, all the alphabet agencies in fact, members of the Senate Sub-Committee on Drug Interdiction Policy, the White House, and Federal Immigration officers in the know, called it "The Trampoline" or "La Trampolina," because it was located in north-central Mexico and drugs were bounced off it into the U.S.

Mexican bureaucrats, army officials, Direccion Federal Seguridad, Federal Judicial Police, well-versed smuggling pilots who'd been around, Central and South American drug lords, and working CIA, DEA, NSA and KGB agents simply called it the Chihuahua Strip.

It was the semi-concealed drug drop-off and redistribution way point for several-upon-several billions worth of illegal drugs and weapons per year.

General Montoya, Carlos, Raul, and a select few other wealthy Mexican gentlemen had an agreement with the South American-based traffickers about the Chihuahua Strip. It served as a highly efficient staging facility for the refueling of vehicles smuggling north, and the redistribution point for hundreds of independents flying in and out of the United States.

The entire southern hemisphere, the CIA's cast of Domestic Operations, many big-time mafioso, operators from all over, shared complicity in the comings and goings of the Chihuahua Strip.

Plane loads of drugs were landed on The Trampoline day and night. Sometimes busy, sometimes slow, consistently in production.

Government officials on both sides of the border, dope bankers, dirty cops, everybody turned their heads to its existence.

Money was money. Who could argue with that? Cash before conscious. Greed spawned the lie.

The Chihuahua Strip was partially concealed in a deep dry gulch. Sand and sagebrush and cactus needles frequently blew over its three concrete runways; blew through the desert-camouflaged hangars that dotted the surface of the once-full basin, across the plane-pounded prospect of a half-dozen other landing sites. There was even a man-made lake to accommodate sea planes. No facet of a smuggler's needs had been overlooked. There were at least a dozen sturdy roads leading in and out as well. Better roads than in all of Mexico so the tractor-trailers would have no problem loading or unloading. Trains too.

Early Friday morning. Not a stilted movement in the environs of the Chihuahua Strip. General Montoya had ordered it that way for the very first time in its history. All flights in and out had been canceled.

The tightly knit upper echelon smuggling community; the group of two hundred bankers and big movers who controlled the entire global drug distribution, had been put on hold. Of these two hundred, the rumor had already reached fifty or so. What would become of the partnership between The Lion: Carlos Deleon, his man Tarrington, and the CIA?

Many such partnerships between smugglers and governments existed, but none so encompassing. The very highest levels of both businesses were involved here.

The Chihuahua Strip in waiting, all the lights doused—landing, loading, and leaving. All but one.

One light was burning, shining a faint glow from inside the large grey and beige painted hangar, adjacent to the largest stretch of concrete tarmac.

Just one. Illuminating three sleepy Mexicans assigned to guard the CIA's first load of the virgin partnership; twenty-eight pallets of hard drugs. Destined for the streets of the good ole U.S.A.

Twenty would be loaded if the CIA showed in the MC-130-H Combat Talon II as was discussed at the Monday meeting in El Paso.

The Combat Talon II's cargo hold was forty feet one inch long, and twenty pallets would fit nicely. The extra eight pallets were in case the CIA brought the extended version of the C-130-H, the Super Hercules. A C-130 with exactly fifteen more feet of cargo space. They were known to do so.

Reclining in the seat of a new lime green fork lift, one of the three Mexican guards tipped his chin, began to snore. The AK-47 assault rifle he held clattered to the floor and startled them. Everybody jumped.

Then a chuckle and the tequila bottle was passed around. Mexican No-Doze. Because touching the cocaine they guarded was an offense punishable by death.

Cocaine.

A kilo of cocaine can come in all shapes and sizes. A popular version is a brick compressed to about two inches thick, ten long, and six wide. No bigger than your average hardcover book. Some kilos come wrapped in dull brown packing paper. Some with the cartel family seal attached, or a like symbol. Some hastily tossed into big silver garbage bags where it cracks into crystalline chunks and crumbles into powder. Still some are vacuum sealed in thick clear plastic. And this is what the Columbians had supplied to the General. Some big blow to kick off the partnership.

Thirty thousand kilos of pure cocaine.

On a pallet there was twenty-eight pounds of coke for every two-inch layer, or three hundred eight pounds per foot. Each pallet was stacked twenty-five hundred pounds high. Just a hair over eight feet.

Of the twenty-eight pallets, twenty were cocaine. The other eight were heroin.

It was Carlos' addendum to Tarrington's plan. Always the businessman, Carlos had hammered a couple interesting twists into the game. One being, "Why not make theese money always." The other was to get his investment back on Tarrington right up to the bitter end. He loved him like a son, but worked him like a favorite pack horse. A good man, like a good horse, Carlos would tell you, was hard to find.

On the eight pallets designated for Carlos' snafu, were sturdy mahogany shipping crates, each perfectly sanded and varnished and made to look like chests of drawers. The pseudo bedroom furniture was completely packed with heroin and stacked two high, two wide, and three deep with fake drawer fronts glued on. All of them wrapped in bubble plastic and ribbed tape. No drawer gliders to be found.

A high density, 160-foot slotted cargo chute with an aneroid cell-activated automatic release system was attached to the top of each crate. The parachutes would open as they passed through a specified altitude.

On the ends of the two crates furthest back in the row of twenty-eight, were two drogue chutes. The last two groupings of fake furniture to go on board the government's C-130 would be the first to fly off, pulled by the drogues as they exploded vertically from the C-130's open tail ramp while airborne. The pulling force to drag these first two crates down the ramp, would in turn drag the remaining six into the sky. Side by side and over the edge.

Standard procedure when utilizing the low level aerial delivery container-release systems that were part of the MC-130's smuggling arsenal. Tarrington and Carlos were banking on this.

It was all part of Carlos' handiwork, part of his forty-three years staying several steps ahead of any authority he couldn't buy. He could not resist beating the American Government one last time. Tarrington had to agree. It was the icing on the cake he was baking.

Just looking at the eight crates of heroin. Even a relatively close up examination, as they would soon be strapped to a forty-foot flatbed, anybody could see it was not a dope shipment at all, but a furniture company at work.

Pretty tricky.

Chapter Forty-nine

Around ten o'clock Friday morning the first load between the Deleon Empire and the CIA was airborne. It was chilly at eighteen thousand feet. Geech and Tarrington hadn't said much since the C-130 Hercules had landed, loaded, and taken off. The CIA had brought the Super Herc, so all twenty-eight pallets were aboard. The twenty with cocaine strapped securely to the metal mesh cargo floor, sequestered toward the nose of the plane.

Geech tried to spark some idle conversation, but Tarrington didn't feel like talking. Personal stuff was awkward, especially through the intercom headsets they both wore. Changing subjects, Geech said the Company would feel much safer landing at a military installation: Holloman Air Force Base in southern New Mexico for starters.

Tarrington didn't want to talk about that either, but reiterated there was no way Carlos' trust could be extended on their first load. Acting somewhat peeved that Geech had even brought it up. They had settled that aspect of things two conversations ago. The coordinates for their ultimate destination will be provided en route, was all Tarrington had to say.

Geech shrugged off the indifference. He knew the pressure being put on Tarrington and could only imagine the distrust some of the agency's previous moves had inspired. So he laid off. Now that the partnership was officially under way, it was time to move Tarrington at a slower pace anyway. Rebuild the shattered ideology. A CIA specialty. Bait and switch, with a wash and wax for the brain.

Even though the cargo bay was pressurized, it was still frigid.

Tarrington was dressed warmly: custom hiking boots, long underwear, heavy denim jeans, red flannel shirt, with a mountain climbing jacket. Geech had ventured a crack about Tarrington's jeans. Nothing was warming the air between them. Oh well.

Tarrington was alone. Sequestered in the tail section of the airplane where the auxiliary controls for the tail ramp were located. These controls were inside a lockable box welded to the inner fuselage of the Hercules.

Because the CIA had brought the bigger aircraft, Tarrington had to alter his plans slightly. He let the overlapping drone of the four Allison 501-D22A turbo props soothe him into a meditative state.

Geech had said the Combat Talon II they planned on flying was down for repairs, so they'd borrowed one of the fifteen Super Hercs Southern Air Transport kept serviced and ready to break laws. Southern Air had long been a CIA front.

Unfortunately, the L-100-30 Hercules didn't have the low level aerial release systems the Talon II had. So dumping the eight pallets of heroin while flying low into the dip of a narrow mountain pass, would have to be done manually. A little more dangerous than anticipated.

Which was why Tarrington flew in the tail section of the cargo hold. Positioned next to the load master controls. He'd insisted he would be the one to lower the tail ramp while airborne. He'd be the one to pull the two rip cords by hand, let the drogue chutes do their job and drag the eight pallets into the sky.

He'd be the one to insure the heroin would land in a clearing at the base of King's Peak. Where some of Carlos and Raul's friends waited; one all-terrain fork lift and a flatbed tractor-trailer ready.

Using his intercom headset, Tarrington relayed the promised drop site coordinates to the pilot, Bob. Belchin' Bob. Drinking an entire six-pack in the short time it took the Mexicans to load the twenty-eight pallets.

Bob was to descend to eight thousand feet just as he crossed the 40.35 longitude mark. There he would be flying among the rocks of Utah's Uintah Mountains. That's where the heroin would be dropped.

Bob reasoned that that particular course would send them directly into King's Peak, he told Tarrington. Nice and cloudy down there.

"No," replied Tarrington, "There's a pass… down there."

And Bob started laughing as only Bob could do after ten or eleven beers. Bob saying something about a similar drop he'd made once a week in Laos flying for the CIA's infamous Air America Corps, during the manufactured conflict in Southeast Asia. Now Bob opened another can of beer over the intercom, making sure Tarrington could hear it fizzing. Bob and his entire crew swilling in typical smuggler fashion.

"That's gonna be an ass-clamper," said Bob. "That pass is ten-three-fifty. This particular Herc, overloaded as it is, will climb at a strained," Bob emphasizing strained, "Seventeen hundred feet per minute."

Bob reminding Tarrington that the vessel they were about to trust with their lives would be five thousand pounds over, even after the heroin was jettisoned. Bob burping and belching through a short lesson on rate of climb. Bob popping yet another beer before he finished.

Tarrington checked his watch, mumbling, "Ass clamp indeed."

Thirteen minutes left before the drop sequence was to be initiated. Eight pallets of fake furniture about to fly from the tail section of the cargo ship.

If Tarrington screwed it up, he'd screw up everything. Yet both of his hands rested placidly on the load master control box.

If Tarrington were to peek around the end of the load, he would see Agent Brenslow. But only if Brenslow was peeking too. Collins had failed to make the trip for some reason.

If Tarrington were to turn his head to the left, he would see Geech halfway up the cargo hold, leaning against the gelid fuselage, facing a stack of cocaine.

The last eight crates of fake furniture were fastened together with coarse-fibered rope. It lay neatly coiled in six tall piles on each side of the bay. Four like-size coils laid loosely atop every other crate. This was to insure no tangles, insure a smooth delivery as each pair of crates was tugged out the rear of the plane. The measure of rope between each was two hundred feet. To make sure the load fell in a precise grouping no larger than a couple football fields. This gave the 160-foot cargo parachutes room to roam, yet condensed the ground crew's task of gathering and reloading the drop onto the tractor-trailer.

Enough precaution and forethought to eliminate any inappropriate risks.

Separating the heroin from the cocaine was a steel cargo net, cotter-pinned and eye-hooked to the cabin walls. This was to prevent the coke from slipping out the rear while the plane climbed out of the valley and over the pass. It was impossible for Brenslow and Tarrington to go forward during this phase. They were stuck in the tail section, resigned to seeing the heroin off. Brenslow to keep the three piles of rope neat on his side, to make sure they unraveled properly. Tarrington to do the same on his.

Pull the rip cords. Stay clear. Hang on for dear life.

Watch the furniture fly. The drug drop.

Tarrington turned his headset back on, relayed the coordinates for the landing strip in Big Timber, Montana. He'd been holding back on Bob.

Bob said, "Oh, so now ya tell me." Bob making fun of Tarrington's cloak and dagger sensibilities. "What, it's some kinda special clearance?" He started with his beer burps again, finished with a long laugh on Tarrington. Then asked, "Thirsty? I'll roll ya a beer.

Used to do it all the time in Nam. Lay it on the flight deck and point her nipples at the sky. Works like a charm. Only lost three good buddies..."

"Just save me one, Bob. Okay?"

"To each his own," said Bob, then began something else but was garbled and came back on yelling, "Three minutes!!! The 40.35! Here she comes!!"

Tarrington checked Geech who checked back. They nodded in unison. Tarrington played peek-a-boo with Brenslow who was up for the game. They stared at each other around the back of the load. Less than three minutes now....

"Tarrington!" blurted Bob, "Tie your shoelaces together!" By sound of him, Bob felt he'd come up with something.

"That's the way man! You'll never fall to the wayside if you keep the laces knotted! Remember that! It's an old CIA trick. We learned it interrogating the man with one red shoe!" And Bob was croaking in between laughs again.

Tarrington was just catching the look on Geech's face when the bottom fell out from under him, sent his stomach wiggling into his throat. He fought for the hand hold, grabbed a shockingly cold steel ring near the control box.

"Yeeeeeaaaaaaaaahhhhhhhhhh!" CIA Bob yelled as he sailed them into the valley toward the drop site. "It snuck right up on me! Go! Go! Go! Lower the Ramp Man! Now!"

Tarrington fought the G force as the plane leveled, snaking his fingers under the metal flap, throwing the switch that started the tail ramp opening. He steadied himself against a crate.

And the world came rushing, light streaming into the belly of the plane, icy cold flooding the cargo bay as the C-130's tail section inched its way down into the blue expanse of sky. Tarrington felt the entire airframe shudder, white knuckling the rip cord.

"Nooooowwwww!" Bob gurgled: it seemed the man had spit up on himself.

Tarrington jerked the rip cord and watched as the drogue chutes catapulted into the misty morning. The first two crates of heroin gathered momentum and tumbled down the tail ramp. His jacket popped and snapped in the wind as the first pile of rope zippered away. His eyes blurring with tears. The freezing gale rippling his face, flapping at his ears.

Then it happened.

Tarrington sneezed.

Geech saw it happen.

Tarrington seemed to be entirely unaware of what he was doing.

Geech's mouth opened to scream, yet the warning came too late.

Tarrington's hiking boot had landed right in the center of the spiraling vortex of rope as he sneezed. The burly strand constricted around his ankle. The vortex became a leg.

Tarrington's face went pale as he was snatched down the tail ramp. Bouncing and banging, his free leg kicked spasmodically at the frigid morning sky.

And he disappeared into nothingness. The green speck of his jacket merging with the mountainous backdrop.

The second pair of crates slipped silently down the ramp behind him. The coldness whistled.

Geech's body sagged as he nearly collapsed against the crate of cocaine before him. "Shit…" he groaned. Then he said it again.

Chapter Fifty

Ever since Tarrington had put several videotaped copies of the El Paso meeting in his hands, Welly had been busy making arrangements for the final curtain of the master plan.

First, he took a copy of the meeting to the headquarters of National Enquirer, hunting the feature editor he'd spoken to just a week ago. This time to show him rare footage: actual CIA agents plotting to smuggle drugs to their own stateside networks.

Oddly, nobody at the Enquirer wanted to touch it.

Welly was off limits. They explained the unexplainable death of their feature editor, the photographer assigned to him, and told Welly enough hot leads for now. His stories were too dangerous.

So he took the video on the road. Barbara Walters, Dan Rather, all the big news breakers. Nobody wanted to be associated with it. CNN even had Welly followed from their Atlanta home offices.

Which is when Welly put the exposé portion of the plan on the back burner and got on with the rest of his duties.

After stashing copies of the video in strategically placed safety deposit boxes, he parked the General's jet in El Paso and chartered one of his own. He also made sure the yacht Tarrington had previously hired was in port, on stand-by. Welly was getting the Tarrington family ready for D-Day.

Collins eventually caught up with Tarrington's father, Welly, as he exited a law firm in Miami. His last con job. They rode down on the elevator together. Alone.

Collins slid behind Welly, removed a silenced .32 caliber Bersa automatic, whispered in his ear that he'd gone too far this time, and shot him three times in the spine.

Welly collapsed on the carpet. D-Day indeed.

Chapter Fifty-one

Scot and Trammel were on the third level, both anxious, checking the meadow from the biggest crack in the cave. The observatory.

There were seventy-two Feds at last count and Trammel's VHF receiver had the CIA landing their cargo plane moments away. Scot had monitored the frequency all morning, now he could hear the DEA's acting load captain talking to some drunk pilot named Bob— Bob telling the DEA man to lighten up, the DEA captain getting that much more serious.

The DEA guy telling Bob the air strip was on the third meadow, big pink stripe like mother nature's puss up there between the mountain's legs. Trying to work with Belchin' Bob, trying to be cool, just as the DEA's "Act Like Your Prey" seminars had taught him to do. Telling Bob to stop on the giant red plus sign at the end. That's the unloading zone.

The DEA captain doing it just like Dirk Feldspar's briefing had conveyed.

Scot was acting like he'd broken out in hives. Itchy, scratchy, couldn't sit still.

Seventy-two plus—Dead Feds. This was a big one for him. Boy, would Enrique be happy. He checked the pile of sod at the beginning of the strip. Where the light discriminator would catch the laser beam. Where the whispery grey plume of the det cord would begin its journey, activating the Claymores and killing the Feds that roved the meadow like ants now.

And the remote-control cameras were recording it all. One copy for posterity, three for Enrique. Scot would use the 300K he was making on the contract, take a nice vacation, sit around and watch his grand scheme on the VCR. For Scot, it was better than sex.

Now he could see the C-130 Hercules on the horizon, flying low, about fifteen hundred feet, heading straight for them, with its tail ramp coming down .. what the?... and one... now wait a minute here... a parachute opening. A man had jumped from the C-130 cargo hold. One less Fed to kill. It made Scot even jumpier.

"Here they come boy," Trammel had the binoculars pressed to his brow, looking out an adjacent crack. Had a big smile underneath that potpourri beard. He checked Scot, "Calm down son, before ya piss yourself. Now git yer ass upstairs and git to flicken yer Bic, boy." Talking about the laser.

Scot was ready to record this one in his personal diary, yet asked Trammel, "Let me see those."

Trammel passed him the binoculars.

"What the...?" Scot murmured.

The pile of sod. Two Feds were about to park right in front of it. Nullify the light discriminator. The laser would never work if they stayed there. "Move..." whispered Scot, no longer antsy, "Move, damn it," he willed them.

"What's goin' on, son?"

"Look."

Trammel took the field glasses. "Well...I'll be. If it can get fucked up, them government bastards will find a way to do it. I told ya son, gots to have a backup." He checked Scot again and it made him cringe. "Goddamn, son. Don't take it out on me. Wipe that death outta yer eyes, kid. Get a grip."

Scot was about to blow. He had to think. He could activate the Claymores with the .50 caliber sniper rifle. He ran it by Trammel.

"Whut the hell? Are you half plum crazy? You go shootin' a gun

314

around here and we'll be hotter than a meat thermometer shoved up a badger's ass! You blow that shot, they'll blast us outta here and string our nuts to the White House flag pole. Hell, the President himself'll cuss us every morning over his first cup of coffee. Don't you dare shoot that thing!"

But Scot had to have his kill.

The Hercules was almost there. The DEA load captain blabbing away on the VHF. Scot could hear it blaring. A DEA suit trying to sound like the Marlboro Man. It was making CIA Bob laugh, asking the DEA guy if he was a snitch or just somebody's little brother.

Scot checked the meadow again. Still the pickup truck was parked in the laser's way. He checked the horizon: four big turbo props echoing in the canyon, the CIA with its gear down, just clearing the first meadow, headed for the waterfall… three thousand yards to go. Still the pickup truck sat there.

"FUUUCCCKK!" Scot lost it, went ballistic with the three stainless steel beads laced into the end of his braided pony tail—swinging, snapping the head, making pebbles, rock spray, sparks, dust, bang, bam, fuuuck, wham, smack, Goddamnit, bang, snapping his head around.

Trammel just backed up, grinnin' at the boy. "Watch it, now. That shit'll give ya split ends, son."

Scot stopped, red faced, fists clenched in front of him, arms flexed, making his palms bleed cause the fingernails were there. "Do you realize what's happening?" Screaming at Trammel, "I'm blowing a job!"

Trammel just chuckled, "More like a fuse, son… look." He pointed through the crack.

After the CIA Hercules cleared the meadow, using the truck as a landing mark, the two Feds in the pickup chased the C-130 down the runway, chased it to the red cross. Time to unload. Unload those Claymore mines too.

Scot got his hands on that fountain of Trammel's thick hair and kissed the man right there on that big wrinkled forehead.

"Ah hell son... git yer ass upstairs."

Scot scrambled up the ladders to where the helium neon laser pointer was mounted on the telescope tripod.

Dead Feds. Scot's self-conceived greatest feat.

———⟫●⟨———

Now he was laughing... and Trammel right there next to him laughing too. Who was laughing harder? You couldn't really tell. Both of them laughing at the futility of it all.

Yes, the DEA unloaded the cocaine. Yes, the DEA rushed the CIA flight crew and cuffed each and every one of them—Bob having a good old fashioned fist fight with three before they wrestled him to the pink pavement.

Yes, Scot had tried to find Geech, but the man he'd been instructed to shoot, the man in the 8-by-10 glossy color print, was nowhere to be found. Yes, just as the DEA was crawling all over the C-130 like mechanical maggots over steel flesh, Scot flicked the switch that would send the helium neon laser into the photodetector, completing the circuit, igniting the det cord, blasting the Claymores, killing the Feds.

But none of that happened.

No.

No.

It was funny.

The pickup that parked on the strip had backed right over the sod pile and crushed the light discriminator. And nobody could really tell till the laser failed. Then Scot took his first look through the 30X Tasco... and sure enough, the light discriminator was indiscriminately pointed at heaven.

It was funny how shit happened no matter how pissed off you got. Most of the time getting pissed only helped shit along.

It was funny.

Funny that the CIA guys had to go into full on salespitch mode, finally convincing the DEA to grab the papers inside the C-130. Told them where to look. Making them use the radio phone and call the appropriate numbers. Convinced the DEA they'd just busted their own. Which got the cuffs off and the DEA fellows mad as hell.

Embarrassed too. Hell, they'd been so intent, so damn serious about enforcing the rules. The CIA so damn nonchalant, so lackadaisical about breaking them. Which really escalated DEA temper. You could see it. Scot could, without the telescope. Bob, in all his drunken glory, just offered the DEA guys a beer. Cool out. After a long day working to completely obliterate a seven-figure tax contribution, the cocktail hour was at hand. It was Miller time.

"At least ya got it all on film, son." said Trammel.

"Yeah, production quality. It sure would've been nice to kill all those dickheads, though."

Trammel put his hand on Scot's shoulder, said, "No doubt a service to mankind, son. But I guess you'll just have to leave it ta God. It's the Lord's work, son. Shit's gonna get straightened soon enough."

"I had no idea you'd found religion, Tram."

"Religion hell. Man don't need religion to know what's right and what's wrong."

Chapter Fifty-two

It was a place called Jerry's Burnt Cow and Cold Brew. You could get a good steak there, if Jerry didn't burn it. And the beer was cold, if Jerry didn't forget to pay the electric bill. Some people called it Jerry's Cold Cow and Burnt Brew. Today Jerry's only son Joe was manning the bar. Jerry had fallen prey to his own beer tap again the night before.

"What do you mean you don't have Perrier?" asked Torren.

"What's that?" asked Joe. "We got Hamms and Oly on tap, got some Budweiser in a can, or I'll fry you a burger. We don't got none of that perrya' up these ways, ma'am. This here's Montana."

"Make it some tap water then."

"See how easy that was," Joe told her, smiling now. "Keep it simple, that's what I always tell the little lady…" He wandered away for a moment, checking for a clean glass.

Torren consulted her watch. She had an appointment to keep. Any moment and her partner would show up.

Joe handed Torren the glass of water. "On the house."

"Thank you." She took a table by the door. There was nobody else in the bar.

She waited. Thirty minutes and two glasses of water later, she heard a car drive up.

The door opened and it seemed like half of Montana's big sky came in behind the man who pushed it open.

He sat at the table with Torren. Using the oil from his scaly fingers, he twisted the ends of his long greying mustache into points. He considered Torren, "It cost a lot of money, I hope you're right."

"You want a drink?"

"No thanks. What's your call?"

"Tarrington is headed straight for La Paz. He's smitten with your daughter. I say he further interrogates her, accepts the lies she's already told him, then lays low with her for a while. A decade maybe. Then he comes back to the game. He's an adrenaline junkie whether he realizes it or not. We'll use him then."

"So you're saying all the money was worth it… letting him play out his fantasies and all that…"

"I'm saying we couldn't have done it any other way. If we'd have done it differently, we wouldn't be as far along as we are now. Besides, me killing all those rats raised my reputation several notches."

"But Tarrington's been several notches higher than that for years." Geech cut in.

Torren finished, "And that's precisely why we had to play him. And why we must continue to play it like we did. Which reminds me, where is he?"

"He's dead."

"What?" Her mouth lulled open, an ashen quality to her face.

"He fell out of the plane."

Now it didn't seem to bother her so much. "That's him… what a better way to write himself off."

Geech couldn't believe how easy she took it. "What are you saying?"

"He and Enrique jumped every time they were together. Enrique was a nut for it. I know Tarrington just went along… he hates taking unneeded chances. Enrique had those B-15 backpack chutes. You can wear one under a suit jacket with nobody the wiser." Torren smiled. "He lost you."

Geech said, "Temporary," and smiled, "Collins took out his father. I have a couple teams watching the airport in L.A. There's a team in La Paz too."

Torren said, "That was a little hard on him, don't you think? Kill his father?"

"It's all about objective. We can't pittle over the corpses. Getting next to Khun Sa, taking over Carlos' operation, not playing footsie with Tarrington, that's the job. Even though I do like the man, his father is immaterial. Who knows what damage those two had cooked up."

Torren frowned, "Perhaps," but eventually she smiled, "What the hell. I'm even further inside now, with or without Tarrington. So it was more than worth it. I also enjoyed myself. And what more is there to life than celebrating the intermingling of flesh and spirit.

Geech said, "or the dissection of flesh and spirit."

She grinned.

"What about the General?" he asked.

It was Torren's debriefing.

"Khun Sa?" she inquired.

"No. Montoya."

"He's getting out, which leaves his daughter Elena with the reins, which puts me even deeper... you see. Elena simply loves me... really." She paused and smiled. "We can start diverting the Juarez warehouse product to our people soon. I've got the General's blessing with Elena."

"And Khun Sa?"

"That's the only place we fell short. The Triangle. And precisely the reason Tarrington is still a major player here. I'm afraid he's the only one besides Raul who can put us in there. The only one in Carlos' operation that is. Of course, we've failed every other time we tried getting to Mr. Sa, so we're left with no real answers there. Khun Sa trusts nobody. The effort to capture the Triangle from the British and the Shan will have to remain as intense as it has always been.

"But look to the sun… the Company essentially owns most of Central America, we've taken control of some half of the contraband and a majority of the politics. The state of our Mexican operation has improved vastly. Carlos is getting out. I'm to be working with Raul soon, I feel it. I've been promoted. Soon we'll have enough intelligence to strong arm the region if finesse fails. I'd say we're ahead of schedule, considering the outcome here."

Geech said, "What about the videos up there in that cave?"

"I'm about to drop in on those two and confiscate all the tapes."

"It makes me sick that Tarrington recorded that meeting in El Paso."

Torren said, "I'm sorry. There was no way I could sabotage that effort. I had no idea he was on that tack. I was killing government witnesses in L.A. Remember?"

Geech said, "Well, everybody's been told not to touch it. Still though, it's embarrassing."

Torren told him, "I don't think too many people are going to tease you about it, Mr. LeCroix."

Geech twisted his moustache, checked his watch, "It certainly was an extravagant ploy…"

"Tarrington's… you mean?"

"All of them, yes."

Torren nodded, a faraway look in her eyes, "Yes."

They stared at each other.

Torren said, "Tarrington was good. It's a shame he didn't roll over easier, or at all for that matter. I fed him all the ideology I could, all of it the truth no less. The Drug War, the government's ultimate stake in it, the coming era of Genocide litigation and Martial Law Rule. Apparently he's yet to contemplate these things objectively. I covered everything but population control. Of course, all he really wanted was to get out, and now he's out... for a while. And Carlos and General Montoya are out too. We've accomplished much. We can already start moving on the markets those two have freed up."

Geech said, "And the Company and my people emerged with very little mud on them, nothing that can't be cleaned up. So it has been a rather successful operation." He sighed, thinking of his responsibility, weary. "There's so much more to do."

He studied Torren for a moment. "Taking over the world is quite an entailing project, if I may say so."

Torren said, "You, Mr. LeCroix, may certainly say so." Then she asked a question that'd been nagging at her, "Is there any possible way Mellonhall knew about my cover?"

"No way possible. Why do you ask?"

"Nothing really. Just the way he was looking at me before I killed him."

Geech licked his lips, "Oh well," he said, and leaned back in his chair, signaling the bartender. "Any beer will be fine," he told Joe over his shoulder.

Joe came from the shadows, the glass clicking as he drew a beer from the Oly tap.

Geech slipped it in before the beer arrived, "Torren, you've done very well. Preston is having a little get-together with some of the people from Paradise Island. I know they'd all like to see you. I think they're interested in using you for some wet work in the Caribbean play."

Torren held up her hand as Joe shuffled towards the table, beer in hand. The glass dripped on the table. They both looked at it. Joe looked at it. They looked at Joe. Joe looked at them. "Run a tab," Torren told him.

"Right," Joe's head bobbed and he strolled away.

Geech was sipping as Torren began, telling him to forget about the wet work. "Tell the boys thanks, but no thanks."

"Going down to see my daughter, then?" He smiled.

Torren said, "The thought has crossed my mind. Let's see if Tarrington shows first. It would be perfect to arrive with him already there."

Geech pursed his lips, raised one bushy grey eyebrow.

Torren yelled, "Bartender!"

"Yes, ma'am?"

"Bring me a beer!"

Now Geech smiled, "You actually liked Tarrington, didn't you?"

"Like," Torren corrected him, "He's a true revolutionary and he doesn't even know it. He's broken all the rules on this one and I'm happy for him to some extent. Maybe he'll stop monitoring all that news and come around one day."

Geech's mind wondered, "So he did have the B-15 on."

Torren said, "He's a real stuntman, Tarrington is."

Geech sounded like a grandfather coaxing his grandson to come fishing when his grandson would have much rather gone out and gotten laid. It was if he really didn't understand. "Rules to break are like goals to a true revolutionary," he said.

"It's a matter of perspective," Torren explained. "Break down those rigid barriers of yours and you'll see the justice of all existence manifest everywhere." With that she downed her beer, and stood. She had to get to the cave and retrieve the tapes from Scot. Before they got out of hand. She told Geech she would see him later and left.

Geech watched her go, called out, "Bartender!"

Joe went over to the table. Geech shot the man in the head.

No witnesses.

Company policy.

Besides, he didn't have his wallet on him. Who would pay the tab?

Chapter Fifty-three

They were moored a mile off the coast of Morocco. The nightlife of Casablanca a helicopter ride away. The yacht was one-sixty by thirty-two, and three stories tall. A nice swimming pool on the top deck, right next to the chopper. A 32-foot Donzi speedboat could be lowered from a stern housing.

Near the pool, two men relaxed in deck chairs. An older, rather attractive woman floated on a smiling rubber crocodile.

An impeccably attired steward arrived with a tray, handed one of the men a cold glistening can of Coors, the other a double Manhattan. He set the woman's Mai Tai at the pool's edge.

Then he addressed the younger of the two men, "Will there be anything else, sir?"

A second steward arrived and placed a stack of newspapers near the younger man's deck lounger.

The man consulted an expensive wristwatch, said, "I have that international ship-to-shore call in a moment. Is a line being prepared?" He tapped the pile of papers, "Very good, thank you," dismissing the second steward with his eyes.

The other steward said, "I believe a line is being readied, sir."

"I'm fine then… Dad?"

The older man said, "Keep the booze running. My back's still a bruise."

The woman in the pool said, "The masseuse is excellent, dear. My legs never felt better."

The older man said, "I've sampled her charms, honey." He told the steward, "Massage at three, after a eucalyptus steam."

The steward said, "I'll inform the staff, sir." He stood at attention, raised his brows at the younger man.

Tarrington said, "That's about it, then. Just bring me the phone," and sorted through the L.A. Times.

"Right away, sir." The steward gave a courtly bow and departed.

Tarrington squared off with his first newspaper and read the headline: Death Penalty in Taylor Trial. He frowned, but said to his father, "Listen to Mom, Pops. She knows what she's talking about." Then he turned the page. A subtitled heading read: Heroin Overlord "Little Nicky" Taylor Maintains Innocence.

Tarrington sucked air through his teeth and let go a loud sigh as if absolutely miserable. But it was the inevitable suffering and confusion "Little Nicky" Taylor was no doubt experiencing that was ruffling Tarrington's empathy.

Seeing this from the pool, Arianna said, "Is it your foot again, dear?"

Tarrington peered over the newspaper at the clunky plaster cast that stretched from toes to mid-calf on his left leg. The sweatbox, he was calling it. Even though it was lying in a special tray of ice. He tried to wiggle his toes but they just glared at him, refusing to budge. Enrique had artfully etched an exquisite marijuana leaf across the front and signed Andy Warhol's name. But beneath the steaming Morrocan sun this had little effect on the foot's morale. Tarrington worked the big toe again and was answered with a searing pain as his mind flashed back to the last load of his career....

When he'd purposely stepped into the vortex of unraveling rope and was jerked from the cargo hold, dragged down the Super Herc's tail ramp, the custom-mounted steel sleeve in his hiking boot had done its job and protected the ankle. Just as he figured it would.

But the rope shifted violently as the next two crates slipped down behind him and practically tore his foot off. Of the numerous bones in his foot, two dozen had been dramatically rearranged. It was a possibility Tarrington had completely overlooked.

He told his mother, "No Ma. The foot's fine. It's more of a pain in the ass."

That's when Welly said, "Listen to Mom about what?"

Tarrington replied, "The massage."

Welly defended himself, "I'm taking one. Am I not? Two yesterday and plenty of anesthesia." He held up his Manhattan and gulped a bit.

Arianna said, "And you're the one who didn't want to wear a bulletproof vest."

Welly looked at his son, "You see why I run around on her?"

Arianna laughed, almost falling off the inflated crocodile. She said, "I'm just sad for you, son. What about the girl? That little bitch broke my baby's heart!"

"Ah Ma... forget the girl. She wasn't my type."

"The cunt." Arianna hissed.

"Relax, Ma."

"Drink your Mai Tai, dear," Welly told her.

The steward brought the phone, said, "Your call, sir. You've been connected," and left straightaway.

Tarrington took the phone, said, "Kiki?"

"Right here," Enrique replied. "How's the weather? They got some great hash on shore. A fine way to spend your retirement, eh?"

"In a hash haze? I'll stick to beer. What's been happening the last two weeks?" He shook out another page of the L.A. Times.

Enrique replied, "Aren't you glad I taught you how to fall out of planes?"

"When I can jump rope again I'll answer that? What about Torren? Was I right?"

"We're almost positive she's bad. I think she can feel the heat, too.

She's showing all the signs; nervous tick, bitten fingernails, bad hair days. And there's heat, by the way, everywhere."

"So how's Chuckie? Sun stroke?"

"Father's fine. A little burnt but he'll make it. He sends his regards."

"Tell him to try a little cocoa butter and aloe. Stay away from the sun block. It causes skin cancer. So he's out?"

"Him," Enrique said, "and everybody else. We've shut down the entire heroin trade. Sent Raul to Burma to explain it to Khun Sa himself. The marijuana's up for grabs right now. I'm still not sure… you know how I feel about it, Taylor. It's gonna be hard to deny people their weed. I'm swimming in guilt already. That's world service stuff, ya know. All the same though, General Montoya's sent his daughter Elena to Montevideo and closed the Juarez warehouse. We've stopped. And ordered all our people to do the same. And everybody's really having pigeons around here. Especially the Columbians, eggs everywhere. You'd think a couple billion would satisfy some people. As far as the assholes go, they're freaking out."

"You mean the CIA?" Tarrington said.

"Yeah. I've already received a couple feelers. They're practically begging. It's just like you said."

"Yeah, but they're still screwing that poor black guy."

"Scapegoats, Inc." Enrique responded. "The government is bent on creating domestic un-tranquility." He leaned into the "Un" part.

"You can't pull any strings for that guy, Kiki?"

"Sorry my hands are full of my own strings right now. If I don't get them all knotted up, I'll give old Nicky Taylor a shot. Promise."

"Use the videos," Tarrington reminded him. "I wasn't thinking about home movies for my golden years when I crashed that party, you know. Didn't Scot hide some?"

"Yeah." Enrique sighed, "It was all just like you said. How'd you figure Torren into all this? That's what broke it open."

"Pillow talk," Tarrington said, then asked, "What about Moni?"

Enrique told him, "That's something I just don't know right now, Taylor. I'm still up her ass with a microscope. Figuring her part in this will take some time. How are you holding up?"

Tarrington took a deep breath, surprised that a tear rolled from the corner of his eye and pooled between the telephone and his face, "I'm drinking a lot of beer, Kiki. You think they're on to me?"

"You mean does Langley think you're dead?"

"Yeah."

"Probably not."

"That's reassuring." Tarrington deadpanned.

"Life's like that."

"And the meek will inherit the earth."

"That's right, buddy. Have another beer. Get meeked."

"I'm meeking right now."

"Cling to that humor," Enrique said, "It'll outlast the money. You're a real dinosaur, Taylor. I love ya."

"You mean I'm extinct."

"What can I say," Enrique elaborated, "It costs to be the boss."

Additional Titles by Sunstar Publishing Ltd.

• *The Name Book* by Pierre Le Rouzic
ISBN 0-9638502-1-0 $15.95
Numerology/Philosophy. International bestseller. Over 9000 names with stunningly accurate descriptions of character and personality. How the sound of your name effects who you grow up to be.

• *Every Day A Miracle Happens* by Rodney Charles
ISBN 0-9638502-0-2 $17.95
Religious bestseller. 365 stories of miracles, both modern and historic, each associated with a day of the year. Universal calendar. Western religion.

• *Of War & Weddings* by Jerry Yellin
ISBN 0-9638502-5-3 $17.95
History/Religion. A moving and compelling autobiography of bitter wartime enemies who found peace through their children's marriage. Japanese history and religion.

• *Your Star Child* by Mary Mayhew
ISBN 0-9638502-2-9 $16.95
East/West philosophy. Combines Eastern philosophy with the birthing techniques of modern medicine, from preconception to parenting young adults.

• *Lighter Than Air* by Rodney Charles and Anna Jordan
ISBN0-9638502-7-X $14.95
East/West philosophy. Historic accounts of saints, sages and holy people who possessed the ability of unaided human flight.

• *Bringing Home The Sushi* by Mark Meers
ISBN 1-887472-05-3 $21.95
Japanese philosophy and culture. Adventurous account of of an American businessman and his family living in '90s Japan.

- *Miracle of Names* by Clayne Conings
ISBN 1-887472-03-7 $13.95
Numerology and Eastern philosophy. Educational and enlighten-ing—discover the hidden meanings and potential of names through numerology.

- *Voice for the Planet* by Anna Maria Gallo
ISBN 1-887472-00-2 $10.95
Religion/Ecology. This book explores the ecological practicality of native American practices.

- *Making $$$ At Home* by Darla Sims
ISBN 1-887472-02-9 $25.00
Reference. Labor-saving directory that guides you through the process of making contacts to create a business at home.

- *Gabriel & the Remarkable Pebbles* by Carol Hovin
ISBN 1-887472-06-1 $12.95
Children/Ecology. A lighthearted, easy-to-read fable that educates children in understanding ecological balances.

- *Searching For Camelot* by Edith Thomas
ISBN 1-887472-08-8 $12.95
East/West philosophy. Short easy-to-read, autobiographical adven-ture full of inspirational life lessons.

- *The Revelations of Ho* by Dr. James Weldon
ISBN 1-887472-09-6 $17.95
Eastern philosophy. A vivid and detailed account of the path of a modern-day seeker of enlightenment.

- *The Formula* by Dr. Vernon Sylvest
ISBN 1-887472-10-X $21.95
Eastern philosophy/Medical research. This book demystifies the gap between medicine and mysticism, offering a ground breaking perspective on health as seen through the eyes of an eminent pathologist.

• *Jewel of The Lotus* by Bodhi Avinasha
ISBN 1-887472-11-8 $15.95
Eastern philosophy. Tantric Path to higher consciousness. Learn to increase your energy level, heal and rejuvenate yourself through devotional relationships.

• *Elementary, My Dear* by Tree Stevens
ISBN 1-887472-12-6 $17.95
Cooking/Health. Step-by-step, health-conscious cookbook for the beginner. Includes hundreds of time-saving menus.

• *Directory of New Age & Alternative Publications*
by Darla Sims
ISBN 1-887472-18-5 $23.95
Reference. Comprehensive listing of publications, events, organizations arranged alphabetically, by category and by location.

• *Educating Your Star Child* by Ed & Mary Mayhew
ISBN 1-887472-17-7 $16.95
East/West philosophy. How to parent children to be smarter, wiser and happier, using internationally acclaimed mind-body intelligence techniques.

• *How To Be Totally Unhappy in a Peaceful World*
by Gil Friedman
ISBN 1-887472-17-7 $11.95
Humor/Self-help. Everything you ever wanted to know about being unhappy: A complete manual with rules, exercises, a midterm and final exam. Paper.

• *The Symbolic Message of Illness* by Dr. Calin Pop
ISBN 1-887472-16-9 $21.95
East/West Medicine. Dr. Pop illuminates an astonishingly accurate diagnosis of our ailments and physical disorders based solely on the observation of daily habits.

- *On Wings of Light* by Ronna Herman
ISBN 1-887472-19-3 $19.95
New Age. Ronna Herman documents the profoundly moving and inspirational messages for her beloved Archangel Michael.

- *The Global Oracle* by Edward Tarabilda & Doug Grimes
ISBN 1-887472-22-3 $17.95
East/West Philosophy. This remarkable oracle may be used for meditation, play or an aid in decision making. It is a guide for the study of archetypes and an excellent introduction to holistic living.

- *Destiny* by Sylvia Clute
ISBN 1-887472-21-5 $21.95
East/West philosophy. A brilliant metaphysical mystery novel (with the ghost of George Washington) based on *A Course In Miracles*.

- *The Husband's Manual* by A. & T. Murphy
ISBN 0-9632336-4-5 $9.00
Self-help/Men's Issues. At last! Instructions for men on what to do and when to do it. The Husband's Manual can help a man create a satisfying, successful marriage — one he can take pride in, not just be resigned to.

- *Cosmic Perspective* by Harold Allen
ISBN 1-887472-23-1 $21.95
Science/Eastern philosophy. Eminent cosmologist Harold W.G. Allen disproves the "Big Bang" theory and opens new horizons to the dynamic principle of cosmic reincarnation, plus revolutionay insight into Christian origins, bibilical symbolism and the Dead Sea scrolls.

- *Twin Galaxies Pinball Book of World Records*
by Walter Day
ISBN 1-887472-25-8 $12.95
Reference. The official reference book for all Video Game and Pinball Players—this book coordinates an international schedule

of tournaments that players can compete in to gain entrance into this record book.

- *The Face on Mars* by Harold Allen
ISBN 1-887472-27-4 $12.95
Science/Fiction. A metaphysical/scientific novel based on man's first expedition to investigate the mysterious "Face" revealed by NASA probes.

- *The Spiritual Warrior* by Shakura Rei
ISBN 1-887472-28-2 $17.95
Eastern philosophy. An exposition of the spiritual techniques and practices of Eastern Philosophy.

- *The Pillar of Celestial Fire* by Robert Cox
ISBN 1-887472-30-4 $18.95
Eastern philosophy. The ancient cycles of time, the sacred alchemical science and the new golden age.

- *The Tenth Man* by Wei Wu Wei
ISBN 1-887472-31-2 $15.95
Eastern philosophy. Discourses on Vedanta—the final stroke of enlightenment.

- *Open Secret* by Wei Wu Wei
ISBN 1-887472-32-0 $14.95
Eastern philosophy. Discourses on Vedanta—the final stroke of enlightenment.

- *All Else is Bondage* by Wei Wu Wei
ISBN 1-887472-34-7 $16.95
Eastern philosophy. Discourses on Vedanta—the final stroke of enlightenment.